# THE RICH PASS BY

Sarah Byrne's story starts with the illegitimate birth of her daughter Angel and her loveless marriage to Nahum Morey, clergyman and governor of the Thomas Coram Hospital for Foundlings. Situated in the fields near Clerkenwell in the City of London, the hospital saved destitute or abandoned babies from the workhouse. Sarah was determined to remain close to the daughter she had lost and when this led her to a role as one of the Foundling Hospital's residential staff, the daily fabric of institutional life there was laid bare ...

GOR
A

Please return / renew by date shown.
You can renew it at:
norlink.norfolk.gov.uk
or by telephone: 0344 800 8006
Please have your library card &  PIN ready

| | | |
|---|---|---|
| 1. 2. 11 | | |
| 14. 2. 11 | | |
| 1a\|J | | |
| 4\|X\| | | |
| 30. 10 E | | |
| | | |
| 6C | | |
| MOC | | |
| 1 1 AUG 2016 | | V. SMITH |

# THE RICH PASS BY

# THE RICH PASS BY

*by*
Pamela Pope

**Magna Large Print Books**
Long Preston, North Yorkshire,
England.

British Library Cataloguing in Publication Data.

---

Pope, Pamela
    The rich pass by.

    A catalogue record for this book is
    available from the British Library

    ISBN 0-7505-1450-7

First published in Great Britain by Century Hutchinson Ltd., 1990

Copyright © 1990 by Pamela Pope

Cover illustration © Melvyn Warren-Smith by arrangement with
P.W.A. International Ltd.

The moral right of the author has been asserted

Published in Large Print 2000 by arrangement with Pamela Pope.

Magna Large Print is an imprint of
Library Magna Books Ltd.
Printed and bound in Great Britain by
T.J. International Ltd., Cornwall, PL28 8RW.

*For my daughters, Alison and Lucie,*
*with my love*

# A TOAST TO CAPTAIN THOMAS CORAM

The rich passed by with outraged mutters
About dead babes in London's gutters.
A seaman came by in bright red coat
And spent his life rocking the proverbial boat.

Groats and sovereigns he collected in hordes
From these outraged ladies—and their lords.
They all thought the seaman—really quite mad.
There are many here who are grateful and
   glad

That this man of compassion and caring nature
From lowly beginnings—but high in stature,
Did not falter from his dream and plan.
Come! Raise your glasses to an honourable
   man.

Reproduced by kind permission of Catherine
Jeffreys, former foundling pupil of the Foundling
Hospital's Berkhamstead School.

# PART ONE

## 1850–55

# CHAPTER 1

The October morning was well advanced and there was quite a congestion of vehicles at the top of Lamb's Conduit Street where the Lamb Tavern had already opened its doors. Horses clattered through puddles left by a recent rainstorm, splashing mud over those on foot, and top-hatted gentlemen with canes walked to the outside of the pavement to shield the wide, swaying gowns of ladies they accompanied.

There was no one to protect the tall girl in a green dress and chipped black bonnet who came along Guilford Street from the direction of Clerkenwell. She stopped at the gates of the Foundling Hospital, a landmark in that fairly gracious area of London. It had been founded over a hundred years ago by a benevolent gentleman named Thomas Coram whose heart had been moved by the plight of unwanted infants. Her eyes were wide with apprehension as she stared at the Coram statue, then at the building, and her loneliness ought to have awakened sympathy. No one noticed.

Her air of dignity was unusual in one of her class, for there was no mistaking that she came from a very different neighbourhood. Mud had dirtied her boots, but her shabby clothes had a clean respectability which showed that at least she didn't make a living on the streets. Her

13

deeply shadowed blue eyes were dull from weeping, and her troubled face was like a lovely rain-washed flower beneath the leaden sky.

She carried a baby wrapped in a patchwork cover, the odd shapes of cotton carefully featherstitched together, the colours faded from washing. The babe was so young it couldn't be seen, and it mewed kitten-like in her arms. She held it closer, warming it with the heat of her own young body, but she was so thin it seemed a lucifer might have done the job better.

Her name was Sarah Byrne.

Sarah was swamped with a feeling of desolation as she looked at the Foundling Hospital at the end of the long drive, and it sapped her meagre strength. The building was so big. It looked cold in spite of the nice red bricks and it was difficult to believe there was any love behind such grand walls, yet she knew that there was. So many poor little city mites had been given the chance of life when they would have had none if their mothers had kept them.

As if to urge her not to delay, the baby struck out feebly at her empty breast. She had no money, and no hope of making any while she had a child in her arms. The only move she could make would be to the workhouse, but then she would lose the baby anyway. It meant everything to her. Everything in the world. But love was not enough when Nature had dealt her the cruellest blow by drying up the milk Angel needed to thrive.

A few days ago she had collected a petition

form from the porter's lodge to ask if the child could be brought up by the charity, and if the answer today was yes, then she ought to be truly thankful. But now the moment had come she felt she was being torn apart.

A man came out of the porter's lodge and squinted at her short-sightedly.

'So you're back,' he said.

Sarah showed him a paper tucked in a fold of the shawl. 'It's Saturday. I've brought me baby, like you told me.'

Fine rain carried on the wind, and dark hair escaping from her bonnet brim was misted with drops as delicate as seed pearls. Her eyes were awash with fresh tears.

'Don't you worry, miss,' he said. 'They'll look after 'im right well. Better'n you could do yerself, I shouldn't wonder.'

'It's a girl.' She held the bundle closer to her face with agonizing affection. 'And she's the most beautiful baby you ever saw.'

'They all say that, ducks.'

It was a strange morning with showers one minute and sun the next. For a few minutes rain came down hard, slanting across the grass with the sharpness of icy needles, and she took shelter in the lodge until it stopped. When the cloud had passed over, a door in the east wing of the main building opened and a crowd of little girls flew out like brown butterflies. They all wore white mob caps and aprons, and as they ran to play on the grass their laughter carried joyfully to the waiting mother and her baby. Relief at seeing them so happy dispersed some of Sarah's gloom. She thought of the sickly children playing by a stream of water through the middle of the alley off Turnmill Street. It was an open sewer breeding diseases of every kind. These children looked bursting with health.

She walked up the drive, wishing she could hide for ever in the peaceful shadows of the white colonnades on either side. So much had happened in the last year, most of it too painful to remember. Pictures haunted her, whether awake or asleep, yet there was danger in banishing them. It was the greatest temptation to keep Angel close to her heart, but if she did that the child would die in the filth and poverty. Here she stood a good chance of growing up healthy like the little girls playing on the lawn.

She had been told to go in by the west front door. At the entrance she stopped again and murmured to the child.

'Don't ever think I abandoned you because I didn't want you, my angel.' She bowed her head over the shawl, and the pain of loving the small mortal inside it seemed worse than the birthing had been. Her arms ached, not from the weight, but from tension which made her squeeze the bundle as if it were possible to take the child back inside her body. 'I'll never forget about you. Never. I'll make you proud of me one day, see if I don't. Then p'raps we'll be together again.'

She was not going to have to face the Governors alone. Another girl was waiting with a baby wrapped in a shawl which had once been white, but was now the colour of gruel. The girl was fair and plump, and she eyed Sarah warily.

'D'yuh reckon they'll ask many questions?'

'Dunno,' said Sarah.

'I hope not,' said the girl. They had been told to wait in the vestibule, and she looked around like a cat sniffing at an unfamiliar place. 'Bloody pictures everywhere.'

Angel began to cry, her tiny face crumpled and red with the effort, and Sarah rocked her gently. 'Hush, my lovely. You hush now.'

'Thank Gawd we'll be rid of 'em in a minute, eh.' The fair girl held her own child against her chest like a bag of laundry.

Sarah was stricken. 'How can you say that? Don't you *mind* leaving your baby here?'

'Glad to get shot of it. I never wanted it in the first place, that's for sure.'

There was a warm smell surrounding them which was unexpectedly soothing after the cold October air. Sarah looked at a leather-covered chair and wondered whether she dared sit down, but before she had a chance the summons came to go before the Governors.

There were eight of them sitting in judgement, all men of middle age or more, and she faced them feeling as if it was an inquisition. They looked kindly enough, but she wanted to rush back to Turnmill Street before they could take Angel from her.

They studied her with varying degrees of interest, one seeing her body, another her heart, another her soul.

17

'Miss Byrne, we have studied your petition, and as far as we can tell there is no reason for us to reject your child.' The spokesman used an eyeglass to see his notes. 'Our schoolmaster has made inquiries into your background and verifies the truth of all your statements.' He paused again, still studying the papers. 'I see you were in domestic service when your father was killed at Smith's Clock Manufactory.'

It was too much for Sarah. The beautiful room blurred and revolved. She closed her eyes and there seemed to be a terrible, indescribable smell of burning which curled through her like the heat and smoke had done that dreadful day. It was a memory which would stay with her for the rest of her life.

Someone brought a chair for her to sit down ...

It was said the fight started because Paddy Byrne was Catholic Irish, and Bill Yardley was Protestant English. No one knew more than that. It ended when Paddy Byrne fell into the furnace, and his dying screams could be heard the length and breadth of the clock factory in St James's Square, Clerkenwell.

Sarah was in the kitchen of the Bradfords' house in Newcastle Place when an apprentice from the factory came with the message. Heat from the range shimmered in the basement room and her sleeves were rolled up past her elbows as she tried to master the intricacies of preparing food for the gentry. The cook was showing her how to decorate a boar's head,

18

which was to be served for dinner that evening in aspic jelly, and the interruption came at an inopportune moment.

'What are you doing here, boy?' Cook eyed his dirty clothes, and even dirtier boots, in disgust.

'Sarah Byrne 'as to come quick. Her father's fallen into the furnace at Smith's.'

Sarah dropped a spoon into the aspic, spattering her spotless apron. A rushing sound filled her ears, and she grasped the edge of the table.

'The furnace, you say?'

'Reckon 'e's done for,' said the boy.

The colour drained from her face. 'Pa! Oh, no!' For a second there was shocked silence. She started to run, then remembered that even in an emergency she had to ask permission. 'Mrs Martin, please may I go?'

'I suppose you'd better,' the woman said grudgingly. 'Though I don't know how I'm going to do anything with this aspic you've ruined.'

Sarah ran from the kitchen and was ahead of the boy as they left the house. The December day had frost in the air, and icy patches made the paths treacherous. Sarah edged people aside in her haste, causing angry shouts as she sent them slithering against walls in Jerusalem Passage. No time to apologize. She didn't even feel the cold, though she hadn't stopped to get a shawl or bonnet.

'Don't die, Pa,' she cried aloud. 'Let me get there quick.'

The last time she had seen him they had parted with a bitter quarrel, all because he had found comfort with a woman who had no right taking the place of her mother.

A carriage was at the factory gate. The horse had been driven fast, and its breath was like plumes of smoke. Sarah rushed through the gate, still pursued by the boy, who took her to the foundry at the east end of the yard. She braced herself to look at the badly burnt figure of her father.

The crowd of workers gathered round made room for her. Above the usual smell of molten copper and zinc there was the sickening stench of scorched flesh which turned her stomach, and she pressed her hands to her mouth in horror.

'A doctor's 'ere, miss. Came as quick as 'e could from the 'ospital.' The speaker turned to a tall young man in beige buckskin trousers and black frock coat who got up from her father's side when he saw her. 'This is his daughter, sir.'

The physician looked to be about twenty-five. He had hair the colour of a newly minted sovereign, a long, handsome face, and hazel eyes which clouded with sympathy.

'I'm Dr James Halden,' he said to her. 'I'm afraid there's nothing I could do for your father. He would have died right away and if it's any comfort I don't think he suffered much.'

He tried to stand in front of the body so that she would be spared the sight of it, but she pushed him aside.

'Was he ill?' she asked. Her voice trembled.

' 'E 'ad a fight with Bill there,' another man said.

Sarah folded her arms across her stomach and rocked with pain and shock. Dr Halden took her by the shoulders and led her away forcefully.

'Is there anything I can do for *you*? What about your mother and the rest of the family?'

'There's only me.'

She glanced up and met the gaze of his heavy-lidded eyes. There was twice the heat in the foundry as there'd been in the kitchen at Newcastle Place and her face became as red as the fire which had cost her father his life. This was the best-looking man she had ever met, a toff into the bargain, and just for that moment she had all his attention. She felt drawn to him by the compassion he so visibly displayed.

'Is there no one else at all?' he insisted.

She clenched her teeth, and her fingers locked together as she gripped them hard. The bitterness she had been harbouring these last months came tumbling out.

'There's Maggie, the woman me father married,' she said. 'She'll have to be told. I ain't seen 'er for weeks.'

Someone had thrown water over the red-hot coke and the place was full of steam which billowed and hissed from the mouth of the Stourbridge-brick furnace. The conical pot Paddy had been handling with tongs had tipped over and the fifty pounds of spilt metal had set in rivulets along the ground.

Bill Yardley was sitting on the wooden casting trough, his black head bowed. There was blood on his calf-length apron, and he was muttering about it not being his fault.

' 'E fell, I tell you. I never pushed 'im.' He looked up when one of the bosses questioned him. 'One minute 'e had the pot in the tongs, then 'e went like 'e was in his cups and toppled into the fire. Gawd, it were awful.'

Sarah returned to her father and knelt down beside him. His charred clothes were wet from a dousing, and she could see down to the bones on his hands which had already been crossed over his chest. The sight made her feel so sick she daren't move.

'He wasn't much,' she said, 'but he didn't deserve to die like this.'

Through the steam she saw the man who had done the fighting. She shrugged off sympathetic hands and went for him, clawing his face with outstretched fingers until she drew blood.

'You killed me father,' she screamed. 'I hope you rot in hell for it.'

'Now, miss, there ain't no call for that kind of talk,' said one of the inspectors.

'The young lady is understandably upset,' said the physician. 'Don't worry, I'll see after her.'

James Halden led her gently away.

... One of the Governors passed over a glass of water, and Sarah took a sip. The faintness passed and she lifted her head.

'I'm sorry, sir. I ain't got me strength back yet since the baby was born.'

'My dear, we understand.' The man who spoke was bald and portly. 'We are concerned with *your* welfare as much as the child's. I hope you can assure us that if we take this baby you will be able to make a new start in the world without your shame being known.'

'Yes, sir. The Bradfords have offered to take me back into service.'

'We've checked on it. The Bradfords are a good Christian family employing a large staff. They believe you left to take care of your stepmother after your father's death. It appears you are a very good worker.'

'Thank you, sir.'

Sarah held the baby's little hand under the shawl, the curl of minute fingers round one of her own making her ache with maternal love. It was going well and she knew they would take Angel, but the certainty caused her increasing misery. They would take Angel away and give her a new name to go with her new life; a name Sarah wouldn't be allowed to know.

'Do you swear on oath, Miss Byrne, that you have never lived with the man who fathered your child?'

'Lord, yes, sir. He dun't know anything about it. He'd have a fit if he did, and so would his wife.'

'Did you know at the time that he was a married man?'

'Not until it was too late. 'E was a gentleman, an' all, but 'e took advantage of me while I was upset about me father.'

No one showed surprise. It was an oft-told tale within these walls.

'So there's no possibility that he could be held

responsible for supporting the child?'

'No, sir. I dun't even know where 'e lives.'

The portly gentleman who had done most of the talking leaned forward and spoke kindly. 'My child, we will take your daughter for you. She will be reared here in the Foundling Hospital until she is old enough to make her own way in the world, but you must understand that you will have no contact with her whatsoever. From this day it will be as if you never had this infant.'

'Yes, sir. Thank you, sir.'

She was trembling with cold, yet the room was heated to a comfortable temperature. A woman came in to take Angel from her. Sarah rested her cheek against the tiny head for the last time, tears spilling on to the fine covering of down like that of a day-old chick. Then she willed herself not to show the extent of her heartbreak, and when she handed the baby over her head was held proudly.

She was given a receipt, just as if she had brought an object in to hock.

'Hospital for the Maintenance and Education of Exposed and Deserted Young Children,' she read. 'The twenty-fifth day of October, 1850, received a female child.' It was signed by the secretary while she was there.

Sarah felt strange with her arms empty. She left the building the way she had come, standing a few minutes at the door to draw breath and quieten her shattered emotions.

It was amazing the way a newborn child had completely enslaved her. From the moment she had entered the world Angel had become the pivot of Sarah's life, and within three short weeks her outlook on everything had changed. All that mattered was Angel's welfare, and Sarah had seen how it would be if she tried to bring her up alone. Misery, squalor, disease and hunger were all she could provide without a job, and no one would give her one while she had a baby to see after. This hospital was the only answer for both of them, and Sarah was not going to waste the God-given chance to prove her worth.

Now the ordeal of parting was over she must look ahead. She opened her blue eyes wide, at last seeing light where before there had been none. She went through the gates bravely, without a backward glance, though she longed to turn just once more to look at the great institution which had swallowed Angel up.

Her plans were quite definite. At seventeen she was about to make a new start in life, not with relief that she was no longer saddled with a child, but with determination to succeed in everything she did for the child's sake. And one day she would claim her, no matter how impossible that might seem right now.

It was plain to see that Peg Wooldridge had come up from the country. Her cheeks were rosy, though the October air gave them a faint blueness, like the bloom on a Victoria plum. It was an experience right enough, coming to London, but she would be glad to be on her way back to the quiet of her home in Chertsey.

She had arrived at the Foundling Hospital yesterday with Betty Gilling, both of them wet nurses, and each had taken charge of a pathetic baby who had been abandoned by its mother. Peg's heart was already won over by the tiny girl she was to look after for the next five years. She had held the baby to her breast and nursed her with intense satisfaction, knowing her own children would adore this precious child. Even Isaac, her husband, might be won over when he saw her.

'Don't know why you want to bring someone else's young 'un into the house,' Isaac had complained. He was burly and kind, but his generosity didn't always extend beyond his family. 'Ain't three of yer own enough?'

'We've room. I've lost six babies before they was a year, Isaac Wooldridge, and now I've weaned our George we can take in a poor waif.' Peg was the stronger of the two and she knew she could convince him. 'Besides, we'll get paid. Farm labouring don't bring in much, so the extra money won't come amiss. Three and six a week we'll get.'

There were about forty women in and around the village who made the fostering of Foundling children their business, and some of the cottages were so overcrowded with children it seemed they must take it in turn to sit down. But Peg's cottage was not too full to make room for one more.

On Sunday morning she wrapped the patchwork cover more warmly round the baby and followed Betty into the chapel. It was the first time she had been in such a beautiful place and she looked round with awe. Stained glass shed bright colours on the pillars along the side galleries, and a painting of Christ blessing children adorned the altar. Above it was a magnificent organ separating banks of pews in the end gallery which Betty had said was where the Foundling children gathered to sing during services. Betty had been through all this before.

Four people were waiting at the altar with the white-haired chaplain. They were to be sponsors. Peg was nervous. She fingered the parchment ticket with a long number on it which she had sewn to the shoulder strap of the baby's gown last night, and wondered what name the wee mite would be given.

'There's the matron and the schoolmaster,' Betty said. 'I think the other two are the steward and the head nurse. Don't worry, they won't eat you.'

Two senior girls in Foundling uniforms took the babies up to the altar, holding them against their white aprons with all the concern of older sisters. Peg's eyes misted. This was nothing like the orphanages she'd heard about. The children looked contented and well cared for, and though the building was vast it had the feeling of an old-fashioned house owned by compassionate gentry. A pleasant warmth surrounded her and she made an effort to follow the baptism service.

The chaplain took Betty's foster baby into his arms and dipped his fingers into the bowl on the altar rail.

He spoke to the sponsors. 'Name this child.'

The matron answered for them. 'Corrie Palmer,' she said.

The little girl lying against the while surplice opened her eyes in surprise when the sign of the cross was made on her forehead, but she didn't murmur. 'In the name of the Father, and of the Son, and of the Holy Ghost. Amen.'

With Peg's baby it was different. She had been restless all morning, and she began to cry as soon as the chaplain took her.

He spoke again to the sponsors. 'Name this child.'

This time it was the head nurse who replied. 'Anna Beckett,' she said.

And Anna, the infant who had been called Angel by her natural mother, voiced her objection to the holy water with all the power in her tiny lungs. The sound carried up to the galleries, and echoed like the cry of a lost soul within the hallowed walls.

Peg Wooldridge and Betty Gilling were given dinner in the girls' dining room, which was very long and hung with pictures. Among them was the portrait Hogarth had painted of Thomas Coram, though it meant little to the two women. They only saw the great man looking eternally down on rows of girls eating meals which his benevolence had encouraged others to help provide for infants who might otherwise have ended pitiably short lives on rubbish heaps. His round face framed by a mass of white hair was forever genial, his corpulence magnified by a large red coat, and at his feet was a globe on which he could chart the voyages he had made as a sea captain.

One of the girls he looked down on in this present decade dispensed baked meat and vegetables from a large dish at the end of the table.

'It's a good place for children to be,' Betty said.

'But it ain't home,' said Peg.

Peg's heart went out to the little girls in their neat brown dresses who were so quiet as plate followed plate down the table in rapid succession until each child had her dinner. While murmuring the grace with them she pictured her boisterous sons at table. They lacked manners, but their happy voices accompanying the noisy scraping of dishes was so different from this. The difference was love. Not that there wasn't any here, but there would be no time to give each child a cuddle, or comfort her if she fell down.

After dinner each woman was given a small parcel of baby clothes, and in return each signed a receipt for the child who was to be in her care.

The matron, a large, capable woman with an air of authority, gave them the customary advice. 'I don't need to tell you these children need the love they have been deprived of by the desertion of their natural mothers. That's why the services of a good wet nurse are so important.'

'She'll be like one of me own,' said Betty. 'I've taken one before, remember.'

'The inspector will visit you every so often to examine the health of the child and see that she's been vaccinated. If there is any sign of sickness the apothecary is to be called at once, and the matter reported to the inspector.'

Peg longed to be away. Isaac would be anxiously waiting for her at home, and she was worried about George who'd been left with a neighbour. She only partly listened to further admonitions. Love was what was needed most, and she had plenty of that to give the little girl in her arms. She'd always wanted a girl.

'Now, the van is waiting outside to take you back to Chertsey,' Matron said. 'You have our blessings, and I know that these will be fine children when they come back here in five years.'

At last Peg gathered her possessions together and wrapped Anna up warmly so that the cold air wouldn't get to her. Betty watched her, but delayed doing the same for Corrie.

'I *do* think that's nice,' she said, touching the feather-stitched covering which was almost as big as a blanket. Her tone was tinged with envy. 'I'd love one like that.'

There was little money to spare in Peg's household, but there was even less in Betty's. She had seven children of her own and she did the best she could for them, but everything was handed down until the latest baby was clothed in garments used several times over. Peg took off Anna's cover.

'You have it,' she said, handing it to Betty. 'I made one that's only been used for George, seeing as I lost the three before him.'

Betty was a thin woman, her pretty hair already white though she was not yet thirty, and when she smiled it was easy to see that she was young at heart.

'Oh, Peg! Thank you. You're a real friend.' Her eyes shone. 'I can put it on me bed, then I'll have to make sure Harry takes 'is boots off.'

They carried the Foundling babies out to where a horse-drawn van was waiting. Peg was thankful to leave the building which was like three sides of a square enclosing so many little souls in the only home they would know until they were old enough to support themselves. She cuddled Anna against her, and was glad it would be five years yet before *this* precious little soul need be subjected to the cold rules and regulations of hospital life.

Neither Peg nor Betty saw Sarah Byrne in her green dress and black bonnet watching them leave.

A keen wind was blowing through the trees, and Sarah stayed out of sight behind the railings in Brunswick Square, her feet and hands numb from the long wait. At last she saw two women leave the Foundling Hospital, one plump, one thin, and in the arms of the thin woman was a baby wrapped in a patchwork blanket Sarah's mother had made. Sarah marked her well.

# CHAPTER 2

When James Halden led Sarah away from the scene of her father's death she had never felt so ashamed. She looked with horror at the fingers which had cruelly raked Bill Yardley's face, and heard her own voice uttering words not even fit to be heard in the alleys. Her mother would never have forgiven her.

'Always speak kindly, Sarah,' her ma had said. 'Remember the meek shall inherit the earth.'

Ma had known her Bible thoroughly and had been fond of quoting it. When she had taught Sarah to read and write it had been her textbook, and it would have broken her heart if she'd heard such a tirade after all her patient teaching.

Sarah twisted away from the physician's grasp and darted back inside the foundry to where Bill Yardley still sat on the trough.

'I'm right sorry,' she cried, falling to her knees on the rough floor in front of him. 'You were shocked like me and I said such awful things.'

The man touched her lovely dark head. 'It's all right, Sarah girl. I understand. Reckon Paddy was lucky to 'ave a daughter like you. He were proud of you, yer know.'

'It wasn't your fault. He was always fighting. Ma told me he killed a man once and that's why they had to leave Ireland. I'm so sorry for what I said.'

She began to weep, hiding her head on the black, oily trouser-legs until the young physician came and once more drew her away.

'It wasn't fighting that killed your father, Sarah. He had some kind of seizure.' James Halden bent his leonine head to make himself heard above the hissing steam. 'Now come away. You need some air.'

There was authority in his voice and she felt a great surge of relief, as if he were plucking at her pain and releasing it.

Paddy Byrne had been a fighting man all his life. He had fled to London in 1828 after the Catholic emancipation bill had been passed, forced to leave his beloved Ireland because his Catholic fervour had led him to kill a Protestant in an argument during the celebrations. He had brought his wife with him, and settled her in the poverty of the Clerkenwell alleys where later Sarah, their only surviving child, was born. Her ma had been a lovely well-bred, dark-haired colleen then, with eyes as green as the meadows in which she'd played before Paddy Byrne had won her heart. Her family had tried to stop the marriage, but she would have followed him anywhere in the world. In London her colour had gradually faded away until only unhealthy red spots stained her cheeks and the cough she developed got worse. Sarah had nursed her mother until she died two years ago. After that Paddy's temper became more fiery than ever.

'If you'd just keep away from the dog fights, Pa,' Sarah had begged.

'You'd have me stop drinking, too, I've no doubt. May as well ask a man to stop breathing.'

Then he had met Maggie. He had taken her off the streets and given her a home because he was besotted with her; the home that Sarah's mother had kept clean and cheerful even when her health was failing. The Lord knew what it was like now.

She shrivelled inside at the thought of having to tell Maggie about the accident. She hated the woman. Her father had only married her to give a name to the child she was expecting, and now he would never see it. Scalding tears brimmed over, and James Halden checked them with the cushion of his thumb.

'Who's going to tell me father's wife?' she asked. She could never bear to give her a name.

'We'll leave it to the factory manager,' James said. 'You've had enough for one day.'

'I must see that he 'as a decent burial.'

'It'll be seen to. Your father worked for a good man.'

She couldn't bear to think of Pa lying under the cold, hard earth, silenced for ever. The glow from the furnace in the steam-filled room was like the flames of hell licking out to show her the place where her father had gone. His covered body was taken out to a cooler resting place, and suddenly the foundry seemed to be going round and round. Sarah pressed her palms to her temples to make it stop.

'Pa, if only I'd made it up with you,' she cried. 'If only you'd never married that whore.'

A choked cry escaped her before she fell to the ground, her legs no longer able to support her. The next thing she knew James Halden was carrying her out through the yard in strong, muscular arms. Her tears had dampened his immaculate waistcoat. It was the first time she had been so near a man with sweet breath and the scent of success about him. His black velour coat was soft and rich, his stock made of silk, and the buckskin trousers fitted him to perfection. The novelty took her breath away.

She wriggled with sudden embarrassment. He was a stranger. Her body became hot, and quite extraordinary feelings affected her limbs and stomach. She was conscious of her own serviceable but dowdy clothes provided by Mrs Bradford, the black dress with the big kitchen apron covering it.

'I've got to go back to work,' she said. 'Put me down. I can walk.'

But he didn't put her down. He continued to carry her out of the gate to his carriage, and lifted her up to the seat. She gripped his hand to steady herself and felt the strong bones. It was the first time she'd been in such a grand vehicle, and when she looked over the side she seemed so high up she was dizzy.

'Sit still,' he commanded, climbing up beside her and taking the reins.

'I work in Newcastle Place.'

'You're not going back there yet.'

'But I 'ave to. If Cook complains to Mrs Bradford I'll get the sack.'

'They'll understand,' James said. He handed her a blanket as she had no shawl and made sure it covered her head to keep out the cold. When he tucked in strands of dark curly hair her skin tingled at his touch. 'You're in no fit state to work straight away after the shock you've had. I've a visit to make. You can come with me. It'll help to take your mind off what's happened.'

She'd never met such a man. There was no arguing with him, and it was very pleasant to have someone caring, so she sat back in the seat without further protest. They set off, passed under St John's Gate and turned right to join traffic heading northwards. Travelling along at such a pace was an experience she would have enjoyed no end on a happier occasion, and even now she savoured the luxury of sweeping by those on foot as if she were royalty.

He drove out past the gardens of Bagnigge Wells House. The derelict remains of the old building were as depressing as the weather and the bare trees dripped with melting frost like chilling tears. He encouraged her to talk about Paddy, asking questions as if he was really interested, and by the time he pulled up she was beginning to feel much better. Just spilling out memories of Pa right back to her childhood eased away some of the pain and she was able to relax a little.

'Now,' he said, turning to her. 'I'm going to visit a lady whose mind is very troubled.

She came to St Bartholomew's Hospital to be operated on, but it's her mind that interests me. I'm sure she'll get better quicker if something can be done about her mental state.'

'Do you mean she's mad?'

'No. A lot of people are classed as mad and shut away without any need. I don't want this lady to be one of them.'

'You're real clever.'

'I wish I was.' He jumped down and tethered the horse. 'Come with me.'

'Not to see a mad woman.'

'Sarah, you didn't listen to what I said. Have faith in me.'

He looked at her with those sensual eyes and she knew how Ma must have felt when she first met Pa. James Halden had a charm which was irresistible. She let him help her down from the carriage and lead her inside a shop where there was a strong, pastoral smell of grain, and Sarah wrinkled up her nose to sniff it. The man who came to serve them was a dealer in songbirds.

'Which one would you like?' James asked her.

There were birds in cages all around, mostly linnets and canaries, and they warbled incessantly, their throat feathers ruffled.

'I like 'em all,' said Sarah, gazing at them with fascination.

'Which one in particular? I'm buying you one.'

'You can't do that. You don't know me.'

'I want to know how you look when you smile.' His masterful manner caused goose-flesh

37

of a most agreeable kind to affect her limbs, and a small, sweet smile tipped the corners of her lovely mouth. His own lips curved to match it. 'That's better. I knew we could salvage something out of today. Now please choose a bird.'

'It's very kind of you, but I'd not be allowed one.' She could imagine what would be said if she arrived with one at the house in Newcastle Place.

'I can see you're a very obstinate woman,' he said.

Minutes later the gift was paid for and placed in her arms, and James went upstairs to visit the man's sick wife.

The linnet she had chosen stopped trilling and sat on the bottom of the wicker cage, its little brown body huddled unhappily beneath the perch. Sarah understood its dejection. This generous man with guinea-gold hair had come into her life so unexpectedly, but she just knew that like a guinea he would slip through her fingers before she had a chance to know him better. The likes of Dr James Halden wouldn't take more than a passing interest in a common domestic servant.

James Halden was hastening towards the Bagnigge Wells Road when he heard the cry that a man had fallen in the furnace at Smith's. He turned his horse and drove under St John's Gate, anxious with the keenness of youth to see if there was anything he could do, but it was obvious from the start that the poor man was beyond all earthly help.

He was about to leave the foundry and continue his journey when an apprentice came rushing in with the loveliest girl he had seen in a long while, and his heart seemed to stop. She was tall and had a slender enough waist for him to have spanned it with his hands, and he was amazed at how strongly he wished he could be given the chance. Then he learnt that she was the man's daughter, and frivolous thoughts were swept away on a tide of sympathy.

She wasn't wearing a shawl, and dark hair escaped from a maid's white mob cap which had slipped half off her head. Her wet boots made footprints on the dusty floor and she still wore an apron over her black skirt, but she had a fine air about her. The trappings of a domestic servant made her seem like a dove clothed in starling's feathers.

She faced the tragedy with courage, acting with dignity even though she was obviously in great distress. James had just finished his years as a medical student and took his vocation very seriously. He hoped eventually to concentrate on diseases of the mind so he was constantly analysing people's actions. He did it automatically when the girl attacked the man who'd been fighting with her father, recognizing it as a natural reaction to shock and grief. And when she was overcome with remorse and apologized so sweetly a few minutes later his admiration for her was boundless. Sarah was a girl with character as well as beauty and he couldn't wait to get to know her better.

He tried to give comfort but it was difficult to find words after such a bizarre accident, except to explain what had happened.

'Your father had some kind of seizure,' he said, sure enough of his diagnosis to be confident. 'He might already have been dead when he fell on the fire, in which case he wouldn't have known anything about it.'

'You're very kind to tell me,' Sarah said.

He took her with him on his visit because he couldn't bear to let her disappear without finding out more about her. The feel of her body close to his in the carriage made him want to hold her, and he was tempted to cover her attractive though work-worn hand with his. Such temptations were unfamiliar to him. He'd been working too hard to spend time with women, and the courting of his wife had been very proper and unexciting. Since marrying her he hadn't cast an eye on anyone else. Until now. Sarah affected him with such unexpected desire he couldn't understand himself. He was certainly too surprised to analyse his own emotions.

When they were driving along he encouraged her to talk about her father and from what she told him he knew it had been a struggle for her even to get a servant's position. It was when she told him where she was working that he was taken aback.

'I'm with the Bradfords in Newcastle Place,' she said. 'They're right kind to me and I like it there. I was real lucky to get the job.'

He knew the Bradfords. His wife was anxiously

40

encouraging him to strengthen the acquaintance as they were influential people, but he was not yet sufficiently advanced in his profession to feel he ought to push for invitations. He had to tread carefully.

So when he bought Sarah Byrne the songbird he didn't deliver her straight to the door of the Bradford house of employment just in case anyone should recognize him and pass comment on the fact that he had taken one of the servants out driving. He apologized and helped her down at the end of the road.

'Forgive me, I must get back to the hospital,' he said. 'I'm already late. But I shall inquire the date and time of your father's funeral and if possible I'll be there.'

'I don't know how to thank you,' she said, giving him back the blanket. She held the bird by the ring at the top of the cage and it had started to trill again. 'I'll be very honoured if you can come, but I'll understand if you can't.'

Her eyes were as blue as the patch of bright sky which had suddenly emerged from between the clouds and when she looked at him he was sure there was invitation in their depths. In spite of the iciness of the day he felt warm and exhilarated, and he was determined that nothing would prevent him from attending.

Maggie Byrne had bought herself a black silk dress from a secondhand clothes shop in Seven Dials to wear for Paddy's burial. Her figure was ungainly in the late stages of pregnancy but she wrapped her red wool shawl well round and kept

41

her hands clasped in front so that it was not so noticeable. Her straw bonnet had a large brim which was usually turned back from her face, but today she didn't want people looking at her grief so she had tipped the brim down.

She was a brown-haired woman of twenty-eight, and not unlike Paddy's first wife. Or so he had kept on telling her.

'Maggie, you're as lovely as the mornin', so ye are.' He would pat her cheek and touch her breast, his beguiling smile warming her. But then the smile would fade, and the melancholy would settle on him. 'You're like my Eileen. My beautiful Eileen. She had the looks of an angel when I first married her.'

Well, now he had gone to find her, but if his Eileen was really an angel she doubted they would meet, for Paddy had been no saint. If he had been she wouldn't have fallen in love with him.

The manner of his death ensured that more than the usual number of people were at the funeral. A hole had been dug for the coffin, next to the place where Eileen had been buried only two short years ago, and boards propped the soil up at the sides. The smell was terrible, worse than anything Maggie had ever known, and on this frosty morning steam came up as if from a dung heap. It seemed to bring a coppery taste to her mouth.

She looked across the open grave at Sarah, her stepdaughter, and it saddened her even more that the gulf between them had never been bridged.

At sixteen Sarah was quite beautiful, but she didn't make the most of herself. Surely she was too thin by far for a man's taste, yet the one at her side today was a toff and no mistake, and it was obvious he cared about the girl by the way he kept looking at her with concern in his eyes. Maggie was intrigued. Sarah had a high opinion of herself, and always stood with her shoulders back and her pretty nose pointed skyward as if she was better than everyone else. Now here she was with a toff! Her father would have had something to say about that. But Maggie had a warm heart and she looked for the best in people. She had always sensed the goodness in Sarah Byrne and for Paddy's sake wished they could be friends.

Clods of earth were thrown on to the stout elm coffin, and the mourners began to leave. Maggie waited. Men Paddy had worked with at Smith's trooped past; so did the neighbours who had stood here before when he had buried Eileen. One or two offered sympathy and would have taken her along with them, but she stayed on with her head bowed until only Sarah and the fair-haired man were left. When she looked up she met Sarah's tear-filled eyes.

She stretched out both hands, as a mother might, unable now to check her own tears, and the girl came round the grave.

'Your father was a good man,' Maggie said. Her lips quivered. 'He gave me pride in meself and made me feel wanted. No one had ever done that before. I don't know what I'll do without 'im.'

Sarah almost took her hands, then drew back. 'You'll be able to go back on the streets,' she said.

The young man frowned, wordlessly reproving her, but Sarah lifted her chin a little higher.

'I'll have 'is child to bring up very soon.' Maggie's voice was still quiet and dignified. 'The streets'll never see me again, not the way you mean. Will you come home with me? There's a few things of yer father's you might like to keep.'

'I'll take you both,' said the toff, extending his hand. 'I'm Dr Halden. My carriage is at the gate.'

Maggie was never one to reject a friendly overture. 'Pleased to meet you, I'm sure. Yes, I could do with a ride.'

'I'd rather go back to work,' said Sarah.

But it seemed the doctor could persuade Sarah to do anything, for it didn't take much argument to convince her that it was wrong to be ungracious.

'This lady can't go back home alone,' he said. 'I shall drive her, and if you don't care to come, Sarah, I'm sure you won't mind walking.'

A bright colour relieved the paleness of Sarah's cheeks. Shadows of indecision flitted across her face, and she looked down at her feet, but the bitterness was seeping away like the ugly water from the trench where her father's coffin lay.

'All right, I'll come,' she said. She took a deep breath, then slipped her arm through Maggie's. 'Let me help you.'

Paddy's daughter was tall like him, and she

had the same air of self-assurance. In Maggie's heart there had always been a prayer that they might be reconciled. Well, perhaps a start had been made, even though it was too late for Paddy. They walked together towards the street, her body heavy but her heart lighter than when she had come.

The alley was too narrow for Dr Halden's carriage. He left it in Turnmill Street where it attracted the interest of a horde of children, and he gave a boy a coin to mind the horse. Garbage was piled high in corners, and Maggie watched Sarah stepping carefully so as not to tread in the filth. She wondered if she had been as particular when she'd lived here.

Most of the timbered houses had windows patched with rags, but the one Maggie entered was slightly cleaner. Sarah hesitated, then drew in her breath and followed.

'I'll wait outside,' said the physician. 'You'll want to talk privately.'

The floorboards groaned, the narrow stairs creaked. Maggie went to the room Paddy had rented for nigh on sixteen years, the only room in the tall lodging house that didn't accommodate more than one family. He had been proud of that. She knew Sarah had been expecting the place to be unfit to live in and was pleased to see her eyes widen in surprise. When she'd gone to work for the Bradfords Paddy had been left on his own and it had got worse than a pigsty then. Now the floor was scrubbed, and instead of sacking round the bed there was a proper curtain slotted on string. A pewter pot

45

and clean cups and saucers were on the table, and there was a rag mat in front of Paddy's chair which he'd said he had carried on his back from Hungerford Market. The chair bore the sagging impression of his big body, and the girl touched it, misty-eyed again.

'I loved 'im, yuh know,' Maggie whispered. 'I looked after 'im well.'

'I s'pose it was better than 'im being lonely.' The admission was grudging, but Maggie's spirits lifted a little more.

Sarah went round the room, picking up objects and putting them down again. Each one must have held memories of her father, but she seemed to be looking for something special.

'What's happened to 'is fiddle?' she asked.

The battered instrument had been Paddy Byrne's most treasured possession and he had played it like a genius when his belly was full of beer. Every Saturday night he had played in a tavern, and he'd been known to take it to protest meetings in Clerkenwell Green to stir up radical fervour with songs. But Maggie had heard him draw notes out of it which rent the air with their sadness, and through his music she'd seen a side of him he'd kept hidden from the world.

'I've wrapped it up,' she said.

'It's the only thing I want,' said Sarah.

She found it behind the chair and picked it up, but Maggie tried to take it from her. It was one of her most treasured memories of Paddy.

'You can have anything but that. I want to keep 'is fiddle.'

But Sarah wouldn't relinquish it. 'Me ma gave it to 'im when they was married. It should be mine now.'

'No,' cried Maggie.

In spite of her bulk she moved swiftly to grab the instrument, and she stepped back for fear it should be taken from her again. The worm-eaten stairs were only a few paces from the open door but she didn't give them a thought. A moment later she fell down them, unable to find the rope against the wall which might have saved her. It was the fiddle which escaped undamaged.

'She must be got to hospital,' James Halden said.

He had been the first to reach Maggie, though her screams had brought people running from all the neighbouring tenements.

Sarah was crying as he lifted the heavy body into his arms. 'Let me come with you. Don't let her die.'

Maggie had no colour at all. It looked as if she had no life in her either, but she moaned as James carried her and laid her gently on the seat of his carriage. He was taking her to St Bartholomew's, the hospital where he was a junior physician.

'There's no room for anyone else,' he said. 'Stay here and I'll come back when there's news.'

She watched him whip his horse and drive

away at breakneck speed. Then she went back inside and sat in her father's chair, shaking with shock and recrimination. If Maggie died she would be entirely to blame. Selfishness had made her want to have the fiddle, and she would never forgive herself for what had happened.

Mrs Bradford had given her the complete day off for her father's funeral and she didn't have to be back at the house in Newcastle Place until six o'clock. She closed her eyes and tried to pray for Maggie, but didn't know where to start. Only yesterday she hadn't cared a farthing for the woman.

Maggie wasn't so bad after all. She wasn't a slut. And she had made Paddy happy in the last few months of his life. Amidst the noise of children shouting, women calling across the alley, and dogs barking, Sarah seemed to hear her father condemning her for the way she had behaved these last months, and her misery grew. He needn't have got married. He could have kept Maggie to warm his bed and no one would have thought the worse of him for it. But Paddy had respected her.

'She's a decent woman who's had no chance to better herself,' he had said, on the day he invited Sarah to witness the simple ceremony before a registrar of marriages. 'Oi can't give her much, but oi'll give her me name, so oi will.'

'You're doing it for the child she's foisting on you. You're a fool, Pa.'

'Oh, the child's moin right enough. She's lived here with me since you moved out.'

'Well, if you put that woman in Ma's place

48

I'll never forgive you.'

'Maggie's nothing loike yer Ma.'

'I don't know how you can even speak of her in the same breath.'

Sarah had refused to go to the wedding. And that was the last time she had seen her father alive. She couldn't bear to remember the dreadful things she had said that day, any more than she could think about what was happening to Maggie now. And only hours after Paddy had been laid in his grave.

Nor did she dare to dwell on what James Halden must think of her. She was ashamed of her false pride. It had seemed so important to make a good impression, to show him that she had risen above the way of life in the alleys, but it was a selfish, uncaring side of her he had seen. And after he'd been so kind, too. When he'd left her at the entrance to Newcastle Place the day Pa died she'd ached with disappointment that she might never see him again.

She hadn't really expected to see him at the funeral, though she had looked forward to the possibility with unseemly excitement considering the solemnity of the occasion. There'd been no call for him to attend. Paddy Byrne meant nothing to him, yet he'd appeared at the graveside this morning. Of course, it was because he'd felt sorry for her, but whatever his motive Sarah had been pleased and grateful.

Her feet and hands were so cold they didn't seem to belong to her, but that was nothing to the coldness inside. She had never felt so wretched and she vowed that if Maggie recovered she would make it up to her somehow. In fact the time to start was now. She couldn't sit around doing nothing while she waited.

She looked around but could see nothing prepared for the arrival of a baby. Maggie seemed to have had no nesting instincts at all. There was nothing that could be used for a cradle so obviously she intended keeping it in bed with her, but Sarah had heard tales of babies being smothered like that and she was surprisingly anxious that her newly expected brother or sister wouldn't end up that way.

She went down to the next floor and called Rosa Kenny.

'Rosa, have you got a box you don't want?'

The five Kenny children came crowding round like little goblins, dirty and ragged, but squealing happily.

'Me old man's got one from the market to burn but you can 'ave it,' said Rosa, who had already started with her sixth child. 'If she comes 'ome Maggie'll need a bit of warmth.'

'I want it to make a cradle.'

'Waste of time. There won't be no baby after a fall like that.'

Nevertheless Rosa produced a wooden box which was just the size, and Sarah went back up to the room that had been her home since childhood. Her ma's sewing bag was still in the cupboard and when she brought out the cotton and needles there was a lump in her throat. Ma had taught her to sew.

A hole in the mattress yielded enough stuffing to make a pillow, and Sarah lined the bottom

50

of the box with it. Next she took off one of her two petticoats which had tucks and embroidery round the hem, and this she cut to cover it and make a frill round the edge. Concentrating on the stitching helped to ease her mind, and the hours passed.

James Halden returned just as she was finishing the last frill, and she jumped up as soon as she heard his steps on the stair.

'James,' she cried, forgetting that she had never used his name before. 'Tell me everything. How is she? And the baby?'

'Maggie Byrne will live,' he said. 'And so will her son, though he's no bigger than a rabbit.'

'Thank God,' she breathed. Then: 'What if you hadn't been here?'

She had known him less than a week, yet it seemed natural to turn to him. He was so tall he had to incline his head to avoid hitting the beams, and his nearness made her tremble.

'If neither of us had been here she would have gone her time.' His tone was critical. 'That poor woman showed great courage today.'

'It sounds like you're blaming me.'

'I didn't say that.'

'You don't need to. I ain't all that proud of meself one way and another, but there's no cause for you to tell me.'

'Perhaps if you could learn a little tolerance. All Maggie Byrne talked about was how she hoped you would accept her. She needs you.'

Sarah drew herself up, full of indignation that he should presume to judge her. 'I was trying,

51

honest I was. But it really ain't none of your business.'

Suddenly the stale air in that tenement room was charged with passionate emotion. From being polite strangers they had become like sparring lovers speaking their minds with a familiarity which was extraordinary in its intensity. Sarah was trembling with anger and roused to a state of excitement she didn't understand until without warning he stopped her in mid-sentence by kissing her soundly. She was so surprised she froze to the spot.

'What is it about you, Sarah?' he demanded. He gripped the tops of her arms, and his voice was hoarse. 'From the moment I set eyes on you I haven't been able to think of anything else. I couldn't wait to get back here to you.'

Her senses were in a whirl but she tried to hold on to her sanity. He was going too fast for her.

'For your information I've been making a cradle for Maggie's baby while you was gone,' she said. 'I ain't heartless like you seem to think.'

He looked round and saw the froth of white cotton in the corner, as pretty a cradle as any woman could want.

'What an extraordinary girl you are.'

She had always kept herself aloof from men, hating their sly looks, their winks and coarse talk. But James Halden was different. His cultured voice and charming manners aroused feelings she had never experienced before. She was becoming agonizingly aware of her body, and she was dismayed by a treacherous longing which made her ache so strangely. Never expecting to meet him again, she had indulged all the week in fond dreams of him, as if he were a character in a journal story, but the reality was infinitely more exhilarating. The way he looked at her sent shivers down her spine. She'd pictured giving herself to a man, but not until the right time and the right one came along. Well if ever there was a right time it was now. She liked this man more than anyone she'd ever met.

He was kissing her again, but with urgency now, the way his lips moved over hers calculated to set up a craving for more. They trailed over her neck to create almost unbearable delight, and she clung to him. He stripped off his coat and her fingers splayed across his back, savouring the warmth of his skin through his shirt. Children appeared in the doorway, chanting and cheering, their dirty faces alight with smiles. When he let go of her to shut the door her impatience for him to return was almost more than her body could stand.

He pulled the curtain away from the bed and drew her on to it while their mouths still met.

'You're so beautiful, Sarah,' he murmured.

James was a powerful lover. He took her virginity with care, giving her so much ecstatic joy in the taking that she scarcely noticed pain. Lying with him was like discovering a miracle. The unleashing of passion brought undreamed of excitement. The uninhibited joining of their bodies was more glorious than anything she had imagined, and the culminating spasm which

53

rocked and arched her body made her cry out with exquisite agony.

In the aftermath she nestled in his arms, forgetful of the time. She revelled in the warmth of his skin, and her fingers twined through the surprisingly dark hair on his chest and down over his flat stomach to his loins. He had the most wonderful body.

'We must find somewhere more comfortable to meet,' James said. He looked with distaste at the rotting timbers above them. The mattress was as lumpy as a bag of onions. He turned on his side and clasped her more tightly as a new wave of passion stirred him. 'If only I had the means to set you up in a house where I could visit you.'

'You mean you'd let me be a kept woman?'

'I'd be very good to you.'

'But you'd never marry me because I ain't good enough, is that it?'

He stroked her hair which massed in thick dark curls on the pillow. He kissed the lobe of her ear, taking it between his teeth and teasing it with his tongue. 'If only I'd met you a year ago.'

'What difference would it have made?'

He was silent a moment. Then: 'I have a wife. It was a marriage of convenience. Had I met you sooner I doubt I would have entered into it, but Maud's father is influential and I hope to gain a better position at the hospital on his recommendation.'

Sarah struggled away from him with un-reasonable disappointment and anger, all joy gone. For all his fine talk he had used her like a whore.

'I think you'd better leave, James Halden. I ain't the sort to be taken for granted, and I sure as hell don't want to be someone's fancy woman.'

She was pulling on her petticoat, and he sprang to his feet and tried to stop her.

'Sarah, come back to me. Let's talk sensibly.'

'There's nothing to talk about. You took what you wanted and now I'm asking you to go.'

'Don't say you weren't willing.'

'No, I ain't saying that, but you've got a wife and that's the end of it. If you've a hankering for something more you'll have to look elsewhere 'cause I ain't obliging.'

He got up and arranged his clothes. 'What did you expect? A wedding ring? You've a mighty high opinion of yourself for a kitchen maid.'

'I ought to 'ave known the likes of you wouldn't do all the things you've done for nothing. Well I've learnt a lesson good and proper and I 'ope I never see you again.'

'Don't worry,' said James. 'There are plenty more like you if I need amusement.'

He departed in such a hurry that a flurry of dust flew up in his wake.

Sarah shouted down the stairs after him. 'I'm a respectable girl, and I shan't always be a kitchen maid.'

Rosa Kenny's children sniggered on the lower landing and jumped aside to let him pass. Shouting was nothing new in Stone Alley.

When Sarah got back to the attic bedroom in Newcastle Place the first thing she did was open the window, letting in damp, wintry air. Then she picked up the wicker bird cage and took it to the sill. The linnet lifted its beak and uttered a few melancholy notes as she opened the cage door. It hopped tentatively to the entrance, then spread its wings and flew away.

Her heart felt as empty as the cage in her hands.

Maggie's baby was a puny infant, but he thrived against all the odds and was baptized Patrick after his father. Sarah took to visiting whenever she had time off, which was two hours every other Sunday, and she never went empty-handed. Cook had been moved by Sarah's grief when she got back from her father's funeral, and when she heard how Maggie had given birth on the very same day she had taken pity.

'You're a good girl, Sarah,' she said. 'Your concern does you credit, and I'll see to it that you have a few things wrapped up for the poor woman when you go to see her.'

'Thank you very much, Mrs Martin. She'll be very pleased.'

'Not a word to anyone, though, mind.'

'No, ma'am.'

'I wouldn't do it for anybody else on the staff, but you're the best worker we've had here.'

The first few days after the burial she had felt like dying herself, mostly of shame, but she had set about her tasks with the same efficiency as always, and if she didn't speak to anyone it was because words would have brought fresh tears. She grieved for her father and worried about Maggie, but most of all she fumed and cried over the affair with James Halden. She ought never to have trusted him.

Patrick was three months old when Sarah knew for sure that she would have James's child before the year was out. The knowledge terrified her. She'd been feeling sick a morning or two, but not so as it interfered with her work, and no one remarked on it. At first she'd given no thought to missing for a month, putting it down to the trauma of losing Pa, but by the time nothing showed for the third month running there could be no doubt that the worst had happened. She was definitely pregnant.

She didn't know how she would live with the shame when it began to show. She started hiding food away instead of eating it so as not to put on any weight, but hunger forced her to have a good meal at least once a week. The Bradfords would soon put her out of the door when they heard she was having a baby, but she didn't know where she would go. There'd been neither sight nor sound of James since that fateful day and no doubt he had forgotten her as quickly as he had taken her, but he must be told there was going to be a child. She would have to have some more money to support it, and it was only right he should pay for the pleasure he'd had.

At the beginning of April she didn't go to Maggie's, but walked instead to St Bartholomew's Hospital. It was such a big place and nobody seemed to know the whereabouts of the junior physician she was asking for. She wandered through corridors, completely lost and tired, until a short, elderly man with a red face and gold-rimmed spectacles took pity on her.

'Who are you looking for, girl?' he asked.

'Dr Halden, sir. No one seems to know where 'e is.'

'I'm sure they don't.' The man took off his spectacles and wiped them on a snowy white handkerchief. 'Were you a patient of his?'

'Yes, sir.' She hoped she wouldn't have to go into details.

'Well I'm afraid he's out of the country so whatever you want to discuss with him will have to wait.'

'Out of the country!' Sarah echoed in dismay. Nausea welled up in her and she put a hand to her throat. 'Will 'e be away long?'

'Young lady, you are impudent to ask, but since the matter seems important to you I'm prepared to say he won't be back much before Christmas. Dr Halden is married to my daughter and has taken her on an extended tour of the Continent.'

'Oh, my goodness.'

'Is there anything I can do to help?'

'No,' said Sarah. 'No, sir, thank you.'

She picked up her skirt and fled from the hospital before letting herself think what James's absence meant. By Christmas her child would be several weeks old, but she'd been forced to survive on her wits since before her ma had died,

58

and she would survive now. There was nothing else for it.

One Sunday in May Sarah walked to Turnmill Street with a slice of meatloaf, a fruit pie and various other luxuries tied up in brown paper to look like laundry. By then she was five months into pregnancy, though no one would have guessed, although she didn't climb the stairs with her usual briskness. She listened for Patrick's cry but the only noise was from the Kenny children as they squabbled over a piece of bread, and Maggie was sitting on the bed with the baby sucking in vain at her scrawny breast. He'd been so sickly from birth and Sarah ached with sadness to see her tiny stepbrother losing hold on life.

Maggie crooned to him and stroked his head. He began to cry fitfully with a keening sound. ' 'E don't grow,' she said. 'Here 'e is five months old and hardly any bigger than when he was born.'

Sarah looked at the mite, and pity drove out every other thought.

'I'll get some warm water to wash 'im,' she said. An acrid smell polluted the room, and the ragged blankets on the bed showed how Maggie had lost heart. 'It might make 'im better.'

'It'll do no good. He's hot and 'is bowels keep running.' She was propped against the cold, damp wall with the baby in one hand and a bottle of gin in the other.

'Give 'im to me,' Sarah said.

Maggie held Patrick closer with maudlin despair. 'You can't do nothing for 'im.' She rolled her eyes and took another swig of gin. 'But you're a good friend. A real good friend, Sarah Byrne, though I never thought I'd say it.' She slid down on the sagging mattress.

Sarah took the gin bottle away and went downstairs. She heard the rattle of a milk pail in the next alley, and the familiar cry of: 'Any milk here?' She bought some and took it back for the baby, dipping her finger in for the mite to suck. He was ravenous.

'You need looking after yourself,' she said to Maggie, sitting beside her on the bed. 'Do you eat the food I bring you, or give it to Rosa's kids?'

She didn't need an answer. The extent of her stepmother's generosity surprised her. This time she made sure Maggie ate the meat and the pie herself, and forced her to drink a cupful of milk.

'You can't feed Patrick if you don't feed yourself, and I'll bet the poor little scrap hates gin as much as I do. If you love 'im, Maggie, treat yourself better than you've been doing.'

Gradually Maggie's colour improved and she leaned her head against Sarah's shoulder.

'You're good to me, girl,' she said. 'I don't know why.'

This was the day Sarah had made up her mind to speak to her stepmother about her own problems. It would be two weeks before she got another chance so she had to take it now whether Maggie was sober or not. She made her sit up.

'Maggie, there's something I've got to say to

you. I need your help. I need it bad.'

The effect of the words was profound. Maggie Byrne was a woman with plenty of love to give, and the best stimulus of all was to know that she was needed.

'Whatever it is you can count on me, Sarah, you know that. Not just for yer father's sake neither.' Her lethargy disappeared and her eyes cleared. 'What is it you want, ducks?'

'I'm having a baby meself,' Sarah said. 'Around September. I'll 'ave to give up me job soon and I ain't got anywhere to live. Can I come here with you and Patrick?'

Tears brimmed on to Maggie's cheeks and she brushed them away hurriedly.

'Dearie, there ain't anything I'd like better. This is your 'ome, always 'as been and always will be.' She didn't condemn even though she was shrewd enough to know who was responsible. 'It were that doctor with the yellow hair, weren't it?' she said. 'Well, I can't say I blame you. He was a right handsome man, and a kind one. And I could see 'e thought a lot of you. Does 'e know?'

'No, and 'e never will.'

Sarah told her about the visit to St Bartholomew's. Maggie put Patrick in his cradle and took her in her arms with motherly concern.

'Well, it ain't the end of the world, ducks. It 'appens to a lot of us and everyone ain't as lucky as I was.'

A ray of sunshine filtered through the dirty window, slanting across the table which hadn't been scrubbed since Paddy died.

Two weeks later Sarah told Mrs Bradford that she would have to leave, making Maggie the excuse.

'I'm sorry, ma'am, but me stepmother's got a sickly baby and she ain't well enough to look after 'erself, never mind him. So I'll have to take care of her.'

Mrs Bradford was a rather severe Christian woman who admired a sense of responsibility in others and was always fair.

'I'm so sorry, Sarah,' she said. 'You've been getting on very well here and I've had glowing reports from Mrs Martin about your work, but if you feel it your duty to go home I understand. And I respect you for it.'

'Thank you, ma'am.'

'Perhaps you'll be able to return to work a little later on when your stepmother's health improves. I heard that she was widowed a few days before the baby was born.'

'Yes, ma'am. Me father died in the furnace at Smith's.'

'So dreadful. Dreadful.' Mrs Bradford went to a drawer and brought out a small inlaid box. From it she took a shilling and gave it to Sarah. 'This may help a little. And when you feel able to work again I hope you'll return here.'

'Thank you very much, ma'am,' said Sarah, and bobbed a curtsey before leaving. She felt guilty accepting the money, but took it gratefully.

She settled in Stone Alley with reluctance,

though Maggie made her more than welcome. For the last few weeks the baby inside her had been making itself felt. Now, as if objecting already to the place where it would take its first breath, it kicked against her stomach wall quite forcibly. She ought to have hated the child she was carrying, it being the cause of her return to squalor after the effort she had made to rise above it, but since she'd felt it move she couldn't reject it. As it grew she would put her hands on her belly and talk to the baby.

'Reckon you'll be as good-looking as yer father,' she would say. 'Not that he'd care, even if 'e knew. Toffs never admit to their bastards, do they. We'll 'ave to just get by on our own.'

Whenever she thought of James Halden a shameful wave of physical longing washed over her until she remembered he had used her and discarded her. But at least her baby would come from decent stock. She began to think of it as *he*, and wondered if he would make something of himself later on in life. Maybe he'd want to be a physician like his father.

The weeks passed and Sarah and Maggie took in washing to pay the rent, but there was never enough money left to buy more than bread and a few vegetables. Sarah's arms and legs were getting thinner every day, and the rag mat she'd started making for the hearth became too heavy to have on her lap. But she was relieved to see Patrick thrive at last now that Maggie had been weaned off gin, and when Rosa's sixth baby arrived she helped with it, gaining experience for when her own time came.

The more tired she became the more bitterly she blamed James. To think a few minutes of thoughtless pleasure could end in this. At the end of the summer she was so hungry she hadn't the energy to move further than Paddy's dilapidated chair and she stitched a baby's gown from her only decent petticoat. Maggie scrounged what food she could, and when Sarah dipped a crust of bread in the cabbage soup she'd made she could see the cracks in the bottom of the dish through the thin liquid. They were like a map of Europe, and that was where James Halden was enjoying a luxurious, carefree holiday with his wife.

Sarah's daughter was born on the last day of September. The midwife rolled up her sleeves and toiled all night by the light of candles stuck in turnips, and just before dawn the baby was delivered on to the same straw mattress on which she had been conceived.

Her labour was not unduly difficult. Sarah pushed and thrust to get rid of the burden she had carried for nine long months, and she screamed until Maggie forced gin down her throat to quieten her. In each lull between contractions memories of James tormented her, and with each new onslaught of pain she mentally tried to inflict the agony on him, cursing him for what he had done to her. When at last it was over she lay back in a sleepy state, as a result of too much gin rather than weakness from the birthing, but she no longer felt like cursing James. The baby had arrived safely and she couldn't continue blaspheming against the man who had fathered it when one glimpse was enough to capture her heart completely.

'You're so beautiful,' Sarah crooned, the next day. 'I think I shall call you Angel.'

The little girl had intensely blue eyes like her own, and a covering of golden down on her head which set Sarah's lips tingling when they brushed over it. She loved this tiny creature so much she didn't know how to contain it, or how to show it enough. She rocked the baby in her arms, refusing to put her down for a minute, and she sang snatches of lullabies she remembered her mother singing so many years ago.

If Maggie was envious she tried not to show it, but it was hard not to make comparisons. 'She'll grow up with rickets like the rest of 'em,' she said, rubbing Patrick's thin legs which failed to support him when he attempted to pull himself up against his father's chair.

'No she won't. I won't let her.'

'There'll be no way you can help it with only charity to live on.'

Sarah rummaged under the bed for a tin box, opened it and brought out a piece of patchwork lined with blanket. 'Me ma made this with bits left over when she took in sewing. When I was little I had it on me bed. Now it's Angel's.'

'Well, that won't feed 'er.'

'It'll keep 'er warm though.' She snuggled the baby in it and rocked her to stop a persistent whimpering.

Two days passed and Angel's cries became

more unhappy. Two more, and it was plain that she was hungry, just as Patrick had been in the first few weeks of life. Sarah began to panic. There wasn't enough milk in her breasts to satisfy the mite. There was no money to buy nourishing food for herself, and no hope of working to earn any. Cow's milk had saved Patrick's life, but when she gave it to Angel she became sick and feverish.

'I'd feed 'er meself if I didn't 'ave me latest,' said Rosa. 'I ain't never been short of milk yet.'

Angel's keening cry became weaker and she lay listlessly in the cradle which Patrick had outgrown, scarcely waking when Sarah tried almost in vain to feed her.

'There must be *something* I can do.' She appealed to Maggie desperately. 'Tell me. Please.'

'Find yer fancy doctor,' said Maggie. 'He's the one who should be providing money to get you out of 'ere.'

'I said I'd never ask 'im for anything.'

'Do you want to keep that child alive or don't you?'

'More than anything in the world.'

Once more Sarah trudged to St Bartholomew's, but James hadn't returned and she daren't ask if he was likely to be much longer. She couldn't wait anyway. She had to find some other way to save Angel's precious little life, and find it quickly.

Maggie had another suggestion. ' 'Course there's always the Foundling Hospital.'

The words hung like icicles in the humidity of the autumn afternoon. They brought a terrible chill to Sarah's heart.

'But I'd never see her again if I took 'er there. I 'eard the Foundling's a dreadful place.'

'You take yer choice. If she stays here like as not you'll lose her anyway. There's more dies than lives in these alleys, if you ask me. One of Bertha Hobbs's kids is down with a fever again.'

'I'd have to leave 'er in a basket at the gate.'

'Where've yer been, ducks!' Maggie scoffed. 'They don't do that no more. Neither do you 'ave to pay a hundred quid like I 'eard it cost at one time.' She put an arm round Sarah's shoulder. 'It's a good place. The best there is for kids like Angel.'

Sarah drew Angel closer and eyed her stepmother with suspicion. 'If it's such a good idea, why didn't you take Patrick to the Foundling?'

'Because I was married to 'is father.' Maggie's tone levelled a rare touch of criticism at the girl she had sheltered these last four months. 'They wouldn't have taken 'im even if I'd been willing to part with 'im, me being a widow. It ain't fair. They only take bastards, to give the mothers a chance to make a fresh start.'

They talked it over endlessly, and the icicles started to melt, dripping on to the rock of objection and wearing it away. While Angel slept, Sarah planned her future with heartbreaking realism. She didn't need Maggie to remind

67

her of the odds against a baby's survival in the alleys, and she loved this one enough to make the ultimate sacrifice.

'Mrs Bradford said she'd take you back,' Maggie reminded her. 'I reckon, that being so, the Governors'll smile on you.'

Sarah studied Angel, committing each tiny feature to memory. 'I'll try it,' she said. 'But if they take 'er I swear I'll not lose sight of 'er. I'll devote me life to getting her back somehow. See if I don't.'

She smoothed the soft baby hair lovingly, and she didn't notice that a few fine golden strands rubbed off on her finger.

## CHAPTER 3

Two days after leaving Angel at the Foundling Hospital Sarah returned to work at the house in Newcastle Place.

'I'm surprised Mrs Bradford took you back,' said Cook. 'I hope you appreciate it.'

'I do, Mrs Martin.'

'And I hope that stepmother of yours appreciates it, too. I don't know what you've been doing to yourself, girl. That dress would hang better on a broomstick.' She picked hold of the loose material round the waist and yanked it with disapproval. 'We must see you get some decent food or it'll be a waste of time paying you a wage.'

'Thank you, Mrs Martin.'

The first days back were hard for Sarah. She hadn't completely regained her strength, and as no one knew the truth about her absence, no allowances were made.

'I reckon if you 'adn't left you'd 'ave bin a parlourmaid by now,' Ella Tomkin said. The two girls were sharing the attic room again.

'Reckon I'll be one anyway before much longer,' said Sarah, with a swish of her skirt.

Her cheeks began to fill out and the hollows by her collar bone were less noticeable, but the dullness in her blue eyes persisted. She tried to go about her tasks with the same thoroughness as before, but too often her mind strayed from what she was doing, and promotion became less and less likely. A dozen times a day she pictured the woman with prematurely white hair who was now holding Angel to her breast, and she ached with longing to change places with her. But the bright enthusiasm with which she had vowed to improve herself was already being tarnished by the increasing breath of reprimand.

'The salt cellar has a finger mark on it, Sarah,' said the housekeeper one morning, after she had spent an hour on the silver. 'You've become a dreamer since you came back here and you're not so careful about things. I found coal dust on the hearthrug in the main parlour yesterday.'

'I'm very sorry, ma'am,' Sarah apologized. 'It won't happen again.'

'You'd better make sure it doesn't.'

But the harder she tried not to make mistakes the more they seemed to occur. It seemed as if she couldn't do anything right and everyone grumbled at her. Yet once she had been a favourite with the below-stairs staff.

'I don't know what's the matter with you,' Ella Tomkin said. 'I reckon that stepmother of yours must've wore you out skivvying. You ain't no fun any more.'

She wished she could confide in Ella, but it was far too risky and she knew she would feel worse if anyone in the house knew about the baby. She was lucky she'd been able to keep it a secret all along.

'I'm just tired,' she said. 'There was never enough to eat.'

Sarah was allowed to dust and polish in Mr Bradford's rooms, a duty given only to trusted servants since it meant moving many of his important papers, but when she went in there after her return she dropped one of his boxes and everything was scattered over the carpet. She picked the papers up hurriedly and put them back before anyone should see, but it seemed Mr Bradford, who was a powerful man at the Doctors' Commons, had complained that they were out of order. There was a great fuss and bother and Mrs Bradford sent for her.

'I'm surprised at you, Sarah,' she said. 'I'm afraid I can't allow such a mistake to go unpunished. I believe you were due for the afternoon off tomorrow. You will work instead.'

The punishment was hard because Maggie would miss her visit, but it was not so bad as losing some of her pay. She was threatened with that a few days later when she was sweeping the

70

back stairs and her rear view was too much of a temptation for the young footman. He playfully pinched her, and Sarah rounded on him.

'I ain't 'ere for your amusement,' she cried.

She was severely scolded for the commotion she caused, but since it wasn't entirely her fault the matter wasn't taken further.

At the end of two weeks she was tired, frustrated, and close to despair. She wished she had taken a chance and kept Angel, for there was no lessening of the pain that parting with her had caused, and no comfort to be found in Newcastle Place. Her emotions were so erratic, changing from anger to jealousy in a moment, and then to resentment of James Halden who continued to torment her thoughts. With Angel gone there was no need to humble herself and inquire if he had at last returned to work. It no longer mattered. But memories of him persisted. Finally she shut herself in the attic room on Ella's day off and sobbed until she ached in body and soul. After that she refused to shed another tear.

That Sunday she took the first positive step towards keeping a check on her child.

She'd thought that Foundling children stayed in the hospital from the time they were taken in. It had been a shock to discover that for the first five years they went to homes in the country where women were paid to nurse them, and it seemed to put a stop to any hope of seeing Angel again. Then she came to the conclusion that it might make things easier. She had seen the two women leave the hospital with babies in their arms, so all she had to do was discover where the van had taken them. After that it would be simpler to make a journey into the country than to find an excuse to walk through the hospital doors.

At the first opportunity Sarah went again to the Foundling Hospital, but she didn't approach by Guilford Street in case the porter came out of his lodge and recognized her. Instead she went round by Mecklenburgh Square and waited by a gate at the rear where there were two smaller buildings. Judging by the warm air and steam issuing from it, the building on the left could be a laundry, and girls with wagging tongues worked in laundries.

After about half an hour a girl came out of the gate, her tartan shawl held round her with rough, reddened hands. Sarah kept out of sight, then followed at a careful distance, swinging a basket. She didn't know how she was going to do it, but somehow she had to get into conversation with her.

The chance came so unexpectedly it took her breath away. The girl lingered at a secondhand clothes shop and was looking at grubby petticoats displayed on iron rods by the doorway, when a young man dressed in a shabby tail coat and check trousers came along and paused beside her. Sarah drew closer, one of a crowd in the busy street. The man smiled at the girl and must have passed some friendly remark, for she looked at him agreeably before returning to her inspection of the petticoats. It was then his hand brushed against her skirt, and two fingers would have slid into the pocket unnoticed if Sarah hadn't been watching. She was near enough now to swing the basket viciously against the pickpocket's hand, making him yell as he extracted the girl's purse, which he dropped as he fled.

The girl spun round in alarm, and gave a cry. 'Thief! Stop him!' She was pale and shaking.

'It's all right,' Sarah said, picking up the purse and giving it to her. 'I'm sorry if I hurt you but it was the only way I could do 'im some damage.'

'That was real good of you.' The girl was almost in tears with gratitude. 'Me wages are in there and I was taking them to me ma. She'd 'ave killed me if I'd gone home without 'em. How can I thank you?'

'I don't want thanks.' A lemonade seller had a place at the kerbside further along, his polished urn reflecting the warm glow from the fire of a trader in hot chestnuts next to him. Sarah took the girl's arm. 'We need a drink.'

She found a coin in her pocket and paid for two glasses of lemonade, then drew the girl into a doorway away from the people.

'You're real kind,' the girl said.

'I know how bad I'd 'ave felt if someone'd tried to pick *my* pocket. Not that they'd 'ave got much. I don't earn enough.'

'What do you do?'

'I'm a kitchen maid. What do you do?'

'I work over at the Foundling Hospital, in the laundry.'

Sarah's heart was beating fast. She was so

73

afraid of losing this heaven-sent opportunity, yet she didn't know how to ask the question she so desperately needed to ask. If she aroused the girl's suspicion all would be lost. She swallowed a mouthful of the lime-coloured liquid and the sharpness stung her throat.

'The tiny babies must make a lot of washing,' she said artfully.

The girl's eyes widened in surprise at her ignorance. 'Oh, we don't have the babies. They're farmed out to East Peckham or Chertsey for five years.'

How easy it had been! Sarah could have hugged her companion right there in the street. After all her worrying she had got the answer she wanted within minutes. By the time she drained her glass she also knew that the last van to leave for the country about three weeks ago had been Chertsey bound.

In parting, the girl squeezed Sarah's hand. She had plump cheeks with dimples and pretty brown hair. 'Me name's Dimsey Turner. I'll not forget what you did. You never know, someday I might be able to pay you back. Me stepfather keeps the pawnshop in Middle Alley off Cowcross Street if yer need me.'

She dodged away among the throng, her red hands now clutching her pockets and the tartan shawl tied over her chest to keep it on. Sarah smiled. She had been handsomely repaid already.

It took a little longer to plan how she was to make the journey to Chertsey, which she had discovered was about twenty miles away. The days were getting shorter and colder, and with Christmas approaching there was so much to do in the kitchen Sarah rarely had a spare minute. But her meeting with Dimsey Turner had revived her flagging ambitions, and she had begun to find favour in higher places once more.

'Mrs Bradford wants someone extra to wait at table,' said Mrs Martin, one morning in late November. 'Mr Priddy reckons you're the most likely, Sarah Byrne. Would you like to do it?'

Sarah's eyes lit up and her pale skin coloured to a pleasing pink. 'I'd like to very much, ma'am,' she said. 'It was kind of Mr Priddy to suggest it.'

'Yes, well ...' Mrs Martin sniffed with disapproval. 'It appears he thinks you're a presentable young woman. Mind you don't get carried away by the honour. Meself, I'd rather judge a girl on her capabilities.'

Sarah had become aware of her looks, which were improving daily, and she began using them to her advantage. She took trouble with her hair, and bathed her face regularly in cold water before rubbing it well with the towel. Her skin seemed to glow, and she discovered she only had to smile at the male members of the staff and they were immediately more friendly. It was a trick worth using.

'Pity to shut you away down here,' Mr Priddy said gruffly when she thanked him for his recommendation. He was the butler, a gentleman full of his own importance and not usually given to conversing with the lower servants.

Her training took long hours. The Bradfords entertained important people, and to correctly serve them food every detail had to be perfected. At the end of a week Sarah's back and legs ached intolerably, but the reward, when it came, was recompense indeed. She was given a whole day off.

'A whole day, Ella! Just think of it. I shall be able to go to Chertsey.'

'Chertsey? What do you want to go there for?'

'There's someone I must see,' said Sarah.

'A fella?' Ella's plain face creased into a mischievous smile. 'He must be special to take you all that way.'

Sarah didn't enlighten her. She discovered that Ella had a sister at Staines, and on the rare occasions she visited her she went on the railway. Staines, it appeared, was not far from Chertsey, but it was a long and tedious journey, and meant travelling by omnibus first of all to get to the big station across the river in York Road.

'I 'as to save up for the fare, and when I get there it's nearly time to come back,' Ella said. 'It ain't hardly worth it.'

Once again Sarah's spirits dropped. It seemed there wouldn't be time to do any prying even if she had the money to go to Chertsey, which she didn't. So the precious day came and went, and the only person she visited was Maggie, who didn't have a lot of sympathy.

'You gave the child up, so what's the sense tormenting yerself trying to see it?' Maggie brushed aside her stepdaughter's problem. She had news she couldn't wait to impart. 'What do you think, Sarah. I'll be moving out of here by Christmas. I've got meself a position, living in like you do.'

The noise in the alleys was deafening that morning, and the smell of the dungheap outside had never been so bad. She sat down, stunned and curious.

'What about Patrick?'

'I can take 'im with me. Mr Wood don't mind. He's a jeweller and he'll be working all day upstairs. 'E lives in one of them tenements in Corporation Lane, on the corner of St James's Passage. I'm to keep house.'

Sarah was far from happy for her. 'You mean you'll be living in sin with 'im,' she said. 'And you'll be right opposite the prison.'

The House of Detention held dangerous men behind bars, some of them Irish, and she remembered how her father had been threatened with it when he'd been caught causing trouble. Turnmill Street was bad enough. At one time so many people from the area were hanged at Newgate it had been nicknamed Jack Ketch's Warren, and according to Paddy it had been known for as many as forty constables to march down with cutlasses to control disturbances. But it wasn't up against dreary prison walls.

'There'll be nowt wrong with the arrangement,' said Maggie. 'Mr Wood's a respectable gentleman, and the house is a right palace compared to this. Be happy for me, ducks. Reckon I deserve a new start as much as you do.'

It would have been churlish to deny it. 'You deserve it more,' Sarah told her. 'And I'm glad for Patrick. It'll be healthier for 'im than here.'

When Sarah was leaving, Maggie thrust a parcel in her arms. It was bulky and badly tied up with paper and string but Sarah didn't need to feel it to know what it was.

'It's Paddy's fiddle,' her stepmother said. 'It was mean of me keeping it, and you could sell it to pay yer fare to Chertsey.'

Sarah's eyes flooded with tears, and she was ashamed of herself for not being more charitable over this generous woman's good fortune.

'No, it's yours,' she said, thrusting it back again. 'Pa would've been livid with me for getting pregnant, and he wouldn't want his precious fiddle going to pay for anything to do with it.' She went to the top of the stairs, then spun round and rushed back to hug Maggie Byrne with spontaneous affection. 'But thanks anyway.'

The Bradfords entertained lavishly at Christmas. Dr John Bradford was a judge at the Doctors' Commons, a very highly respected man at the top of his profession, and Elizabeth, his wife, was well known for her hospitality. Their dining room that Christmas of 1850 was the scene of a sumptuous dinner attended by family and friends, and it was the first important one at which Sarah Byrne was allowed to serve. It was an occasion she would never forget.

The day began like any other, except that the bells of St James's Church seemed to peal with more exhilaration than they ever did on a Sunday, and Sarah pictured the ringers jumping up and down for joy at the ends of their stout ropes. Two carriages took the Bradford family to early morning service, though it would have been no distance for them to walk. She caught a glimpse of them filing down the front steps in their best clothes, prayer books clasped in hands which no doubt itched to be unwrapping parcels. Two children arranged themselves in the first carriage, Bradford grandchildren with their parents up from Bristol. An older man joined Dr and Mrs Bradford in the second. He was Mrs Bradford's brother, so Ella said, a reverend gentleman by the name of Nahum Morey.

The air of excitement was as great below stairs as it was above. Once the early morning jobs were done there was a relaxing of discipline, and when the family returned from church everyone on the staff, from Mr Priddy down to the newest domestic, was invited to the second-best parlour to receive a small present. Sarah was given a new apron to wear for work and an embroidered handkerchief for herself, a very pretty one with lace round the edge which was much too good to use.

Christmas dinner for the Bradfords and their guests was not until six o'clock. The servants had theirs at two, gathered round the scrubbed table in the big kitchen. Firelight shone on festoons of holly, making the berries glow like rubies, and nothing could taste better than the chicken and the plum pudding Mrs Martin had cooked.

'I give a toast to you all this joyous, happy Christmas,' said Mr Priddy, raising a glass of homemade raisin wine. It was warm and smooth on Sarah's tongue, nothing like the terrible gin Maggie had given her which she never wanted to taste again.

Later she helped Mr Priddy to set the dining table upstairs. She preferred it to preparing food, and took the greatest care to see that each piece of cutlery was exactly an inch from the edge of the snow-white damask cloth. She folded napkins to look like coronets and gave the crystal glasses a final polish before positioning them in groups to the right of each place. In the centre of the table was a bower of holly entwined with Christmas roses, and the candlesticks were garlanded with festive trinkets which sparkled in the firelight. Sarah had never seen anything look so lovely, and she danced from one end of the table to the other to admire it.

Cook had said she must be more smartly attired to work in the house, so she had a new black dress for the occasion. She pulled the strings of her apron until the bow at the back was just right, and perched her white cap at the correct angle on her head to make it sit pertly on her dark curls. Her new position made her nervous but she kept breathing deeply to conquer it, and looked forward to proving herself worthy of the promotion.

At six o'clock everyone assembled for dinner and Mr Priddy signalled that the first course could be taken in, a heavy tureen of mock turtle soup which was to be served from a side table. Sarah carried it carefully, but when she entered the dining room and glanced across at the guests she almost dropped it. There immediately behind the silver platter of Salmon à la Régence, was James Halden.

Luckily he had his back towards her. A pain gripped her heart, and its beat became so erratic the soup slopped on her apron. Sarah hurriedly put it down, her hands trembling, and Mr Priddy looked askance at her, no doubt thinking she was intimidated by the company. She was afraid to look round again, but the other housemaid was ready to carry soup bowls to the table and she had to do the same.

Sarah's confident manner temporarily deserted her and she tried to keep behind James as much as possible, hoping not to be noticed. Like as not he wouldn't even recognize her, and he'd made it clear she was merely one of a number of girls who accommodated him. It was a year now since she had seen him, and he was more handsome than ever. His burnished gold hair curled over the high collar of a royal blue coat, and he wore a black velvet waistcoat sprigged with silver leaves, an expensive-looking garment for a young physician unless he had private means.

Seeing him made Sarah think with anguish of their child. My goodness, what a commotion it would cause if she announced to all these posh people that James Halden had once seduced her. Not that they would condemn him. It was an everyday occurrence for the gentry to bed maidservants. She pushed the thought away, praying instead for Angel on her very first Christmas.

James was talking to the person on his right, a vivacious lady who Sarah recognized as Mrs Bradford's daughter. On his left was a small, plump girl with round brown eyes which she blinked rapidly, as if smoke from the fire made them smart. Her fair hair was worn in a tight knob at the crown of her head, while ringlets covered her ears in the style made fashionable by Queen Victoria. Her shoulders were covered by a lace-trimmed mantelet, and pink ribbons decorated her lavender wool day dress. Sarah guessed she must be James's wife, and thought she looked like the pink jelly which wobbled on a dish near the salmon.

When she had to set a plate before him she could smell pomade on his hair, and her gaze was drawn to the long, clever hands which had once touched her body so intimately and unprofessionally. The sight of them sent a warmth stealing through her veins, and she was afraid her new dress might soon smell of sweat like the old one.

After the soup came courses of fish, meat, game and poultry, followed by a ragout with truffles. Then the eagerly awaited plum pudding arrived to the accompaniment of clapping and cheering, and a plume of blue smoke from the brandy flames was like the tail of Halley's Comet.

Before the pudding was cut the Reverend Morey stood up and rapped the table to attract attention. He was a man of about forty, and he wore a black jacket buttoned to the throat with only a glimpse of white stock appearing above it. His dark hair was thinning on top, but he had bushy side whiskers as if it had all slipped downwards, and his chin was a dimpled mound seeming to support an ever-smiling mouth.

'Dear friends and relations, I think this is the moment when we should be aware of how lucky we are to be partaking of such excellent food and spare a thought for those less fortunate.' There were murmurs of assent, though Sarah noticed the children eyeing the plum pudding impatiently. 'I hope you agree that we should show our gratitude for God's gifts in a concrete way, by supporting a charity. What could be more appropriate at Christmas than to remember children who have been deserted by their mothers and know only a hospital as home. I refer, of course, to the Foundling Hospital.'

'A worthy cause indeed,' said James Halden.

Sarah felt as if the room was spinning round, fearing that everyone would glance in her direction. In fact she almost expected them to accuse her of causing the conscience-prodding dip into their pockets. But there was only good-natured laughter and the jingling of coins as the men tried to outdo each other in their generosity.

James Halden, of course, had no idea that he was helping to support his own daughter. What consternation it would cause him if he were to find out.

'Nahum, dear,' said Elizabeth Bradford, 'we're all used to your fondness for parting us from our wealth, but may we ask what prompted you to choose the Foundling Hospital this year?'

'Ah, you may well ask,' said the Reverend Morey. He tucked his fingers in the neck of his coat and puffed out his chest like a pouter pigeon, his smile widening. 'Standing before you is a new Governor of the Hospital. As you know, for many years I have devoted time to families in my parish who foster babies for the charity, but now I feel I can do more. A vacancy arose on the committee and I am proud to have been asked to fill it.'

There was a murmur of congratulations, and Mrs Bradford came round the table to kiss her brother's cheek. Then the pudding was served, and dinner resumed, much to the relief of the children.

Sarah was trembling. The totally unexpected mention of the Foundling Hospital, coming on top of the shock of seeing James, had shaken her so much she scarcely knew how to complete the rest of her tasks. But she thanked the Lord that Reverend Morey hadn't become a Governor sooner, for then everyone would have known about Angel, and James's plump and prissy wife might have discovered her husband had fathered a bastard.

When a signal was given for the ladies to retire, leaving the men to their port and cigars,

Sarah hurried to the kitchen, scurrying like a rabbit for shelter.

'Whatever's the matter with you, girl?' Mrs Martin asked. 'I knew it was a mistake giving you responsibilities.'

Soon there was the dining room to clear. Family and guests could be heard playing charades and blindman's buff in the drawing room, and Mr Priddy snuffed out the candles, replacing them with new ones ready for tea at about ten in the evening when the table would again be laden with sweetmeats and delicacies. But the joy of the occasion had dimmed for Sarah. She got down on hands and knees to sweep away crumbs, and in the gaslight she looked paler than ever.

She was so busy she didn't hear anyone approaching. Someone had dropped jelly on an expensive rug and she was attacking it forcefully with a brush to relieve her feelings when the bristles came in contact with a pair of smart leather shoes. Her hand stilled, and she raised her eyes to see grey trousers close to her shoulder. Up and up she looked, to a black waistcoat sprigged with silver, and the intense gaze of James Halden.

James was aware of Sarah Byrne from the moment she came into the dining room carrying the soup tureen. He saw her through a gilt-framed mirror on the opposite wall, and that first glimpse of her brought him more joy than a dozen Christmases put together. He'd thought of her constantly, hoping she still worked for the

Bradford family, and the invitation to Christmas dinner with them had caused him more elation than Maud, his wife, though he hadn't dared show it. And Sarah was here. Wonderfully, miraculously she was here, and lovely as ever though she looked tired. At all costs he had to avoid catching her eye.

When he had left Sarah at Maggie Byrne's hovel that fateful day last December he had told himself she was no different from a hundred other girls. For weeks he had pushed thoughts of her out of his mind, and it hadn't been too difficult at first.

In early spring Maud, his wife, suffered her second miscarriage, and with the accompanying trauma it was a wonder James managed to finish the last of his studies at the hospital. He became angry and frustrated, having struggled so hard to rise above his humble background to become a physician, and the marriage he had seen as his link to success was more like a chain binding him to the spoilt daughter of the man whose position he envied. After the miscarriage Dr Rollerson, Maud's father, had insisted on paying for them to make an extended tour of Europe, so that Maud could regain her health, and James's dream of a permanent post at St Bartholomew's Hospital was indefinitely postponed.

While Maud rested on balconies overlooking Lake Garda, the Matterhorn, the Bay of Naples and the Tuileries Gardens, James took himself for long walks. The truth was, Maud bored him. He found it trying having to listen to endless complaints about her weight, her tiredness and her inability to carry a child. Maud had become petulant. Each night she retired to bed a few minutes earlier, and he saw it as an excuse to avoid the means of starting another pregnancy, though she was in the best of health.

It was not his way to admit that he had made a mistake. In the beginning he had found Maud appealing, and on their wedding day he had really believed that he loved her, but ambition had clouded his vision. Her father, Richard Rollerson, was the physician to whom James was attached at St Bartholomew's, and he had cultivated Maud Rollerson's friendship early for the purpose of improving his status with his tutor. A word from Maud and he had been given one of the four coveted places as a dresser, which meant he had more chance to learn the great man's skills. James intended one day to be equally celebrated, and as a dresser he was privileged to be at the bedside while the physician examined a patient. He took every opportunity to learn while arranging pillows and giving comfort.

From boyhood James had wanted to become a physician, but even if he had been taken seriously there would have been no money to cater for such an extravagant ambition. His father was a land agent who ran an estate in East Anglia belonging to John Bradford's brother. The job provided the Halden family with a home and enough money to live fairly comfortably, but with four sons and five daughters to bring up there had never been any to spare. James had gone round the village with his father as soon as he was old enough, visiting tenants in cottages with no sanitation. Sickness caused by overcrowding, and the damp, fetid conditions had appalled him. He spent hours with the local clergyman who had his own private store of medicines such as Epsom salts, gentian, laudanum, and quantities of port which he believed built up the strength, and he had seen for himself how garlic had done wonders for children with whooping cough. But it had taken Duncan Bradford's vision to persuade his agent that James was gifted enough to be worthy of the expense involved in letting him study medicine.

'He has the ability to become a physician,' Duncan Bradford had said. 'I've seen the way he gives confidence to the sick, in spite of his youth. What is more, he has a social conscience, and as a result of his persuasion I intend to see that our labourers' cottages have better sanitation.'

James's father was angry. 'But I've been recommending such improvements for years.'

'But you have only used the cottagers' convenience as an argument,' said Duncan. 'James has seen that their health would be improved, and consequently their work. I find that a worthwhile observation.'

In fact he was so impressed he agreed to make an allowance towards James's student fees at St Bartholomew's, but it had not stretched to comfortable accommodation. The only lodgings James had been able to afford were so squalid he had scarcely been able to concentrate on his studies for the cold each winter, and the thought of a house and wife to warm his bed had been added incentive to pursue marriage plans with Maud Rollerson.

Then Sarah Byrne disrupted his cosy life.

When he first saw her on the day of her father's accident, something happened to him. His system reacted to contact with her in ways he had never experienced with Maud, or with any other woman. He wanted to give comfort, and protect her from the cruel blow life had dealt her. More than that, he wanted to act on the impulse to touch her and experience the thrill of holding a girl whose very presence caused him exceptional physical excitement. He had carried her in his arms as naturally as if he had been doing so for years, and she had felt right there.

He watched her go down Newcastle Place with the bird cage in her arms, and pity rose up like yeasty dough in his chest, restricting his breath. She was so lovely, so young, so innocent, and she had such courage.

The next day he went back to the factory and found out the time of the funeral. When he stood beside her at the grave he longed to hold her hand, and the sight of smudges on her cheeks from weeping made his heart ache. She was so dreadfully alone.

He hadn't meant to make love to her. It happened with the same naturalness that had first drawn them together, and in taking her he felt the greatest fulfilment of his life. Then like a fool he had spoken of Maud, and Sarah had seen him as nothing more than a philanderer.

What a powerful thing his pride had become. He'd looked around that shabby dwelling and smelled the poverty which he had vowed to help alleviate in his dedicated youth, and to his shame he had thought only of escaping from the fleas he might have picked up from that terrible straw mattress.

On his long, solitary walks in Italy, Switzerland and Paris, he began to long for Sarah. He pictured her mane of dark hair which was so beautiful to touch, and her unblemished skin, like silk beneath his fingers. And more than once he lost his way because he was remembering the bluest eyes he had ever seen. Yet she was not a conventionally beautiful girl. Compared with Maud she was too tall and thin, and her mouth was too wide, but she had a simple grace which remained in his memory long after her features were blurred by time.

Immediately he was back in England he longed to seek her out, but his acquaintance with the Bradfords prohibited it. The last thing he wanted was word to be passed to Maud. Once he went to the house in Stone Alley and was met at the door by Maggie Byrne, but she only wanted to talk about the undersized child in her arms whose life he had saved. When asked about Sarah she turned up her nose and sniffed.

'I can't tell you where she is.' Maggie looked at him suspiciously. 'What would you be wanting with her anyway?'

He couldn't tell a woman like Maggie Byrne

that thoughts of Sarah were blighting his relationship with his wife, and turning him to celibacy. She would have roared with laughter.

But this Christmas an invitation had come to celebrate with the Bradfords, and he had found her. His spirits soared. He glanced over at the mirror every time she came near, longing to speak, and he drank in her loveliness like a man who has crossed a barren desert. She was more mature than when he had last seen her. Her waist was still slender enough to span with his hands, her eyes were full of mystery, and her control of the situation was admirable. He alone could tell she was nervous. He sensed the bond between them, and knew she was aware of it too, though she gave not the slightest outward sign.

He bided his time until there was an opportunity to seek her out. Under cover of a game of blindman's buff he slipped into the darkened dining room, and to his relief she was there, on hands and knees by the table. When she looked up at him the year just passed faded away like an unpleasant dream.

'Sarah, I must speak to you.'

'We've nothing to say.'

He clasped her arm and made her get to her feet, but she shook herself free immediately.

'Where can we talk?' he asked.

'I told you, I've nothing to say to you.'

He followed her when she went towards the door, and detained her. 'Sarah, please! Do you think I wasn't aware of you every moment of that interminable dinner? Every time you came near me I wanted to put my arm round your waist.' He tried to do it now, but she dodged back into a corner. 'Say we can meet somewhere and start again.'

'Does this mean you no longer have a wife?'

'Of course I still have a wife, but there's no need for you to worry your pretty little head about it. Since meeting you I've thought of no one else, I swear.'

He put one hand against the wall, close enough to touch a strand of her hair which had pulled free from the cap, and he imprisoned her in that dark corner. Her rapid breathing was proof that her emotions were stirred as much as his, but she shrank away, flattening her body against the cold wood rather than succumb to his persuasion.

'Your swearing doesn't impress me one bit,' she said, turning her head aside to avoid a kiss. 'If you've thought of me at all since we last met I'd be very surprised.'

'My dear Sarah ...'

'I'm not your dear Sarah.' She tried to slip free, but he moved round so that he could see her face more clearly. In the gaslight her blue eyes flashed, and her anger only increased his need of her. 'I have me pride, James Halden, and I'm ashamed I ever let you come near me.'

'I'm sure there have been plenty of men since,' he said, considerably piqued. But the thought of anyone else knowing her intimately produced a wave of incredible jealousy.

'There's been no one. Mrs Bradford don't

allow followers. And she'd be none too happy if I told her I was being bothered by one of her guests.' She clutched the brush against her, unaware how provocatively her hands were thrusting up her breasts. 'Now, if you don't mind, I've work to do.'

'I'll not let you go until you promise to let me see you.'

'Then we'll be here all night.'

'What a delicious thought. I'd like nothing better than to spend the night with you.'

His teasing upset her. 'I wish you'd never come here. Oh, I wish it so much.' She stamped her foot. 'I thought you'd left the country for good.'

So she had been asking after him. He drew in his breath with elation, but he could see by the way she bit her lip that she hadn't intended to let the confession slip.

'How did you know I'd gone abroad?' He bent his head and cupped her face between his hands so that she couldn't look away. 'My little sparrow, I do believe you regretted our quarrel as much as I did. And you must believe me when I tell you I'd rather have been with you than in any of those exotic places.'

He attempted to take her in his arms, thinking the matter was happily resolved, but she was adept at dodging, losing none of the dignity which was so exceptional in a common maidservant.

'I don't hold with philandering,' she said. 'I intend to make something of meself, so I'd be obliged if you'd treat me with more respect.'

'Hoity-toity!' James scoffed. Such airs she gave herself! 'The only way a girl like you gets on in this world is if she has something worth selling. I'd not expect your favours for nothing.'

He was immediately ashamed of the outburst. For a moment she looked stricken, then she lifted her head proudly. 'If ever I'm that desperate for money I'll come and ask you for it,' she said. 'But it won't be for the reason you think.'

She walked away with a poise unmatched by any woman of his acquaintance, and he stared after her with angry fascination.

# CHAPTER 4

The meeting with James upset Sarah very much. He was an arrogant man who thought he had only to crook his finger and she would come running. Well, she had shown him she couldn't be swayed by his good looks or his fancy words; not any more. But the fire in her body when she lay in bed thinking of him that night warned her that she had to be strong or she wouldn't be able to reject him if he tried again.

Strangely, she wasn't so upset by the revival of a strong physical attraction. She could control that by reminding herself of the terrible consequences it had led to the first time. What troubled her more was the memory of James's kindness when they first met. It had meant so much to her and she longed for his compassion again, but it was too late now for him to be told about Angel. He would never forgive her for abandoning his child.

Last night there had been Christmas bells ringing all over London. Tonight when she tried to sleep there was a dog howling, and the dismal sound expressed everything Sarah was feeling. But just as she was burying her head beneath the blanket in utter dejection Ella came to bed, and she passed on the most extraordinary piece of news.

'You know you was talking about Chertsey,' Ella said. 'Well Reverend Morey comes from there. Ain't that a coincidence?'

Sarah's eyes flew open. 'Did he say so?'

'I 'eard Mr Priddy telling Cook.' Ella never missed anything that was said in the kitchen.

It was the only thing that could have made Sarah temporarily forget about James, and she was still awake with her thoughts when Ella's snoring rattled to the rafters of the narrow attic room. God works in mysterious ways. She had learnt that from her ma, but she had never understood until recently. First there had been Dimsey Turner, and now there was the Reverend Morey. Somehow she was going to get to Chertsey to see Angel before too long. All she had to do was work out a plan.

The next morning breakfast was laid ready in the dining room for the Bradfords' guests to help themselves at whatever hour they chose to rise. Sarah was kept busy replenishing dishes, and every time she had to go down to the kitchen she was afraid of missing the Reverend Morey, but he appeared last of all. Luck was with her again, for he breakfasted alone.

'Excuse me, sir,' Sarah said. She bobbed a curtsey to give a good impression. 'I was here when you was collecting for the Foundling Hospital yesterday, and I wondered if a shilling would help. It's all I have, you see, but I don't need it with Mrs Bradford providing everything for me. I'd be glad if you'd take it.'

Nahum Morey wiped his mouth on a napkin, and gave her his full attention.

'My dear, kind girl.' He positively beamed as he took the coin and held it up between his thumb and index finger. 'This is indeed the widow's mite.'

'It's a whole shilling I'm giving you, sir. And I ain't a widow. I ain't been married.'

He laughed, and stood up. 'What's your name, child?'

'Sarah Byrne, sir.'

'Well, Sarah Byrne, you've strengthened my faith in human nature, even though I can tell you don't go to church.'

'I don't have time, sir.'

'Hmm.' He stroked his round, dumpling chin. 'You should go and hear the Foundling children sing in their wonderful chapel. I'll make it right with Mrs Bradford for you to have time off next Sunday, then you must go and listen to them.'

'Me, sir?' Sarah's face lit up.

'I rent my own pew, of course. But the public are admitted to the galleries, providing they make a small donation.' The light was extinguished as quickly as it had come, and her shoulders curled with disappointment. He held the shilling out to her. 'How would it be if I returned your gift so that you can give it at the door?'

'That's very kind of you, sir. I'd be more than pleased.'

'Consider it settled then.'

Nahum Morey was a man of middle height, and Sarah could look into his dark brown eyes. She did so with such innocent flirtation he should have been discomforted, but he met the look with his usual amusement. And something more. She was learning to recognize the effect she had on men, and to her surprise she saw the hint of desire creep into his gaze. His smiling lips almost curved into an invitation which his calling would not permit him to express.

She thought over this new development carefully and decided to encourage it. With a little guile her visit to Chertsey might even be achieved quite soon.

That was Thursday. She had to wait three more days until Sunday, and it was difficult to hide her excitement. It was also important to think what she should wear, for if any of the Governors who had interviewed her only three months ago saw her at the service they would know why she was there. Ella, whose curiosity had to be appeased with little white lies, was persuaded to lend her best bonnet. It had a deep brim which widened towards the chin so that in profile the face would be hidden, and before she put it on Sarah brushed her unruly hair until it looked smooth, then she parted it in the middle and drew it tightly back. It altered her appearance considerably, making her look older and quite severe, and in her new black working dress she could have been taken for a widow.

'I don't know what you're up to, Sarah Byrne, but I know you ain't religious,' said Ella. 'So there must be some other reason you changed yer time off. Don't you tell me again you ain't got a fella 'cause I shan't believe you.'

Sarah neither confirmed nor denied it, but went off with a smile.

She needn't have worried that she would be recognized. A constable was at the door to regulate the stream of people going into the chapel, and she was directed to the eastern gallery. Her face was pleasingly flushed from hurrying, but now she walked with her head held high, taking slow, dignified steps so that no one would have thought she was a domestic servant.

Once in her seat she was able to look round, and she quietly absorbed the lovely surroundings. When every seat was taken the Foundling children filed to their places, filling the gallery where the organ stood like a turreted castle, girls on the left in snowy white, and darkly dressed boys on the right. One day Angel would be among them. Sarah blinked back tears. It was harder still to restrain them when the singing started, for she had never heard anything so glorious. There was a professional choir as well as the children, and the sound of hymns being so brilliantly performed made the Foundling Hospital chapel the most popular place of worship in London. Her meagre shilling donation was an embarrassment in this wealthy company, but she refused to think of it.

During the sermon Sarah's attention wandered. She spotted Nahum Morey in his rented pew, his legs outstretched and his head tipped back against the wood as if he were concentrating on the sermon's message, but she was suddenly aware that their eyes were meeting. She looked away hurriedly, confused in spite of her resolution to encourage him. He was old enough to be her father, and she convinced herself that she was suffering from too much imagination. Surely a man of the cloth wouldn't look at her with the same sort of craving as James Halden. The thought was odious.

She pictured James with his intense hazel eyes and nose that was too big. Since Christmas Day her feelings for him had been in such a chaotic state she didn't know whether she loved or hated him. Whichever it was the emotion was so strong it made her attempted flirtation with Nahum Morey seem cheap. James would have plenty to say about it if he knew. She could almost hear his language. But she was doing it for their child, and in order to make sure that Angel was happy she needed the Reverend Morey.

The children began to sing Handel's anthem. 'Blessed are they that consider the poor', and Sarah dared to glance once more in his direction.

This time there was no mistaking his scrutiny. As soon as their eyes met he inclined his head in acknowledgement.

After the service it took time for the galleries to empty. Sarah was worried because it was getting late, and when at last she was out of the hospital she started walking quickly towards Clerkenwell, but she hadn't gone far before a hackney cab drew up.

'Allow me to give you a lift, Sarah,' said Nahum Morey, leaning out.

The night was dark and a fog was coming in from the river, but she hesitated. Things were happening too easily and it made her nervous, even though he was Mrs Bradford's brother.

'I don't know that you should, sir.'

'Nonsense. We're going to the same destination.' He alighted and offered his hand to help her in. When she was still unsure he patted her shoulder. 'Your reluctance does you credit, but you've no need to be afraid. My respect for you is increasing by the hour.'

She'd never been in a hackney cab. Once inside she wriggled into the corner of the seat to make room for him, and prepared to enjoy the novelty. But she was soon aware of his fat thigh pressing against hers, and each time they passed a gas lamp he turned to look at her. She had to distract him.

'Reverend Morey, do you really visit babies from the Foundling Hospital in your parish?'

'Regularly,' he said. 'There must be forty or more.'

'As many as that?' Her surprise was genuine.

100

He chatted on about them for the rest of the journey, as she had hoped he would, and she learnt that they couldn't be better looked after.

'They're treated like part of the families caring for them. In fact I often hear the children calling their foster parents "mother" and "father". The sad thing is that the tie is broken when they are five, and the little ones can get very distressed.'

Sarah was quiet. The thought of Angel calling another woman mother made her heart ache anew.

'I wish I could do something for them,' she said, and the concern in her voice was now innocent of duplicity.

Nahum Morey, too, fell silent. Along the cobbled road the steady clop-clopping of the cab horse echoed through the fog-laden evening, and they were enclosed in a very private world. He was a good man. She was ashamed of causing his inner disturbance which she sensed by the restlessness of his hands, and she wondered if he was praying.

He breathed deeply before speaking again. 'Miss Byrne, I've been a widower these last three years, and the rectory where I live is big and lonely.' Under the next gas lamp it was Sarah who looked at him, but he stared straight ahead. Then he cleared his throat and made a quite extraordinary proposal. 'For some time now I have been thinking I should marry again. I know we haven't long been acquainted, but will you do me the honour of becoming my wife?'

'Oh!' she gasped.

He turned to her quickly and took one of her hands in both of his. 'I know it must come as a shock to you. Indeed it has to me, too, but I'm certain you've been sent into my life. I feel the compassion in you. From the first moment we spoke I knew you were a girl with great sensibility, and I admire you very much. I need someone to share my duties in the parish, someone with understanding of family problems and poverty, and a love of children. Please say you'll marry me.'

Like someone drowning, Sarah saw her past life in detail; the filthy room in which she'd grown up with no privacy and no sanitation, the painful joints on Ma's fingers from too much sewing, Paddy's brawls, and the incessant noise and smell of Turnmill Street. She shut out memories of James, and thought hard about Angel. Had she been asked the same question in different surroundings her amazement might have been tempered with doubt that Nahum Morey was in his right mind, but in this confined space she began to share his conviction that they had been drawn together by their various needs.

'You don't know anything about me,' she said doubtfully.

'All I need to know is in your demeanour. We shall soon grow to know each other better.'

She daren't think of the future. The last thing in the world she had thought of becoming was a parson's wife, and if she were to consider it for any length of time she would refuse through lack of courage. But he was expecting a decision now, and with Angel firmly in mind there could only be one answer.

She said, 'Thank you, Reverend Morey. I think I should like to be your wife.'

He sighed with satisfaction and carried her hand to his lips. The touch was not unpleasant.

One day in February, just six weeks after Sarah accepted Nahum Morey's proposal, Edward Wooldridge ran home from the Chertsey Infants' School on the corner of St Anne's Road as fast as his six-year-old legs would carry him. Usually he lingered by the stream to throw in stones, but today he didn't stop. He rushed along London Street and Bridge Road so fast that he puffed and staggered the last few yards to the cottage where he lived with his parents and two younger brothers.

'How is she, Ma? Has the inspector been?'

'He's been,' said Peg. 'Not long since, and he's sending the apothecary. I wish he'd hurry.'

His mother was bending over the baby in the basketwork cradle his father had made for the first Wooldridge child, and she was mopping the fevered little body with a damp cloth.

'Do you want me to go and find him?' Edward asked.

'You're a good boy.' Peg paused and ruffled his hair affectionately, then handed him the cloth. 'I must get yer father's tea. It'd help me more if you keep Anna cool. But don't make her wet or she'll get worse.'

Anna didn't belong to them. When Ma had

come home from London with her there'd been great excitement, and Edward and his brother Billy had looked at the mite as if she were a fairy found among the budding snowdrops. She was different from George. Different from all of them. Edward had watched over her for hours, even refusing to go down to the lock with his friends for days, though he loved to play there. He fetched and carried things for Ma when she was nursing her, and never grumbled the way he'd done when George was sucking.

'It's no good getting too fond of her,' Ma had said. 'We've only got her for five years, then she has to go back to the Foundling Hospital.'

But five years was a lifetime, and every day Edward loved Anna more. If she cried he rocked the cradle and sang to her tunelessly. If he had the chance he picked her up in his sturdy little arms and kissed her downy head the way he saw his father do when he thought no one was looking. Anna had found a place in all their hearts, but nowhere so strongly as in the heart of this young boy.

She'd had a fever since last night, and all day at school he'd been thinking about her. He didn't want her to die like so many babies did. For weeks now she'd been recognizing him, her eyes following him round the room, and she tried to pull herself up in the cradle to see him better. He made funny faces to amuse her, and when she smiled at his antics he would go on to tickle her toes until she gurgled happily.

'She's going to have dark hair, Ma,' he

said one morning, when Anna was nearly five months old.

'It's coming on dark after all,' Peg agreed. The baby fluff had disappeared and the new hair that was growing was quite a different colour.

Today her eyes were as dull as a puddle. When he bent over her she cried, like she'd done all night, and he wanted to cry with her.

The apothecary came in his pony and trap just before Pa got home. He was a small man with a shock of white hair, and a ruddy complexion from his liking for port. He brought with him a bottle of his own herbal remedy for fevers and scarcely looked at the baby before worrying about his fee.

'I take it the hospital inspector will be paying me,' he said.

He placed his flabby hand on the hot little forehead, and Edward expected the fever to disappear like magic. Instead, Anna's limbs suddenly began to jerk alarmingly and for several seconds she thrashed her head from side to side until tiny bubbles of foam appeared on her lips. Then she was still.

Edward began to cry. 'She's dead, Ma. She's dead.'

'The child has had a mild fit,' said the apothecary, turning Anna on to her stomach. He didn't seem too concerned. 'Quite a common occurrence in babies with a fever. Dose her with the medicine I've brought and she'll be better by tomorrow.'

'But what if it happens again?' Peg had gone

very pale and her hands fluttered over Anna anxiously.

'It won't. She's a strong child.' The man picked up his bag and went to the door. 'The hospital will have to be informed, of course. I'll tell the inspector to mention it in his report.'

The fit had frightened Edward, and he wouldn't leave Anna's side even when Ma told him it was time for bed. His pa had been worried, too. He'd picked up the baby and held her while Ma gave her the medicine, and his face had the same look as when Billy had fallen in the river. But the apothecary had been right, and by morning Anna was almost like her old self, crying at last to be fed instead of turning her head away.

'Thank God for that,' his father said. He'd always gone to the fields long before Edward was up for school, but today he was still wrapping his lunchtime bread and cheese in a cloth. 'Don't like to see little 'uns ill.'

'You was worried about her, Isaac, same as all of us,' said Peg, and she gave Pa one of those nice smiles that made you feel warm inside. 'I'm glad you was. It shows you're a good Christian.'

Pa shrugged himself into his coat and tied a muffler about his neck to keep out the cold February wind. 'Better tell that to Reverend Morey next time you see him.' He collected the stout stick he always took with him, and pulled on his cap. 'Forgot to tell you, Peg, I hear the rector's taken hisself a wife.'

'He never has!' said Peg with disbelief. Then:

'So that's why he's been away more than usual. Is she someone posh?'

'Dunno. But from what I 'eard she's a bit of a thing little more than half his age. Some blokes have all the luck!'

'Get away with you, Isaac Wooldridge.'

Edward creased up laughing as Ma chased Pa with a broom outside into the bright, crisp morning. When he went to look at Anna before going to school her eyes were once more as blue as the sky, and she curled her fingers round his as if she didn't want to let him go. He was so happy he wouldn't have changed places with anybody.

Nahum Morey rarely drove in his carriage up to London now that the railway had come to Chertsey. The city streets were so congested with vehicles it was a slow process getting up the Strand, and in winter horse manure was apt to splash up unpleasantly. He found the train far more to his liking.

On the day he married Sarah Byrne at St James's Church in Clerkenwell he was impatient to travel home, there being no reception to mark the occasion. His sister Elizabeth had preferred not to attend the ceremony for fear of appearing to condone his alliance with one of her housemaids, and the Bradfords' staff had been equally disapproving of one of their number presuming to move up into such illustrious circles. The only witnesses had been Sarah's stepmother, and an ecclesiastic colleague who envied him his good fortune.

107

After Christmas he had wanted to arrange for the marriage to take place straight away, before he could change his mind, but it was difficult to fit it in with his new duties as a Governor of the Foundling Hospital which required him to spend one day a week in town. In fairness to Sarah he had wanted to devote a whole day to her, but the pressure of his work had made it impossible, and he had been forced to settle for an afternoon wedding, following a Governors' meeting, so that he and his bride could depart for Chertsey on the last train.

He tried not to think of the shock his sister had expressed so strongly when he had told her of his intentions.

'You should be ashamed of yourself, Nahum,' Elizabeth had said. 'Poor Adelaide must be turning in her grave if she knows you mean to put a domestic servant in her place. It's too disgraceful for words. Why, you don't even know the girl!'

'I'm sure she will be quite suitable.'

'Whatever will the family say? Really, Nahum! If you're so desperate to marry again please wait until a lady of the proper class comes along. I can introduce you to several of my acquaintance.'

'Thank you, Elizabeth, but I have already proposed to Sarah, and I'm quite happy about it.'

Happy indeed. Sarah was now his wife, and he had only to look at her to know he had done the right thing.

She had never been on a train before and the

speed, which must have been twenty miles an hour, made her as excited as a child.

'I ain't never travelled so fast. It's bloomin' marvellous,' she cried.

'Haven't,' he corrected. 'You must stop saying "ain't", my dear.'

'Yes, Nahum. I'll try to remember.'

She was already dutiful and anxious to please him, and she looked so pretty in a dress of sprigged cotton he'd given her the money to buy for the wedding. Her lovely hair had been coaxed into ringlets which bounced out beneath her bonnet, and he longed to feel the spirals curling round his fingers. When he recalled how he had felt on first seeing her he had to push the sinful thoughts out of his mind.

When they arrived at Chertsey her excitement increased. She looked around with a bright smile, which turned to surprise and a hint of dismay.

'I didn't know it was such a big place,' she said as they drove through the gaslit streets from the station in a hired carriage. 'How will I get to know people?'

He laughed. 'Anyone would think you had come from the country.' But he was pleased because it showed she intended taking seriously the duties of a rector's wife. 'I shall introduce you to my parishioners on Sunday morning.'

'I want to be a credit to you, Nahum.'

'You will be, I know.' He took the liberty of holding her hand briefly.

She twisted in the seat to peer at every building, her eyes seeking the upper windows

109

above shops rather than the goods on display, as if she were looking for someone.

'Where do the Foundling babies live?' she asked.

His smile broadened with growing satisfaction. 'My word, what interest I kindled when I spoke of the hospital at Christmas. I find it very heartening, my dear.' His hand now rested lightly on her knee. 'I'm especially pleased you have such a fondness for babies. Adelaide and I were never blessed with children, but it has always been my dearest wish to have a family.'

For a girl born and bred in the slums of Clerkenwell she showed surprising embarrassment at the discreet mention of his hopes. She lost the colour which had tinted her pale cheeks to the velvety beauty of pink rose petals, and her lower lip was drawn in slightly. For the rest of the short journey she sat beside him uneasily, no longer so taken with her surroundings.

The rectory was a dour red brick house with ivy-clad walls where birds would soon be nesting. It had an iron gate almost indistinguishable from the railings, and he preceded her through it to the front door which was centrally placed between tall windows, with a bow window above it belonging to the bedroom they would be sharing. In answer to his ring the door was opened by a short, stout woman dressed severely in black.

'Ah, Mrs Deacon,' said Nahum, striding in and drawing Sarah after him. 'Allow me to introduce you to the new Mrs Morey.'

110

There were deep lines at the sides of the woman's mouth which pulled her lips downwards ungraciously. She had been his housekeeper since he had first moved into the rectory with Adelaide, and she looked after him with a devotion bordering on obsession. He'd informed her of his intention to remarry, and she had commented favourably, so he was quite unprepared for her look of horror when Sarah stepped into the house.

'Pleased to meet you, I'm sure,' she said, keeping her hands firmly clasped over her bombazine-covered girth. And there was no welcoming smile. 'Your dinner's close to spoiling, sir. I expected you back sooner.'

The house was cold. He took Sarah through to the parlour where the glow from a fire lent a more cheerful appearance to the book-lined retreat which had been exclusively his own since Adelaide's death.

For the first time he felt awkward with this tall girl who was young enough to be his daughter, and he wished he had warned Mrs Deacon what to expect. With a single look she had made him feel faintly ridiculous. Such withering disapproval had curled those drooping lips after her initial consternation, and Nahum was so inwardly uncomfortable he forgot to consider Sarah's feelings.

'From tomorrow, Sarah, I should like you to wear your hair in the style in which it was dressed when you attended the service at the Foundling Hospital,' he said, forcing the smile which gave him a jovial reputation. 'The severity will be more in keeping with your new responsibilities.'

He meant it would make her look older and plainer.

Sarah came through the first week of marriage with few hopes of real happiness, though she was pleased enough with her elevated circumstances. It was gratifying to have people shake her hand who once wouldn't have given her the time of day, and when she walked through the dreary rooms where evidence of the late Adelaide Morey still abounded she had trouble convincing herself that she was now the mistress here.

She detested Mrs Deacon, who was like a sterner, more forthright edition of Mrs Martin. But she remained amiable no matter how much she was provoked, and each day she gained a little more confidence. In time she would put the disagreeable widow in her place.

Nahum was the one she aimed to please. She didn't love her husband, or even have any great affection for him, but she was mindful of the predicament in which he had placed himself by marrying so far beneath him, and she was going to make certain he never had cause to be ashamed of her. She listened to the way he spoke and began imitating his careful diction, and her natural grace was an asset when she walked at his side. He bought her two new gowns of a sombre colour at a shop in Guildford Street, a pair of good shoes, and a bonnet which shaded her lovely blue eyes. Her hair no longer showed signs of its natural curl.

He was fascinated by her hair. When it was loose at night he gathered it in his hands and buried his face against it before kissing her, and it seemed to give him more satisfaction than the hurried, clumsy act of love which followed. Sarah closed her eyes when he lifted her nightdress and entered her with no show of sentiment. It was just the mating of two bodies, essential for procreation, but certainly not meant to be enjoyed. She endured these attentions patiently, and hoped that she would not become pregnant.

Above all she had to suppress thoughts of James Halden. She was still haunted by the look in his eyes at Christmas, and memories of his strong, lean body made her ache with a longing which Nahum's undignified fumbling would never be able to satisfy. If she allowed herself to think of James at all tears came close to the surface, and she knew she would never feel the same with anyone else.

On Sunday she heard Nahum preach for the first time, and she met the assistant curate, a young, delicate-looking man by the name of Daniel Marsh. Neither impressed her. Her husband's sermon was too long and hard to understand, and the curate was so self-effacing she had difficulty getting a word out of him. It could have been that he was overcome with shyness, for he gazed at her almost with awe and stumbled over his words.

'You are ... you have ... I mean, the Reverend Morey is a very lucky man, Mrs Morey. If there is anything I can do for you ...'

According to Nahum he was indispensable. He practically ran the church, especially now that Nahum was away so much on Foundling Hospital business, and Sarah felt sorry for him. His eagerness to please ensured that he was put upon, and judging by the worn state of his clothes she guessed he was paid a pittance for it. Pity made her more friendly towards him than she might otherwise have been.

'It's kind of you to make me so welcome,' she said, dazzling him with a very personal smile. 'I'll remember your offer.'

The young man went on his way with a lighter step, and he made an effort to project his almost non-existent chin.

But more than anything else Sarah craved for even a glimpse of Angel. During that first week she went out with Nahum in the trap he used for visiting in the parish, and she was continually looking for a young woman with white hair and a baby. She'd thought it would be easy to find her. It was going to be nothing of the sort. To her disappointment Nahum only seemed to visit the old and sick, and after the first few days he no longer took her with him, having suffered embarrassment each time he introduced his new wife whose youth couldn't be disguised. She was amused and saddened by his dilemma. She was also frustrated.

It was on Tuesday, the day before Nahum paid his weekly visit to London that Sarah met Peg Wooldridge. She supported a baby of about six months on one hip and carried a bundle of laundry.

'Good morning, Mrs Wooldridge,' said Mrs Deacon, letting her in by the back door.

'Parson's washing, Mrs Deacon,' said Peg. 'I'm real sorry it's a day late, but the baby's been ill.'

Sarah was in the kitchen when she arrived, and her heart gave a sudden leap as she recognized the plump, rosy-faced woman as one of the two who had driven away from the Foundling Hospital that fateful day. Full of new hope, she waited by the table.

The housekeeper took the bundle of laundry and money changed hands. She said: 'There's more this week, with an extra one in the house.'

'I'm Mrs Morey, the rector's new wife,' said Sarah, going towards Peg with an outstretched hand as the housekeeper didn't have the manners to introduce her. 'I'm sorry your baby's not been well.'

'She's had a fever and now she won't let me out of her sight, so I 'ad to bring her.'

The baby's head was buried against Peg's arm. Sarah touched the dark hair springing up in a quiff. 'What's her name?'

'Anna Beckett. She ain't mine, ma'am. I foster 'er.'

Anna looked up, and her blue eyes fixed on Sarah for several seconds. Her skin was sallow since the fever, and her little face was pinched with the cold so that there was nothing attractive about her. All at once she began to scream, turning her tiny head away, and Peg bounced her against her shoulder with soothing murmurs until the outburst ceased. Then she picked up the dirty washing and went to the door.

'I hope the baby's soon better,' said Sarah, with all the diplomacy of a clergyman's wife. Not that she really minded. She couldn't take to the child.

'Thank you, ma'am.'

Peg left. After a moment Sarah followed her. There was a knot of excitement in her stomach and her breathing was erratic.

'Mrs Wooldridge, did you know my husband's a Governor of the Foundling Hospital now?' she asked, catching the woman up.

'I'd heard, ma'am.' Peg's expression was wary. 'There's nothing the matter with Anna that need trouble him. She's well looked after.'

'I can see she is. I only wanted to tell you I'm really interested in the Foundling babies and I hope to visit some of them for my husband. There's another about Anna's age, I believe.'

'Betty Gilling took one the same time as me, but Reverend Morey knows there'll be no troubles there. Betty's fostered before.' Anna was crying again and Peg cuddled her into the folds of her own shawl where it was warm. 'Now if you'll excuse me, I must get home to me boys.'

Sarah stayed outside a few minutes longer, her spirits lifting wondrously, and she felt as happy as a robin singing among the branches

116

of the oak tree. The sky was blue, the air crisp and clear, and the sun was shining on a patch of yellow crocuses. It was the loveliest day imaginable now that she knew the name of Angel's foster parents.

The following morning Nahum set out on his visit to London, just seven days after their marriage, and Sarah watched his departure.

'I shall miss you, Nahum,' she said.

Nahum kissed her fingertips. He rarely kissed her lips. 'You make it difficult for me to leave. I've never had a better incentive to hurry home. Goodbye, my dear.'

She waved until he was out of sight. An hour later she went to the church and looked for Daniel Marsh.

'Mr Marsh, I wonder if I might accept your offer of help,' she said when she found him in the vestry. 'I thought I'd visit some of the mothers with Foundling babies today.'

'That's very commendable of you, Mrs Morey,' said Daniel. His large Adam's apple moved up and down as he swallowed his nerves.

'So I'd like you to drive me in the pony and trap, just till I know where people live.'

'But, Mrs Morey ...'

'I'm sure my husband won't mind. The first person on my list is a Mrs Gilling.'

Daniel took more persuading than she had expected, but finally agreed to spare an hour later in the morning. She watched him get the pony ready, learning all the time so that she would be able to harness it herself in future when she wanted to drive out in Nahum's absence. When she was seated beside him Daniel's discomfort was noticeable. It embarrassed him to be sitting so close to the rector's wife and he kept as far to the side as he could so that no one would think he was enjoying her company.

Sarah was too excited to worry what anybody thought. And too preoccupied to hold a conversation. She was picturing her daughter, her beloved Angel, and as the pony stepped daintily over the cobbles she was counting the minutes until she was with her for the first time in nearly six months.

They drove the length of London Street and Bridge Road in silence until the first glimpse of the sun glinting on the river by Chertsey Bridge prompted Sarah to comment.

'It seems to be a long way.'

'Harry Gilling is the lock-keeper,' said Daniel. 'It's a small cottage for a large family.'

When they reached it Sarah counted four children playing near the turf-sided lock, and fears for Angel's safety immediately sprang to mind. Not far off she could hear rushing water where the Thames tumbled over a weir, and two more children were running along the narrow bank separating the lock from the river. The whole area seemed fraught with danger.

Betty Gilling was at the cottage door, her white hair knotted prettily on top of her head and her arms folded over the mound of her stomach where her eighth child was curled, almost ready to be born.

'What brings you, Mr Marsh?' she asked. 'Has that old skinflint parson sent you to check up on me?'

Daniel's face turned crimson. 'Madam, allow me to introduce you to Mrs Morey, the Reverend Morey's wife. She has kindly offered to visit the Foundling children.'

'Should you need anything, Mrs Gilling ...'

'If I need anything, ma'am, I call the inspector. But I don't need nothing.'

'If I can just see the baby.' Sarah's legs were trembling. There was a patch of ground at the side of the cottage where washing was strewn to dry on the bushes, and she saw Angel's patchwork blanket.

'There's nowt wrong with Corrie. I earn me three and a tanner.'

'I'm sure you do. I only want to see her a moment.'

Betty stood aside grudgingly. 'Yuh'd best come in.'

The cottage was warm and surprisingly tidy, considering the size of the family, but Sarah saw little of her surroundings. Her eyes went straight to the wicker chair by the window where a baby was just waking from its morning sleep. She went over to it, her mouth dry, her pulses racing, and when she looked down at the cherubic child with bright golden hair she had to grip the arms for support. Without asking permission she lifted the baby and held it against her heart, crying silently.

# CHAPTER 5

There was no doubt that Paddy Byrne's greatest gift to his daughter Sarah was the passing on of his irresistible Irish charm which enabled him to get his own way. Sarah knew well how to use her gift.

She had been married to Nahum Morey for two years when the staid Mrs Deacon died of influenza. There had never been any warmth between the women, but they had learnt to respect each other, and Sarah had become accomplished at running the house. With subtle flattery she had gradually been accepted by the housekeeper. With humility she managed to convince her husband that she was obedient to his every wish. Had either realized her knack of manipulating it might have been a different story, but Sarah never allowed her determination to show.

After Mrs Deacon's death there was no change in the pattern of life at the rectory, and Nahum's comforts remained the same. His meals were always ready, his clothes clean and pressed, and his vestments for the Sunday service were immaculate. After his visits to London his wife was waiting to welcome him as if he had been away for weeks, and she was always dutiful in bed. She visited the sick, made gifts for the poor, and ran bazaars to raise money for the church. She also made a point of keeping in touch with every woman who fostered a baby from the Foundling Hospital as the charity was so dear to her husband's heart. In all she was a model wife, and earned the esteem of everyone in the town.

Sarah herself was reasonably happy. She had achieved her purpose in being able to watch Angel grow, but often she was homesick for Clerkenwell and the friends she'd known since childhood. Life was so different in the country and she couldn't get used to the fresh air, the slower pace, the cleanliness of everything. Sometimes she longed for the sound of traffic and street cries. There was no soot in the mists and fog which came from the river, and no garbage in the gutters like there was in London. She was awakened in the mornings by cocks crowing, and it was so quiet in the evenings it seemed everyone must go to bed before dark.

If she hadn't kept busy all the time she would have thought too much about James, and about Maggie. She missed Maggie, though once she would never have believed it possible. The bond which had drawn them so close before Angel's birth was strong and sometimes Sarah longed to be back for a brief time in that dilapidated house in Stone Alley, free of the sanctimonious atmosphere of the rectory, until she remembered Maggie wasn't there any more either. Once she started writing her a letter and had filled a sheet of paper before she realized that Maggie couldn't read so there was no sense in sending it. Perhaps the jeweller she kept house for could read, but the things Sarah wanted to say were not for a stranger's eyes.

For several weeks after her wedding she had entertained the silly idea that James might look for her, but she was thankful that he never came even though he soon heard about her marriage to Nahum.

'How very kind,' Nahum said one day as he was going through his morning correspondence. 'My sister's friends, Dr Halden and his wife, have written to send good wishes on our marriage. They hope we'll be very happy. Pity Elizabeth wasn't as kindly disposed.'

Good wishes! Sarah's heartbeats quickened. James's message had been meant for herself, an oblique way of saying that he was no longer interested. She knew it was best, but she couldn't help wondering what would have happened if she hadn't been so proud on Christmas Day.

Gradually she got used to thinking of Angel as Corrie, but it soon became clear that she would never be able to claim her as her own. Such dreams were defeated by the means she'd first thought would make it possible for her baby to be returned to her. Nahum would be horrified if he discovered she had a child. His disappointment at having a second wife barren was, to him, the only flaw in their marriage, and her deception would never be forgiven.

But there were ways of increasing her contact with Corrie. Sarah schemed for several weeks before daring to put forward a proposal.

'Nahum, am I doing everything I should now

that Mrs Deacon is no longer with us?' she asked. It was a warm spring evening and she was sewing by the window while he checked the weekly accounts. His careful way with money was well known.

He looked up and smiled. 'My dear, you are coping perfectly. I'm very proud of you.'

'If only I didn't feel so tired,' she said. She let the sewing drop on to her lap and her shoulders drooped a little. Her complexion was always pale, but she had dusted her cheeks lightly with flour after the evening meal to accentuate it. 'I don't want to neglect anything.'

Nahum got up at once and went to her side, his concern tinged with ever-present hope.

'Do you think, Sarah, this might mean you are expecting a child?'

'I don't think so,' she said but she expressed the truth so artfully it sounded almost as if there was a possibility. 'What I need, just in case, is some help with the heavy work.'

'We already have a housemaid.'

'Who should be free to help me with the food. And she would be if I could have a woman come in to scrub the floors.'

He returned to pick up his account book and totted up some figures. 'That would mean paying out almost as much money as when Mrs Deacon was here.'

'I'm sorry, Nahum,' said Sarah. 'I shouldn't have suggested it. Of course I can manage.'

Her subservience never failed. Nahum was immediately contrite, apologizing for his hesitation and assuring her that her health was more important than anything else, especially if there was the longed-for reason for her tiredness. She could have a woman come in twice a week.

'I'll find someone suitable tomorrow,' he promised.

'I already have someone in mind,' Sarah said. 'I sometimes visit the lock-keeper's wife who has a Foundling child, and she's a good worker. She could do with the extra money.'

She had learnt long ago that Nahum's chief interest in the Foundling Hospital was the boost it gave to his own ego being on the Board of Governors, a position acquired mainly through the generosity of his brother-in-law, John Bradford, who always supported the charity financially. Nahum was content to let his wife do the local visiting, and reports on the children's welfare came regularly from the inspector, so there was little required of him in Chertsey. In this respect Sarah had made herself as indispensable as Daniel Marsh.

However, Nahum was not out of touch. 'But the Gillings have a horde of children,' he protested.

'And you know how I love them, Nahum, dear. The oldest are working, and their father is always on hand to keep an eye on the others. Mrs Gilling can bring the two youngest with her.'

She knew Nahum wouldn't refuse.

Betty Gilling started work the following week.

It was a long walk from the lock, but Harry had made her a box on wheels in which to push the two little girls, Corrie Palmer and her last child, Lily, who was seven months younger. She thanked the Lord there had been none since Lily. Already there were six in one bed, three at the top and three at the bottom, and they would soon have to make room for Matt, the boy born before she took in Corrie. She had more than enough to cope with, but the chance of a job to bring in a few extra shillings was not to be scorned.

The rector's wife was a bit of a mystery, and Betty couldn't really make her out. She seemed to have taken to the Foundling child the moment she set eyes on her, and there was no doubt in Betty's mind that Corrie was the sole reason for her being offered the work. The girl seemed to love kids, but like the first Mrs Morey she didn't produce any. It weren't fair that one woman should fall every time her husband used her, while another never fell at all. She sighed as she thought of the constant drudgery. No wonder her hair had turned white at twenty-five. Then Lily touched her hand to show her something, and love welled up in her like treacle. Not for the first time she found herself pitying Sarah Morey.

'The children can play in the garden,' Mrs Morey said when they arrived.

A short time later Betty stopped her scrubbing and looked out of the kitchen window. Mrs Morey was outside, seated on a wooden bench with Corrie on her lap and Lily beside her, both children enthralled with a story she was telling. There was no doubt she was a beautiful woman. Since marrying the rector she had filled out, and she had such clear blue eyes which reminded Betty of others she had seen, though she couldn't place where it was. Usually her hair was drawn back tightly until the skin pulled at her temples, but today it was loose, and so pretty Betty was quite envious. Some said she was a girl from the slums of London that Reverend Morey had taken pity on, but Betty didn't believe that. It wouldn't be pity that any man felt for Sarah Morey.

As she watched she saw Sarah put both arms round Corrie and hug her with a joyful laugh. Corrie was a loving child who inspired affection. She was also a delight to behold with her golden curls, and the two formed a real picture out there in the garden. It made Betty Gilling strangely uneasy.

A routine was established which went on for more than a year. Betty came to the rectory on Wednesdays, when the Reverend Morey was in London, and on Saturdays to see the place was clean for the Sabbath. While the scrubbing was done Mrs Morey found an occupation which would involve the children, and going there was the highlight of their lives. But as they grew older it no longer seemed necessary to take them with her, and one Wednesday morning Betty arrived on her own.

'Where are they?' Sarah Morey demanded. Her disappointment was so acute she was wringing her hands. 'Why haven't you brought Corrie?'

'There's no need now, ma'am. They're big

enough to stay with the others and do jobs at home.'

'I want you to bring them with you,' said Sarah. 'They're just becoming useful when there's the silver to clean, and they gather fir cones for the fire. They can do a dozen small jobs.'

Betty didn't come without them any more for fear of losing her job, but she wasn't blind or daft. She could see that Mrs Morey was besotted with the Foundling child, and she began to feel sorry for her. She was a woman in need of a child to love, and having none of her own she was lavishing it all on Corrie Palmer, which was sad because in another year she would have to be returned to the hospital.

On rare occasions Peg Wooldridge came with the laundry as late as Wednesday, and now that Mrs Deacon was no longer there it didn't seem to matter. On Wednesdays the mistress was in such a good mood you could get away with anything.

'I'm sorry, ma'am,' Peg would say, and find one excuse or another.

And Sarah Morey would tell her that it didn't matter, though on any other day she would have been irritable at the delay. As long as the rector's wife could hold Corrie Palmer's hand she was happy, as Betty soon told Peg.

'It's a shame really,' she said. 'For Corrie as well as her. The kid dotes on her, and it's making her difficult. Spoilt like. You're lucky it wasn't Anna she took to.'

'There ain't much about Anna that would

'appeal to her,' said Peg.

They stood a moment by the kitchen window and compared the two Foundling girls who were playing with Lily in the garden. Anna was growing tall, and her black hair was so unruly Peg had plaited it to keep it away from her pale face. She was as fearless as the Wooldridge boys who involved her in all their mischief, but sometimes Anna would stand and stare, as if she was seeing things that others couldn't see. She was a strange child.

Betty frowned. Now she knew who it was with eyes like Sarah Morey's. Anna and Sarah both had surprisingly light blue eyes considering the darkness of their hair. The stamp of the Irish, Harry had said, when they were talking about Mrs Morey. Perhaps both had Irish blood in them.

Sarah refused to think about the inevitable separation from Corrie when it was time for her to be returned to the Foundling Hospital. She lived in the present, loving her more each day and experiencing the secret joy of sharing in her child's upbringing. But as the months became years she could no longer hide her feelings. She made little dresses and pinafores for Lily and Corrie, but Corrie's were decorated with ribbons and lace. She always brushed Corrie's beautiful hair when she came to the rectory, and though she began teaching both children the alphabet it was Corrie who received the most attention. She would cuddle the child and sing to her, always trying to keep her near, but sadly Corrie wanted none of it. She would wriggle away from Sarah's attention as soon as she could and hide in the garden.

'My beautiful, precious child,' Sarah crooned one day. 'I don't know what I'd do if you didn't come and see me.'

'I'm not yours,' said Corrie, darting off. 'I'm not anybody's.'

When the sun played on her golden hair it was as bright as the copper warming pan which Sarah put between the sheets on winter nights. The lovely reddish gold curls were so similar to the colour of James's hair it took her breath away, yet she could see no other likeness. Corrie had a short, snub nose and rosebud mouth, and her eyes were a smoky grey. Nor was she growing tall like her father or Sarah. She was nowhere near the height of Anna Beckett either, who was shooting up like a sapling.

Anna made Sarah feel uncomfortable. Whenever she came to the house with Peg she would look about with solemn curiosity, and her blue eyes dominated her wan little face. Sometimes she would stand in front of Sarah and stare at her in the most curious way, saying nothing. The child gave her goose pimples and she never encouraged her to stay, though Anna clearly wanted to.

'You're a pretty lady,' she said one Wednesday. She reached out to Sarah longingly, trying to hold her hand, but Sarah thrust her away, unmoved by the quivering lips and tear-filled eyes her rejection caused. She just couldn't take to Anna Beckett at all. Perhaps it was because she compared so unfavourably with Corrie.

Being so preoccupied with her child helped Sarah to ignore the change in her husband. Nahum was no longer so kind or considerate, and he was prone to strange moods. He stopped her from going visiting in the town, and whenever Daniel Marsh was near Nahum became angry, taking it out on the poor, innocent man whose only role in life was to serve.

'My wife doesn't want you hanging around her like a pet dog,' Nahum said to him after the service one Sunday morning. Daniel had been offering to lend her his favourite book of poetry as she had developed a liking for it. His head sank so low that his collar dented his bottom lip, and Sarah had touched his arm in sympathy, earning an even stronger rebuke herself.

Nahum was becoming a feverishly energetic lover. Perhaps he thought powerful attacks on her might produce the result he longed for. He would pump away until he was exhausted, as though by sheer force he could inject her with fertile seed. It left Sarah sore and bruised. His weight had increased since their marriage, and she began to dread his nightly activity, but she accepted it without complaint as the price she had to pay for Corrie.

Sarah's downfall came through being over-confident.

As it drew nearer to Corrie's fifth birthday she began desperately seeking a way in which to keep her in Chertsey. To lose her now was going to be ten times worse than when she had left her at the Foundling Hospital, and she was making herself ill with worry.

The solution came to her one evening when Nahum commented on her excessive pallor.

'My dear, you're not looking well,' he said. 'I do hope you're not sickening for anything.' After all this time his hopes could still be rekindled, so the comment was made cheerfully.

Sarah sighed. 'I'm such a disappointment to you, Nahum.'

The summer evenings were getting shorter and she was lighting the wick of the lamp on her husband's desk so that he could see to write his sermon.

'I will admit we don't have the fulfilled marriage I had hoped for,' he said. 'A house is not a proper home without children, and I quite thought there might have been three at least by now.'

'It's all my fault.' Sarah always took the blame, though she knew it wasn't the truth. Then, as the flame of the lamp flickered and grew, she saw the most wonderful answer to her problems. She drew in her breath at the simplicity of it, wondering why she hadn't thought of it before, and it excited her so much she put forward the suggestion without stopping to think if it was wise. Clutching his sleeve, she said: 'Nahum, we could adopt a child and bring it up as if it were our own.'

Her husband's smile, which she had long since discovered to be a deceitful thing, wavered on his lips like a breeze over a cornfield, and he was slow to answer. 'I don't know that I care for the idea. I've no wish for someone of unknown parentage to inherit after my death.'

'Oh, Nahum, shame on you,' she chided. 'I'm not thinking of money. I'm talking about giving a home and love to a child. Wouldn't it be a very Christian thing to do?'

Her heart was beating like a drum while he considered. Then: 'For your sake, Sarah, I shall give the matter thought. My sister Elizabeth does a lot of charitable work in orphanages. She may know of a suitable baby.'

'But I want one of the Foundling children,' Sarah cried, much too eagerly. She went down on her knees beside him. 'I want the little girl who comes here with Betty. Her name's Corrie Palmer. Please, Nahum. I really love her.'

'Impossible,' he said, his small eyes hardening. 'You know all Foundling children have to be returned to the hospital. Not even foster parents are allowed to keep them.'

It was the first time she had ever begged him for anything, but she knew it was likely he could be persuaded with flattery. 'You're a Governor, Nahum. You can do anything. Say you'll try to get Corrie for me.' Her blue eyes beseeched him. Her hands cajoled, touching his face with tenderness and trust.

He frowned: 'I've seen the unhealthy affection you have for the child. I should have put a stop to it.' He removed her hands from his person and deposited them in her lap. 'There's nothing I can do to prolong the girl's stay here, even if I wanted to.'

Sarah's eyes filled with tears, which she allowed him to see before burying her face against his ample knees. His trousers were rough against her skin and smelt fusty like the church where he spent so many hours praying, presumably, for guidance.

'But you can try. Please say you'll try.' Her longing for her daughter outweighed all else and she began to sob.

'There, there,' he said, as if she were a child herself. 'We'll think of something.'

In the days which followed Sarah never let him forget, but Nahum was adamant.

'Corrie Palmer has become an obsession with you,' he said. His patience was dwindling and for the first time in four years of marriage she could see he was on the point of losing his temper. Yet still he smiled. 'I think we'll consider the subject closed.'

Sarah was heartbroken. She couldn't eat and began to lose weight. Her hair lost its lustre. By the end of September she had lost interest in everything, and waited with dread for the news that Corrie was to be taken back to London. It was like the fear of death.

Anna could hear Edward calling but she kept in her hiding place, covering her mouth so that he wouldn't hear her laugh.

'Anna, where are you? Anna!'

She loved Edward more than anybody in the world. He worked now with his father at the farm, going every morning as the sun came up and not getting back until it was due to set again, so she hardly saw him unless she hid from Ma when it was bedtime. He always came looking for her.

Sometimes on Sundays he would take her to the fields where he had been helping with the harvest, to see the rabbits, or a nest of mice. He taught her to make easy corn dollies. Once he had made a crown of poppies for her hair and a daisy chain for her neck, and she had danced all the way home, feeling like a princess.

Edward was eleven now, and nearly as tall as Isaac. Anna, too, was tall for her age. She had quickly outgrown any tendency to baby fat, and her legs were like beansticks. Her little heart-shaped face was lost amidst the abundance of black hair, her nose was too big, and her mouth with the upper lip thinner than the lower showed her determination to have her own way. She was a very strong-willed child, and not a particularly attractive one. Peg tried to keep her hair tightly braided, but the moment it was done Anna would shake it free. Freedom was everything. She would make George take her down to the river, or get Billy to run away with her for hours, never fearing the punishment. Edward was the only one she obeyed without question.

This evening she was hiding behind a pile of rush mats and baskets in the shed at the back of the cottage. She liked the reedy smell of them. It reminded her of the river bank where Pa and the boys went to cut rushes at weekends so that Ma and Billy could work all week. Sometimes she had to help with the weaving, and her fingers were sore from bending stems round the spokes.

'Come out of there, Anna,' Edward said, pushing aside the baskets. She squealed at the fun, but he wasn't laughing.

'Boo!' she cried, jumping up to frighten him. Then her mouth drew in with disappointment. 'You always know where I am.'

Edward looked serious. 'You've got to come indoors. The inspector's here.'

Her little fists clenched in defiance, and her mouth set stubbornly. 'I don't want to see him. I don't like him.'

She dreaded the inspector coming because he always asked a lot of questions, and told her how lucky she was that she would soon be able to go to a big place in London where there were lots of other girls and boys. She didn't want to go to London. She didn't ever want to leave Ma and Pa, and she would die if she wasn't near Edward.

Edward was pale and she wondered if he'd been eating pork crackling again which didn't agree with him, but he didn't seem sick.

'Ma'll get into trouble if you don't come. Besides, you should be in bed.'

The sun was so low it looked through the dirty window at her, touching the reeds with golden fingers so that they were bright yellow. She pulled a basket over her head and crouched down again.

'Say you can't find me,' she commanded, her voice muffled.

He clambered over and pulled off the covering so quickly her hair brushed out like a halo.

'I'll come with you,' he said. He put his arms round her thin little body and squeezed it. 'Come on.'

The inspector was a big man with a thatch of grey hair which brushed the beams. Anna would look no further than his leather-gaitered legs as she was hauled in front of him, and she wore her most sullen expression. He had come to say something nasty, she could tell. Ma was twisting a handkerchief in her hands, and her nose was as red as the apples Anna had been forbidden to pick in the garden because they were to be kept till Christmas.

'Well, Anna, the time has come,' said the inspector. He had a loud, jolly voice which rumbled round the room. 'In two weeks I shall be taking you and Corrie Palmer on the train to London. Isn't that exciting news?'

'When will we come back?' Anna asked.

Ma came and picked her up, holding her so tight she could hardly breathe. There was the smell of flour and dripping on her apron front, lovely cosy smells which gave a safe feeling, but there were tears on her cheeks.

'You can't be our little girl any more, Anna, love,' Ma said. 'We've got to let you go.'

'No! I don't want to go anywhere.'

'I know you don't, and we'd like to keep you for ever. But you belong at the Foundling Hospital and we were only able to borrow you for a little while. We've always taught you to give borrowed things back, haven't we? Well, now that's what we've got to do.'

'You will have a lot of children your own

136

age to play with,' said the inspector, leaning too close.

Anna began to kick and scream. Her face was stricken and the walls of the warm kitchen seemed to start spinning round her.

'Edward!' she screamed. Ma could no longer hold her and she ran to the boy she thought of as her older brother, clinging to him. 'Don't let this horrid man take me anywhere. *Please* don't let him.'

There was a nasty loud noise in her head, and a strange feeling started moving up through her body from her feet until she couldn't stop shaking. And then she fell down, not knowing anything more until she woke up in Ma's big bed.

The apothecary was bending over her, mumbling words she didn't understand. 'It was a slight convulsion, Mrs Wooldridge. Nothing to worry about.' He placed a cold hand on Anna's forehead. 'I don't think there's any need for blood letting, but if she's still not well tomorrow you could give her an infusion of mistletoe. It sometimes works.'

Anna opened her eyes and wondered why they were fussing round her. The last thing she remembered was the sun perched on the shed window ledge like a big golden ball, and Edward telling her it was bedtime.

Nahum Morey was not at all happy about his wife's attachment to the Foundling child. He hadn't realized she was allowing her feelings to run away with her to such an extent and he was worried about the situation. It put him in a predicament.

Being a man of faith he believed in the truth, so he had no delusions about his feelings for Sarah. He loved her passionately. Not the way he had loved his gentle Adelaide, to whom he had been devoted, but with a lust which made him ashamed. Sarah was a beautiful, sensual woman and she aroused in him the kind of emotions he had always condemned as sinful in others. He enjoyed her body, though he wouldn't allow himself to dwell on the pleasure it gave him, and being away from her, even for one day, was a kind of purgatory. To his dismay his weight problem was causing him to become increasingly short of breath and he would soon have to restrict his carnal pleasures. It made him frustrated and angry when he didn't intend to be, and he deeply regretted the outburst which had made Sarah so unhappy.

His love also made him jealous. He couldn't bear to see Daniel Marsh fawning round his wife like a besotted mongrel, and any other man who looked at her was to be immediately discouraged. Now, to his intense shame, he found he was even jealous of the child, Corrie Palmer, who had wormed her way into Sarah's heart so thoroughly there seemed no dislodging her. And Sarah believed he could bend the rules of the Foundling Hospital so that she could have the child with her always.

For many nights Nahum lay on his back in the big double bed, knowing Sarah was weeping into the pillow beside him. He listened, and his heart ached because he knew if he failed her she would hold it against him for ever. So on the day that the inspector called on Peg Wooldridge, Nahum Morey was in London, asking to see papers at the Foundling Hospital which were strictly confidential.

He had been thinking the matter over very seriously as he travelled from Chertsey on the train. Apart from his emotional objection to bringing up a child which was not their own, there was another consideration, one which he hoped to keep from his wife. His financial state was very worrying indeed. As a Governor he was expected to be continually generous, and it seemed he was always having to spend more money than he could afford. He knew Sarah thought he was mean, but the truth was his capital had dwindled away, and his stipend was insufficient for his needs. Two years ago Mr Gladstone had promised that by 1855 taxation would drop to sixpence in the pound, but the war in the Crimea had put a stop to such plans. In another few months Nahum could see he would have to resign his Governorship, if only to save the expense of his weekly journeys by train.

Being a Governor gave him the right to know details of any child's parentage, but in his case the necessity to study the books had never arisen. Today, however, he used his privilege to check on the background of the child his wife idolized, more out of curiosity than any inclination to relax his stand against trying to procure the child for her. Private information was immediately made available. The consequential shock he suffered all but paralysed him.

The papers were kept in the office of the treasurer's clerk, and fortunately he had the room to himself while he pursued his investigations. He found Corrie Palmer's name listed under the twenty-fifth of October 1850. The mother was an unmarried girl by the name of Mercy Barnett, a street trader's daughter, ill used by a seaman who had made off to the other side of the world rather than face up to his responsibilities.

Nahum was about to close the ledger when his attention was caught by the entry above the one he had been reading. Under the same date, neatly inscribed in copperplate writing with sepia ink, was the name Sarah Byrne. His stomach churned.

There was no mistake. Suddenly he was reading the most terrible things about his own wife.

'Sarah Byrne, unmarried, of Stone Alley, Turnmill Street, Clerkenwell, left a female infant, subsequently baptized Anna Beckett. Father married and untraceable. Unencumbered, the mother able to return to work in Newcastle Place.'

He pressed his hands to his eyes to shut out the dreadful picture. His heart hammered painfully, and he was so angry he couldn't move, even when he heard the treasurer's clerk returning, though he managed to close the book before eyes other than his own fell on the damning evidence of Sarah's treachery. He felt so ill he almost vomited over the leather-bound cover.

All their married life she had been living a lie. So many confusing facts battered his brain he didn't know how to start sorting them out. He didn't know if he wanted to. For one thing he would have to acknowledge that Sarah was not barren, so it must be his own fault she hadn't given him children. It was a wicked blow to his pride. The possibility that she might have been raped should have made him pause and perhaps pity, but his savage jealousy allowed no room for it. Sarah had produced a child by another man, and that made her a loose woman.

'She's a common whore,' he breathed against his clenched knuckles. 'And to think she's fooled me all these years.'

No wonder she'd been desperate to have contact with the Foundling Hospital. Having left her bastard to be brought up on charity she had then schemed to stay near it. No wonder she was now inconsolable at the prospect of the child being returned to London. How easily she'd tricked him! How gullible he had been. But she wouldn't get away with it.

It didn't occur to him until he was travelling home that in learning the truth he had also acquired the means of getting his revenge.

Pleading illness, he excused himself from the Governors' meeting that day and took an earlier train home. He was staring out of the carriage window, seeing nothing of the countryside because the image of Sarah with Corrie Palmer in her arms was superimposed on everything he looked at, and it was then he remembered something important. The child born to Sarah Byrne had been baptized Anna Beckett.

The significance dawned on him like a sword piercing his anger. He didn't know how it had happened, but Sarah was giving all her maternal love to the wrong child. By prodding his memory he placed Anna Beckett as the strange, dark little girl who was fostered with Mrs Wooldridge, his laundry woman, and with his new knowledge he thought he could see a slight resemblance to Sarah, though it would never be remarked upon.

He was breathing quickly, his nostrils pinching in as he thought of the coming confrontation with his wife. Daniel Marsh usually met him at the station, but today Nahum was early. The only transport available was a dog cart, which he hired of necessity, but the slowness made his temper worse, and by the time he reached the rectory he felt as if he would burst with fury. He had never been so overwrought in his life. When he stormed in the door it was as if a gale of wind was behind him, and he shouted his wife's name at the top of his voice.

'Sarah! You whore, where are you?' He had never used such language, and shouting the word aloud added fuel to his temper. 'Liar! Bitch! You've deceived me all these years, but you'll never do it again.'

Sarah came running from the parlour, her face colourless. 'Nahum, whatever's the matter? Are you ill?'

She was lifting her skirt as she hurried to him, and he could see her ankles. 'You shameless creature. You made use of me, didn't you?' He took hold of her by the shoulders and began to shake her with all his strength, forcing her back through the hall towards the staircase. 'All that pretence about wanting to help Foundling babies! The only one you wanted to help was your own.'

'No, Nahum!' she protested. She tripped on the rug and his grip tightened.

'What a fool you made of me, Sarah Byrne. I saw your name in the ledger, so don't deny it.'

'Nahum, let me explain ...'

He was sweating profusely, and an iron band seemed to be clamped round his chest. His perpetual smile became an ugly grimace. 'But you haven't made such a fool of me as you've made of yourself. You don't even have the sense to *know* ...'

The truth he had been about to disclose never passed his lips. Instead he suffered an excruciating pain which made him clasp his heart, and he let go of Sarah so violently she crashed against the newel post. Blood gushed from a wound on her temple, running down into her eyes, but she saw Nahum Morey's fatal collapse just before she crumpled into unconsciousness at the foot of the stairs.

# CHAPTER 6

In the October of 1855 Sarah returned to London, just five years after she had left her baby to be cared for in the Foundling Hospital.

When she got off the train from Chertsey she didn't have enough money to take an omnibus. She had to walk all the way to Clerkenwell with a canvas bag containing all her belongings, and her feet dragged as she grew more reluctant every minute to face the destitution she thought she had left behind for ever.

It was a month since Nahum's death, and she didn't know what to make of this new turn her life had taken. After five years as the wife of a country rector with no financial worries she had suddenly become a homeless, penniless widow. All she had left was the clothes she wore, the second gown Nahum had bought her, and her wedding ring. Nothing else, for the rectory belonged to the church, and she had discovered that her late husband's public generosity had run him into considerable debt.

She pushed her way through the narrow, crowded street of Southwark and crossed the river by Blackfriars Bridge so that she wouldn't have to pay a toll. Her legs ached already from the walk which once would have meant nothing to her. But as she kept to the inside edge of the footpath to avoid being splashed by the congestion of horse-drawn vehicles her gaze turned to the heart of the city, and all at once her spirits lifted. She loved London. She belonged here.

The sky was heavy with rain-filled clouds which pressed down on the dome of St Paul's as if to deflate it, and the wharves and warehouses bordering the river cowered like black giants in the smoky gloom. Bales of goods thumped from even blacker openings in the walls into barges at landing stages, and tiers of narrow windows rose upwards with all the hopefulness of blinded eyes seeking light. She had been homesick for this city, and the years of marriage to Nahum slipped away. Living with him had made her feel middle-aged, yet she was still only twenty-two, and it was wonderful to be free again.

What was more, her darling Corrie had also returned to London. It would have been unbearable in Chertsey without her, but Fate had once more intervened to bring them close together.

She wished she knew what Nahum had been going to say just before he died. She could remember very little about his fatal collapse, no matter how many times she went over it in her mind.

For several days after his death she had lain in the sagging double bed with a bolster by her side to stop her rolling into the hollow created by Nahum's bulk, unaware that he would never again make the springs protest at his weight. In the moments when she had drifted nearer to consciousness she'd thought she saw Corrie sitting on the bed, but when she had tried to lift her arms to gather her close the vision faded away.

Someone bathed her head. A woman. When she called Nahum to know who it was he didn't answer, and it was almost a week before she recognized Elizabeth Bradford. Incredibly, Nahum's sister was sitting by the window with some needlework.

'What's the matter with me?' Sarah asked. 'And where's Nahum?'

She knew something dreadful must have happened for Mrs Bradford to be visiting. Since her marriage there had been no communication with her former employer, not even at Christmas, and she could never think of her as a sister-in-law.

'My brother had a heart attack,' Elizabeth Bradford said, putting down her sewing. When she bent over Sarah there was no sign of sympathy, yet she was known for her kindness. She was older than her brother and she wore a black lace cap over her grey hair. Her gown, too, was black, and the high-necked bodice was closed with a mourning brooch. 'In trying to break his fall you were knocked against the newel post. He collapsed on top of you.'

'But why are *you* here?'

'Poor Nahum is dead. Someone had to see to everything as you were incapable.'

The news caused such pain Sarah had to shut her eyes again. Then she remembered why Nahum had come home in a terrible

146

temper and called her unrepeatable names. He'd found out about Corrie. She turned her head away, scalding tears coursing down her cheeks and on to the pillow which had absorbed her earlier grief.

The hours passed, daylight faded, and the sounds of a warm September evening came in through the open window. When she partially woke again she could smell honeysuckle and new-mown grass in the churchyard.

She remembered being told that Nahum was dead. Over the years she had grown to love him in a familiar, comfortable sort of way, though of late a change in temperament had made him difficult. She was not grief-stricken the way she had been when her father died, but sorrow was a weight which kept her from opening her eyes on a world where she would sorely miss his company.

He had loved her, of that she had no doubt. But she didn't find out he had made no provision for her in the event of his death until Elizabeth could no longer withhold her sentiments.

'I knew no good would come of such a marriage,' she said. 'You tricked my poor brother into it, Sarah, and I fear you must also have squandered his money.'

Sarah could only protest feebly. 'How can you say such a thing?'

'My husband has looked into Nahum's affairs, as there was no one else to do it, and has been shocked to find that debts were mounting weekly.'

'I knew nothing of them.'

'A good husband would naturally not discuss such things with his wife, but you must have had some idea. For Nahum's sake, so that no stain will be on his character, Mr Bradford has cleared those debts, but you, Sarah, will have nothing. I blame you for his death. It was worry that caused his heart to fail.'

Sarah had been too ill to defend herself, and besides, in a way Elizabeth Bradford had been telling the truth. She *was* to blame. The shock of finding out about her child had been responsible for her husband's fatal apoplexy, and she would feel guilty for the rest of her life.

A week later Elizabeth had departed, taking with her everything of Nahum's which belonged in the family. Sarah was still too weak from her head injury to make any protest at the way they were treating her, but as soon as she was able she had sold the rest of Nahum's possessions to repay the debts which John Bradford had settled, preferring to lose everything rather than owe the Bradfords a penny. They would never be able to say that she had accepted their charity.

Without the help of Daniel Marsh she would never have survived those dreadful days. He helped her to make the house ready for the next occupant, and though she protested he gave her the money for her railway journey back to London. Had she encouraged him he would have given more. He was almost in tears when he took her to the station, and when he said his farewells his reedy voice was quite unsteady.

'You've been treated very badly, my dear Mrs

Morey, but I hope you will remember that you have a true friend here in Chertsey, should you ever need one. If at any time you would like to return ...'

'I'll never return, Mr Marsh,' Sarah had said.

'This terrible thing should never have happened to you.'

'But it has, and now I must leave.'

'Mrs Morey ...'

'Goodbye, Daniel.'

His face had coloured at the use of his Christian name, and he'd grabbed her hand with renewed courage. 'Don't go ... Sarah.'

But Sarah had stepped into the railway carriage with relief, unable to feel anything but pity for the curate whose heart she had unwittingly stolen.

Now, as she crossed into Farringdon Street and saw familiar landmarks, she stopped and put down her bag, gazing about her with the pleasure of someone who has come home after a long absence. Yet there were changes, and not all for the better. Work was about to start on a new street through to Clerkenwell Green and excavations were under way to raise the level of the road by several feet. There had recently been a very bad storm, leaving mud everywhere, and it seemed the sewers had overflowed in Saffron Hill, for the filth was worse than she had ever seen it. A bridge had been carried away in Castle Street, so likely there had been a flood tide at the time.

The bag was bumping against her legs as

she turned into Corporation Lane. She hoped that Maggie was still looking after the jeweller whose name Sarah had a struggle to remember. Mr Wood. Yes, that was it. An urchin showed her which tenement house was his.

The boy who answered her knock was scrawny still, with dark hair and roguish eyes like Paddy's, but his expression became cunning when he saw her neat dress and bulging bag.

'You must be Patrick,' Sarah said. This was her half-brother, and for two pins she would have hugged him. 'Is your mother at home?'

'Ma!' he called. 'Ma, there's a woman to see you.'

Maggie's voice came from upstairs. 'Who is it?'

'I'm your sister, Patrick.' Sarah went to touch him, but he backed away.

'I ain't got no sisters. Only brothers.'

Brothers! Sarah marched into the house belonging to Abel Wood.

'Maggie, where are you? It's Sarah.'

Maggie came hurrying down the stairs, followed by two little boys of about four and three.

'Lawks, girl, where've you sprung from?' She rushed to Sarah and threw her arms round her. 'I don't know what brings you, ducks, but it's good to see yer.'

She had filled out a little since Sarah had last seen her and she was no longer drab. She wore a taffeta dress the colour of port wine and a white lace cap, and there was a happier air about her, though the lines of care had deepened with the

150

extra years. Maggie had become motherly.

'What've you been doing to yourself, Maggie Byrne? I can't believe it's you. And with two more boys!'

'I'm a respectably married woman again, I'll have yer know. Maggie Wood I've been these last four years.' Maggie let go of her and called up the stairs. Patrick disappeared down the street before she could shut the door. 'Abel! Sarah's here. Come and meet 'er.'

She led the way to a room at the back which served as living room and kitchen, chattering non stop. It was all reasonably clean, and a smell of cooking reminded Sarah that she hadn't eaten since early morning when Daniel's landlady had given her breakfast. 'You can take yer bonnet off and sit yerself down. We can talk while I get dinner.'

The two younger boys, Dick and John, clung to her skirt as she told Sarah how good Abel was to her. Maggie had done well for herself. Abel had his workshop on the first and second floors of the tall house and made intricate jewellery which he sold to a shop in Hatton Garden. He had made the ring which adorned her finger, and the brooch at the neck of her dress.

'Seems to me you have everything you want,' said Sarah, trying not to sound envious. Maggie had been stewing meat, and now she rolled out pastry with a heavy glass roller like the one Mrs Martin had used in the Bradfords' kitchen. 'I'm pleased for you, that I am.'

The backs of her eyes and nose were burning, and a single tear found its way on to her cheek.

Maggie put down the rolling pin.

'Here's me goin' on about *my* life, and you haven't told me about yours. How long are you visiting for? Is the Reverend Morey calling here to take you back home?'

'Nahum died a month since.' Sarah lifted her chin, determined to talk about it unemotionally. 'All he left was debts, and I've nothing but what you can see.'

'Oh, Sarah. Oh, ducks, I'm so sorry.' After a few stunned seconds plump arms enfolded her. 'Have you no home either? Yer can stay here for a bit. Abel won't mind, I'm sure.'

'What can I do with my life now? There's nothing left ... except Angel.' Sarah slipped back into using the name she had called her child at birth.

Maggie said: 'Yer've seen 'er then.'

'Twice a week. Sometimes more. She's beautiful, and she's got golden hair just like James Halden's.' She told Maggie about Betty Gilling and Peg Wooldridge, and how she had almost persuaded Nahum to adopt Corrie. 'That's her name, Corrie Palmer. It's what they baptized her at the Foundling Hospital.' Sarah buried her face in her hands to hide her misery. 'I nearly had her back, Maggie, but now she's right out of reach. What am I going to do?'

'Well, to my mind you're a fool,' said Maggie, her sympathy evaporating. 'A fool I said, and a fool I meant. If you'd left well alone and not tried to see the child you'd 'ave saved yerself a lot of heartache. By now you'd 'ave forgotten you ever had 'er.'

'Never,' said Sarah. She sat forward in the worn chair. 'The most foolish thing I ever did was take her to the Foundling. I ought never to have listened to *you*. I could have brought her up myself, the same as you've done Patrick.'

'And what would you have done for money? Answer me that. You'd have been on the streets, girl, that's where you'd 'ave been.'

Their voices rose in heated argument, and at that moment Abel Wood appeared. He was a thin man with a hooked nose and dark stubble on his chin which made it seem too weighty for his cadaverous face. His head was bald, and his shoulders curved from continuous bending over intricate work. His short-sighted eyes blinked at the stranger in his kitchen.

Maggie hurried to his side. 'Abel, this is Sarah, me stepdaughter. She needs somewhere to stay and I said she could stop here.'

'So you're Paddy Byrne's daughter,' he said. He assessed her as if he was looking for flaws in a jewel. Then: 'I s'pose you can stay a short while. But if you cause trouble like Patrick, out you go.'

'Abel!' cried Maggie. 'Sarah was married to a parson.'

'I don't care if she was married to a bloody prince. If she upsets you, Mags, I'll kick 'er out meself.'

He spoke as if she wasn't there, and Sarah's temper increased tenfold. 'That's a dreadful thing to say. Perhaps I'd better leave now.'

'Take no notice, ducks,' Maggie shouted. 'You should be ashamed, Abel Wood. Sarah's just lost 'er husband, and she can stay as long as she likes. Yer've no right judging 'er by Patrick. He's a boy with high spirits.'

'He's the devil 'imself.'

'You've got to forgive him, Sarah. He looks after me right well, but Paddy's son is just too much for 'im.'

The boy in question burst in noisily from the street, chanting obscene words. Maggie clipped his ear, making him yell, but undeterred he began to torment the two younger boys who had crouched quietly in a corner, watching.

'Patrick, take Sarah upstairs,' said Abel. 'She can have your bed. You can sleep in the workshop.'

Patrick scowled, but did as he was told. Sarah followed him up the narrow stairs with her bag, her eyes on his thin, dirty bare legs and ragged trousers. The other children were clean and decently fed, but this one had a smell of the gutters about him and looked like he could do with some good food to fatten him up. Her heart went out to him. It seemed there was no love for the boy in this house, and though Sarah could hardly believe it, Maggie had let her own well-being be bought at Patrick's expense.

The room had one dirty window overlooking a wall of the House of Detention yard. Patrick went and gazed out.

'That's the prison,' he said. 'I wish I could see over them walls. I can hear men shouting sometimes.'

'Is that where you heard the bad words you used just now?'

154

He grinned. 'Reckon I did.'

'They're bad men in there,' Sarah said. 'You don't want anything to do with them, do you?'

'I 'ate to think of them shut away.'

'But they've done wicked things.'

Patrick flung himself on the mattress which Sarah was to use, and jumped up and down on his knees, full of boyish energy. Then he stopped, and stared at her.

'Are you really my sister?' he asked.

'My father was your father, too. You're like him, Patrick.'

He was thoughtful a moment. Then he said: 'He was Irish. Ma said so. Are you Irish?'

'I suppose I am.'

'Then I think I'll like you,' Patrick said.

Anna hated the Foundling Hospital, but she didn't cry all the time like Corrie Palmer. She sat in a corner of the playroom, dressed in the brown serge dress and white apron she had been given, and tried to think how she could run away. She had to get back to Ma and Pa, and Edward.

She didn't understand why she had been taken from them when they loved her and wanted to keep her. It wasn't fair. That hateful inspector had dragged her away, even though Ma had been weeping enough to fill a kettle.

'She's such a wee thing,' Ma had said through her tears. 'She needs a proper home like she's got here, not a great institution. It's cruel.'

'Not cruel, Mrs Wooldridge. Anna was

brought to us when her life was not worth anything. The hospital took her in, and you knew she had to go back there time she was five. Rules is rules.'

'But we love her.'

Ma had held her so tight the buttons of her dress had pressed into Anna's chest until they hurt. She had clung equally hard, her little arms binding like rope round the warm, soft neck.

Saying goodbye to Edward had been worse.

'I made this for you, Anna,' he had said, presenting her with a small wooden doll. 'It ain't very good but it's the best I could do.'

She'd cried then, because she had loved the doll so much and the inspector had tried to take it from her.

'She won't be allowed to keep it, I'm afraid. Everything is shared at the hospital.'

She had clung to the doll tenaciously, until the awful feeling she'd had once before stole up through her little body from her feet to her head, and the next thing she knew she was lying on the floor with her head in Ma's lap. The inspector stood over them.

'Another of her fits,' he'd exclaimed. 'It's time she was back at the hospital.'

' 'Tis only the third one,' Pa had said. 'And they're mild. She'll soon grow out of them.'

Pa knew all about it. He'd brought home some hairs from the cross on the back of a donkey when she was cutting her teeth, and Ma had made a little black silk bag to put them in so they could hang round her neck to keep the funny turns away. She'd never had any more until the inspector had come to say she must go back to London.

Edward's doll was in Anna's apron pocket. She had refused to be parted from it, and leniency had been shown during her first few days in new surroundings. She and Corrie were allowed to play while the other children attended lessons in alphabets and multiplication tables, but they sat at one end of the long playroom like wilting flowers, still too unhappy at their uprooting to do anything. And Corrie continued to cry.

'I want Mrs Morey,' she sobbed, her pretty lips perpetually curving downwards. 'She said she wouldn't let me come here.'

'Mrs Morey, Mrs Morey!' scoffed Anna. 'She's all you think about.'

'I want Ma, too,' wailed Corrie.

When Matron came in that afternoon everyone stood up and shouted 'Hooray'. It seemed a silly thing to cheer about and Anna remained sitting on the floor until a group of older boys appeared with musical instruments which they took to a bank of seats at the far end. Someone else brought in toys, and when the music started Anna was given a horn which didn't make any sound. She threw it down in disgust and took a drum which Corrie showed no inclination to use, thumping it furiously to express her feelings. Then she discarded that, too, and left Corrie's side for the first time to join in with the other children. A small boy gave her his wooden sword and she brandished it the way he had shown her.

Presently Anna turned round to see a girl of about six shaking Corrie by the shoulders.

'Why don't you stop crying?' the child asked. She was making Corrie worse. 'We don't like cry-babies.'

'I want my ma,' sobbed Corrie.

'You haven't got one. None of us has, so stop howling.'

The wooden sword in Anna's hand landed across the aggressor's legs. 'Leave Corrie alone,' she shouted. 'She can cry if she wants.'

In the ensuing pandemonium the young musicians played on, but Matron came and took Anna away, scolding her gently for bad behaviour which would not be tolerated once she was settled in. She was told unruly children were placed in solitary confinement and given only bread and water for a week.

The next day Corrie's misery was worsened by the barber. She shrieked when he went near her with the scissors, and had to be held down by the nurse so that he could take off about twelve inches of her golden curls.

'I don't *want* my hair cut,' Corrie screamed. 'Mrs Morey says I've got beautiful hair and she brushes it for me.'

'You'll have it cut, child, whether you like it or not,' said the nurse. 'A penny a head the barber charges and we're going to see we get our penn'orth.'

When it was done the reddish gold hair licked round the edge of her mob cap like a straight silken fringe, and there was no consoling her. Anna's turn followed, and the opposite happened. Once the heaviness dropped away her black hair formed into tight curls, and for the first time she looked almost pretty.

An older girl helped Anna and Corrie to dress each morning as soon as it was light. She tied the strings of their aprons and did up their buttons, and she sat between them at their bread and milk breakfast which was at half past seven. Dinner was at one o'clock. Anna quite liked dinner, and soon she would know each day by what there was to eat. Monday and Wednesday meant mutton. On Tuesday and Thursday they had beef boiled into soup with rice, while on Saturday there was either rice or suet pudding. Sunday was best of all with cold roast beef and potatoes or bread. At six o'clock there was always bread and milk for supper, and at eight o'clock it was bedtime, but no warm arms cuddled her. There was only a nurse to help untie and unbutton the morning's fastenings before she undressed and climbed into a bed in the long, crowded dormitory.

Once the first week was over the two small girls joined others in the schoolroom. A mistress in a plum-coloured dress began to teach them sewing so that later on they would be able to help with needlework that was taken in. Anna found she could do it quite well, but Corrie had no aptitude at all, though when it came to learning Foundling hymns she excelled. Most important of all was to know the Catechism, and they had to repeat it over and over until it could be said without faltering.

They were in their second week when a nurse

came one morning to take Anna Beckett over to the infirmary to see a physician.

'I don't want to see him,' Anna said, remembering her inoculation on the first day back, and how it had hurt.

' 'Fraid you've got to, ducks,' said the nurse, whose name was Teresa Thorpe. She was a nice enough young woman, well-rounded like Peg, and until now Anna had liked her. 'Something to do with you having fits.'

'I don't, I don't, I don't,' cried Anna.

'Well, we'll see.' Teresa held her hand as they left the main building by a back door and crunched over the path to the infirmary, Anna dragging her feet. She had to be scolded. 'Yer'd better behave. The physician runs a madhouse, I've heard, and he'll take you there if you're not good.'

Anna hung back even more, frightened by the threat, though she wasn't sure what it meant. The infirmary was quiet like the chapel and had a strange smell. She shuddered when she looked in an open door and saw grey-faced children in beds with blue curtains round, propped up on pillows.

The doctor was very tall and had hair nearly the same colour as Corrie's. He wore a smart black tail coat and silk waistcoat, and a gold chain was draped from a buttonhole to the pocket where he kept his watch. He stood over her for a moment, smiling gently, then he sat on a chair so that she didn't have to look up at him.

'So you are Anna Beckett,' he said. 'And you

160

sometimes have "funny turns".'

'Yes, sir.'

He took off her mob cap and touched her dark hair which sprang up in unruly profusion. There must have been some magic in his fingers because they made her head tingle. She opened her blue eyes wide and smiled back at him, the curve of her mouth imitating his.

'Tell me how you feel when you have these funny turns,' he said, his exploring fingers moving to her temple.

'I go round and round till I fall down. Shall I show you?'

She wanted to please him. She darted away and began spinning on one foot in the middle of the room, but he quickly took hold of her and drew her back.

'No, Anna. If you go round and round any more I might have to prescribe some medicine for you.' He looked intently into her eyes, and she thought he was sad, even though he smiled. His eyelids were like shells beneath his sandy-coloured brows, and he seemed to hide behind them. 'What do you think made you feel funny the last time?'

Remembering made her answer tearfully. 'I didn't want to leave Ma and Pa. And Edward. And the inspector took away my doll.'

The physician sighed deeply. His arms closed round her momentarily, and the feel of rough, male clothing against her was like being back with Isaac. It was comforting.

'You were frightened, then,' he said, and she nodded. 'Well, there's nothing to frighten you

161

here.' He stood up, and he towered above her like a golden figure in one of the hospital's many paintings. Trustingly she slipped a small hand into one of his, and she would have gone with him anywhere, but he detached her fingers after giving them a reassuring squeeze. 'Nurse, I shall leave instructions for Anna's treatment, should it be necessary. The child obviously has mild epilepsy, and should it recur she must be exposed fortnightly to intense cold in a bath for an hour, then put in a warm bed until a fever is induced. But she seems healthy enough now. I hope she stays that way.'

'I hope so too, Dr Halden,' said the nurse.

James Halden returned to a tall, red-brick house in Clerkenwell, a private asylum where he was employed as permanent physician. Professionally the years had been good to him, though it was a great disappointment to Maud that he had specialized in diseases of the mind. She considered the insane unmentionable, and the care of them the least attractive area of the medical profession, but in accepting the position in Claybury's Private Asylum the financial rewards had enabled him to buy a house in Calvert Terrace, just off Myddelton Square, an address which certainly won Maud's approval.

Maud liked to be associated with the right people and be seen in the right places.

'I'm to be on the committee of the Society for the Relief of Distressed Widows,' she told him one day. 'Such an honour, don't you think, dearest?'

162

The endearment was affectation. She had borne James three children in the last five years, but none had survived infancy, and she accused him regularly of not trying enough to save them. The fact that all three babies had been born with an incurable heart condition was characteristic of the Rollerson side of the family, but Maud preferred to blame her husband, and the marriage suffered as a consequence.

James took refuge in his work. He was already a respected physician in his field, and his opinion was often called for in public hospitals and institutions, which was why he had been to the Foundling Hospital today. Principally the visit had been to see a senior boy with lifelong problems who had suddenly become unmanageable and would have to be admitted to an asylum, but while there he had been asked to assess Anna Beckett, a child who had moved him strangely.

He was finding it difficult to change old methods of treatment at Claybury's. The elderly lay proprietor, Miss Cordelia Claybury, had inherited the madhouse from her father who had made a good living out of the rich and insane. The man had not been deliberately cruel or corrupt, like so many non-medical people who licensed their houses for this purpose, but he had stuck to the principle that the violent needed continual restraint, and his daughter still feared more progressive methods.

'Miss Claybury, the most successful way to treat insanity is with kindness,' James told her when she insisted that a particularly deranged woman of middle age should remain chained by the ankle to her bed.

But Miss Claybury was adamant. 'Mrs Duncan's family pay well to keep her here but we can't have her attacking the other patients. For her own good and everyone elses she must be restrained.' She would not allow the manacle to be removed, and her word had to be obeyed.

James had done training under Dr John Conolly at Hanwell, the Middlesex County pauper lunatic asylum, and to him the insane were the most pitiable of all human flotsam. He wanted to improve their lot, as John Conolly was doing, but with Maud always wanting every luxury he couldn't afford to leave this lucrative private madhouse.

Today he heard screams coming from Mary Duncan's room on the first floor as soon as he entered the house. A man wearing a hat he'd painted and twisted into an unrecognizable shape shuffled along the corridor, pointing upwards with a contorted grimace.

'It's 'er again.'

'It's her again,' repeated a woman with red eyes and dribbling mouth.

James hurried upstairs, calling for an attendant, and found Mary Duncan trying to reach the iron-barred window, her shackled ankle attached to the bed which she was dragging along inch by inch behind her. The noise she made was like a cry from hell, and James knew her suffering had turned this place into hell itself.

'It's all right, Mrs Duncan,' he said gently,

appalled at the poor woman's distress. Her hair was like a bird's nest, her skin grey, her leg bleeding. One of his rules, which Miss Claybury could not contest, was that all patients must be spoken to kindly, but it was hard to make himself heard above the noise. When he was near enough she went for him with clawed hands. 'I won't hurt you. I want to help.'

His soothing voice reduced her screams to a quieter moaning, and she huddled on the floor against the bed in a pathetic foetal position.

'Get the key to this devilish contraption,' James ordered the attendant, a blowsy woman with the strength of a man. 'Hurry.'

When the manacle was unlocked a weeping ulcer was exposed, and he was sickened, not by the sight of it, but because he had failed her in not acting sooner.

'Be careful,' the attendant warned. 'She's violent.'

'She's in need of different treatment.' The room was unsanitary. Mary's clothes were wet and dirty, and the smell was appalling. 'I want this room cleaned, and I want a warm bath got ready for Mrs Duncan.'

'I can't bath her, sir. It ain't safe.'

'Then we'll do it together.' James never expected anyone to do things he was not prepared to do himself.

Three hours later Mary Duncan was back in her bed. Her wound was dressed, her body and clothes were clean, and her hair was neat. The chain had not been replaced, nor would it ever be, and warm, fresh blankets covered her. She muttered incoherently but the sound was happy, and her eyes had lost the terrible haunted stare of madness.

'P'raps she should be in a strait-waistcoat tomorrow,' said the attendant. There were four scratches across James's cheek from Mary's fingernails.

'Tomorrow Mrs Duncan will be treated with kindness,' said James. 'She will have well-ordered meals nicely presented, and for a short time she will mix with the other patients. From now on we must keep her mind free of stress and I guarantee she will improve daily.'

'But tonight ...'

'She'll have no restraint. I've given her a mild sedative and I'll sit here with her myself until she sleeps.'

It was soon dark, but a watery moon penetrated the iron grille and made silver stripes across the floor. Long after Mary Duncan was asleep James continued to sit beside her, his thoughts disturbed by the day's events, and little Anna Beckett, whom he had seen that afternoon, kept tugging at his conscience.

She was a strange little girl, advanced for her age and surprisingly sensible for one afflicted with the symptoms of epilepsy. Perhaps she'd intrigued him because she had such lovely eyes, unusually blue against the dark hair, and clear and direct like those of Sarah Morey.

His memories of Sarah were as strong as ever, but he thought of her with mixed emotions. He would never understand why she had married a pompous clergyman. He had wanted her himself so badly, and when he'd heard of her wedding he had been insanely jealous. For days he'd been in the blackest of moods, furious with her for wasting herself on a man old enough to be her father, and even more furious with himself for not having taken her forcefully after that Christmas evening when he'd known her feelings were as inflamed as his own. He hadn't dared to dwell on her in those aging arms lest his raging should drive him to deeds he might regret for the rest of his life.

Mary Duncan stirred in her sleep. James touched her hand, and she smiled. Several hours passed while he sat there, knowing that Maud would be inconsolable at having missed a charity dinner.

He made up his mind to tell Miss Claybury in the morning that things must change, otherwise he could no longer stay in her employ. The case of Mrs Duncan influenced him strongly, but for some reason it was Anna Beckett more than anyone who made up his mind. He kept thinking of her pirouetting, her small face impish, then her eyes filling at the memory of her lost doll. The Foundling Hospital was generous towards its inmates. He had heard that forty pounds a year had been paid for a girl to be looked after in the asylum of Dr Perfect in West Malling. At some future date it might become necessary for Anna Beckett to be admitted to a private asylum. The knowledge worried James. He couldn't bear the thought of a child like Anna ever being subjected to the indecencies and ugliness of a house such as

Claybury's, and he vowed that from now on he would work only to make life for lunatics stress-free and tolerable, even if it meant less money for himself.

Maud must understand.

There were still scratches on his face on Sunday. If the weather was fine Maud liked to walk in Hyde Park, not so much to see as to be seen, her small hand slotted lightly into the bend of his arm. That day in early November when a warm sun was turning the autumn trees to gold, they entered the park by Grosvenor Gate and passed a group of young chimneysweeps in the Ring playing pitch-and-toss. It was then that James saw Sarah.

Sarah was watching the chimneysweeps with a rapt expression, and holding the hands of two small boys, while one a bit older had to be reprimanded for trying to climb a tree. James stopped at the sight of her, making his wife almost lose her balance. His heart began to beat like a native drum and his palms ran with sweat.

So Nahum Morey had given her children. The discovery was painful, and his heavy-lidded eyes narrowed to shut out the picture she made with them. She was pale but more beautiful than ever, and her dignity was pronounced in spite of having to cope with three boys.

'What's the matter, James?' Maud asked irritably.

'Surely that's the wife of Nahum Morey over there,' he said. At that moment he felt as if the chain he had taken from Mary Duncan now fettered him to his wife. 'Perhaps we should speak to her.'

'Definitely not. Elizabeth Bradford would never forgive us.' Maud's hand tightened on his sleeve as she urged him to walk on towards the Serpentine. 'I spoke to her the other day at a charity meeting and she was telling me that her poor brother died recently. Apparently the servant girl he married squandered every penny of his and Elizabeth says she has no pity for her now she's destitute.'

James hid his feelings well. No one could have known that he no longer heard the park sounds for the pounding in his temples or that his feet felt iron-clad as he walked away from the woman he longed to hold in his arms. It wouldn't do for them to meet now. With great effort he averted his gaze from the sight of Sarah Morey with her family, but he promised himself that one day soon he would look upon her intimately, now that she was free once more.

## CHAPTER 7

Patrick didn't know what to make of his sister Sarah. She wasn't like his ma, or any of the women in the street. She gave herself airs and spoke more like a toff, but she made a fuss of him and she'd mended his trousers.

He liked it when she spoke about his real father, because Ma always shut him up when he asked questions.

'Our pa was a devil sometimes, but he could be a wonderful man,' Sarah said one day. 'He could make my mother laugh even when she was ill, and when he played his fiddle no one could keep their feet still.'

'Ma keeps 'is fiddle in a cupboard. I wish I could play it.'

'Perhaps one day she'll let you try.'

'No she won't. She belted me when I touched it once.' He was a restless child, always on the go, and he jumped off the bed where they'd been sitting so that he could dance a jig. His boots clattered on the boards, and Ma was soon yelling at him to stop. He made a rude face in the direction of the door, then stood in front of Sarah. 'I'll tell you a secret. I *can* play the fiddle.'

She laughed and wagged a finger. 'Don't tell fibs, you naughty boy.'

He liked sharing secrets with Sarah, but she never shared any with him. She went out nearly every day and was gone for hours. When she came back Ma would look at her strangely, sort of angry-like, and one day she said: 'I don't know why you don't go and work in the bloody place.'

Sarah'd been upset. 'You know I can't do that.'

He heard her crying sometimes. His stepfather made him sleep in the workshop on the top floor, but draughts came up through the floorboards and he would lie awake, freezing cold and frightened by eerie shadows. He'd taken to creeping downstairs to the bedroom as soon as the house was quiet, and curling up on the rug mat under the window. At first Sarah didn't know, but one night after Dick and John were asleep she was sobbing into the pillow, and he climbed in bed beside her like a stray cat in search of warmth. Sarah held him tight, moulding his thin little body close to her own, and he was still there in the morning, happier than he'd been for a long time. After that they always shared the narrow bed.

She never told him why she was so miserable but he supposed it was because she was a widow. Some widows wore black and cried over everybody, but not all of them. A woman in the next street had sung 'Good riddance' when her old man snuffed it, and she'd swigged gin until she couldn't sing any more. It'd been the funniest thing Patrick had ever seen.

Soon he decided to find out where Sarah went every day. He waited until she got to the corner, then he followed her stealthily along Bowling Green Lane and Farringdon Road, on and on until his legs began to ache and he thought she was never going to stop. She didn't pause until she came to a big red-brick building with a long drive in front and a statue at the gates. There she hurried round to the side and waited until a crowd of little girls came out to play. She was hidden behind some bushes, but when she saw the children she leaned forward eagerly, as if she longed to snatch one for herself, and she lost her unhappy look. Patrick was jealous.

Things had been better at home since Sarah

came. She made him feel wanted, which nobody else did. He couldn't remember living anywhere different, but Ma was always telling him he should be grateful Pa had moved them away from Turnmill Street and given them a good home. He wasn't so sure. He knew Pa hated him so he kept out of his way, and Ma cared only for his sickly looking brothers, sneaky John who was her favourite, and grizzling Dick. They didn't want him and he didn't want them. The dirtiest jobs were kept for Patrick, like emptying slops and carting coal, and he was beaten if he skipped doing them. Pa said that come the new year he'd be sent out to work. He tried not to care.

But now there was Sarah, someone who took an interest in him at last. She was so pretty, even though she always looked sad, and he wondered what she was thinking when she sat so still. Pa stared at her a lot, mostly when Ma wasn't there, and his fingers would be wiping dribble from his lips. It made Patrick feel scary, and he wished he wouldn't do it.

Today he waited ages while Sarah watched the little girls, and for the first time her eyes were bright like they should be. It was a rum game. Presently the children went inside again and he was so keen to see where they went he forgot to keep out of sight. The next moment he felt Sarah's hand grabbing him by the neck of his tattered shirt.

'And what do you think *you're* doing here?'

Patrick gulped. He stuttered and didn't know what to say, and the more he wriggled the tighter she held him until the shirt ripped, exposing his dirty back.

'Well?' she prompted.

He looked up at her with pleading eyes and bit his lower lip hard. 'If you want a kid so bad, won't I do?' he asked. 'I'd be good, I promise.'

Sarah didn't say anything for a moment. Her anger evaporated and she knelt down on the path to gather him close. 'Oh, Patrick.'

'Ma dun't want me,' he said.

He twined his arms round her neck and the smell of her skin was sweet. Rain came spilling from a wintry sky in a sudden shower, and she drew him under her shawl, kissing the back of his head where sometimes lice made it itch.

She said: 'I love you, Patrick, and if I'd somewhere to go I'd take you with me, but right now I must stay with your mother. And she *does* love you, even though you don't think so. I was there when you were born and she wanted you badly.'

'Well now she only likes me when Pa ain't there.' They started walking back towards Clerkenwell, silent for a long time. He was deep in thought. They'd got as far as the bottom end of Coppice Row when he asked the next question. 'Ain't you got no money?'

'Not a penny.'

'Then I'll get you some,' he said, and pranced in front of her with excitement. 'I'll get some for us both.'

'No, Patrick,' she cried. 'I won't have you stealing.'

173

'I ain't never stole nothing.'

The last declaration was shouted over his shoulder as he darted off in the opposite direction from home. His legs were no longer tired. The winter evening was quickly drawing in and tallow candles were lit in the shops. He went dodging and weaving through crowded alleys, an urchin who knew every inch of the area, and he almost fell under the feet of a coal hawker's horse in his haste. The keys scattered from a locksmith's barrow as he tipped it in regaining his balance, earning a string of abuse, but he was off again before anyone could catch him.

In a few minutes he reached Saffron Hill. He scanned the dim length of it and soon saw a group of street musicians returning home from a day spent entertaining in richer streets.

'Giuseppe!' he called. 'Giuseppe, I want to play your fiddle.'

A boy of about twelve walked along scraping a bow across the strings of a violin with more rhythm than melody. Another carried a harp, and a third was singing like a jaded nightingale which he held out his cap for rewards to loiterers who'd finished a hard day's work.

Giuseppe stopped. 'No more you play my violin. The padrone forbid it.'

'But I want to earn some money, like you do.'

'We have no money.' Giuseppe wore a tall hat which had a curly brim and he knocked it sideways as he started to play again. 'The padrone he take it all. He beat us if we not

174

take it home. Now you go.'

Patrick knew he meant it. Today must have been a bad day.

He'd made friends with the Italian boys several months ago. They came from a place called Napoli where the padrone had bought them from their parents, and they all lived together in a big, dirty house and ate something funny called macaroni. The padrone provided it, but he was crueller than Abel Wood and they were frightened of him.

Lots of Italians lived in Saffron Hill and most talked a language Patrick couldn't understand. He heard them shouting inside a filthy shop behind him which reeked of sour milk. Nearby was an ice depot and early every morning men with barrows filled the street, gabbling away in their strange tongue as they mixed ice with milk and then went off to sell it. He'd often been down here to see them, and once Giuseppe had bought him a halfpenny ice. Now it was dusk the barrows were returning, to be unloaded and packed close together in courts and yards, and the sound of their wheels dragging up the hill drowned the violin music.

'Please, Giuseppe, let me play,' Patrick begged.

A swarthy man with a large stomach came out of the milk shop, his greasy hair a shiny black and his moustache as bushy as a brush. The Italian's eyes glinted as they rested on Patrick Byrne and he grabbed him before he could escape. It was the padrone.

'You heard what Giuseppe say.' His voice

was syrupy and he held Patrick by his torn shirt, making the hole bigger. 'I not have you disturbing my musicians.'

'I only wanted to play the fiddle.'

'Then you come to live with us.' He lifted him by the scruff of the neck until his feet were off the ground. 'You make money for me, eh?'

'No,' yelled Patrick, wriggling like an eel.

The padrone set him down again, but landed into him with his fist before letting go, and he roared with laughter as Patrick sped away. 'You Irish banshee, you stay away from my boys.'

Patrick ran all the way home with blood running from his nose which he kept wiping on the sleeve of his shirt. He wasn't going to cry. He crept in the door and peered down the passage to make sure Ma was in the kitchen, then he took off his boots so he wouldn't make a noise going upstairs. He wanted to crawl into a corner like a dog to lick his wounds, but Sarah prevented it.

'Patrick!' She caught him before he could reach the bedroom and her face was shocked. 'You poor boy. What happened to you?'

Her concern took him off guard. Ma would have shouted, and he would've shouted back and known where he was. He wasn't used to a gentle voice. Suddenly his lip quivered and he buried his face against her skirt. At that moment Pa came down from the workshop.

'What's the matter with 'im?' he asked Sarah roughly.

'I don't know yet,' said Sarah. 'Looks like someone's hit him.'

Pa yanked him away from her. 'Well he must have deserved it,' he said, and boxed his ears. 'That's another to go with it.'

Now Patrick yelled for all the house to hear, and Sarah clutched him close once more.

'That was a wicked thing to do, Abel Wood.'

'Who provides for that kid, you or me?' Pa demanded. '*I* give 'im a home, madam.'

'And that makes you responsible for treating him better.'

Patrick looked up from the folds of Sarah's skirt and saw Pa raise his arm as if to strike her as well, but he thought better of it. His face was red and his eyes glittered, but Sarah just stared back at him until he thumped down the stairs muttering with suppressed anger.

The days following James's visit to the Serpentine with Maud were fraught with questions and problems. Seeing Sarah with her children had unsettled him badly and he found it difficult to concentrate on his work. For five years he had resisted all temptations to visit her even though he could have found an excuse which wouldn't have made Nahum Morey suspicious, and he knew he'd been right. One glimpse of her had been enough to fire his blood, and it was not enough. He desperately needed to see her again.

Maud must never know the effect her disclosure had had on him. The news of Nahum Morey's death had made him want to shout for joy. He didn't care about the allegation that Sarah had squandered his money. He didn't dwell on the fact that she had a family. He told himself his main interest was to make sure she was all right and wanted for nothing, but in moments of honesty he admitted his greatest wish was to revive the passion she aroused just by her presence. There was no other woman like her and he craved to be with her no matter for how short a time. Surely there was nothing to stop him now the old man was dead. Nothing except loyalty to his wife.

For a fortnight he delayed making any positive decision. It wasn't that he would feel any real guilt about being physically unfaithful to Maud. It wouldn't be the first time. What worried him was the much deeper regard he had for Sarah Morey and he was afraid that once he was with her again he wouldn't have the strength to leave. She excited him mentally as well as sexually and he had to push thoughts of her away by becoming more involved with his patients. Long hours spent at Miss Claybury's asylum were the only way he could be sure of keeping his own sanity. But his willpower grew less as the days became shorter.

On the next Sunday when Maud was paying a routine visit to her father James gave way at last to the insistent voice within him which urged that he shouldn't delay his search for Sarah any longer. He ordered his carriage to be brought round and set off for the back streets of Clerkenwell, his first destination being the house in Stone Alley where her stepmother lived. He remembered Maud repeating Elizabeth Bradford's account of her brother's wedding, to which she had not been invited, and it seemed Maggie Byrne had been Sarah's only witness, so their differences had been patched up. In her widowhood it was likely she might have turned to Maggie again.

'Maggie Byrne moved long since,' said a neighbour. 'Went awf with 'er kid to keep 'ouse for a jeweller. Heard tell she married the man.'

'And where does the jeweller live?'

'Corporation Lane,' another woman volunteered. 'Abel Wood's the name of the man.'

James rewarded them generously, though no one had heard of Sarah Morey. He needed to get away from the smell and dirt of the alley as quickly as possible.

Corporation Lane was slightly more wholesome. He drove along the narrow street, studying the tall tenement houses which looked out gloomily on the wall of the House of Detention. There were plenty of people about and he had to slow his horse to walking pace. Two houses up from St John's Passage was where he'd been told he might find Maggie, and when he reached it the door was standing open. From inside came the sound of a woman screaming, but no one passing by took any notice. Only James made it his business to investigate, gripped by a sudden, irrational premonition.

The problem of Patrick worried Sarah very much, and eased the heartbreak she suffered in not knowing what to do about Corrie. In a very short time Patrick had found a place in her heart and she was distressed at the way he was treated.

'Have you no thought for that poor child?' she asked Maggie after the confrontation with Abel. 'Don't you care that your husband hits him? My father must be turning in his grave.'

'Paddy Byrne was no saint,' said Maggie. 'Likely Patrick would've been worse off with him than he is with Abel. Anyway, it's none of your business.' She thrust a bucket into Sarah's hands. 'The step ain't had a scrub in years. Pull yer skirt up and get on yer knees. Reckon they've forgotten what they was meant for.'

'Nahum said they were meant for praying.'

'Humph!' snorted Maggie. 'Prayin' don't bring in money. You'll 'ave to find work, ducks. Abel's fretting about keeping you.'

'I help all I can. I go to the market and I take the children off your hands.'

Her stepmother took a battered tin from the warped chest of drawers. 'I want some more money in this by the end of the week, or out you go. Stop wasting time round that bloody Foundling Hospital and do something useful,' she said harshly. Then she softened a little. 'Forget about the kid. Or find yerself a real man and have some more. That way you'll not have time to mope.'

Sarah hated being dependent on the Woods. She had already sold one of her two dresses to a second-hand shop to help pay for her keep, and the coppers left over were hoarded in a purse tied inside her skirt so that she would have something to put in the collection plate when she went to the Foundling Chapel on Sunday evenings.

Her well-ordered life with Nahum had made it hard to adapt to the scarcity of refinements in Corporation Lane.

The trouble was, Nahum had given her a social standing which made the return to her roots that much more difficult. She would have liked to become a governess, but that was impossible with no education, and she'd never served an apprenticeship so there was nothing much she could do except housework. The alternative was to go into a factory, but lurid tales of sweat shops made it an unbearable thought.

A strained atmosphere was developing. Maggie was on edge and had little to say, while Abel said nothing at all. Every day he shut himself in his workshop from early morning until evening, and on Sundays he drank himself into a stupor.

The only joy in Sarah's life was a glimpse of Corrie if she walked to the hospital, but even that was more painful than pleasurable since she could only watch her in secret. And she cried when she saw what they had done to her beautiful hair. Soon, she knew, she would have to take any work she could get so that she could rent a room somewhere and claim Corrie as her own. Life without her was empty.

The tall house was as gloomy as a tomb, and just about as depressing. No sunshine ever penetrated the windows, little warmth came from the smoky fire, and in places the wallpaper was peeling with the damp. Sarah had been living there for three weeks when events took an extraordinary turn.

It was Sunday. Maggie had taken John and Dick to see a friend over at St Giles, and Abel was drowning his sour moods in liquor at the nearest tavern, so it was unusually quiet. The day was cold, frost making patterns on the kitchen window as if new lace curtains covered it, and Sarah was sewing in front of the meagre fire when Patrick startled her.

'What're you doing?'

'I'm making you a coat out of the tails of one of your father's old ones.'

'You're clever,' he said. His energy never flagged and he turned a somersault on the mat before sitting cross-legged in front of her. 'I'm clever, too. Ma's out so I could show you how I can play the fiddle.'

Sarah put down her sewing. The boy was persistent in his claims and she decided to put him to the test.

'All right,' she said. 'You can show me for five minutes.'

With a yelp of delight he climbed on a chair and took Paddy's fiddle from a cupboard. She hadn't realized how the sight of it would bring back memories, and she touched it lovingly before Patrick tucked it under his chin like an expert. To her amazement he started to play a tune. It was not anything she knew, but someone had taught him the rudiments of music and his little hand on the bow was almost as sure as her father's had been. The gift brought a lump to her throat.

Paddy Byrne would have loved this boy of his. He would've been so proud. It was as if his life carried on in the thin little body, making the child old beyond his years, and it was hard to believe he was only six.

The front door opened while he was still playing, and Abel Wood burst in like a raging bull. He was so drunk he lurched from wall to wall, his face red as fire, yet he steadied himself remarkably when Sarah stood up and ran to protect Patrick from the trouble she could see in his eyes.

'Give me that bloody thing,' Abel shouted, trying to grab the fiddle. 'Yer mother's forbidden you to touch it, you varmint! Give it 'ere I say.'

'I let him play it,' said Sarah, and when she took it from the boy he scrambled between his stepfather's unsteady legs, scuttled from the room like a hare, and was gone through the open front door.

'Give it to me!' Abel reached again for the instrument, but she too darted out of his way. 'Damned thing's caused more rows in this house than enough. I'd like to smash it over that kid's head, so I would.'

'The fiddle belongs to Maggie.'

'It's a relic from Paddy Byrne, and she never lets me forget it.'

In the midst of her anger Sarah felt a curious elation. If Paddy's fiddle meant so much to Maggie then she had lied when she said this man made her happy.

183

He was a frightening man when he was drunk, aggressive and foul-mouthed. Obscenities poured from his lips and she longed to get away from him, but she had to put the precious fiddle back in the top cupboard before he could do it any damage. Like a fool she stood on the chair Patrick had used, and the next moment she screamed in terror as Abel swayed towards her and lifted her skirt. His hands shot up to her thighs and she could feel the clammy heat through her cotton drawers. She kicked and struggled, but she was no match for him, and he began to laugh with ugly enjoyment.

'Beast!' she yelled. 'Take your hands off me this instant.'

She was afraid if she wriggled too much the string of her drawers would break. Frantically she stowed the fiddle on the shelf so that her hands were free.

'Parson's widow!' said Abel. 'Was he man enough to handle a wench like you?'

'Stop it!'

She managed to dislodge the hateful, exploring fingers before they reached up any further, and when he teetered backwards momentarily she jumped to the floor. Her heart was racing, and fear drummed in her ears as she tried to dodge past him. She had to escape, as Patrick had done. But before she could reach the door he had caught her again, this time by the arm, tearing her dress.

'You ain't going nowhere, Mrs Parson's wife. Not before I find out what pleasures he 'ad.' He swung her round so roughly it felt as if her arm was breaking and she was piniioned against him. 'No sense letting the likes of you go to waste, is there now?'

His breath was foul, and she jerked her head from side to side to avoid his seeking mouth. At any moment she thought she would be sick over him.

'Leave me alone.' She kicked his shins but lust made him impervious to pain.

'Yer'd better be nice to me, or you'll not have a roof over yer head,' he said, trying to undo her bodice. 'I ain't providing for any more of Paddy Byrne's family. I want payment.'

Sarah was sobbing with fear and anger. Her hair fell loose and she tried to bite the hand which now touched her breast. Finding it impossible, she attacked his face with her fingernails instead, drawing blood, and he was so incensed he let out a roar before forcing her to the floor. Somehow he levered himself out of his coat while holding her down, and his arms extricated themselves one at a time from his braces. He smelt of sweat and intending lechery, and as his body covered hers she screamed loudly enough to awaken the dead.

Help came just as Abel Wood was fumbling once again with her skirt, mercifully impeded by his drunken state. A tall man strode in, brimful of anger and calling for the madness to stop. Strong hands wrenched the weight from her and Abel was dragged to his feet. Sarah scrambled aside the moment she was free, but she was too shocked to stand and she lay with her head buried in her arm, sobbing with humiliation and relief.

'Blast yer to 'ell,' Abel snarled. 'May yer guts rot. You ain't got no right 'ere.'

'If you lay hands on her again I'll kill you.'

'I can do what I like in me own 'ouse.'

'Not to Sarah you won't.'

At the sound of her name Sarah rolled over and peered up through the smoky atmosphere to see the stranger who had come to her rescue. Only he was not a stranger. Amazement forced the breath from her body and she gave an anguished cry, for the last person she had expected to see was James Halden.

'James! Help me.'

It had all happened so quickly. So brutally.

'It's all right, Sarah. He won't trouble you again.'

'So yer've a fancy man, 'ave yer.'

Abel bellowed with fury and his fists clenched ready to attack, but his wrists were caught in a powerful grip and pulled behind his back so deftly they were rendered immovable. A clout to his chin put an end to his struggles as he fell headlong. He remained spreadeagled on the floor, his trousers round his ankles, so undignified he would have been a laughable sight if his crime hadn't been so serious.

James bent down to Sarah who was sitting on the floor amidst the ruins of her reputation, dishevelled and frightened.

'It's all right,' he murmured.

'You've killed him.'

'No. He'll come round presently but you'll be out of here long before then.'

He caressed her hair briefly to reassure her and she responded to his touch, such gentleness making the previous strength in his hands incredible. Her body felt bruised. She grasped the edges of her bodice together for the sake of decency, then let him help her to her feet.

'Find your children and bring them with you,' James said, buttoning her dress for her as if she were a child herself. 'They're not safe with a drunk like that around. We must leave straight away.'

Cold air was blowing down the passage from the front door and she began to shiver. She was too dazed to comprehend his instructions.

'What did you say?'

'Your children,' he repeated. 'Where are they? Go and get them quickly.'

'I haven't any children,' she said. 'There's only me.'

James looked as if he wanted to argue but Abel grunted and twitched. Time was precious. 'Well, we can't stop for luggage. Anything you want will have to be collected later. Come with me. I've got a carriage outside.' He kicked Abel Wood lightly, and the sot grunted again like a slumbering pig. 'I doubt if he'll remember what he did by the time he's slept that off.'

He took Sarah's arm and made her walk to the door. The afternoon was sinking into a wintry sunset and the pinkish gold sky had a luminous quality which turned the colour of James's hair to pure copper. His hazel eyes settled on her, mysterious under the shade of his heavy lids, and his mouth was unsmiling.

The sight of him there made her unsteady legs even weaker and she crumpled against the doorway. He had to carry her from the step to his carriage.

Hardly knowing what he had done, James took the reins and urged his horse out of Corporation Lane with all speed. But to what destination?

Having located the whereabouts of Maggie Byrne he had intended paying a simple social call that Sunday afternoon to inquire after Sarah, since it was most likely she had gone to her stepmother when she became homeless. The last thing he had envisaged was leaving the house with her in his arms.

He looked at her sitting beside him, so wan and dishevelled, and his heart behaved quite uncharacteristically. For five years he had imagined seeing her again, and fire spread through his body every time he thought of possessing this girl who had become almost an obsession. Yet now he didn't recognize his feelings.

The screams coming from the tenement house had chilled his blood, and perhaps because he was used to dealing with screaming situations he had rushed in through the open door without stopping to consider the wisdom of it. All he'd seen at first was a drunkard intent on rape. Handling the insane gave him the knowledge and strength to remove the attacker from his victim without any trouble, but he'd almost let go of him again when he saw who had been lying bruised and terrified beneath him. His

188

instinct had been to strangle the wretch, but when he fell and was no longer a threat James had turned his attention to Sarah.

She was like a limp doll when he'd picked her up. Before putting her in the carriage he'd savoured the feel of her in his arms, and the inhabitants of Corporation Lane who had gathered curiously round the house of Abel Wood were just hazy figures in a mist of anonymity. He had no idea where he could take her but she had to be removed from this hideous environment.

Sarah was now huddled dejectedly in a travelling rug, her head lowered and eyes closed.

'Are you all right?' he asked, turning into Rosoman Street. He had to talk to her but there would be no chance while they were driving along the busy thoroughfare leading out to Islington, so he took the entrance to Spa Fields and sought an enclosure where there was a semblance of privacy. Once there'd been a view from here of the hills of Highgate and Hampstead, but not any more. He pulled up beneath some trees which shielded them from the encroaching houses, and gave Sarah his full attention. 'Did he hurt you badly?'

'No,' she said.

'Has it happened before?'

'No.'

'Who is he?' His questions were curt, but too much sympathy at this stage might have caused her to break down. Besides, he was still unsure of his own reactions.

'He's Maggie's husband, and I've loathed him since I set eyes on him.' Her words emphasized her loathing, clearing her of the dreadful suspicion James had fought against, that she might have given the man encouragement. She glanced up at last, still showing signs of fear, but she was breathing more easily. 'Was it a coincidence you came, or were you looking for me?'

'I've been trying to find you since I saw you near the Serpentine with the three little boys I thought were yours.'

This gave her something else to think about, and she was reproachful. 'If you saw me why didn't you speak?'

'I was with my wife.'

'And *your* children?'

'I haven't any either.'

It was quiet beneath the smoke-stunted trees, except for some dogs playing nearby. The urgency of escape was past, and now that they were alone he felt awkward. They were like strangers. Five years stretched between this day and their last calamitous meeting, and the conversation he had rehearsed for when he found her would be out of place after the afternoon's events.

He longed to touch her, but he was afraid if he did she would shrink from him. After the experience she had just been through he didn't want to frighten her anew. Her shoulders were tense. She raked her fingers through her tangled hair, and clutched the neck of her black dress nervously with her other hand.

190

'What am I going to do, James? I can't go back to Maggie's, and there's nowhere else I can go.'

The appeal in her eyes made him unreasonably angry, though it could be that he took refuge in anger to stop himself succumbing to a protective urge. He needed to beware of this kind of involvement.

'I'd heard you are now a penniless widow,' he said, remembering his disillusion when he'd learnt how she had schemed to marry poor Nahum Morey. Many would say she deserved her present impecunious state for being too ambitious.

'Obviously you are still friendly with the Bradfords,' said Sarah. She was regaining her poise, and her eyes were cold as she took up the implied criticism. 'My husband was over-generous. And before you assume, like everyone else, that *I* spent his money, let me assure you it was not so. Nahum had run up large debts before he died and everything had to be sold to repay them, or rather to repay Mr Bradford who kindly settled them from his own pocket.' She paused. 'I was ill, you see.'

'So it's true you were left with nothing?'

'I would rather be destitute than in Mr Bradford's debt.'

Her bitterness spoke of the Bradfords' un-acceptance of her. He guessed her life had not been easy, and the mention of illness worried him.

'Would you like to talk about it?' he asked more gently.

She fell silent again, gazing into the distance. In profile her face was perfection; her nose small and straight, intelligent brow sweeping to the hairline, lips soft as flower petals, and her firm chin lifted even now with the spirit he remembered. Yet she had changed. Her voice was cultured, and she spoke with a maturity which had been lacking in their previous encounters.

She sighed. 'A short time ago I was a clergyman's wife with very few worries. I had my household duties, I went out visiting, and ... children came to see me.' She stopped, and covered her face with her hands as if too pained by the memories to go on, but after a moment she recovered. 'I loved the children. They were fostered in the village from the Foundling Hospital. I wished they were my own.'

'And did you love Nahum Morey, too?'

'Yes, I did.'

Her hands clasped tightly together to stop them trembling, and her distress made him ashamed of his irritability. The reason for it was all too clear. He had sought Sarah Morey with the intention of talking her into a clandestine affair, certain he would have more success than on the previous occasion, before she had embarked on marriage. His physical need of her had dictated his approach and he had almost banked on the outcome. Instead he'd been forced into the role of rescuer, and now sympathetic listener to the sad twists her life had taken. His emotions were too confused for him to pursue his original course, and frustration followed the necessity to subdue his sexual craving.

The light was fading from the sky. A lamplighter was busy illuminating the cold streets at the back of them, and arcs of pale light shimmered in the icy air. James's horse snorted impatiently, one hoof digging at the frozen soil.

'I haven't thanked you for what you did,' she said. 'I'm very grateful. Now I mustn't delay you any longer.'

Before he could answer she threw off the rug and jumped down from the carriage, nimble as a goat.

'Sarah, where are you going?'

He was unprepared for her sudden flight. She began to run, her dark clothes causing her to merge into the dim background of trees and houses. He quickly tethered the horse to a tree, then followed, calling her name. His heart was beating like a steam hammer, not from exertion but from the challenge she now presented. The chase was exhilarating. He ran with loping strides, covering the ground like a lion, and when he caught up with her he grabbed her wrist, swinging her towards him.

'Just what was that in aid of?' he demanded.

His arms closed round her and she panted against his chest.

'There's nothing else you can do for me. Surely you ought to be getting home.'

'And what about you?'

'I'll find somewhere to go.'

'You can't go back to Corporation Lane.'

She shuddered, and for the first time began to cry. Great sobs shook her as delayed shock took hold. He touched the top of her head with his lips, and his hold on her tightened, but he managed to convey reassurance even though hot blood coursed through his veins, inflaming his loins. He wished he could draw her unhappiness into himself so that he could suffer it for her.

She seemed to belong in his arms. He had never felt such closeness to anyone. Certainly not to Maud, who avoided any show of affection. Sarah was slender and supple against him, and in that moment he felt at one with her and deeply concerned. He cared very much that her life was so disrupted. He cared that Nahum Morey hadn't provided for her in the event of his death. He was incensed at the behaviour of Maggie Byrne's husband, and with Maggie herself for not seeing that Sarah was given a safe haven after her bereavement.

The depth of his feelings amazed him, and he discovered the truth about his earlier change of heart. He loved her.

He was shaken by the revelation, which for everyone's sake must be known only to himself. Once the spasm of weeping had passed he moved her away with a show of impatience, annoyed with himself for falling into such a trap and determined to put the situation back in perspective. But there remained the question of how best to help her.

He gave her his handkerchief to dry her eyes.
'We must be going.'
'Where to?' she asked with a note of despair.
'I'm taking you home with me,' James said.
Foolish, impetuous decision.

# CHAPTER 8

Maud Halden was upstairs when James returned home. She had been in a pique when he left because he had refused to take her visiting in Newcastle Place, and she had spent the Sunday afternoon consoling herself with a box of sweetmeats.

Her husband had no regard for social correctness. A return visit to the Bradfords was long overdue, and Maud was very much afraid of offending them. His connections with such an influential family had partly swayed her decision to marry James, but he was obstinate in his refusal to encourage a closer friendship with them, even though he knew it was her dearest wish.

She heard Nessie open the front door, and she waited a few minutes longer before going down to greet him so that he would know he was not forgiven. Her small hands, emerging from lace undersleeves, smoothed the full skirt of her pink flower-sprigged silk day dress, and she drew the fringed wool cape a little higher round her shoulders in preparation for leaving the warmth of the bedroom fire.

Nessie came running up the stairs.

'Master says can you come, Mrs Halden,' the girl said. She was plainer than a lump of dough, and Maud was tired of telling her to walk sedately instead of hurrying as if time was biting at her heels.

'Is there any reason for the urgency?'

'Don't know, ma'am, but there's a woman with 'im.'

Maud was intrigued. She primped in the mirror, patting her cheeks which were already pink from sitting near the fire, and tweaked the lace edging of the muslin cap on the back of her head. A woman? How mystifying.

She peeped over the banister but saw nothing, James obviously having taken their visitor into the sitting room. Her slippered feet made no sound on the stairs and she was listening for voices which might enlighten her before the meeting. All was quiet. She drew back her plump shoulders and stood as tall as she could so as to enter the room with dignity in case someone of importance had accompanied James home, but her carefully arranged smile of welcome froze on her lips when she recognized the young woman who had worked for Elizabeth Bradford and seduced her gullible brother.

James came forward. 'Maud, we have a guest who will be staying a few nights with us. I'd like you to meet Mrs Sarah Morey.'

She was astounded at his impudence. In fact his stupidity robbed her of speech for several seconds. She didn't know whatever had possessed him to bring this woman into the house at all, never mind expecting her to stay. But no one could accuse Maud Halden of bad manners. Questions must wait until later.

'How d'you do,' she said, but kept her hands primly clasped.

Sarah Morey inclined her head. She reached to James's shoulder, a stately creature in spite of her dowdy black gown, and there was pride in her bearing which was at odds with her rough background. By gad, the girl had taken more from Nahum Morey than his money. She had used him to give herself airs above her station.

'Mrs Morey needs your help,' James said. 'As you are on the committee of the Society for the Relief of Distressed Widows I know you'll have sympathy for her present situation and want to do something about it.'

'I hardly think ...' Maud began.

'You're already familiar with some of her story.'

'And I don't want to know any more. I hardly think she is a deserving case ...'

'She needs shelter until a small allowance can be arranged which will enable her to rent lodgings and find work.' He came to Maud's side, leaving the widow Morey standing alone. 'I know you'll not refuse, my dear.'

Maud was at a disadvantage, having been taken completely by surprise. The imposition required thought, but James, in his usual forthright way, wanted immediate action, and she was being pushed into a decision without a chance to argue.

Meanwhile the girl found her voice. 'I think perhaps you're right, Mrs Halden. I shouldn't be bothering you.'

She started to walk towards the door, but James detained her, placing a hand on her arm with a certain familiarity which caused Maud new uneasiness.

'My wife would be very upset if you left with nowhere to go,' he said. 'Nessie will take you upstairs to the guest room.'

'Have you no luggage?' Maud asked.

'I have nothing.'

Her diminutive height had never troubled Maud before, but in the presence of Sarah Morey she wished she could be of equal stature. The girl was too self-confident and not in the least humiliated by her reliance on charity. It would have given Maud more authority if she could have looked directly into her eyes, but as it was she had to issue orders to Nessie while their poised visitor stood like a genuinely invited guest. The situation was not to be tolerated.

When Mrs Morey was safely upstairs and out of earshot, Maud faced her husband, all pretence of cooperation gone.

'This is an outrage, James. How dare you bring that woman into our house? And how did you come to meet up with her, may I ask?'

'I visited her,' said James. 'You are constantly regaling me with the importance of charity work, so I felt I should take a positive interest.'

'We have a Lady Visitor to call on those in need. If she is satisfied the applicant is genuinely deserving it is then up to the committee to

198

decide if she is sober, chaste and of good character.'

'Mrs Morey is all of those things, I'm sure.'

'How are you sure, James? I should very much like to know.'

There was something very strange about this affair and Maud was determined to get to the bottom of it. She didn't think her husband had been acquainted with the girl for long. She knew him well enough to trust his faithfulness, mainly because his work absorbed him to such an extent he rarely had time to call his own, and if there had been anything clandestine between them he wouldn't have had the audacity to bring her here. So there had to be a good reason for his interference.

He settled into his favourite chair, stretching his long legs across the hearthrug. 'Elizabeth Bradford is a hypocrite,' he said, letting the statement linger a second or two. 'A friend she may be, but I'm bound to say her compassion for those in need is all outward show if it doesn't extend to her family.'

'Mrs Morey isn't her family.'

'She is her sister-in-law. Yet Elizabeth had no compunction in allowing her to be turned out on to the streets. When I heard I was horrified, and I've made it my business to do something about it.'

'But it has nothing to do with us.' Maud bit her fingers with anxiety. James had always had a social conscience. She remembered him telling her how his concern for the plight of the poor in his village had led to John Bradford's brother paying for him to study medicine. 'I can't possibly ask Mr Chalmer, our chairman, to consider the case, and I want the young woman out of our house before the Bradfords hear what you've been doing.'

'She will stay until someone helps her.'

He was adamant. The argument continued, but Maud knew that once James had made up his mind nothing would change it. She would have to find some other way to get rid of the embarrassing girl, and pray that Elizabeth didn't get wind of what was happening in Calvert Terrace.

Mrs Morey refused to take dinner with them, pleading a headache, and in all fairness she didn't look well. Maud ate in aggrieved silence, but in her mind she went over conversations at the last committee meeting of the Society for the Relief of Distressed Widows which she had attended in Sackville Street.

'Mrs Shaw, is it true that a widow must live within a two-mile radius of Charing Cross to qualify for the bereavement grant?' she had asked.

'Indeed yes,' Mrs Shaw had said. She was one of the four ladies and one gentleman who served on the committee. 'They must also apply within two months of the husband's death in order to get it. The rule is very strictly observed.'

Maud now did some mental calculations, and was exultant. She was almost certain Elizabeth had said her brother had died in September, and as it was now early December the time limit had been exceeded if Sarah Morey was hoping to claim benefit. James could not argue with that.

She put down her fork and left the rich pastry dessert which she normally enjoyed. 'I've realized that we can't help Mrs Morey, James, so I'm afraid she must leave,' Maud said. She almost purred with satisfaction. 'She has been widowed too long for any money to be allowed.'

James seemed unconcerned. 'Then I think we should employ her ourselves. We could do with a more responsible person than Nessie about the place, and she could take over the cooking from Mrs Vallery, who has never pleased you.'

'No,' cried Maud, her elation banished. 'I won't have it. It will make us enemies of the Bradfords, and we shall be ostracized by the rest of society when word gets round.'

'I don't care a fig for society. But I do care about justice, and I'll not let this lady be treated like scum.'

'Lady! The girl was a jumped-up kitchen maid.'

'For five years she was the wife of a respected clergyman. Kindly remember that, my dear, and I'm sure the two of you will get along very well.'

Maud fumed. She had never been so angry about anything, but James was too masterful for her to compete against in a battle of wills. She would have to pursue a more subtle strategy, because she was determined that Sarah Morey wold never settle here permanently.

Tomorrow she would start investigating. There

had to be a means of getting rid of the interloper post haste.

Nessie, the parlourmaid, was sent with the invitation for Sarah to dine downstairs, but she was dealt with curtly. Sarah was in no mood to suffer the barbed remarks made by James's wife.

'Please thank Mrs Halden and tell her that I have a headache, and I prefer not to inconvenience anyone.'

Poor Nessie didn't know whether to bob a curtsey or not. She half sketched one and backed away nervously. 'Yes, miss, ... er ... ma'am.'

When she had gone Sarah opened the guest room door an inch, but she couldn't hear what James was saying even though she strained her ears. His deep, throaty voice was just an authoritative sound which carried up the stairs and nearly caused her heart to stop, for she could tell that his wife had no hope of changing his mind.

She pondered on this new situation, one which had developed with such amazing speed she was still breathless. The combined shocks of Abel Wood's attack and James's timely intervention had robbed her of the ability to make a decision, and now she found herself in a most embarrassing position. She had allowed James to bring her here because she was too frightened to return to Corporation Lane, but she couldn't remain under his roof, in close association with his wife, and the sooner he came up with an alternative suggestion the better.

The comfortable bedroom was luxury after the conditions at Maggie's. She loved the way the quilt dimpled under her hand as she tested the softness of the feather mattress, and there was water in a pitcher on the wash-stand to pour in a bowl for freshening up. For the first time since leaving the rectory she was able to sit at a dressing table and see herself in a mirror, and she drew a silver-backed brush through her tangled hair.

Maggie would be worried by her disappearance. Tomorrow, when Abel had shut himself in his workshop, Sarah would have to collect her things and give some kind of explanation. None would've come from Abel himself, she felt sure, and she didn't want to distress Maggie too much when she had to go on living with the wretch. And after that would come the problem of finding somewhere else to live.

The suggestion that she was eligible for charity made Sarah very uncomfortable. She was aware that James had invented it on the spur of the moment as an excuse for her presence here, and in truth her financial state did warrant it, but she had developed a fierce pride since marrying Nahum and didn't want to be dependent on anyone. She certainly didn't want Maud Halden meddling in her affairs. Somehow she had to find an opportunity to speak to James alone, but it was going to be very difficult.

She was in a dreadful dilemma. Seeing him again after five years had caused havoc to her system, and she was suffering from curious palpitations which made her feel as if the wings of a dozen birds were fluttering inside her. A lump seemed to have formed in her throat, making swallowing difficult, and the thought of food was nauseous. When a tray was sent up she returned it. She couldn't have eaten anything if she'd tried. It was feast enough to think of James, and she curled up on the chaise longue to try to make sense of her emotions.

His hair was still the same glorious colour, like a lion's mane, and in the gaslight downstairs it had reminded her so much of Corrie's it had hurt to look. The attraction which had drawn them to each other after Paddy's death was as strong as ever, and in Spa Fields she'd known that mysterious forces had been at work, compelling him to seek her. There had been none of the previous brashness about him such as he had displayed that Christmas at Newcastle Place, but no doubt the circumstances of this latest meeting altered things, and he was that much more mature. Of one thing she was certain. He must care about her deeply, otherwise he would never have risked bringing her here.

Nessie came with a warming pan later in the evening.

'Master says you're to rest, and come the morrow Mrs Halden'll tell you what's been decided,' the parlourmaid said. She slid the copper pan down the bed until it was heating the place where Sarah's feet would go, then she straightened. 'Beggin' yer pardon, ma'am,

204

but you seem to 'ave put the cat among the pigeons, so to speak. I thought you ought to know Mrs Halden's right upset, so I'd tread carefully tomorrow if I was you, particularly if you want her help. Mrs Halden ain't a very easy person when she's roused.'

Sarah smiled for the first time. 'Thank you for the warning.'

'You ain't a *real* guest, are you? I mean you won't be angry with me for speaking out of turn.'

'Nessie, I've a feeling Mrs Halden thinks I'm the scum of the earth.'

'Oh, I wouldn't say that, ma'am. I'd say you was a lady what's hit on bad times, and I hope as how they soon improve.'

No one else came up to Sarah's room, and when she heard the crier calling nine o'clock she began to undress, feeling like a prisoner. Her neck was sore taking off her gown, and there were bruises at the base of her throat where Abel's hands had gripped. He could have killed her. She bathed them carefully, and the cold water cooled them down. There were bruises, too, on her legs when she removed her stockings, but they were not painful like the others and she hoped they would soon be gone. After her marriage she had taken to wearing a whalebone corset which minimized her waist. This she also removed, but as she had no nightgown she kept on her drawers and high-necked chemise for decency's sake.

The warmth and comfort of the bed made it possible, eventually, to drift into an exhausted, dreamless sleep, so she heard nothing when the bedroom door opened some time later. A frosty moon filled the room with eerie light, silvering everything it touched, and in repose Sarah was more beautiful than the most delicate porcelain with her dark hair spreading over the blue-white pillow.

She was disturbed by a breath against her cheek, so soft it was scarcely detectable, but she was subconsciously aware of a protectiveness surrounding her. She opened her eyes slowly, afraid to disperse such a comforting feeling, and James was there with his back to the window. The moonlight changed his hair from gold to platinum, and he wore a black silk dressing gown tied with a wide sash. When he saw she was awake he put his finger to his lips to caution her not to make any sound.

'Don't be afraid,' he whispered. He came to the bed and sat on the edge of it. 'I only want to talk to you.'

Sarah sat up, drawing the sheet to her chin. 'How did you get away from your wife?'

'Maud and I have separate rooms. She prefers it to being disturbed when I come home very late.' He smoothed the back of his hand over her cheek, and she quaked inwardly as if he had stirred a swarm of bees which buzzed from her stomach to her head. 'I wanted to tell you I've arranged for you to work for us and live here.'

She protested. 'James, I can't ...'

'Are you too grand now to do housework?'

'No, of course not.'

206

'Can you cook?'

'I satisfied Nahum.'

'Then it's settled.'

Their muted voices throbbed in the midnight room. He leaned forward and lightly brushed her lips with his, but she turned her head aside before he could pursue such a course.

'It's courting danger,' she said. 'I can't possibly live here, not in any capacity. It would be sinful.'

'Only if we committed a sin, and that won't happen, I promise.' He moved to a safer distance to show he had no dishonourable intentions. 'I can't allow you to go back to Corporation Lane.'

His concern frightened her because she longed to respond. It would be so easy to become dependent on his strength, but in the circumstances it would also be foolish, so she hid her feelings in resentment.

'You don't own me. I can live where I like,' she said. 'I want to make a home for Patrick. My little brother's being ill treated and he needs me.'

'Patrick is Maggie's child,' said James, a stern note creeping into his voice. 'Every child needs its mother and he belongs with her, so stop worrying your lovely head about him.'

'Sometimes a mother has to give up a child for its own good.'

'Any woman who allows the bond to be severed between herself and her offspring is weak and selfish. Love will overcome hardship. It's as vital to an infant as its mother's milk.' He jerked his head, as if to shake away the disharmony. 'What an inconsequential argument.'

James's views were dagger points piercing her conscience. Sarah covered her ears, letting go of the sheet as she did so, and her breasts were provocatively visible through the fine cambric chemise.

'I'm leaving tomorrow,' she said, fearful of hearing any more.

He was silent a moment, and when their eyes met a fierce spark was ignited. It blazed into angry passion, unvoiced, unacknowledged except for the sharp intake of breath.

'Leave then!' His words were a low, bitter withdrawal of his previous concern. 'Go back to Abel Wood. Perhaps I shouldn't have interfered this afternoon.'

'James!' She no longer needed to pretend indignation. 'That was cruel and uncalled for. Get out of this room.'

'Are you really so chaste? You weren't once.'

He pulled back the bedclothes and pressed her against the pillows, then claimed her mouth harshly before she could twist away. Within seconds her lips parted under his, answering the eagerness which had driven him to go back on his word, and gradually the kissing became a hungry yearning for each other. He caressed her nipples through the thin material and the sensation sent waves of ecstatic shivers coursing through her. Her arms encircled his neck and her fingers raked through his thick, shining hair, conveying a desperate need for him. His hands trailed downwards over her body. But just when her actions were inviting him to undress her completely he let her go and flung the covers over her again.

'You're a very exciting woman, Sarah,' he said, as if in condemnation. 'Who could blame any man for wanting you?'

After he had left, Sarah stared at the ceiling, trying to rid her body of the intense ache which was neither pleasure nor pain. She was ashamed of her weakness. James had only to touch her and the world was spinning faster than it had ever done. That intimate kiss, calculated to prove a wantonness, had been more like an insult, yet she knew it had affected him with equal potency. They could never be together without sparks flying.

His suggestion that she should stay in the house and work was preposterous. She didn't want to be Maud Halden's servant, and she could never live compatibly near James. But the alternative was to leave in the morning without seeing him again, and he had just made that an unbearable thought. She would have to stay. She was bound to him strongly by a feeling of inevitability.

She was bound to him by the existence of their daughter, though his views ensured that he could never be told.

It was growing dark when Maggie returned home with her two small sons that Sunday afternoon. The lamp hadn't been lit so she had to feel her way down the passage with the boys giggling and clinging to her skirt. There was no sign of Abel or Patrick, the fire had gone out in the gloomy kitchen, and she had to search blindly along a shelf just inside the door for the lucifers. She was about to make for the table when she almost fell over a huge black mound on the floor. A scream rose to her throat, but before she could utter it the mound produced a series of loud snoring noises, and alcoholic fumes were added to the stale air.

'Abel, you great oaf, get up this minute.' She'd seen him drunk regularly, but never in such a state as this. 'You boys get on upstairs while I see to yer father.'

Her hands were unsteady as she coaxed the wick of the oil lamp to burn, and she dreaded coping with her husband. Paddy Byrne had possessed an unpredictable temper, volatile and unpleasant while it lasted, but over in no time and afterwards he'd been full of remorse. Not so with Abel. She'd learnt soon after marrying him that his temper was evil and she would do anything to avoid incurring it.

Sometimes she wished she had stayed in Stone Alley with Patrick and taken a chance. The boy would have been happier. It grieved her to see him running wild, but if she showed him the affection he deserved it only made it worse for him with his stepfather who belted him for the least offence. These last few weeks she'd seen Patrick open up like a flower bud in the warmth of Sarah's attentions, and Maggie's conscience was troubled. All the boy needed was love, but Abel's vindictiveness prohibited it.

The house was too quiet. There was no sign

of Sarah either, and Maggie began to feel very uneasy. Something bad had happened while she was out and the sourness of it lingered.

Now there was some light she could see to revive Abel. She dipped a cloth in water and bent over him to wipe his face which was lying in vomit. The stench made her retch, and she was so angry at his disgusting condition she didn't notice at first that his braces were down over his hips and his trousers had slipped. When she did water dripped on to his nose from the cloth poised in her paralysed hand. Oh, God, what had he done?

Maggie felt very sick. She forced herself to minister to him, but her suspicions grew by the second and her quick, fragmented breathing was more like dry sobs. The ugly word rape formed on her lips but she couldn't utter it. If only Sarah would come through the door and tell her she was wrong.

His failure to come round was an added worry. A deep stupor such as this couldn't be caused by alcohol alone.

'Will you stir yerself, Abel Wood, and tell me what the hell's happened here. Where's Patrick? And where's Sarah? Come on, you devil, answer me.'

Abel groaned and opened his eyes which he seemed to have a job to focus, and his gaunt face looked greyer than ever. When he had struggled to a sitting position he nursed his chin as if it hurt. Draught from the window made the lamp flicker and shadows danced round him like goblins while he grunted some more.

'Damn bitch of a girl!'

'Explain yerself. What've you done to Sarah? And yer'd better tell the truth.' She was shaking. With Patrick gone too it was likely that Sarah had taken him out of harm's way, but who knew what kind of mischief had driven her to it? 'Tell me you didn't touch her.'

'I didn't touch her,' Abel said, repeating the words parrot fashion. 'Not but what she don't deserve a thrashing for the way she spoils that kid.' He shook his head to clear it. 'Must've fallen.'

He got awkwardly to his feet and his trousers fell round his ankles, exposing thin, dirty legs beneath his shirt tails.

'What happened to yer braces then?' Maggie demanded.

'What always happens to 'em when I relieve myself.' He pulled the trousers up, replaced the braces, and pushed her aside furiously as he staggered to the door. 'Get out of me way, woman. And don't ever accuse me of anything again.'

Maggie stared after him, afraid to say more, but her mind was not at rest. She wanted to believe him. He'd never lied to her before, not that she knew, but her suspicions wouldn't go away. It was partly because he hadn't flown into a rage, which he definitely would have done if he'd been as innocent as he'd made out. There were times when she'd had bruises just for complaining that he drank too much.

When Abel's sons had been put to bed, lashed by her tongue for playing up, she returned to the kitchen and re-lit the fire, ashamed of her impatience. It wasn't their fault they had such a fiend for a father. The chair she sat in had a broken back and it creaked with every movement, so she remained motionless as she dwelt on Sarah's disappearance. Being Sunday she'd probably gone to the Foundling chapel to drool over the child she idolized since she'd never had the bother of bringing it up.

Presently the door opened a little way and Patrick inched his way through. Timidity was not in his nature, so his wary entrance was a sure indication of unpleasant happenings.

'Ma? Where's Pa gone?'

'Out,' said Maggie.

His little body straightened up and he came to the fire. By its light she saw his grubby face was tear-stained, and her heart contracted with unexpected pity. He cried so rarely.

She asked: 'What's the matter, son?' It was the nearest she'd got to a term of endearment since giving birth to Abel's children.

'He's taken Sarah away and I don't know where she is.'

'Who's taken Sarah where? Yer pa's up in 'is workshop.'

Patrick glanced fearfully towards the stairs, looking ready to take flight if they so much as squeaked under a boot. Lord, what *had* the drunken wretch done to frighten the boy like this?

'It were a man what came,' he said. 'If 'e hadn't ...' His little mouth quivered. 'If 'e hadn't ...'

'Out with it, boy.' His mother was running out of patience, already troubled enough with suspicions. Patrick's strange behaviour acted on her nerves like a flame to a fuse and she began to shake him. 'I want to know what happened here. Was it *your* fault?'

The child's teeth were chattering. 'I ain't done nothing.'

'Yer father then ... What did *he* do?'

'He was hurting Sarah.' His eyes filled, and tears trickled into grooves in the dirt already prepared for them. 'He was mad 'cause I was playing the fiddle to 'er, and I 'ad to get out of 'is way. Then I 'eard 'er screaming. It were awful, Ma.'

'And the man who came? Who was he?'

'I dunno. He was a toff. I looked through the window and saw 'im hit Pa for what 'e was doing to Sarah. Then 'e carried 'er out to 'is carriage and took 'er off.'

Maggie frowned. 'This toff, what did 'e look like?'

Patrick screwed up his eyes as he tried to remember and find words to describe what he'd seen. Then: 'He was big, and 'e 'ad yellow hair,' he said.

'James Halden,' murmured Maggie after a moment.

She moved away to absorb this new turn of events. It didn't take much imagination to fathom out what had been going on, and she gripped her stomach to stop sickness rising to her throat. She had no idea what had brought James Halden to these parts, but she hoped he'd

214

arrived in time to prevent Abel getting what he'd been after.

Patrick tugged at her skirt. 'I want Sarah,' he fretted.

His little figure looked crumpled and forlorn, and his need touched a chord in Maggie's heart at last. She sat down in Abel's chair and drew her son on to her lap.

'Hush, boy. She'll come back.'

'Do you promise?'

She kissed the top of his head, and the feel of his curly black hair brought warm thoughts of Paddy Byrne flooding into her mind. Abel, in his determination to eradicate memories of her first husband, had made her neglect this child, but he would never do it again. Her arms closed tightly round Patrick. Some good had to come out of today's evil deeds.

'I can't say for sure, but I reckon it's time you and me stuck together, dearie.' Maggie rocked him against her breast as if he were a baby, and he cuddled deeper into her lap. 'I ain't much for words, but I love you, son. And I reckon I'll call you Paddy from now on, same as yer real father was called.'

When Sarah didn't return to Corporation Lane the next day, Abel Wood's work suffered. His lack of concentration was due to three things: anger, frustration and a determination to track down the interfering stranger who had entered his house uninvited and used force to spirit Sarah away. He'd yet to find out who it was, but when he did the fellow would wish he'd never poked his nose into business that didn't concern him. He'd get his own back somehow. Meanwhile frustration dogged him whenever he thought of Sarah Morey and how he'd been cheated out of possessing her. The fact that he'd failed made his longing for her worse. He'd never felt so desirous of a woman as he did that one, and he wouldn't rest until he'd tamed the proud bitch.

His conscience plagued him, too. He hated having been made to look a fool in front of his wife, and she was giving him a hard time. Maggie was even sheltering Patrick from his wrath and took the boy's word against his. He hadn't known she possessed such a temper. In a curious way he respected her for it, and it made him anxious to put things right between them.

The second day after Sarah's disappearance he stayed in after supper and put fresh kindling on the fire.

'Mags, I'm sorry,' he said, settling into his chair. 'The way things looked on Sunday you'd a right to be angry with me, but I swear it weren't bad like you thought.'

Maggie sniffed. 'It weren't good either.'

'I'd been outside to relieve myself, like I told you. When I came back there was a bloke struggling with Sarah, and I went for 'im. I was trying to protect 'er, but 'e was right strong and I ain't no fighter.'

She looked at him straight, arms folded while she tried to decide whether to believe him.

'Why didn't you tell it this way before?' she asked.

216

'Because you'd no bloody right to doubt me.' He almost let his temper rise again.

'So 'e knocked you out and made off with Sarah?'

'That's it, plain as a pikestaff, but I didn't get an ounce of sympathy, or thanks for me efforts.'

She sat on the chair with the broken back, and it groaned at her indecision. 'Well, I s'pose it could be true, and if so then I'm sorry, too. If the man were James Halden, Sarah wouldn't have gone with 'im willingly.'

'Halden did yer say?' His eyes were as crafty as a ferret's. 'So yer've known all along who came 'ere.'

'It's only a guess,' said Maggie.

'It ain't no guess. You know more'n you're saying, woman. Who is he? Where do 'e live?'

'All right, I *do* know it were 'im,' she said, with a touch of defiance. 'You don't think Sarah'd let me worry meself silly, do you? She sent someone round to tell me yesterday that the Haldens are giving her work, but I don't know where they live, Abel, Gawd's honour.' It was clear she was worried. He gave her a few moments, and soon she became confidential. 'I feel responsible for 'er. She 'ad a bad time once through Dr Halden and I'd hate for it to happen again.'

'What did 'e do to 'er?'

'She 'ad 'is baby. He never knew, though.'

Abel was astounded. It was impossible to analyse his immediate reaction. To think that devil of a physician had stormed in like an avenging puritan when all the time he'd been guilty of the very act he'd been so keen to prevent. It took some digesting. It also gave Abel a deadly weapon to use in retaliation.

'When was that?' he asked, trying to sound calm. 'And where's it now?'

'It were before she married Nahum Morey.' Maggie looked down at her hands. 'She ... lost it.'

From then on she was mule-stubborn and refused to be drawn or pushed any more, but Abel Wood had gleaned enough to plan a subtle revenge.

The next day he made inquiries and discovered that Dr James Halden was in charge of a private madhouse in Clerkenwell belonging to a Miss Claybury, but he didn't live on the premises. His home was in Calvert Terrace where he lived with his wife. They had no children.

He chose midday to call at the house in Calvert Terrace, knowing the physician would be away. He wore his decent black suit and his top hat which he'd blackened along the rim with boot polish to hide where the silk had worn. With gloves and cane he felt he was presentable enough to use the front entrance, but there was an important matter to attend to before doing so. He had to make sure Sarah Morey was absent, which was why he had taken the precaution of giving a copper to an urchin to accompany him.

'You're to go to the back door and tell whoever comes that Patrick Byrne is crying for

218

Mrs Morey, his sister. Then take Mrs Morey on a goose chase. I want her out of the way for at least half an hour.' Abel showed him another coin, but held it out of reach. 'If you do the job properly this could be yours as well.'

'Yes, sir,' said the boy, who scuttled off while Abel stationed himself in a place where he could watch unobserved.

Shortly afterwards he saw Sarah leave the house with the boy, and was unprepared for the inner disturbance the sight of her caused. He had to turn his eyes away quickly in order to concentrate on the business in hand, and as soon as the way was clear he went up the steps to the front door and rang the bell.

'Good day,' he said to the housemaid who answered. 'My name is Abel Wood, jeweller of Hatton Garden, and I've called to see Mrs Halden privately.'

'I'll see if Mrs Halden is expecting you,' said the girl.

He touched her arm to detain her, giving a conspiratory smile. 'Dr Halden, er ...' He hesitated diffidently. 'My visit is to be a surprise.'

'Oh, I see, sir. Come this way then.'

He removed his hat and walked carefully down the carpeted hall behind the maid, wishing his boots didn't squeak. He was shown into the front parlour which was so warm it smelt of stuffiness and a cloying perfume. The walls were covered in pictures, with framed silhouettes grouped in the alcoves either side of the fireplace, and he had never seen so many knick-knacks. They were displayed on occasional tables, the mantelpiece, the piano top, in fact every available space, and Abel was almost distracted from the purpose of his visit. A woman with fair hair drawn down beside her cheeks and swept into a bun at the nape of her neck, rose from a chaise longue. She was small and well rounded, tightly buttoned into a dress of blue striped silk.

'Who are you?' she asked. 'Why did you not leave a visiting card?'

'Begging yer pardon, ma'am,' said the maid, 'the gentleman's a jeweller, and 'e's come with a surprise for you.'

'Abel Wood of Hatton Garden, ma'am.'

Mrs Halden's expression changed to childish anticipation. 'Thank you, Nessie. You can go.' She indicated a chair for Abel's use, and touched a gold locket on black velvet ribbon which adorned her neck. 'And what is this surprise, may I ask? Has my husband ordered a special trinket?'

Abel sat on the edge of the chair and turned his hat round nervously, unaware that blacking was coming off on his fingers. 'I'm sorry to disappoint you, ma'am. I'm afraid the surprise is of a rather unpleasant nature. You see, you are harbouring my wife's stepdaughter, Sarah Morey, and we're anxious that she should return home straight away.'

Her round eyes grew rounder, and the

excitement vanished. 'Why didn't you come to the servants' entrance and speak to her yourself?'

'I was afraid she was being kept here against her will.'

'Why ever should she be? What an extra-ordinary idea. I don't understand.' The woman was flustered. 'My husband brought her here because she was widowed and destitute, and we are acquainted with relatives of her late husband. We took pity on her and agreed to give her work.'

Abel took hypnotic hold of her attention. 'Your husband, madam, has known Sarah for six years, and she had a child by him before she married the Reverend Morey. When my wife heard that Dr Halden came on Sunday and left with Sarah she was inconsolable, and I myself am very concerned for 'er welfare. For my wife's sake I've 'ad to find the courage to confront you with this truth and ask that you tell Sarah we forgive 'er and want 'er back.'

The woman's face drained of colour. 'This is terrible. I can't believe you.'

'It wouldn't benefit me to make up such a lie.'

'No.' She clenched and unclenched her hands until the knuckles were white. 'What happened to her child?'

'It died.'

A clock on the mantelpiece chimed the half hour. Maud Halden's features were working, and her hands continued to move as she struggled with her emotions. Abel didn't expand on the statement. He couldn't, since he knew nothing more.

Finally she found courage to challenge him. 'It *is* a lie,' she said, her high voice sharp with anger. 'I refuse to believe such a dreadful accusation against my husband. I insist you leave immediately, and you can take Mrs Morey with you.' Without removing her eyes off him she pulled the bell cord, and the housemaid appeared so quickly she must have been hovering near the door. 'Tell Mrs Morey I want her, Nessie. And show this ... man ... out.'

'Mrs Morey's not in, ma'am.'

Abel got to his feet. 'In that case I'll not detain you any longer. But perhaps yer'll be good enough to tell Sarah we want 'er to come home. We don't like the thought of 'er being near the man what ravished 'er before.'

'Get out!' cried Mrs Halden.

Abel had to admire her dignity, and he felt sorry he'd had to hurt her, the innocent victim of her husband's treachery, but the job was done and he certainly didn't regret it. He had the feeling she was not a woman who would allow herself to be humiliated, and as he left the house he banked on her making life as unbearable as possible for James Halden.

Sarah, of course, would once more be left with no alternative but to return to Corporation Lane.

# CHAPTER 9

There was no sign of Patrick anywhere. Sarah searched Myddelton Square and the churchyard of St Mark's Church with the boy who had brought her the message, but Patrick was not lurking behind wall or bush or railings.

'Reckon 'e must 'ave made awf,' said the urchin.

'Where did you meet up with him?'

'End of Rosoman Street. Said 'e were told you was in Calvert Terrace, but 'e didn't know where it was. So I brought 'im.' Seeing she was doubtful and inclined towards returning to the house he skipped in front of her. 'P'raps 'e's gawn in the church.'

She went into St Mark's to humour him but it was quiet and empty. Not the sort of place where Patrick would go. Sarah was mystified and a little uneasy. She walked up the aisle and lifted her eyes to the light from the painted glass in the east window which spread fingers towards the fine organ in the western gallery. If Patrick had really been crying for her he would have knocked on the Haldens' door himself once he knew where she was, not left it to a strange boy he'd never met before. She looked round to tell the urchin so, but he had disappeared.

There had to be a reason for this puzzle. The boy didn't know her and wouldn't have come with such a message for nothing. She started to retrace her steps, acknowledging several other pedestrians with a nod and a smile, just as if she were still a clergyman's wife instead of a servant once more. She still had to get used to her reduced circumstances.

She was just turning into Calvert Terrace when she saw Nessie showing Abel Wood out of James's house. Her blood turned to ice. She dodged into a doorway, clutching her skirt tightly round her legs to stop a feeling of panic as she remembered his hands exploring her thighs. Even the air seemed tainted with his foul breath and she wanted to be sick. She hadn't reckoned on her reaction to seeing him again. He was the most hateful man she had ever known, and she feared him greatly.

As she watched he put on his hat and gave it a satisfied tap. His expression was smug. Whatever his business had been he was clearly pleased with the outcome, and there could be no doubt that it meant trouble. Neither was there any doubt that the message apparently from Patrick had been a piece of fabrication to get her out of the way.

He must have made a determined effort to find her. Sarah huddled in the doorway long after Abel had disappeared into Myddelton Square, afraid to contemplate what mischief he might have stirred up while paying a secretive visit to James's wife.

Perhaps he'd been trying to get her to go back to Corporation Lane. He'd complained about keeping her, but lechery was a powerful thing.

He might want her under his roof once more where he could subject her to his attentions. Or there could be another reason, one which made her heart thud, and set up a painful drumming in her ears. She had always trusted Maggie not to speak of the past to anyone, but confidences were apt to flow between man and wife. If anything had been said about Corrie, Abel could have been on a very meddling errand indeed. She shook at the thought of it, and knew she must get away immediately.

She hurried down the steps to the basement of James's house. Mrs Vallery, the cook, was an indolent woman who was more than happy to let Sarah do the work, and she'd been checking the pantry, paying particular attention to a gin bottle, when the boy had called. Luckily she was still there, and Nessie seemed to be occupied elsewhere. Sarah crept stealthily upstairs to the bedroom to gather up her few belongings which fitted into her pockets.

Thank goodness James was not at home. It had been an impossible situation from the start, fraught with danger, and she realized it was a relief to be quitting. She had only seen him briefly since he had risked coming to her room in the night. In Maud's presence he had told her formally that she was to be employed in the house, and just seeing him had been enough to warn her that their emotions were highly inflammable. The more she thought about him the more imperative it became that she should move on. All she had wanted was breathing space to plan what course to take next, but it was impossible to think of anything other than the renewal of her yearning for him. And from the way he had kissed her she knew James was affected much the same. The threat of discovery perpetually hung over them, and she owed it to him to leave before his marriage was ruined.

She took off her apron and washed away the smell of the kitchen with a little water from the pitcher. In a few days she had spent here she'd appreciated how much she had missed the comforts of her home in Chertsey. Now she was going to be fending for herself once more with no idea where to go, since a return to Maggie's was out of the question. The one thing she would never do was end up in a workhouse, so she had to find some means of earning a living, but with no money she didn't know where to go while she looked for work.

As she dried her hands she twisted Nahum's ring round her finger. It was the only thing she had of any value, and she had resisted selling it when repaying the debt to John Bradford, but now she could no longer keep it. She was sad that it would have to go. Poor Nahum would have been appalled at the reason, and it was almost as if she could feel the weight of his disapproval.

She had intended to slip out of the house without a word to anyone, but from the hall she saw Maud Halden in the sitting room, looking out of the window. By her expression it was doubtful if she was seeing beyond the barrier of her troubled thoughts and might not even

226

have noticed, but she deserved the courtesy of an explanation.

'Mrs Halden, forgive me for intruding but I saw Abel Wood come here.'

Maud swung round. 'How dare you come in without knocking.'

'The door was open, ma'am.'

'It was not an invitation for you to enter uninvited.' She looked down her nose at Sarah with a regal air. 'And I have no intention of discussing anything of a private nature with a servant.'

'He came about me, Mrs Halden.'

'You sound worried, Mrs Morey.'

'I should never have let Dr Halden bring me here, and as I respect your feelings I've decided to leave.'

Maud was surprisingly flustered. 'No, you can't. You can't go until things have been discussed with my husband. I forbid it.'

'There's nothing to keep me. I just wanted to thank you for giving me shelter even though it's obvious how much you dislike me. Goodbye, Mrs Halden.'

She was turning away when Maud issued an imperative command.

'Stop!' The small woman was full of indignation. 'Don't think you can walk out without answering a few questions, madam. I'd hoped to confront you with them when my husband was present, but I'm forced to ask them now.' She came up to Sarah and raised her eyes to hers. 'The obnoxious Mr Wood came here to inform me you bore a child some years ago, and said that it was fathered by Dr Halden. Is that true?'

Sarah's worst fears were confirmed, but she remained outwardly calm and hoped her inner turmoil wouldn't be seen.

'Abel Wood is an evil man,' she said. 'He tried to rape me, and now he wants to blacken my name. I hope you didn't believe him.'

'I asked you if it were true.'

'Would I have married the Reverend Morey without telling him if I had a child to support?'

'You're fencing with me, but I advise you not to,' said Maud. 'I know the baby died, but the fact that you had one is the important issue since my husband is being blamed. I shall have the truth from him, you may be sure.'

A faint colour crept into Sarah's pale cheeks. 'I only saw Dr Halden on two occasions, the first on the day that my father died in a fire, and the second at the funeral. He was very kind to me. You may question him yourself by all means, and I'm sure he'll be as surprised as you to hear such news. Any suggestion that he acted improperly is cruel and malicious, and it takes someone like Abel Wood to invent such a tale, but if you wish to believe him, Mrs Halden, I'm sorry for you. He wanted to cause trouble and apparently succeeded.' Her black skirt rustled as she swept out of the room, speaking her farewell over her shoulder. 'Good day to you, ma'am.'

She held her head high as she left Calvert Terrace, and no one would have guessed that her legs felt so weak they could scarcely hold her. She hadn't told any lies, but for James's sake she had managed to avoid telling all the truth.

What troubled her most, though, was the fact that she had denied Corrie's existence.

The choir master, Mr Marfleet, stopped the lesson and tapped his baton on the top of the piano.

'Corrie Palmer, you are singing flat.' He had positioned her in the middle of the front row as she was the smallest pupil. 'Yesterday I gave you the chance of tuition because you had a sweet voice and showed promise. Today you sound like a toad.'

Corrie's lower lip quivered. The slightest reprimand upset her, but tears promoted jeering so she had quickly learnt to hold them back.

'My throat hurts,' she said, rubbing her eyes with the backs of her hands.

'Nonsense. You're not trying,' Mr Marfleet dragged the hands away and made her clasp them in front of her apron. 'We will sing the scale again.'

Normally she was happy when she was singing and she could follow the other children easily, but her throat felt as if it was all closed up and she could hardly swallow. She hadn't told anyone because she was afraid of being sent to the infirmary. Anna had told her children died there, and she didn't want to die.

Icy December draughts cut through the high-ceilinged chapel. It was cold enough for the choir of juniors to shiver and look pinch-faced, but Corrie's cheeks were burning. She felt so poorly she longed for the comfort of Ma's lap, and homemade lemonade to cool her throat, but no amount of longing would ever again produce such precious things so she struggled on, miming when she knew she couldn't hit the note properly.

She was perpetually miserable at the Foundling Hospital. Anna had hated it too, at first, and had been full of plans to run away, but now she never mentioned it. Anna had made friends with other girls. Corrie could only pine for the Gilling family back in Chertsey and keep wishing Ma and Pa would come and take her back there.

She had pined equally for Mrs Morey, and had tried to have faith in her promises. That lovely lady with the soft, musical voice and pretty face had been the shining star in Corrie's firmament, the most wonderful being in all the world, and Corrie had believed her when she had said that no one would take her to the big place in London.

'Corrie, my sweet Corrie, soon perhaps you'll be my little girl,' Mrs Morey had crooned, only days before the inspector had come to take her and Anna away on the train. 'I'm going to see if Reverend Morey will let you live here with us.'

The rectory had been such a big, warm house, and she would have loved to grow up there. She'd boasted about it to Anna.

'*I'm* going to stay with Mrs Morey for ever and ever,' she'd said.

Anna had looked at her in a funny way, and

then she had shrugged her shoulders and said 'Amen' just like the parson did after the Lord's Prayer in church on Sundays.

But Mrs Morey had done nothing to stop the inspector removing her to London, and now Corrie hated her. She hated her more than she hated being in this big, noisy place where no one had any sympathy when she cried, and she never wanted to see her again, unless it was to take her back to Chertsey after all.

She couldn't swallow her bread and milk at supper time. A nurse took the spoon and tried impatiently to force it down her, but Corrie's throat was so tight she could hardly breathe, and the woman clucked when she put a hand on the little forehead. It felt as if she was burning up.

'You should be in the infirmary,' the nurse said. She pulled back Corrie's chair. 'Come with me.'

Corrie tried to stand but suddenly the floor seemed too far away and she began to fall, as if through space. She wasn't aware of being picked up and carried out of the long dining room under the inquisitive gaze of dozens of girls, but when the sharp, cold air outside struck her it set up an uncontrollable shivering and she croaked painfully as she tried to cry. In the infirmary another nurse undressed her and bathed her feverish little body with cold water, then she was tucked up in a bed and left on her own while voices outside the door discussed what might be wrong with her.

'Better get the apothecary in,' one said.

'The physician more like,' said the other. 'And better keep her isolated until 'e says whether it is or not.'

Corrie's eyes filled with scalding tears. If they knew what was wrong with her they didn't give a name to it, and she was very frightened.

'They die in the infirmary,' she remembered Anna saying. 'I saw them looking awful, all white and skinny.'

Her throat felt swollen and her mouth kept filling with water which she couldn't swallow down. The last thing in her mind before she lost consciousness was a picture of Mrs Morey's smile, full of love and promises, but Mrs Morey had failed her, and it hurt too much to think about her any more. It was all her fault she was in this dreadful place. All her fault.

At first Sarah didn't know where to go when she left James's house. Without money she had two alternatives, return to Maggie's or sleep in a doorway, and she didn't fancy either. Nahum's ring still encircled her finger, the only thing she had of any value to sell, but she was reluctant to part with it permanently. It was while she was twisting the ring she suddenly remembered Dimsey Turner, the girl she had once followed from the Foundling Hospital when she'd been desperate to find out Corrie's destination in the country. Dimsey had said her stepfather took things for hock. Sarah's spirits lifted a little. Of course, the thing to do was visit the area of Clerkenwell where pawnbrokers thrived better than anyone. Dimsey might even be there still.

She stopped at the wooden-fronted shop in Middle Alley off Cowcross Street which displayed a sign with three red balls on a blue board. Some writing in the window advertised the advancement of money on china, glass, jewels and wearing apparel. When Paddy had been alive she'd pawned things often enough, but she'd got out of the habit. Now she was afraid to go inside, but she had to get enough money to last until she found work, otherwise she'd find herself having to pawn her stays since she'd nothing else of value.

And the sooner she could recover her wedding ring the better. She wouldn't feel right not wearing it.

It was a noisy neighbourhood where tousled, flea-ridden heads appeared at upper windows and coarse humour somehow kept despair at bay. The smell of nearby slaughterhouses made her press her fingers to her nose, and she felt conspicuous in her tidy black gown. A man rolled from the gin-shop across the way and tripped over a mangy dog, sending him staggering in her direction. She shrank back when he tried to clutch her arm to save himself, horrified at the thought of his hands touching her, and without further hesitation she opened the pawnshop door.

The shop was crowded. It sounded like a cage of monkeys babbling, and Sarah pushed her way through to a passage where several doors opened into little closets facing the counter so that she could speak to an assistant in semi-privacy. Dresses adorned the walls, draped on nails which could do no good to the flounces. Flat irons, old boots, tools, an assortment of cutlery, and jewellery of all descriptions filled the shelves, ticketed and numbered.

A man with grey curly hair was entering each transaction in a book. He wore a frock coat and beige trousers of such good quality Sarah wondered whether they had been unclaimed stock.

'Yes?' he asked. No deference here. People in dire need of money were all treated the same.

Sarah took the ring off her finger and handed it to him. 'I'd like to know how much you can advance me on my wedding ring,' she said, attending to business before asking for Dimsey.

He weighed it in his hand like an expert. 'Two shillin',' he offered.

'But it's gold. I must get more than that for it.'

'Two shillin',' said the shopman. 'Take it or leave it.'

He'd started to hustle her away with impatient patter when he was interrupted by a female voice in the background.

'Wait, Pa. Yer can't send 'er away.' A girl poked her head round the corner of the booth and smiled at Sarah. She was plump and dimpled, and brown ringlets bounced like springs against her cheeks. Sarah recognized her at once, though she'd been afraid she wouldn't. 'Remember me, ducks? You rescued me purse from a pickpocket once. Me name's Dimsey Turner.'

'Yes, I do remember,' she said. There seemed no need to say she'd been looking for her.

'Down on yer luck are yer then?'

'For the moment.'

'Then hop under the counter and come on upstairs with me.' She helped Sarah through. 'I never did know yer name.'

'Sarah Morey.'

'Give Sarah back 'er ring, Pa,' said Dimsey. The man with grey hair did as he was told, then proceeded to serve the next woman who had pushed immediately into the vacated space. Flaking brown paint covered the walls and it was so dark Sarah had to feel her way up to the next floor, but Dimsey's slippered feet skipped up in no time, her grey skirt swinging from well-rounded hips dusting the stairs as she went.

'Ma, I've brought a friend,' she called.

Sarah followed her into a room so full of bundles and sacks all tied up with string and labels it was difficult to find a place to put her feet, and dust hung in the air like a cloud of pepper, stinging her nose. A consumptive-looking woman had been leaning out of the window gossiping with her neighbours but she brought her head back in so quickly a potted plant wobbled dangerously near the edge of the parapet.

'Who is she?' the woman asked, squinting at the unexpected guest.

'The girl that saved me losing me wages once.'

'How d'you do,' said Sarah.

235

Dimsey's mother coughed. 'It were when I started being ill.' The coughing racked her thin body for several seconds. 'I remember Dimsey telling me. In them days no wages would've been a calamity and no mistake, so ye're welcome. I'll make some tea.'

Under the conglomeration of bundles there was furniture, some of it worth a bob or two, and when Dimsey had stacked the bags on top of each other against the wall there was room to sit down.

'Me stepfather's doin' right well,' she said. 'He reckons we'll 'ave Ma out of 'ere come next year.' (Sadly Sarah was of the opinion that Dimsey's mother would be leaving sooner than that, but not to a new earthly home. She scarcely had strength to lift the kettle.) 'Now tell us how we can 'elp you. Where d'you live, and why was you putting yer wedding ring in hock?'

'I've been widowed these last three months.'

'And yer've no family?'

'No. No home either right now. I wanted enough money to rent a room, and then I need to find work.'

Dimsey's cheeks dimpled into a smile. 'Yer can stay 'ere ternight, can't she, Ma? Mind, yer'll have ter share me bed, but I don't mind if you don't.'

All Sarah needed straight away was a roof over her head, so the offer was more welcome than a heap of sympathy. 'I wouldn't mind sleeping on the floor,' she said. 'But a bed sounds like the answer to a prayer. Thank you.'

'I looked for you after that day,' said Dimsey. 'I always wanted to thank you properly for what you did, but I ain't seen you around.'

Downstairs in the shop the rabble continued to banter and argue. In the narrow court below a woman with a basket of vegetables was shouting her wares in a raucous voice, accompanied by the mangy dog's incessant whining. Sarah was given tea in a cup which would have elegantly graced Maud Halden's table, and as she recounted a little of what had happened to her in the past five years she wondered if the pawnbroker was doing too well to move from his lucrative business in Middle Alley.

She tried not to show impatience to know what Dimsey had been doing.

'And what about you?' she said when the right moment came. 'Do you still work at the Foundling Hospital?'

'Lor, yes. This is me day awf. I got took on as a nurse after I'd done time in the laundry and I like that fine, but me stepfather's insisting I give it up to look after Ma. I bin living in, see.' Dimsey stirred the fire which belched smoke into the overcrowded room, and soot settled on a clutch of daintily painted vases beside it. Then she put down the poker and turned to Sarah with a triumphant light in her eyes. 'Now why don't *you* take me job? Yer can come with me tomorrow, ducks, and I'll put in a word for you.'

'I can't,' Sarah protested. But the very idea made her heart race.

Dimsey was indignant. 'Why not? Ain't it

good enough for you? You bin a parson's wife, so you ought to be able to look after children. I reckon it were meant, you coming 'ere today.'

Sarah thought of Corrie with her bright golden hair the same colour as James Halden's. The longing to be near her again was so strong she held her breath, and her elbows dug into her sides to suppress the excitement she felt at such an opportunity. Maybe Dimsey was right. Maybe it was another of the Lord's mysterious ways and she ought not to dismiss it. She had always been willing to take risks for the sake of her beloved child, and things had turned out right before. With Dimsey Turner to speak for her there was less chance of awkward questions, but in the event of any she must be prepared to lie, even though untruthfulness went against her conscience.

'All right,' she said. 'Thank you, Dimsey. I'll come with you tomorrow.'

James returned home that evening with a sense of anticipation. He hadn't been alone with Sarah since that first night, but the knowledge that she was near filled him with joyful satisfaction, and he hadn't felt so happy for as long as he could remember.

It was dangerous, of course, harbouring a girl he cared about more than anyone in the world. In time Maud was bound to find out, but by being discreet he hoped to ward off the discovery until he had installed Sarah in a house of her own, and if Maud wanted to protect the respectable façade of their empty marriage she would have to accept that he had taken a mistress. He had no doubts as to Sarah's willingness. She had demonstrated her feelings so well he had scarcely known how to control the passions she invoked, and since that night his physical need of her had given him no peace. But he had vowed to have patience and not cause a scandal while she was in Calvert Terrace. It might not have to be for much longer. Already he had a small dwelling in mind to purchase, only a few paces from Miss Claybury's institution, and as soon as he had the key Sarah could be removed there to live in comfort.

Such were his thoughts as he took off his redingote and beaver hat in the hall and handed them to Nessie. His complacency was to be short-lived.

'Mrs Halden says will you go straight into the parlour, sir,' said Nessie. She looked flustered, as if it hadn't been a good day.

James raised his eyebrows. 'Mrs Halden knows I always retire to my study before supper.'

'Beggin' yer pardon, sir, but it sounded important.'

'Hmph.' He delayed obeying until the girl had disappeared down the basement stairs. If Maud was in one of her bad moods her voice was inclined to shrillness and he didn't want private business being repeated in the servants' quarters.

He went into the parlour and found his wife sitting very straight in a high-backed chair by the fire, more like Her Majesty than ever. Her mouth was pursed, her chin jutting, and her hands were clenching the chair arms as if they could squeeze the wood to pulp. She didn't get up.

'Good evening, my dear.' Whenever he addressed her James felt as old as her father. Maud inspired impeccable manners.

'There's no supper,' she said. 'Mrs Morey has left, and Mrs Vallery is ... incapacitated.'

His good humour vanished. 'Where has Mrs Morey gone?'

'So you're more concerned about her than you are about your supper.'

Her tone was sharp and there was a dangerous glitter in her eyes. Something serious had happened in his absence and he questioned her with equal sharpness in his anxiety to know what it was.

'I am concerned that you may have driven her away with your unkind tongue.'

'Are you indeed? Your concern would do you credit if it were not suspect.' Maud stood up and shook her skirt into place as if agitating for a confrontation. 'I had a visitor this morning by the name of Abel Wood.'

'My God!'

'I hope not!' said she tersely. 'But I take it you know the man?'

James closed his eyes momentarily to shut out the revolting picture of Sarah being subjected to gross indecency. 'I pray you didn't let him make off with Sarah. The wretch tried to rape her.'

If Abel Wood had taken her back to Corporation Lane there'd be hell to pay. He'd go after her and create such an uproar it would be the last time such a trick was ever tried.

'Sarah? I didn't know you were on first-name terms with Mrs Morey,' said Maud.

He wanted to shake her. 'Tell me where she went.'

'I'll tell you what Mr Wood told me, then you can give me a truthful explanation.' She was infuriatingly determined not to answer his most important question. 'According to him, James, you fathered Mrs Morey's child.'

He was staggered. His utter amazement showed in the sudden dropping of his jaw, but he recovered immediately. 'And *you* believed him?'

'Should I have done?'

'Most certainly not. The man's a liar and a troublemaker. Mrs Morey has been married to a clergyman these past five years, as you well know, and she has no children.'

'You seem to have more than a passing acquaintance with the girl,' said Maud. 'How interesting that you know so much about her and had no difficulty finding her address.'

He raked his fingers through his mane of hair in exasperation. 'What matters is that she hasn't gone back to it.'

She sighed irritably. 'Mrs Morey was out when Mr Wood called. She saw him at a distance, though, and came to tell me she was leaving. I asked her to remain until you returned home but she wouldn't wait.'

Suddenly he felt sorry for his wife. She'd suffered a humiliating visit from a most objectionable man, and must have been tormented ever since by the lies he had spun. James's expression softened and he put an affectionate hand on her shoulder.

'Maud, I'm sorry you're so distressed. The truth is simple. Several years ago I was called to Smith's Clock Manufactory when Sarah's father met his death in the furnace. She was very young and very upset, so I took her home to her stepmother, Maggie, who is now married to Abel Wood. At no other time have I set eyes on her, except when we visited the Bradfords that Christmas. A few weeks later we heard she had married Nahum Morey.' He looked into her face with such candour he could almost see the worry lines ease away. 'You must believe me.'

But she was still angry. 'The man's trouble-making has deprived us of a good cook. Whatever else she might be, Mrs Morey was proving to be very useful in the house, and I might have been able to make it right with Elizabeth Bradford.' She jerked the bellpull. 'His lies were so believable. According to him his wife told him all about the child.'

'There is no child.'

'No. It died.'

At that moment Nessie answered Maud's summons, and James had never been more pleased at an interruption. The last statement from his wife had cut razor-sharp into his complacency. She had made it sound so certain that a baby had existed, and a gnawing fear took hold in his mind. He left her to salvage some kind of evening meal, and went upstairs to his room where he paced back and forth for several minutes.

He'd never considered that Sarah could have become pregnant after their brief time together. Their meeting at the Bradfords' had occurred about a year after Paddy Byrne's death and he'd presumed there had been no break in her employment during that time, but supposing she had lived through further heartbreak and tragedy, experiencing the birth and death of their child. If he had caused her such pain she had given no indication. Surely she would have approached him for help, or reproached him for bringing such shame upon her, but there had been no word. He longed to hear from her own lips that Abel Wood had fabricated the whole story. Yet he wouldn't know how to broach such a delicate subject, even if she were around.

Presently he came down again to put on his outdoor clothes. He'd hoped to leave the house without Maud seeing him but he was just shrugging himself into his coat when she appeared at the parlour door.

'Where are you going, James?'

'Sarah must be found,' he said. 'She has no money and nowhere to go.'

He set off on foot, intending to search the streets of Clerkenwell. Both mind and body ached with the complexity of his emotions but he strode out boldly, determined not to return without her. The main reason for her flight had to be fear of Abel Wood, but if Maud had repeated to her the malicious tale she had just told James, and it was not true, then the poor girl would be feeling too embarrassed to face him. He had to find her, if only to put matters right, but he didn't know where to start looking.

The only place he knew she would *not* be was at Maggie's house.

He didn't know if she had any other friends who would take her in, and he was desperately worried for her safety. How little he knew at all of his beautiful, sensual Sarah who was almost as much a stranger to him as on the day they had met, but who held his heart in a most mysterious way. The moment he found her he would tell her so. He ought to have told her that night instead of denying every natural instinct in favour of discretion.

His first inclination was to head for Newcastle Place, but he decided against it. Knowing the emotional climate he didn't think she would have sought refuge there either, but there were questions he would have liked to ask Elizabeth Bradford before he approached Sarah herself.

He walked for over an hour, searching the area around Turnmill Street where she had spent her childhood. He looked in lighted shops and doorways, in churches and community rooms, then ventured warily into the unsavoury alleys. It was like looking for a rose on a dungheap. He was accosted by prostitutes, invited into a brothel, and children in rags ran alongside him begging. His well-dressed appearance made him too noticeable and he daren't linger in the dark courts where shifty characters lurked round every black corner. He kept his hands in his pockets, his watch chain hidden beneath his coat, and his eyes peeled for shadows keeping pace with his own. He'd been a fool to enter his thieves' den.

At the place where Turnmill Street became Cowcross Street he was uncomfortably aware that his precautions were insufficient. Two girls in thin cotton dresses and battered bonnets were loitering by the open door of a particularly disreputable public house, and though he saw their signal to someone inside it was impossible to push through the cluster of people who seemed set on delaying his progress. He was trapped. The ruffians, one in a sailor's uniform, the others in moleskin jackets and trousers and cloth caps, burst into the alley from the pub and set upon him.

'This ain't no place fer you, guv'nor.'

'Slummin' it, ain't yer?' They taunted him, prowling round like wolves while he tried to break free. Argument was a waste of the breath he was going to need. 'Let's see what ye're worth.'

James was a tall man who possessed exceptional strength but alone he was no match for the band of murderous robbers. He felled one and crippled another with a well-aimed kick. Two more received body punches which doubled them up, but as soon as they were disposed of others came to join in the fight. His fists struck home again and again, causing swearing and cursing which would scorch the paint off wood, but he didn't really stand a

245

chance against such odds.

The mobsman with a knife was younger than the rest, better looking and better dressed. He didn't soil his hands or his clothes in the affair, but waited until James was close enough to drive the blade into his back. Even then James pursued his attackers until blood was gushing from his wound and he finally collapsed. He was dragged into the shadows, stripped and robbed of everything, including most of his clothes, and left for dead.

Like the priest and the Levite everyone passed by the figure lying cold and injured in a corner of the alley, though in fairness he was well hidden among piles of rotting vegetables and other accumulated rubbish. Luckily the night was humid for December and no frost touched him, but rats scurried about their business, sniffing at him with an air of anticipation as if waiting until the body had lain long enough to acquire a taste. Slops were emptied over him from an upper window. His burnished hair turned dark with the wet, and congealing blood mixed with the mud beneath him, but James Halden had more stamina than a bull terrier and he fought to keep a hold on life.

The Samaritan was a bargeman on a visit from the river with a bushel of wheat removed without permission from his vessel under cover of darkness. He was making his delivery just as dawn lightened the sky, and he saw a movement from a body lying amidst the rubbish beside the bakery which was his destination. He bent down and felt for a heartbeat. Finding one, he removed his guernsey and wrapped it round the poor blighter, then gave his familiar rap on the crumbling wooden door.

'Bloke 'ere needs savin', Gabriel Smith,' he said. 'Reckon 'e's almost a gonna, but it's worth a try.'

Between them they carried James into the warmth of the bakehouse and laid him on a dough trough.

Less than half an hour later Dimsey Turner set out for the Foundling Hospital where she had to start work at seven o'clock. She took Sarah Morey with her, and they passed the alley off Cowcross Street without knowing anything of the previous night's events, which were common enough to be quite unremarkable.

# CHAPTER 10

Sarah entered the Foundling Hospital through a side door. In the early morning light the ceilings seemed high and the walls all-enveloping as she followed the girl whom she must have been fated to meet again, and she was filled with nervous excitement. Muted sounds of morning industry filtered through the corridors, and when she breathed in deeply there was the same warm smell of polish and soap which she remembered from the day when she had deposited Corrie, wrapped in her patchwork blanket, into the arms of a nurse such as Dimsey Turner.

Her memories were filled with the grief of that parting from her baby, but now there was this extraordinary opportunity to be near Corrie after all through her childhood years, if only she could secure the job which was so tantalizingly within her grasp.

'We'll go to Matron first,' said Dimsey. She took Sarah up a flight of stairs with an iron rail above the wooden banister and iron spikes along the length. Seeing Sarah's horror she hastened to explain. 'A boy was killed sliding down these banisters once, years ago. Since then any child caught trying is shut in the dark and fed on bread and water, or given a few lashes. The schoolmaster reads the rules to all the kids.'

Sarah touched one of the dreadful spikes with a shudder. All her senses were keener than they had ever been, and every sight and sound was important in this building which was now Corrie's environment.

They were in the boys' wing. She caught sight of small figures in brown trousers and jackets emerging from a long room ahead of her, and an older boy with a bugle hanging from a cord over his shoulder wished them a polite good morning as he passed. If only they could have come through the girls' wing instead. Sarah's impatience was mounting by the second, but must be curbed if she was to create a good impression.

Matron was a woman of medium height who had a forbidding air of authority. A white cap covered her hair completely so that it was impossible to see what colour it was, and her brown dress had a puritan plainness relieved only by a small green shawl. Her room was equally plain, containing nothing which wasn't essential to her station.

She inquired sharply after Dimsey's business. 'Well, miss? I thought it was settled last week that you are to leave us to look after your mother.'

'Yes, Mrs Grant, but I hope you might consider a friend of mine for me job, ma'am. This is Sarah Morey and she's a widow with no children.'

'Morey?' The woman's brow furrowed in an effort to place the name.

'My husband was a Governor, ma'am,' said Sarah. Her heart was beating uncomfortably fast.

There was a surprised pause. 'And you wish to become a nurse here! I've never heard anything so extraordinary.'

Sarah's lovely blue eyes filled with tears quite unexpectedly. She was alarmed at her lack of self-control and feared it would put paid to her chances immediately, but though she didn't know it they acted in her favour, accompanied as they were by unrehearsed words which would have touched the stoniest heart.

'My husband, the Reverend Morey, was a very generous man, Mrs Grant,' she said. 'And his love of the children here was an inspiration. For his dear sake I want to carry on the good work to which he devoted his time and money, but all I can offer is myself, if you will accept me. You see there was nothing else left after his death.'

'Well,' said Mrs Grant, visibly moved. The two women studied each other for several seconds. 'I must consult the treasurer's clerk, but it seems to me your motives are very commendable.' She dismissed Dimsey, then invited Sarah to sit down. 'Have you no family at all?'

'No, ma'am.'

'There's no need to ask if you are Protestant, of course, or to question your character. You must also know that staff here must always promote the interests of the charity, and that the most important thing is the welfare of the children.'

'Yes, I know all that.'

'I take it you never drink?'

'No, ma'am. Never.'

Another pause followed, during which Sarah was subjected to a suspicious stare, and the question which followed was calculated to upset her story if there were discrepancies in it.

'And how do you come to be a friend of Dimsey Turner's?'

Sarah decided the complete truth was her only course. 'I once saved her purse from being taken by a pickpocket,' she said, with as much modesty as the truth allowed. 'It seemed as if the Lord meant us to meet again yesterday. Dimsey told me the sad news that she can no longer leave her mother, and there was I hoping to offer myself for the kind of work she does here for the children. My dear Nahum would have said it was Divine Intervention.'

Mrs Grant smiled at last, the skin around

250

her mouth creasing into tight, strained lines where she was unused to smiling. 'Indeed it does sound that way.'

Sarah's black dress was almost as severe as Matron's brown one, though there were tucks and lace trimming on the high-necked bodice. Her hair was drawn tightly back and plaited in a coil on her crown, and over it she wore a straw bonnet with a small veil which was tied beneath her chin with black velvet ribbon. Today she looked older than her twenty-two years. To her relief Mrs Grant showed no interest in what Sarah's life had been before she had married Nahum. It was as if Nahum, in judging her fit to be his wife, had given her a character reference requiring no further investigation, and for that she sent up a little prayer of thanks.

What seemed to concern Matron more was whether Sarah would be able to adapt to the routine and rules of the hospital. 'You do realize that if you live at the hospital you won't be allowed out later than nine o'clock in winter and ten o'clock in summer without the treasurer's permission?'

'There's nowhere I should want to go, Mrs Grant,' Sarah assured her.

The woman took a deep, catarrhal breath which caused a wheezing sound to rattle beneath the brown merino. She was no longer quite so awe-inspiring, and Sarah guessed at her quandary.

'Well, Mrs Morey,' she said, at length, 'it seems to me that if you have an education you are more fitted to be a teacher than a nurse, but that must rest with the treasurer.'

A teacher! Sarah's spirits sank. She would never be able to teach. She remembered the alphabets her mother had made her learn until she could write her name, and blessed her for insisting that she persevere with reading which she did so well even Nahum had been surprised at her ability. But that was not an education.

An appointment was made for her to see the treasurer's clerk. His office was near the Court Room where she had once stood in front of the examining committee of Governors, and when she entered it she felt as if she were once again the young girl with a baby, begging for help. She remembered the man. Pray God he wouldn't remember her.

He extended his hand. 'Mrs Morey, this is a strange situation. Matron has acquainted me with the details and I must offer you condolences on the loss of your husband. The Reverend Morey was a very respected member of our committee. We are devastated by his untimely death.'

'The Foundling Hospital meant everything to him, sir,' said Sarah. She kept her chin high, and her eyes met his steadily. There must be sincerity but no humility in her approach.

'And now you wish to continue his good work I hear.'

'It's my dearest wish, for Nahum's sake as well as my own.'

He stroked his bearded chin. 'You must be a very good Christian woman.' Both thumbs disappeared into pockets in his waistcoat and his fingers danced while he debated the matter silently. Then: 'May I ask what is your God-given name?'

'It's Sarah, sir.'

'And your husband's parish was in Staines I believe?'

'No, sir, it was in Chertsey, as you very well know. Nahum's deep interest in the welfare of the Foundling children came about through contact with babies being cared for there.' She sat on the edge of the chair, aware that she was being tested. 'I can bring you my marriage certificate should you doubt that I am who I say I am.'

To her relief he brushed aside the offer. 'No, no, dear lady, that won't be necessary.'

She didn't know what she would have done if he had wanted to see it. He was an astute man who might well have had a better memory for names and facts than he did for faces.

He went on. 'What bothers me, Mrs Morey, is that we don't have a vacancy for a teacher at this moment, nor the money to pay for an additional one. A nurse's job hardly seems fitting for a lady such as yourself.'

'I'll be happy to work in the humblest capacity,' Sarah said, hiding a smile at his description of her. She leaned towards him a little and spoke more confidentially. 'You may have heard that my dear husband gave everything he had to charity, and as our house belonged to the church I am left with nothing. It's a dreadful thing to have to admit, but if I don't come here then I don't know what will become of me.' She drew in her lower lip which trembled slightly. 'His sister, Mrs Bradford, would support me, I'm sure, if I were to ask her, but I would much rather be independent, and I've set my heart on continuing with Nahum's work.'

The treasurer's clerk cleared his throat, as if embarrassed by her candour. 'Very well, Mrs Morey. I respect your sentiments and you may take the place of ... er ... Dimsey Turner.' He consulted a note Mrs Grant had given him. 'Your duties will be to keep the children neat and clean, help to mend their clothes, see they rise and go to bed at the proper time, and attend to their meals. The other important thing, which should be no trouble to you, is to make sure they know the Catechism, and you will be responsible for their good behaviour in the chapel.'

'Thank you.' She could scarcely hide her elation. 'You may be sure I shall do my best.'

'There will be no privileges.'

'I expect none, sir.'

Sarah left the office with a spring in her step which hadn't been there since the Chertsey days when she had lived for the times when Mrs Gilling brought Corrie to her. There were no guilty feelings about the exaggerated story she had told. Since Nahum had left her nothing except his good name she had no hesitation in using it to obtain the one thing in life she desired more than anything else, to be near her daughter.

She would live like a nun here. The threat James Halden posed to her peace of mind would be over for ever. And she would tell no one where she was living, especially not Maggie who had betrayed her trust.

It was well into the morning and Sarah walked sedately past labelled doors on her way back to the matron's room, still unable quite to believe her luck. Her arms ached to hold Corrie once more, but she knew the absolute necessity for caution and schooled herself not to show the strength of her emotions on seeing her again.

Perhaps this wasn't exactly the life she had imagined leading, but she would do anything for her child's sake and she couldn't wait to see the joy on Corrie's little face when they were reunited.

Maggie was returning from Covent Garden, laden with vegetables in a basket, her youngest child balanced on her hip, and had just reached her door when a hansom cab came to a stop beside the kerb. Cabs were an unfamiliar sight in Corporation Lane so Maggie's curiosity was natural. When the cabby got down from his perch at the rear and helped his elegant passenger to alight she was even more surprised.

The lady stepped down as if afraid to soil her shoes and gown upon the unswept pavement. She was small but dignified, her plum-coloured skirt so wide that it was obviously supported by a hoop, and her fur-trimmed cloak added to the impression of bulk. Her bonnet was edged with lace and decorated with roses, sweet as a summer's day, but her expression was as cold as the winter wind which whipped between the tall houses.

She glanced up at the tenement, then addressed Maggie who had a foot on the step. 'I'm looking for Mrs Wood,' she said.

'I'm Maggie Wood.'

'Then I'd like to talk to you. May I come in?'

'If yer can get down the passage,' said Maggie, eyeing the hooped skirt doubtfully. Dick was grizzling so she set him down and patted his behind to send him off in search of his older brothers. 'And who might you be, ma'am?'

'I'm Mrs James Halden. Unfortunately we have a mutual acquaintance in your step-daughter, Sarah Morey.' She turned to the cabby. 'This won't take long. You may wait.'

Her skirts touched the walls on either side as she preceded Maggie into the dim interior and she lifted them delicately, showing an inch of lace on the hem of her pantaloons. So this was Maud Halden. There was no hesitancy about her, and the reason for her visit was a puzzle.

'I'll make some tea,' Maggie said.

'No thank you. I merely wish to know if the young woman has returned here.' Maud looked around, her small nose wrinkling at the indelicate odours.

'Of course she ain't here. I thought Sarah was working for you.'

James Halden's wife took a small handkerchief from her reticule and fluttered it gently to release a faint scent of violets into the stale air.

256

'My husband brought Sarah Morey in our house, Mrs Wood, on the pretext that she was a homeless, penniless widow, and in spite of many misgivings I took pity on her. Yes, she worked for me for a few days, until your husband visited me with an urgent request for her to be returned to you. Did you know of this?'

'No,' said Maggie. 'No, I didn't.'

She suddenly turned cold, and she put a poker into embers in the grate to stir up a little warmth as well as to hide her dismay. So Abel had been interfering! That accounted for one or two strange goings-on in the last couple of days. Gawd, there were going to be words about this.

'Have you seen her?' Maud asked impatiently.

'No, I ain't.' There was a mystery here sure enough, and a serious one at that to bring her ladyship slumming. 'I take it she ain't with you any more neither since ye're asking me, but if you didn't want 'er in the first place ain't it a good riddance?'

Maud Halden twisted her gloved fingers together. 'I want to know whether there was any truth in the story your husband told me about Sarah having had a baby which died. A baby he accused James of fathering.'

So that was it. Abel had gone blabbing his mouth off. Maggie thanked the Lord she hadn't let him know the whole of it. She didn't want to cause Sarah any more trouble even though she'd been mad with her for coming to the house three days since when there'd been only Paddy home and not stopping to tell how things

257

were. Sarah had taken all her belongings in the canvas bag she'd brought from Chertsey, and disappeared without a word. Now it seemed she had a mighty big reason. Mrs James Halden was on the warpath.

Maggie dithered, playing for time. 'I ... don't know what ye're talking about.'

'Nonsense, woman. Of course you know.' Maud's courage in pursuing the subject had to be admired. 'I've already made discreet inquiries from the late Reverend Morey's sister who employed Sarah before her marriage, and according to her she gave up her job for several weeks ostensibly to look after you. Is that true?'

'Yes, it's true. Me first 'usband had just been killed in a fire.'

'And did she give birth to a child in that time?'

Direct questions were the hardest to answer. Smoke began to billow from the stirred ashes and Maggie coughed as she bent over to put on some sticks.

'Yes, that's true, too,' she said reluctantly. 'When she lost it she went back to the Bradfords.'

The other woman went deathly pale. 'And its father?'

'That were Sarah's business.' Maggie had put the loaded basket on the table and she set about removing the swedes and cabbages which had made it so heavy. She hated being caught up in other people's problems. 'I don't know why yer can't let it rest. It's all in the past, and if

258

she's gawn then there's no 'arm done.'

'Do you know where she is?' Maud persisted.

Maggie was getting angry. 'Look, lady, I ain't Sarah's keeper. She's a grown woman, and a widow at that, so she don't 'ave to tell me where she's going.'

The twisting fingers gripped tightly together, and Maud lifted her shoulders in a gesture close to despair.

'I'm asking because my husband is missing as well. He went out to look for her three nights ago and he hasn't returned. Nor has he been to Miss Claybury's institution where he is employed as a physician. I'm at my wits' end. What am I to think?'

There was silence a moment. Then Maggie said: 'I think I will make that cup of tea. Best sit yerself down.'

She put a kettle on the hob, thrusting it into the newly kindled flames with unnecessary force. Things were worse than she could have ever imagined and if Sarah'd been here this minute she would have berated her unmercifully for being so stupid. The poor woman, whose dress completely hid the chair she'd thankfully accepted, had every right to be worried. She'd lost her husband to a trollop, for that was what Paddy Byrne's daughter had become.

No wonder Sarah had come so stealthily to collect her belongings. No wonder she'd told no one where she was going. If she'd let out so much as a hint that she was running off with James Halden she would have felt the length of her stepmother's tongue.

'I am right, aren't I?' said Maud. 'You think they've gone away together.'

'Reckon it looks that way,' said Maggie.

James's wife bent her head and the violet-smelling handkerchief was pressed to her eyes. For a moment she couldn't say any more, and Maggie guessed it was a very rare occasion when she was lost for words.

'I don't know how I'm going to live with the humiliation,' Maud cried. 'How could he have done this to me? I've always made him a good wife, and if it wasn't for me he wouldn't be so respected in his profession.'

'Looks like 'e's thrown the whole lot up.'

'And for what?'

'For Paddy Byrne's daughter.'

Outside the cab-horse snorted and clonked its hoofs into the cobbles with a steady drumming sound. A few flakes of snow were falling, and children sitting in the gutter lifted their faces and opened their mouths to catch them on their tongues. When Maud Halden was leaving a short time later she stopped on the step to make her final pronouncement, and snowflakes settled on her rose-bordered bonnet.

'I shall never forgive him,' she said. 'Not even if he crawls to me on his knees.'

From the moment Sarah started working at the Foundling Hospital her thoughts were all of her child and she expected to see Corrie as soon as she took up her duties, so it was a great disappointment when she was asked to take care

260

of a little boy newly arrived from a foster home in East Peckham.

'Poor little blighter. I feel real sorry for 'em when they first come back 'ere, but they've got to get used to it,' said Dimsey, who was showing Sarah what to do.

She wondered how long it had taken Corrie to adjust. The thought of her being unhappy was like a thorn in Sarah's heart, but she had to curb her anxiety in order to give this small boy the attention he needed.

'I want to go home,' he said, stoically refusing to shed tears. He was a fighter and he tried to cover his misery in a fit of aggression, kicking out at offers of comfort. Sarah buttoned his trousers and waistcoat, tied the brown bow beneath the smart white collar, and fastened his waist-length jacket.

'This is home now,' she said. 'There, we've finished dressing before the others so there's time for a cuddle.' She sat on his bed and took him on her lap. He was so small and vulnerable, and tears of sympathy for his loneliness stung her eyes. 'Soon you'll be glad you came. You've got all these other children to play with.'

'I'll look after 'im,' said an older boy. Kindness among the children was one of the first things Sarah noted.

She saw that he ate his bread and milk, and after breakfast deposited him in the playroom. Immediately she was given enough jobs to occupy her for the rest of the morning; making beds in the boys' long bedroom gallery, taking soiled linen to the laundry, checking drugs from the apothecary's shop; and then there was the never-ending pile of mending to tackle.

'You're good at sewing,' said the nurse she'd been sent to help. Her name was Teresa Thorpe and she held her needle as if it were a garden trowel. 'Likely you'll be put on to dressmaking.'

'My mother taught me,' said Sarah.

'You'll get on all right with Matron then. She dun't like sending the kids' clothes out to be made. A rum 'un she is. Reckon her petticoats are starched like they been out in a hard frost, so as no man can lift 'em.' She started telling Sarah about the rest of the staff, painting swift word pictures. 'The porter now, he ain't allowed to let in anyone loose or disorderly, and he's supposed to stop riots. Him! When he stands straight a dog could run through 'is bow legs. Then there's a coatmaker. He has dinner at the menservants' table along with the gardener and the baker, and 'e talks like 'e's got a mouthful of pins. And when the laundrymaids come in to dinner they look like a bunch of pickled beetroots.'

Sarah smiled as she took her place at one of the dining tables later, recognizing people from Teresa's clever descriptions. She was to eat with the mistresses, her position as a nurse being above that of the maidservants who dined at a separate table, as did the menservants. Five other nurses, three infirmary nurses and four mistresses dined with her.

'There should be four nurses from the infirmary but there's been diphtheria over there,' said Teresa, who had appointed herself Sarah's tutor when Dimsey left. 'They have to stay separate if they've been with someone infectious so as not to spread it.'

Sarah was also sharing a bedroom with Teresa. It proved to be a bare, narrow room much like the one she had shared with Ella Tomkin at the Bradfords'.

'Will I get to work with the girls sometimes?' she asked that night. Her frustration had increased when the afternoon had been busier that morning and there'd been no excuse to visit the girls' wing.

'Like as not you'll be sent to the east side tomorrow, seeing as ye're learning the ropes. Do you like girls best?'

'No. But at the same time as I left Chertsey there were two little girls due to come back here and I wondered how they were getting on.' She didn't trust herself to speak Corrie's name in case her voice should tremble.

'They're fine, I shouldn't wonder.' Teresa's reply wound down into a sleepy sigh as she turned over to face the wall, obviously too tired to talk any more, and Sarah was left with her thoughts.

She couldn't sleep. Tomorrow seemed such a long time coming, and anticipation welled up like bubbles, carrying precious memories of Corrie. She kept picturing her with her original tumble of golden curls, and wondered what James's reaction would be if he were ever to find out that he had such a beautiful daughter.

She hadn't dared to dwell on him since her

flight from Calvert Terrace. Maud Halden had naturally been very upset by Abel's visit but Sarah hoped she had convinced her of James's innocence. However, even if Maud had thought better of repeating the tale she would have had to find some other reason for Sarah's hurried departure, and there was no knowing what she might have made him think. Sarah was cold with dread that Maud might have turned him against her for ever, yet it was probably better that way than continuing with the impossible situation she had allowed to develop.

One thing she knew: James had not sought to question Abel Wood.

She had carefully chosen the time to pick up her canvas bag from Maggie's house. On certain days Abel sold his work in Hatton Garden and he always came back with money for Maggie to go to the market, then spent the rest in a pub on Clerkenwell Green, so the house was empty around noon, except, on that particular day, for Patrick.

'I knew you wouldn't leave me for good,' he'd said.

It had been heartbreaking to say she couldn't stay. 'Has anyone been asking for me, Patrick? A man with lots of fair hair?'

'You mean the one what took you away in 'is carriage. No, 'e ain't been. Nobody 'as.' He clung to her. 'I thought you didn't love me any more.'

'Silly boy, I'll always love you, and if you need me when you're bigger I'll make sure you can find me.'

James had reminded her that he was Maggie's child and Maggie's responsibility, and she'd had to remind herself of his words. She'd left with all her belongings before blood ties forced her to remain too long, or made the temptation to take her half brother with her too strong to resist. And though she knew it was foolish her heart had been heavy with the knowledge that James Halden had not cared enough to come asking for her.

Next morning Sarah reported to Matron and was instructed to help with the girls. On winged feet she hastened through the corridors, past the chapel where the sound of vibrant organ music touched her soul, and up to the long bedroom identical to the one where she had been yesterday in the west wing. She was happier than she had been since the evening when she had almost persuaded Nahum to consider adopting Corrie.

In the dim light she saw little girls of varying sizes getting into their clothes. With pulses racing she scanned the length of the room, believing she would spot Corrie straight away, but they all looked alike in their brown dresses, all with short hair which was partially hidden by the high-crowned white caps. They chattered like birds in a bush, older girls helping the younger ones, but before the nurse on duty could reach Sarah there was a shriek from the far end of the room.

'Mrs Morey! Mrs Morey!'

A small, barefoot figure darted down the middle of the room, brushing aside anyone in her way, and she flung herself against Sarah's apron, her arms clasping her round the hips. Sarah hugged her wordlessly with eyes closed in ecstatic pleasure. Then she looked down and saw black bushy hair like an untidy mop and the little pinched features of Anna Beckett.

'Anna,' she said, after a moment in which disappointment tasted bitter in her mouth. She held the child away from her, trying hard to suppress that disappointment, for Anna was not to blame. 'Let me see if you've grown.'

'Have you come to take us away, Mrs Morey?' Anna bounced up and down with excitement. 'I knew you would. I told Corrie you wouldn't leave us here. Oh, I am glad.'

'Where is Corrie?'

The other nurse came over, a serious young woman with heavy brows and a figure laced so tightly into a corset the pain of it showed in her expression.

'Good morning, Mrs Morey. I see you're already acquainted with Anna Beckett.'

'I know several of the children,' Sarah said. 'My late husband was a clergyman at Chertsey.'

'Ah, yes. I had heard.' The woman removed Anna from their presence, sending her back to finish dressing. 'So sad about the other little mite who came back here at the same time as Anna.'

Sarah felt as if the floorboards were coming up to meet her. Her hands went to her breast where fear struck like a physical pain, and her legs would scarcely hold her.

'What happened?'

266

'Diphtheria,' said the nurse.

'Oh, my God.' Shock temporarily paralysed her. Nausea rolled through her in sickening waves, and caution was impossible. 'Excuse me,' she gasped, and fled from the room.

She ran down the stairs as if the devil were after her, only the balls of her slippered feet touching each step. Corrie was dead. Like a dirge the dreadful words kept repeating themselves.

Out through a back door and on to the gravel path, the stones now chipping into her thin soles. It was all her fault. If she hadn't brought her here she might still be alive.

Past the fishpond. A yellow, wintry sun touched the water and turned it to gold. Gold like Corrie's hair. She had to see the place where her child had died and hear from those who nursed her what a wonderful child she had been.

Up to the infirmary door. She stopped and glanced up at the façade with loathing. Corrie, in all innocence, had died here never knowing how much her real mother had adored her. No punishment would be too great for the wrong she had done to her when she had deprived her of the most important thing in life, a mother's love.

She went inside and breathed in the smell of carbolic soap and Condy's fluid. Dark walls seemed to close in on her like a tomb, and the brooding quietness was broken only by intermittent coughing from a ward on her left.

'Where do you think you're going?' A very irate nurse appeared. Over her arm she carried a tiny brown dress, underclothes and an apron. 'No visitors are allowed here under any circumstances. Kindly leave at once.'

'I've ... started working at the hospital,' Sarah stammered.

'Well, I could do with some assistance. Have they sent you over here to help me?'

'Yes.' She didn't care if disobedience cost her the job. There was no longer any reason to protect it. 'Can you tell me about Corrie Palmer.'

'I'm just taking the child's clothes to be cleaned and smoked with brimstone. Why do you want to know?'

'I lived in Chertsey. I know the family who fostered her. They'll be very upset to hear that she died.'

The woman raised her thin eyebrows. 'Who said she was dead?'

Sarah took a step forward, hope rushing in like a torrent filling a dry riverbed. 'You mean she's not dead?'

'Certainly not, and I hope that isn't the story going around in the main building. Corrie's making a surprising recovery, thanks to Dr Moore.' The nurse beamed, as if talking of someone hallowed. 'He actually cut the membrane so that the child could breathe. I've never seen anything like it.' She became carried away by the miracle that had happened, going into details Sarah didn't understand. Then: 'Dr Moore says she's no longer infectious so I suppose it won't hurt if I take you to see her. Might cheer the mite up to see someone she knows.'

Suddenly the sun was shining in Sarah's heart. She'd awakened from some terrible nightmare, and was filled with a joy no words could express.

She followed the nurse into a ward where girls of various ages were lying in narrow iron beds, woven blue coverlets tucked tightly round, pillows stacked behind them, and each one separated by blue curtains draped like canopies. The floorboards creaked.

Corrie was in a bed at the end, and Sarah hardly recognized the little girl who had played in the rectory garden not many months ago. The plump cheeks were sunk in, her skin seemed transparent, and her once beautiful hair was straight and damp against her head. She looked like a wax doll and her eyes gazed out from deep hollows.

But at least she was alive. Sarah couldn't hold back the tears of relief.

'Corrie, it's me. I've come to see you,' she murmured, approaching softly so as not to frighten the tiny convalescent. 'I'm so glad you're going to get well.'

The child stared up at her blankly for what seemed an age. Then she started to scream.

'Mrs Morey! Don't come near me.' She pressed herself back against the pillow. 'I hate you, I hate you, I hate you.'

'Corrie!' cried Sarah, her hands flying to her mouth in consternation.

The physician came rushing in to see what

the commotion was about.

'Send Mrs Morey away,' Corrie sobbed. 'I hate her for ever.' She hid beneath the blanket and refused to come out.

'You'd better go,' said the physician.

'But I don't understand. What have I done?'

'You've done nothing, I'm sure. The child has been at death's door and isn't very rational yet.'

She leaned over and gently touched the mound beneath the bedclothes. 'I'll come and see you again, Corrie.'

The little waxen face appeared once more, and the accusation in her baby eyes hurt Sarah more than a physical wound.

'Go away. I hate you. You don't care about me. You let me come here so I'd die.'

Sarah left the infirmary with leaden feet, past the fishpond which had now turned as grey as the overcast sky, and the fish which ventured near the surface were like drops of blood.

So this was to be her punishment. Not total loss, which in time she might have accepted, but something worse. Her daughter had lived to condemn her.

# PART TWO

## 1867

# CHAPTER 11

In the summer of 1867 Anna Beckett was apprenticed to a milliner, Mrs Fanny Cobham, who had premises in Burnet House on the west side of St John's Square, Clerkenwell. The building had once been the town residence of Gilbert Burnet, Bishop of Salisbury, but had long since been partitioned off into a rabbit warren of apartments occupied by numerous families, many of whom pursued trades in the very rooms where once the prelate had entertained his distinguished guests. Mrs Cobham rented a room on the ground floor with a window where she could display her creations, and it was possible to see who passed through the bricked passage in the centre of the house leading to Ledbury Place, a row of small tenements built on the bishop's former garden.

Anna finished stitching a piece of pink ribbon down one edge and drew up the thread the way Mrs Cobham had shown her so that it made a rosette, then she attached it to a white chip bonnet along with the others she had made. She liked being an apprentice. The millinery shop was a quiet retreat shut off from the noisier residents who made everything from shoes, boxes and stays to picture frames and clock cases. Behind Mrs Cobham's door was a more genteel industry which had been judged suitable for a girl whose apprenticeship had been delayed by uncertain health, and the lady herself had satisfied the strict inquiry as to her good character.

'You're a clever girl, Anna,' Mrs Cobham said. 'It's lucky for me the Foundling Hospital didn't think you were strong enough to do housework.' In her youth she must have been almost as tall as Anna, but years of bending over making bonnets had caused a curvature of the spine and her poor body was so contorted she couldn't stand straight. 'You were well taught in the art of using a needle.'

'I made clothes for the babies who're sent out to be nursed,' said Anna. Her eyes clouded momentarily. 'Mrs Morey taught me before she became Matron.'

She always suffered a peculiar ache when she thought of Mrs Morey. Over the years she had never completely got over her disappointment that Corrie Palmer was the favoured one, and though the days of favouritism were long since passed she still sometimes craved for one of the magical smiles Mrs Morey had bestowed on Corrie. The girl had become a dull companion after her illness. Anna had seen no reason to stay close to her once the ties of babyhood were broken and she had made other friends, but Corrie had clung like a leech.

'No one cares about me,' she would complain. 'I wish I could read like you can. Please help me.'

Anna had always done her best, but Corrie's learning ability had been hampered by her lack of confidence and her perpetual complaint that Mrs Morey was to blame for everything. It had all been so silly. Now, though, Corrie was apprenticed at a big house in Myddelton Square and she had seen nothing of her for several months.

As for Mrs Morey, in Anna's view she was not very happy. She had changed so much since those wonderful days at the rectory when her love for the children had shone radiantly. She had been such a lovely lady and Anna would have done anything to feel the warmth of those arms which had always scooped up Corrie Palmer. It had been a privilege to sit by her knee, but it would have been heaven to nestle against her breast. She was still beautiful of course, even more so now that she held a position of authority, but she had become unapproachable, and rarely smiled any more.

The day was hot and tiring. One of the things Anna didn't much like about being with Mrs Cobham was the tiny bedroom she had been given at the back of the house which had no ventilation. She found the airless conditions difficult to get used to after the long dormitory at the hospital with its row of windows, and she couldn't sleep at night. Her eyes were heavy and her cheeks pale as she arranged the rosettes in a cluster against black lace trimmings.

'You look tired, Anna.' Mrs Cobham was an observant soul with a kindly disposition. 'There's a box to be picked up at the bonnet-shape makers. You can collect it for me. A change will do you good.'

Anna jumped up at once. It was a novelty to be able to walk along the streets on her own and she never missed a chance to do so.

'I'll go now, Mrs Cobham,' she said.

'And be back in ten minutes.'

'Yes, Mrs Cobham.'

The bonnet-shape maker had a shop in Jerusalem Passage, just across the square, and as soon as she set out her weariness disappeared. A man with muffins in a basket, which he carried on his head, smiled at her as she stepped out of the door and a newspaper boy dodged out of her path.

Anna, at sixteen, was turning from a duckling to a swan. In the last year she had been allowed to let her hair grow. It was now tightly looped back and tied with a black bow, but short curls escaped from the severe style and framed her face so prettily they might have been put there just for decoration. Her features had filled out a little and softened with the approach of womanhood, showing good bone structure, though her nose was too big for her to be considered beautiful. Her blue eyes were exceptional, considering the darkness of her hair, but mostly she kept them hidden beneath heavy lids which gave an impression of sensuality. And her determination to overcome disability showed in the set of her mouth.

Since the onset of puberty she had become more prone to fits, though they were never serious and she had got used to the strange feeling which started in her leg and progressed through her body. Recognizing the symptoms

276

made it easier to cope with an attack, which often produced no more than a numbness and jerking in her limbs, and the nurses at the hospital knew exactly what to do. Sometimes she was seen by the physician, but as she had a sharper mind than many of the children who never had a day's illness it was decided that nothing need be done about it.

She was still in the doorway waiting for a cab to pass before she could cross St John's Square when a tall, clean-shaven young man approached. He wore a brown tweed sack coat, brown and white check trousers and a red neckcloth which even Anna knew to be countrified. His head was bare and he had straight brown hair which flopped on to his forehead. It was obvious he was looking for an address and he stopped to inquire.

'Excuse me,' he said. 'I'm looking for a milliner by the name of Mrs Cobham.'

'This is Mrs Cobham's,' said Anna. 'I work for her.'

The young man regarded her keenly and a slow smile of satisfaction and sheer joy transformed his face. 'Yes, of course you do. I should have known straight away. You're Anna, aren't you? Anna Beckett? Don't you remember me?'

Anna suffered a curious pounding in her temples, and strange shivers of recognition made her limbs incapable of movement. She knew his voice. She knew that very ordinary, but very lovable face.

'Edward?' She breathed the name nervously.

'Yes, it's me. I've been inquiring after you ever since I came to London.'

Had she still been a child she would have flung herself into his arms, but she was an adult now and had been taught that adults must be dignified at all times. And he was a grown man.

'Fancy you thinking of me,' she said.

He touched her cheek with gentle affection. 'I've never stopped thinking of you. When the inspector took you away it was the worst day of my life. We all loved you so much.'

Pleasure coloured her face a delicate pink, and to cover a completely new shyness she looked down at her feet. There was a joyous feeling flowing through her veins, a cramping of her stomach muscles, a tightness in her chest from holding her breath in case there was some mistake.

'How did you know where to look for me?'

'I asked at the Foundling. Cagey they were. Didn't want to tell me, but I wouldn't give up. I flattered one of the maids and she gave me the name of the milliner and said that's where you were.' He took her hands in both of his. 'I'd've knocked on every door rather than go back home without seeing you, that I would.'

'Oh, Edward.' She laughed with delight.

'Are you pleased to see me?'

'Of course I'm pleased.'

'You haven't really changed much. Only grown more pretty.'

'You haven't changed either.' She gripped his fingers as if afraid he might disappear again. 'Tell me about Ma and Pa. Are they all right?'

'They're as fit as fleas, and so are me brothers. They all said I was to give you their love if I found you.'

'Oh, Edward,' she said again. She didn't know how to express her excitement, and her eyes didn't leave his face. 'I've never forgotten you all, never for a minute. And seeing you again is just about the best thing that ever happened.'

'There's so much to say.'

'I know.' From the yard of Smith's Clock Manufactory came the sound of the hour striking. In a panic Anna gathered up the skirts of her dark blue dress which she had been allowed to make for herself before venturing into the outside world. 'Oh, my goodness, I can't stop. Mrs Cobham said I must only be ten minutes.'

'But I can't let you go so soon.'

She glanced up anxiously to see if Mrs Cobham was looking out of the window. 'Tomorrow I can have an hour off in the afternoon while Mrs Cobham visits the bank. Will you still be here?'

'I have to be back in Chertsey tomorrow night.'

'Then come to Mrs Cobham's shop at two o'clock. We can talk privately.' She wanted to reach up and plant a kiss on his cheek, but the shyness persisted and spontaneity had given way to self-conscious deliberation. 'Come to the door in the passage through to Ledbury Place.'

'I'll be there,' Edward promised.

She watched him walk away and couldn't believe he was real. She'd always dreamed of seeing Edward again, but the prospect of it ever happening had grown less and less likely over the years, perhaps because institution life was so insular it sometimes seemed as if there was no life outside the hospital walls.

It had been strange to find their faces almost on a level. The last time they had been together he'd been able to carry her. At the memory a strange heat affected the most personal part of her body, adding to the discomfort of the humid day, and she didn't understand the reason for it. All she knew was that it felt as if a miracle had happened.

Sarah Morey was informed that a young man from Chertsey had been asking to see Anna Beckett.

'Said 'is name was Edward Wooldridge, ma'am,' said the nurse. 'He wanted to know where she'd gone but we never told 'im.'

'You did right,' said Sarah. The girl was new, replacing one whom Sarah had dismissed a week previously for giving strong liquor to one of the boys. Punishment for breaking the rule forbidding it was immediate discharge and a ban from working in the hospital ever again. She smiled at the new girl. 'The children lead a sheltered life and it's our duty to see that they are protected at all times.'

'Yes, Mrs Morey.'

It was her day for checking the children's instruction and after talking with the nurse she went outside, intending to see the boys who worked a forcing pump which supplied the infirmary and the main building with water, but she changed her mind. The warmth of the June day was oppressive and the noise of the machinery would make her head ache. Instead she walked through the garden.

She'd thought the news had meant nothing to her, but she was wrong. It was a long time since she had thought about her old life in Chertsey, but the name Wooldridge had brought memories flooding back.

So Edward Wooldridge had not forgotten the little dark-haired waif his mother had looked after for five years. It surprised her when she considered how plain the child had been, and she couldn't understand what had appealed to the boy to make him anxious to renew her acquaintance. Admittedly she had never spared much thought for Anna in those days. The girl had been no more than a cover to give the impression that Sarah's interest had been in children generally rather than Corrie in particular.

Of late, though, Sarah had taken more interest in Anna Beckett. Her close links with Corrie from birth gave her a special place in her heart and she felt more responsible for her than for other girls. Anna had changed a great deal, both in looks and ways. She had a gentle nature but plenty of spirit still, and she coped courageously with her illness. And she was clever with her hands. There were times when Sarah looked at her guiltily, almost wishing that Anna had been

281

her daughter instead.

It was nearing lunch time and boys in a double row were doing drill exercises before going into the dining room, the tallest in front, shortest at the end. Some looked so young it seemed incongruous that they were already breeched and into coats and waistcoats. How quickly they grew and left babyhood behind.

Corrie had caused her much sadness. In the first five years after the child had rejected her there'd been little change in her attitude and it had tested Sarah's love for her cruelly. The almost fatal illness had left Corrie with delicate health and for some time she'd been frequently in the infirmary, but if Sarah had gone near her the condition had seemed to become worse.

'I don't want to see Mrs Morey,' she would say, hiding her head under the blanket. As she got older she would restrict herself to polite answers when Sarah asked after her.

It was hard to sustain a love which was continually spurned and many a night Sarah had lain awake wrestling with her conscience. It had been a great temptation to tell Corrie she was her mother, and if she'd thought it would help she might have risked doing so, but she knew instinctively it would have made matters worse. The cherubic infant with warm, affectionate ways had become a flighty child with few friends, and Sarah had looked in vain for reasons in herself to account for such a disposition. There'd seemed to be no way she could identify with her daughter. But perhaps disillusionment and the loneliness of her responsible position at the hospital had made her far too introspective.

Not only could she see no likeness to herself in Corrie, Sarah could see no likeness to James either, and that perhaps more than anything caused her disappointment. Even the golden hair had become darker.

The few days spent in James's house had proved to Sarah that the extraordinary attraction she had felt for him when they first met had not been a transitory thing. No man had ever come near to affecting her the way he did and she had long ago resigned herself to the truth that here was another love doomed to be unreturned. She hadn't seen or heard of James Halden since she had left Calvert Terrace. In the beginning she had fostered a hope that he might learn where she was and try to make contact, but weeks passed, months turned into years, and there had been no word.

Her greatest comfort now was that things had improved between herself and Corrie. Thankfully there had been an easing of the tension once childhood was behind her, and as Corrie grew stronger in body she also matured in outlook. Before she had started out on her apprenticeship six months ago Sarah had spent a precious hour with her alone in her office, and some of the misunderstandings between them had been aired. She went over it regularly in her mind.

'The family who've agreed to take you are very suitable, Corrie,' Sarah had said. 'I've made strict inquiries and you are to be apprenticed to the housekeeper.' Her only worry was that the house was too near Calvert Terrace, but that was something she had to keep to herself.

'Thank you, Mrs Morey.' Corrie had sat on the edge of the high-backed chair so that her feet could touch the ground, and her eyes were downcast. 'Before I go, I want to say I'm sorry I've always been so nasty to you.'

The apology was so surprising it had robbed Sarah of her usual caution.

'You mean a lot to me,' she'd said.

'I know, and I don't deserve it.' For a moment the girl had hunted for the right words. 'You see ... I idolized you. I thought you were so wonderful and you wouldn't let me be sent here. You promised me ...'

'Oh, Corrie.'

'It wouldn't have been so bad if you hadn't promised. I believed you, and then you let me down.'

For the first time Sarah had glimpsed her daughter's acute feeling of betrayal, and she had understood. But she'd had to make her own position clear.

'Didn't you know that my husband died at the same time as the inspector took you from the Gillings? I was ill myself for a while.'

'I know now,' Corrie had said.

The meeting had brought them closer together, but it hadn't fired Sarah with a renewal of the all-consuming love she had once borne for Corrie. It had kindled a feeling of friendship instead, and she had the sense to know that it was a much healthier emotion as long as their relationship was not known. She had at one time intended to tell Corrie who she was as soon as she reached an age to leave the hospital, but such a disclosure could only ruin the fragile basis of their new understanding.

Sarah carried on walking under one of the shady arcades which lined the front drive and the lawns. At thirty-three she was a very beautiful woman. The slenderness of her neck was emphasized by the way her hair was drawn away from it into a chignon which was covered by a spotless white cap. She was dressed in unadorned grey, the bell-shaped skirt of her gown just touching the ground, her arms covered with long, close sleeves. The simplicity of her clothes heightened her beauty at a time when frilled and flounced crinolines were all the rage.

For three years now she had been matron of the Foundling Hospital. Her work as a nurse had been exemplary, and on Mrs Grant's retirement there had been no one better qualified to fill the post. Sarah's love for the children, her dedication to their needs, and her exquisite sewing all contributed to the decision to appoint her. But more than that, through Nahum she had acquired a knowledge of keeping books, and as a late Governor he had provided her with an impeccable background, making her the only possible candidate. Perhaps also it had eased the minds of the other Governors seeing her promoted to a position more in keeping with her status.

As for Sarah, she devoted her time entirely to her job and rarely left the grounds. Her days were completely taken up with her duties, which had become her whole existence. She was in overall charge of all the children, the nurses and the mistresses, and was responsible for the conduct of her staff. The hospital food was also her responsibility, as were the linen, the bedding and clothes, and besides that she had to keep account of materials bought for work undertaken by the children. There was no longer much to tempt her outside the Foundling gates, but had there been she would have been hard pressed to find time for absence.

She strolled as far as the porter's lodge. The man who had given her the application form requesting Corrie's admittance had departed before Sarah came to the hospital, but had he still been there he would never have associated the pathetic girl in a tattered green dress with the poised woman who tapped on his door.

'Good morning, Mr Rooke,' she said, going inside.

The present porter, a burly man with excessively long side whiskers and clean-shaven chin, got up from the table at once. 'Good morning to you, Mrs Morey. What an unexpected pleasure.'

Sarah disliked his effusive manner. 'Mr Rooke, I believe you are only expected to let in gentleman visitors with specific business here, except for when there are services being held in the chapel.'

'That's right, ma'am. No one unsavoury gets past me.' He was very conscious of having been sworn in as a constable in order to do his job.

286

'Yet you allowed a young fellow access to the main building to ask after one of our girls.'

The porter scratched his balding dome thoughtfully. 'Would that be a Mr Wooldridge, ma'am? If so the young gentleman was very respectable. Nicely spoken and a traveller from the country. I thought him genuine.'

'Hmm,' said Sarah. 'Well as long as you considered him desirable I suppose there can have been no harm in it.'

'Thank you Mrs Morey. I reckon meself a good judge of character.' Mr Rooke smiled ingratiatingly before going on: 'Now there was a young ruffian 'ere yesterday who was asking for *you*, but the likes of him I'd never let inside the gate.'

Sarah raised her eyebrows in surprise, thinking that perhaps an ex-Foundling boy had come back, as sometimes happened.

'Did he say who he was?' she asked.

'Yes, ma'am. Said 'is name was Patrick Byrne and I was to tell you 'is ma's not well, but it didn't seem the sort of message to bother you with.'

She left a few minutes later, hoping the man hadn't seen that the message bothered her very much. Even more than the news that Edward Wooldridge had called.

It was the first time Patrick had tried to get in touch with Sarah, though for years he had known where he could reach her.

'I'll tell *you* where I'm going, Patrick, but no one else must know, not even your mother,'

Sarah had said, when she had waited for him outside the charity school one afternoon. 'She'd tell your father, and if there's one person I'm afraid of it's Abel Wood.'

He hadn't been old enough then to know why his pa frightened Sarah so much, but he'd known it was serious and he never again wanted to see her as scared as she'd been that day when the bloke with yellow hair had taken her off. So he'd told no one.

Ma had created at first when Sarah disappeared. She'd used words to describe her which always earned him a cuff round the ears every time he used them himself.

'Run off with that bloody doctor, would she!' Ma had stormed. 'Well good luck to 'er, but she won't be welcome in this 'ouse again.'

He'd known it wasn't true that she'd gone off with a doctor, but he hadn't enlightened Ma. Best leave well alone. What Sarah did was her own business, and if she was happier shutting herself away with a load of kids what nobody wanted then he had to keep her secret. But he'd missed her. It'd caused a pain in his belly for weeks and he'd moped around like a stray dog wishing she would come back.

But now Ma wasn't well. She'd developed a cough that wouldn't go away and sometimes she would spit blood. He knew what that meant. The lung sickness. Pa said there was nought wrong with her, but Patrick was worried and he'd decided it was time to tell Sarah.

The old cove at the gate of the Foundling had looked down his nose at him good and proper, but he didn't care. A labourer could never pass for a toff, and he dressed for his job as an odd-man at Covent Garden market. His coat and trousers had been torn on rough wooden boxes, sweat stained his neckcloth, and his hard round hat had been flattened out of shape by carrying baskets on top of it, but there was no sense in spending good money on new togs.

He got good commission as an odd-man. Sometimes he could make as much as two quid in a week if he was lucky enough to get paid twice over for the parcels he carried, once by the tradesman whose flowers he was delivering, and again by whoever received them. He'd no compunction about accepting double the money. By rights he ought to have had a little put by for the days when he didn't earn anything, but having struck up a friendship with some of the Seven Dials Irish he spent more than he should on liquor. He'd have to watch his drinking habits though if he wanted to keep the ticket which allowed him to ply for work in the market. There'd been a complaint already that he'd arrived drunk at a customer's house.

Patrick had become a very good-looking young man. He had inherited a fine head of black curly hair from his father, and his eyes which were as blue as his half-sister's always held a roguish twinkle. His shoulders were broad, his muscles strong from hard manual work, and his height and strength meant he could easily sweep the girls off their feet, which he often did. But girls, like liquor, cost money, so he never rose above his impecunious state.

He was walking back through Rosoman Street after his visit to the Foundling, and he had reached the boundary wall of the House of Detention when two youths of about his own age stopped him.

'Would I be right in thinking you're Paddy Byrne?' asked one. The movement of his small mouth and sharp nose was rat-like, and he had a distinctly Irish accent.

'That's me name,' Patrick said.

'We've been told you have sympathies for the cause,' said the second youth, who was better looking and had an even more pronounced brogue. 'Would that be right now?'

'What cause would that be, and who's been talking about me?' Patrick asked. He had always been a good mimic and he found himself imitating the accent.

'There's only one cause worth fightin' for, boy-o. Ireland. Freedom for the Irish! Have you not been taught that from yer father's knee?'

'Me real father's dead, but he was loyal to the last, so I'm told.'

'We heard that too,' said the second youth, whose name Patrick later learned was Tam O'Mara.

Ratty's name was Shaun Connell. 'Yer father played 'is fiddle at meetings on the Green, did 'e not?'

'That he did.'

The two youths slapped him on the back and started walking along with him. 'If you're interested, Paddy, there's a meetin' at the Bull's Head next week.'

'What sort of meeting?'

Shaun looked up and then down the street. Tam glanced at the high walls of the prison.

'Can we trust you?'

'Best ask the Seven Dials Irish,' said Patrick, miffed at their secretive air and lack of confidence in him. He'd been thick with the Irish labourers ever since he'd started working at the market.

'It was them who put us on to you,' said Shaun.

'Then yer know you can trust me.'

Tam put a conspiratorial finger to his nose. Shaun again looked up and down the street, and they waited until a pair of women had waddled by.

'It's the Fenians,' Tam told him. 'They're starting up a band locally. Why don't you come along?'

'I might just do that,' said Patrick, grinning widely. He was proud of his Irish parentage and pleased that they wanted to include him. 'Would it be all right if I bring me father's fiddle?'

Tam and Shaun both roared with laughter.

'You'll be welcomed with open arms, Paddy me boy,' Tam promised. 'Providing yer can play it.' Then he put his mouth close to Patrick's ear. 'You do know it wasn't a musical band we was talking about, don't you, boy-o?'

He was angry at that, angry and embarrassed that they should take him for a fool. 'There's some music that can stir men to fight battles,' he said. 'As well me father knew.'

They parted company and Patrick headed

for home. He'd heard a bit about the Fenians recently. It was a secret brotherhood that had been started in America by a man who'd set his heart on an Irish republic, and word had it that Irish labourers and the like were flocking to take the oath of conspiracy. Now the movement was spreading to England, and it was no kid's game.

He pictured himself taking part in a militant uprising, and the thought sent his spirits soaring while his stomach started to knot up with a fearful excitement.

Edward Wooldridge was in St John's Square by half past one on the day following his meeting with Anna, half an hour early. He walked back and forth between St John's Gate and Jerusalem Passage pretending he had legitimate business there, and he looked so often at the church clock he witnessed its hands move. The cobblestones were hot beneath his feet and he found London far too crowded, dirty and noisy for enjoyment.

He'd spent a sleepless night at the lodging house in Holborn where he had been staying. Seeing Anna again had dispelled all the tiredness of his first visit to the city, and he couldn't get over how lovely she had become. Her skin was so delicate, pale as cherry blossom against a dark, moonlit sky, and her slender body looked as supple as the river reeds he gathered each autumn. He hadn't expected to find such a graceful creature. The Anna he remembered had been a boyish child, always playing pranks and getting herself so untidy Ma had pretended to despair. In those days he had loved her like a brother, and it was brotherly love he had carried all these years in his heart.

But what now? From the moment his eyes had met hers yesterday he had been captivated.

At a minute before two a woman with a bent body emerged from the passage to Ledbury Place and set off towards the Gate. Edward waited a little longer, more nervous than he had ever been, and when he saw Anna at the milliner's window his pulses began to race. He didn't know what he was going to say to her. His tongue felt trussed up like a chicken.

Anna, it seemed, had no such difficulties.

'I've been counting the minutes, Edward,' she said as she let him in. 'I kept telling myself I only dreamed I saw you yesterday, just in case you didn't come today. It would've been so awful.'

'I've been counting the minutes, too,' he admitted. The last thing he had expected was that he would feel awkward with Anna.

She showed him in to a small room overflowing with boxes of ribbons, laces, threads, silks, satins and a host of other things required for fashioning hats. They spilled from shelves which lined the walls and cupboards under the window, and on the narrow table where she had been working there was a half finished bonnet which even Edward's inexperienced eye could see was going to be a creation fit for royalty. Who would have thought she would develop such talent?

'Tell me why you came to London,' she said. 'And I want to hear all about Ma and the family. There's so much news to catch up on.'

'The farmer that Pa and I work for has started rearing cattle,' he told her. 'He's already got a small herd and wants to know the best way to market it. I've been finding out about sending cattle by railway, and whether it's worth renting a market stall regular.' He was on safe ground talking of things he knew about and he warmed to his subject. 'Did you know there's going to be a big new market at Smithfield? I've been to see the excavations and there must be hundreds of navvies shifting the earth.'

Anna laughed. 'Of course I know, silly. It's a stone's throw from here.'

'When it's built I reckon I might be coming to town often.'

'Then we could meet.'

'Every week if I could manage it.'

'Oh, yes.'

A current of emotion flowed between them. He saw Anna's breast rise and fall as she took quick, fluttering breaths, and he knew that, like him, she was disturbed by a sense of elation which couldn't be put into words.

'Do you live here?' he asked.

'I've got a room at the back. It isn't much.' She hesitated. Then: 'I'll show you.'

Anna lit a candle and carried it high as they left the workroom and went down a dark passageway draped with cobwebs which looked as thick as fur in the flickering light. She opened a door at the back of the house, and left it open when they went inside. The windowless room was so small there was space only for a bed and a chair.

'You sleep here?' Edward was horrified. The air was stale, it was unbearably hot, and it looked more like a prison cell. 'I can't bear to think of it.'

'It's my own,' she said. 'I don't have to share it with other girls.'

'But if you lived with us in the country you'd be able to open a window and look out on green fields.'

She pursed her mouth slightly. 'That privilege was taken away from me, if you remember, but they tell me I've had a better life at the Foundling Hospital than ever I would've had if my real mother had kept me. That's something I can never prove, but one thing I *do* know. Any woman who can give up a baby, for whatever reason, must be cruel and selfish.' She put the candle on the chair because her hands were shaking. 'When they took me away from your ma and shut me up in that great institution I felt as if I was being punished, but I never knew what I'd done to deserve it. I needed love, Edward.'

'I went on loving you. We all did.'

'Did you?' her voice was wistful, only half believing.

They fell silent, remembering so many things, and the eerie illumination cast deep shadows over them. The candle flame spluttered as a draught caught it.

He touched her face with the sensitivity of a

blind man, exploring every feature with great tenderness, and when he reached her chin he tipped it upwards so that her gaze was captured.

'I love you still,' he said. 'In fact never so much as I do at this minute.'

'Then hold me,' she whispered, 'because you've always meant more to me than anyone in the world.'

Edward's arms closed round her, and as her body moulded against his he didn't know how to contain the tumult of feeling she aroused. He'd had a few girls. There was one in Chertsey who hid in the barn to wait for him if he was slow in asking for favours, and another who hoped he would put a ring on her finger. But there had never been one like Anna Beckett.

He kissed her lips and found them sweeter than honey, but he didn't linger over them. He was afraid of frightening her.

'I want to take you back with me to Chertsey, Anna. Will you come? I can't leave you here.'

'I have to finish my apprenticeship.'

'But that might take years,' he protested.

'All the same, I have to stay. Each Easter Mrs Cobham has to give me a testimonial of good conduct to take to the hospital Governors.'

She rested her head against his chest and he smoothed her dark hair. He remembered how he had felt when the inspector had taken her away from him and knew that even as a boy of eleven his heartbreak had been of adult proportions. Anna had belonged to him. He knew now why he had never cared deeply about any of the girls he had bedded, and why this opportunity to come to London had filled him with more excitement than was natural. He'd been determined not to go back home without finding her, and anticipation had been as potent as parsnip wine. Even so, it had never been his intention to make the declaration which followed.

'I don't want you to be a milliner,' he said, kissing the top of her head. 'One day I want you to be my wife.'

Anna tensed in his arms and he felt her tremble, but he didn't know whether it was from joy or apprehension. He ought not to have been so forward. After all she was still very young. Slowly she raised her head and she made a little noise in her throat like a cat's purr. Then she flung her arms round his neck and almost strangled him.

'Oh, Edward! How *wonderful* that would be.'

He needn't have worried about frightening her. She pressed her mouth to his in a fervent kiss which took his breath away and made him fear for her sweet innocence. The old Anna still existed beneath the trappings of womanhood, as impetuous as ever and twice as lovable. He crushed her to him and had no more compunction about letting her know just how much he wanted her.

Neither of them heard footsteps down the passage. Mrs Cobham held on to the doorpost to straighten up, and what she saw caused her to scream in disbelief.

'Mercy! Is this the way you behave, Anna

Beckett, as soon as my back's turned. You trollop! Disgusting, wicked little trollop.'

Edward let go of Anna immediately and they sprang apart. 'Mrs Cobham, I can explain ...' Anna began.

'You'll explain to the Foundling Hospital Governors, miss. They'll have plenty to say about such behaviour.'

'But, Mrs Cobham ...'

She gave her no chance to get a word in. 'I shudder to think what would be happening if I hadn't come back to fetch my purse. Inviting a man to your room! It's disgraceful.'

Edward tried to come to Anna's defence. 'It isn't what you think, ma'am.'

'And how long has she known *you*, pray?' The woman's tone was so scathing it made him feel as small as one of the silverfish scurrying across the floorboards. 'Pack your things, girl, this minute, and get on back to the Foundling. I shall make my report, and I don't ever want to see you again.'

At that moment everything started happening. To his horror Edward saw Anna begin to shake in a most extraordinary way and he remembered how she had suffered from fits when anything had shocked her as a child. He hadn't given it a thought until now.

'Anna!' He cried her name in anguish but before he could do anything she had fallen to the floor with foam bubbling from her mouth. He accused Fanny Cobham. 'Now look what you've done.'

Mrs Cobham let go of the doorpost too

quickly. She tottered forward, caught her foot against Anna's prostrate figure, and grabbed at the chair with the candle on it to regain her balance. The candle toppled over. Straight away the flame licked at the bedcover and it caught alight.

There was only one thing to do. Edward took off his best coat, the one his mother had bought with a little money she had been saving to buy herself a new dress, and smothered the fire with it before it could take hold. After that he didn't know who to help first, his dear Anna or the woman with the bent spine who had caused all the trouble.

## CHAPTER 12

It was Wednesday, the day in the week when carriages belonging to the Foundling Hospital Governors waited in the spacious courtyard at the front while the committee sat to discuss applications for admission and various other items of business. This Wednesday they were longer than usual, leaving little time to spare for customary drinks in the Lamb Tavern nearby. The case of Anna Beckett had arisen.

Sarah sat beside Anna, knowing something of what she felt as they faced the row of elderly men sitting in judgement at the long table, but she seemed to be composed. Her spine was pressed against the back of the chair.

Her hands were loosely clasped on the apron covering her sapphire-coloured dress, and her feet in black boots and stockings were placed neatly together. Never for a moment did her clear blue eyes leave the face of the treasurer's clerk who was the spokesman.

'The charge against you is very serious, Anna,' he said. 'You were apprenticed in good faith with Mrs Cobham and would have received a gratuity, but I'm afraid that will no longer be paid as the lady cannot present you with a certificate of good conduct.' He had a full grey beard which hid his neckcloth, and his red waistcoat matched the florid colour of his cheeks. He looked at the papers in front of him. 'You entertained a young man in your room alone, I'm told, and Mrs Cobham was very upset to find you ... er ... in a compromising situation. Have you anything to say?'

'No, sir,' said Anna.

One of the Governors, an impeccably dressed man with a trim figure, glanced at his watch and yawned. 'The girl is sick,' he said. 'There's no point in asking her questions.'

His lack of sympathy made Sarah angry. And she was impatient with Anna for saying nothing in her own defence. There'd been some mitigating circumstances which should be taken into consideration and she felt obliged to speak, though her presence there was only to chaperon.

'Gentlemen, permit me to say that the young man in question had come from Chertsey to see Anna. As a child she had been fostered with his family, and I'm sure any show of affection Mrs Cobham witnessed was of a brotherly nature.'

'In her bedroom?' The clerk allowed time for the committee to digest the information, then questioned Anna again. 'Is this correct?'

'It is, sir,' Anna said. 'And I'm not sick. I had one of my strange turns.'

'Ah.'

A look passed between the assembled group of men which made Sarah's spirits sink. She'd hoped the matter of Anna's fits would not be discussed, but it seemed as if they were going to be very much a part of the case against her. When Edward Wooldridge had brought Anna back to the hospital in a hansom cab, still suffering from the after effects of her latest attack, Sarah had been as sad as if it had happened to Corrie. Without realizing it she had allowed her feelings for the girl to deepen considerably in the last few years.

'These strange turns of yours have been getting worse of late, have they not?' said the clerk. 'This last one actually put the lives of a great many people in danger. It caused a fire in fact.'

'I don't remember, sir.'

The magnificently carved antique table across the room had a glass above it, and reflected light from the window dazzled the girl sitting so straight and poised. At that moment there certainly seemed to be nothing wrong with her at all.

'Do you always lose your memory when you

suffer convulsions?' asked the oldest Governor, leaning forward.

'Briefly, sir.'

'A devilish business,' he murmured, and Sarah almost expected the old fool to cross himself.

The clerk cleared his throat. 'Gentlemen, this girl is an epileptic, and she should be with people who have experience of her type of illness. It is no longer wise to allow her to be in the company of normal people and I'm sure she will be happier in the care of nurses who will be sympathetic to the peculiar workings of her mind.'

'We agree,' said the well-dressed man.

'In that case I shall make arrangements for Anna Beckett to be taken to an asylum where she can be suitably cared for.'

Anna's eyes widened and she got up from the chair, her hands clenched into tight, angry fists.

'You can't send me to one of those places. I'm not a lunatic.'

'Please sit down again,' said the clerk.

'No, I won't. And I won't go to an asylum. You can't make me.' She made her protest loud and clear. Her back was rigid with defiance.

Sarah wanted to help her, to add her own protests to Anna's, but she didn't have the power to oppose these men. They were always fair, and they had made their judgement on the evidence presented to them.

Another Governor, his manner kinder, tried to give some reassurance. 'Child, if you were

302

left to your own devices and allowed to go out into the world alone it's certain you would be lured into gin-shops before many days. And from there the step to prostitution is easily taken. From what we've heard you are even now inclined to respond too readily to male attentions. Unsavoury men would soon play on your fragile state of mind, I assure you, so please think of it as a kindness that we are offering to have you cared for in a safe home.'

'No! It's cruel and you've no right to make me go anywhere like that.'

Sarah's heart ached for her. On one of the walls was a great religious painting, Will's interpretation of Christ showing a child as the emblem of Heaven, and she wanted to beg them to look at it and reconsider the fate to which they were condemning Anna. But her plea would have fallen on deaf ears, for in their eyes Anna was no longer a child.

The treasurer's clerk rang a handbell to summon a maidservant and the clang of brass against brass was painful to the ears. 'The final decision will be in the hands of a physician from the hospital in Hanwell, Anna,' he said. 'I asked him to be here at noon and if he is in agreement with us he will take you back with him.'

'No!' Anna screamed. 'I'm as sane as any of you and I won't be shut in a madhouse. I won't, I tell you.'

Suddenly she began to tear at the buttons on her apron and her face became contorted with ugly grimacing. She started to mutter incoherently, her limbs shaking without control, and when the men attempted to hold her it was almost impossible. Foam bubbled from her lips. She fought them, scratching and clawing like a wild thing, and had the strength of two her size.

'Mrs Morey, there's no time to lose. See if the doctor's arrived. If not fetch Dr Moore from the infirmary.'

Sarah Morey picked up her skirts and fled.

She left by the nearest entrance and ran round to the front of the building to save time, frightening a squirrel which darted up a tree. The August weather was still warm and she grew uncomfortably hot as she hurried. Anna had never been violent before. The sight of her struggling like a demon had made Sarah want to weep, but there'd been no time to indulge in emotions of her own. She had to get help as soon as possible.

To her relief a cab had just drawn up at the main entrance and a tall man in a curly-brimmed hat got out. Sarah ran to him while he was still paying the cabby.

'Excuse me, are you the physician from Hanwell?' she asked breathlessly.

The man turned round, replacing his wallet in an inner pocket of his coat. 'Yes, I'm Dr Halden,' he said.

Sarah's hands flew to her face in consternation. James became immobile. They stared at each other in disbelief for several precious seconds, and her legs shook. He took off his hat.

'Sarah?'

'You!' she gasped.

He had changed. Grown older. His hair was no longer so brightly golden. Now that it was turning grey it had become the colour of light sand silvered in the sun, but it was just as thick. His face was more gaunt, his nose more pronounced, and there were hollows beneath his cheekbones, yet the change suited him. His air of elegance made him very attractive and as his heavy-lidded hazel eyes held hers she felt as if she would never be able to breathe normally again.

With reluctance she remembered the urgency with which she had sought him.

'Will you come to the Court Room at once, please,' she said. 'Anna Beckett has become violent.'

James remembered the name. Anna Beckett was the child who, several years ago, had impressed him so much he had returned to Claybury's intent upon improving the lot of the mentally ill. He could even remember her vivid little face and the way she had danced to show him that she was not ill.

He rushed into the west wing with Sarah, not daring to spare a thought for their totally unexpected meeting. Side by side they hurried through the corridors to the Court Room, where he saw the girl lying unconscious on the floor. Two of the Governors were on their knees trying to revive her but they stood up when he came in.

'The girl is mad,' the treasurer's clerk declared. 'The sooner you can take her to

Hanwell the better, Dr Halden.'

'She has epilepsy,' said James.

'Which is a sickness of the mind.'

No one disputed it.

James picked her up in his strong arms and her head fell limply against his shoulder. 'She must have suffered a severe shock,' he said. 'Is there a quiet room where I can take her until she regains consciousness?'

'There are beds in the infirmary.'

'No,' said the clerk. 'She may be a danger to others there. We can't risk that.'

'A quiet room, please,' James repeated.

'She can lie in my room for a while,' said Sarah quickly. 'There'll be nothing to disturb her there.'

'Show me where it is.' Anna was stirring in his arms and he was alarmed by her pallor. He didn't want her regaining consciousness in the presence of these men who had obviously brought on the attack by telling her she was to be committed to an asylum.

Having received the Governors' consent Sarah said: 'Follow me.'

They went up a flight of stairs, and at a door labelled 'Matron' she selected a key from the bunch hanging from her belt and let them in. It was a pleasant room with turkey carpet to walk on and pictures on the walls to please the eye. The quilt, made of silk shapes pieced together, had been sewn by a gifted needlewoman and he urged her to remove it before he laid Anna down on the bed.

'I find it very sad, James, that anyone with the

306

falling sickness should be classed as a lunatic.'
Sarah was standing at his side. 'Anna is loving
and highly intelligent. I can't bear to think of her
spending the rest of her life among imbeciles.'

He removed Anna's mob cap and a cloud of
black, unruly hair spilt over the pillow. 'Perhaps
you'll be good enough to undo her apron and
loosen the neck of her dress.'

Her hands were as graceful as ever. He
watched her unbutton the V-shaped apron top,
then the top of the dress edge, and it brought
a constriction to his throat. She fetched a bowl
of water and he bathed Anna's face, but all the
while his thoughts were with Sarah.

Finally he murmured: 'Have you been here
all along?'

'For eleven years,' she said.

He had never seen her look more beautiful.
Life in these almost cloistered surroundings
agreed with her. It had given her an air of
serenity which kept her pale skin flawless, her
mouth tender, and a caring quality to all her
movements. But the reason for the sadness
he saw in her eyes must be more than her
present concern for the girl lying so still on
the bed. Surely their blue depths were clouded
with long-standing pain which made her extra
sensitive to suffering in any form.

He was not conceited enough to believe that
he might have been the cause of it.

'And you?' she asked, bringing a chair to the
bedside for him. 'What have *you* been doing?'
She looked down at her hands so that he
couldn't fully see her expression, but when she

307

went on there was censure in her tone. 'I once thought that you would try to find me when I left Calvert Terrace, but no doubt your wife poisoned your mind.'

James checked Anna's pulse rate, keeping his eye on the second hand of his pocket watch, but it was an effort to time the beats when his own pulses were throbbing.

Glancing sideways he met with the grey poplin of Sarah's gown and it became the background for pictured memories of the dreadful days following her flight from Abel Wood's evil gossip. Though he tried to suppress it there were times when it was impossible to forget what had happened in the alley off Turnmill Street ...

'What d'yer reckon?' asked Gabriel Smith that December night of 1855. Watched by a street doctor he supported James with strong hands beneath his armpits while a flat-faced young woman applied Arabian Family Ointment to the wound on his back. 'Is it 'ealing?'

The itinerant doctor surveyed the patient from a distance. His job was to sell his cures, not to administer them.

'He's doing well enough, but you can't expect miracles from the penny box. Now if you was to spend 'alf a crown I'd be pleased to provide you with an ointment which never fails.'

'You know I ain't got 'alf a crown. Me last penny paid for this and if 'e don't get better soon I'll be asking for parish relief.'

James groaned as a wad of material was

pressed against the wound. He knew the cloth wouldn't be clean but he was too weak to protest, and Gabriel was a good man who was doing his best to save him. The woman, he had discovered, was his mentally retarded daughter Dolly who never spoke, but whose short, stubby fingers had a healing touch all of their own.

'Who is 'e anyway?' asked the doctor.

'Dunno,' said Gabriel, 'but I reckon 'e's a clever cove. Cleverer than the likes of you.'

'How about a blood purifier to help?'

James opened his eyes and moistened his lips with his tongue. 'Keep it,' he murmured to the dapper little man who hadn't even bothered to remove his hat before entering the house. 'It's nothing but burnt sugar and sassafras.'

The street doctor closed his bag angrily. 'Too clever for 'is own good, I'd say. I'm not the usual crocus, y'know. Good 'ospital training I 'ad.'

After he'd gone Dolly smiled and dribbled as she eased James down again on to the straw mattress. When he'd first regained consciousness, almost drowned in the quantities of gin being forced down his throat, it had been a shock to find her ministering to his every need, but mercifully the alcohol had deadened his sensibility as well as the pain, and he'd got used to her being there day and night, gazing at him round-eyed with the devotion of a mongrel.

She made some soup from cabbage leaves and carrots, and she fed him as if he were a child. One strong arm was round his shoulders, pressing him against her full breasts, and she crooned to him in a tuneless voice which nevertheless conveyed the love she showered on him. The measure of his progress was that he could now support himself on one elbow while the hot liquid was spooned into his mouth, and in spite of the meagre diet he was very slowly gaining some strength. He swallowed the lot, though its flavour had nothing to recommend it. Without nourishment he would never leave this hovel alive, and the thought of dying here was so abhorrent he was exerting a willpower he hadn't known he possessed just to survive.

He was also aware that he owed poor Dolly more than he could ever repay.

'They call 'er Daft Dolly round 'ere,' said Gabriel. 'But she ain't so daft as they think. When you was brought in she washed yer wound and kept you warm like you was a baby. Instinct, I s'pose yer could call it.'

James didn't know what day it was, where he was, or how long he had been lying on the straw mattress spotted with mouse droppings, and he hadn't the energy to ask questions. Apparently he'd been robbed of his clothes and his money, and he was wearing a ragged shirt which smelled of yeast and flour, but he had no idea how he had come to be in such a place as this where rats gnawed at the floorboards, cockroaches were as numerous as ants, and the ceiling was as black as pitch. The single window had rags stuffed in it to hold the filthy glass in place, and it was impossible to see out.

He watched Dolly pad barefoot about the

place, always singing in her tuneless fashion, and he no longer saw her outward ugliness.

'What worries me,' Gabriel confided, 'is what'll 'appen to 'er when I'm gawn. I ain't young and me bones ache something chronic, but I can't go to me grave knowing Dolly'll be shoved into Bedlam.'

When James was well enough to leave, Gabriel found him some clothes and gave him the last coppers from an old tin box with which to pay for a cab to take him home.

Home. There was no loving wife to welcome him back, no shred of relief that he had returned almost from the dead, not a sign of sympathy for his weak state or any interest in how he came to be reduced to it.

'How dare you come back here,' Maud stormed. 'You look like a crossing sweeper, but that's only to be expected, I suppose. Mix with the uneducated and you'll end up like them.'

'Maud, I was almost killed.'

'Fighting, were you, over that slut you had the audacity to bring into my house? Well it serves you right if you got hurt. *I'm* hurt. How do you think I felt when you went off with that doxy? I have never been so humiliated in my life, and if you think you're coming crawling back here then think again because I won't have you in the house.'

Physically he was still very weak, but he had never lost his strength of mind and he refused to tolerate such outspokenness from his wife.

'Your coldness almost amounts to inhumanity,'

he said. 'You've obviously judged me by such rigid standards there's no room in your heart for an allowance that you could be wrong.' He was longing to soak in a tub of hot water and put on a set of clean clothes, but he had to get things straight with Maud. 'Firstly, if it's Sarah Morey you're referring to by such uncouth names, I haven't seen her since before the visit of your lying informant Abel Wood. Secondly, the house is mine, not yours, and if anyone leaves it will be you, Maud.'

Her vindictiveness fizzled out like a spent squib. 'You know I could never leave. Where would I go, and how would I face the humiliation?'

'I'm sure your father will be sympathetic if you repeat all the opinions of me you have just made so colourfully clear.'

'But I can't admit that my marriage has failed.'

It was not often he took the role of irate husband. It made life easier if he allowed her to express herself freely, but his ordeal had robbed him of patience.

'You've always found fault with me,' he said. 'Perhaps you'll be happier if we part. Tomorrow I'll have a word with John Bradford at the Doctors' Commons and see if he can advise how you may start divorce proceedings.'

'James!'

Every scrap of colour drained from Maud's face. Her shock at the suggestion registered like a death knell and he almost felt ashamed of resorting to such cruel tactics.

'Is that not what you want?' he asked.

'Oh, James, no. The terrible shame. No!'

'Then we must be more understanding of one another.'

She swallowed hard. 'You didn't find Mrs Morey, you say?' The question trembled out.

'No. I was set upon by thieves before I'd been out half an hour.'

'Oh dear.' She delicately helped him out of the shabby coat which was stained with tobacco juice and smelt of sweat. 'I'll get Nessie to heat some water for you. Later you can tell me exactly what happened.'

Her spirit was not broken, though. Just before he went upstairs she had the last word, bringing a smile to his lips. 'I do think you could have found some way of letting me know.'

Two days later he returned to Gabriel Smith's and gave him a sum of money which would make life easier for several weeks to come. He also gave him a letter to keep somewhere safe with instructions that James should be notified in the event of Gabriel's death so that he could personally make arrangements for the care of his daughter Dolly Smith.

Anna's eyelids were flickering and James knew it wouldn't be many minutes before she regained consciousness. He let her hand fall gently on to the bedcover, returned his watch to his pocket and stood up, anxious not to waste the precious few moments he would be alone with Sarah.

He moved her away from the bed and spoke in an undertone. 'You left without a word. Did you mean me to believe what Abel Wood had told my wife that day?'

Time had taken the sting out of what had once been a subject too delicate to discuss. In retrospect he realized he had partly blamed her for what had happened to him and a certain bitterness still lingered. If only she had stayed to set matters straight he would never have needed to go out searching the streets for her.

He had been shaken to find her here at the Foundling Hospital, and in a position of authority. For months after she had disappeared he'd glanced twice at every tall girl with dark hair he passed. He'd often gone through streets where she might be even though it took him out of his way, but there'd been no sign of her, and finally he had ceased to look. If she had still been in Clerkenwell their paths would surely have crossed sooner or later. When they didn't he presumed she must have returned to Chertsey, perhaps to marry the curate she had once mentioned warmly.

This was the last place he would have thought of looking for her, yet now it seemed the most obvious. Nahum Morey had been a Governor. Sarah had needed refuge. If only he'd had the sense to think of it before.

'Don't resurrect the past, James,' Sarah said. 'Whatever motives we had for doing what we did are long since forgotten and it's best they're left that way.' She moved with such grace. He remembered how it had irritated Maud that a girl of Sarah's class had an air of breeding. She asked: 'Are you still living in Calvert Terrace?'

'I reside at the hospital. As a medical officer it's required of me. My house is closed up.'

She looked at him in surprise. 'And what about your wife?'

'I took Maud to Egypt one summer,' he said. 'She'd set her heart on going because it was somewhere none of her friends had visited. Sadly she died there of typhoid so she was never able to make them envious.'

Her hand covered his in mute sympathy. He smiled in acknowledgement. That brief contact was a key which opened a floodgate, releasing feelings he had kept under tight rein for so long, and it took willpower to resist the temptation to respond. He had tried to convince himself she meant nothing to him, but all it had taken to reveal the true nature of things was a slight touch of the hand.

Anna Beckett uttered a small sound and Sarah quickly moved back to the bed. The girl's eyes opened slowly and she looked from James to Sarah and back again.

'It's all right, Anna.' Sarah smoothed the hair away from her temples. 'You're in my room and when you've had a little rest you'll feel better.'

James gave her water to drink, and a faint colour returned to her cheeks. He knew she wouldn't remember him, yet it was as if his presence eased away the fear she had suffered earlier.

Her mouth curved into a small smile. 'You won't let me go to a madhouse, will you?'

'Not a madhouse,' he promised. 'But I'm

going to take you to the hospital where I work so that I can look after you for a little while.'

He felt a great need to comfort her. Perhaps it was because her eyes were exactly the same shade of blue as Sarah's. Blue as delphiniums in a country garden.

His heart was weightier than the medical books he leafed through many a night in search of new treatment for afflictions of the mind. He had never returned to Miss Claybury's institution. Instead he had applied to work with John Conolly at Hanwell Asylum so that he could learn from that gentle, sympathetic physician who had spent all his working life trying to improve conditions for the insane. When the great man had died in March of last year James had become a senior medical officer, and in this capacity he had been asked by the Foundling Governors to approve Anna Beckett's admission to the hospital where mental illness was treated with compassion.

But he was strangely reluctant to comply with their wishes.

While James was away making final arrangements with the treasurer's clerk Sarah stayed with Anna Beckett and was moved to trail the backs of her fingers across the wan cheeks. Anna's blue dress, so carefully stitched, was crumpled and needed an iron, and her black hair fell unrestrained over her shoulders in a tangle of curls which would take ten minutes' brushing at least to tame. She touched that too, stirred by strong emotions.

316

'Don't be afraid, Anna. Hanwell won't be like a madhouse, not with Dr Halden there. It's just another hospital.'

Anna was sitting on the chair with her hands clasped in her lap, but her body was tense and there was bitterness in her expression.

'You must believe that I'm not mad,' she said.

'I know.'

Sarah knelt down and held the girl gently against her, feeling a great desire to weep. Anna allowed the embrace for a few seconds, then eased herself away.

'Yet you did very little to try and convince the Governors.'

The accusation caused Sarah further pain. 'You need help, Anna. The Governors were right. And with Dr Halden looking after you I know you'll be in good hands.'

'You know him?'

'Yes.' A quiverful of memories pierced her heart momentarily, and she couldn't elaborate. All she said was: 'He's a kind man.'

There was very little rapport between them. Anna wouldn't permit it. Her feelings were now well under control and she had an air of self-restraint which was like an invisible wall around her to keep out Sarah's sympathy. It was too late to try to break down that barrier.

'Please don't tell Edward Wooldridge where I'm going.'

'But he'll want to know.'

'I'd rather he didn't,' Anna said.

'Then what must I say? He seemed to care

about you very much when you were brought back here from Mrs Cobham's.'

'He'll soon forget me again. And I don't need him. I don't need anyone.'

The girl was too self-contained. It wasn't good for her to keep her emotions so concealed, but Sarah's compassion quickened as she recognized the pride and fear of further pain which made Anna trust no one but herself. In her youth Sarah had reacted similarly. She wished there was some way she could give support to Anna who was setting out into forbidding territory.

James returned, and Sarah was filled anew with amazement that he had come back into her life. The change in him had at first seemed purely due to the aging process, but seeing him with Anna had shown her that it went much deeper. His concern for the girl was genuine. His kindness made her tragedy more bearable, and Sarah could tell that he was dedicated to his work.

She'd touched his hand when he had told her that Maud was dead, but not with condolence. The loss of his wife might have saddened him but there wouldn't have been any great pain, and her passing must have released him from a lifestyle which hadn't suited him, since he had closed up the house. For the first time she felt closer to his world, and it was that which had prompted her to show understanding.

Her own feelings about Maud's death would have to be examined later. She was not sure yet if she wanted to extend this new beginning with James. Nor was she confident that he would want to pursue a strange relationship which caused turmoil whenever their lives touched briefly.

He went straight to Anna. 'There's a cab waiting outside.' He bent over and smiled to give her confidence. 'I'm going to carry you downstairs and we'll be on our way.'

'I can walk,' Anna said. But she swayed when she stood up, and James swept her into his arms.

An extraordinary panic affected Sarah. For many months after her father's death a terrible smell of burning had stayed in her imagination. Now, for the first time in years, she was tormented by it again, and her skin seemed to shrivel with the never-forgotten horror. The reason for it was the sight of James carrying Anna. For one moment it was as if she had been taken back in time and was watching herself being carried from Smith's Manufactory in those same strong arms, and the sense of repetition was so strong she had to stifle a cry.

It was all nonsense, of course. Jealousy perhaps. Waves of emotion she had thought long since buried were now surging through her body like a river in spate, and as she followed the tall man and the girl downstairs her surroundings faded into a mist. The man and the girl were all that mattered. She felt linked to them by a thread of fate which pulled and tugged to draw them together. If it had been Corrie in his arms she would have understood, but it was Anna Beckett he was taking away.

A small group had gathered by the steps to

see Anna leave. As the cabby flicked the reins and the horse headed down the drive, emptiness engulfed Sarah, and for the first time since she had been at the Foundling Hospital she broke down and wept in front of them all.

## CHAPTER 13

Maggie was nothing but skin and bone. In the eleven years since Sarah had seen her she had become an old woman, and the house in Corporation Lane was hardly fit to live in. Nor was there a welcoming smile when Maggie saw who it was standing on her doorstep.

'Look who the devil's brought!' she exclaimed, wiping her hands on an apron already hardened with grease and dirt. Her hair was grey and her face was hollowed and sallow. 'Who asked you to come?'

'Patrick left a message for me,' Sarah said. 'He thought I should know you've not been well. Thank goodness he did. Sounds like you've not been eating enough so I've brought you some food.'

'I don't want yer charity. And how did Paddy know what hole yer'd hidden yerself in?'

'Can I come in?'

'Suit yerself.'

Sarah had to steel herself to walk down the passage to the kitchen where Abel Wood had once tried to rape her. The stench was indescribable. From the damp and filth everywhere she guessed the closet must have been overflowing for months, and she fought down sickness, for she had never seen anything worse even in the alleys. A rat ambled among the garbage, the walls were the colour of bleached soot, bed ticking hung at the window, and a string of clothes which showed no improvement from washing stretched across the fireplace. Her eyes streamed with tears, partly from the acrid smell, but mostly with grief that Maggie had been reduced to this.

'How could you let things get this bad?'

Maggie shrugged her thin shoulders. 'I 'ave to go out charring to keep us. I ain't got strength to do nothing else.'

'But what about Abel? Doesn't he give you any money?'

'He's always too drunk to earn any.'

'You mean he doesn't make jewellery any more?'

'He ain't never here. The pub's 'is home.'

'Then what about the boys? Don't they help you?'

'John's learning to be a watchmaker, and I ain't seen Dick since 'e went awf to work on a barge. Paddy only sees what 'e wants to see, and that's mostly girls, drink and 'is Irish friends. Reckon 'e thinks 'e's got more important things to spend 'is money on.'

Sarah still held the basket of food. There was nowhere to put it down. She was so shocked she wanted to run from the house as she had done once before and never come back, but

Maggie's plight filled her with too much pity. She couldn't possibly leave until something had been done.

Abel's chair was now a sagging wreck with the springs protruding, but there was nowhere else to sit so she covered it with her shawl and gently pressed Maggie into it.

'I'm going to start cleaning up,' she said. 'While I'm doing it you can eat a pasty and some peas. If I'd known what to expect I would've brought soup.'

'You don't 'ave to do nothing,' Maggie protested. 'You ain't come near me all these years so I don't want yer 'elp now. I can manage on me own.'

Guilt at her neglect added to Sarah's depression and she didn't know how to make amends, other than to set about doing things to improve her stepmother's lot. The thought of wading into such filth was so distasteful she felt like vomiting, but it had to be done. She took off her gloves and her round velour hat with the ostrich plume, and rolled up her sleeves.

'Yer'll ruin that la-di-da dress,' Maggie warned.

'Then I'll take it off.' Sarah unbuttoned the grey gown she always wore and stepped out of it, deciding to risk Abel Wood coming in rather than return to the Foundling Hospital looking as if she had fallen in the Fleet Ditch.

The old-fashioned houses in the Lane had been built for better-class tenants. This one now looked like it belonged in the St Giles slums. She began by clearing the grate and setting fire to all the rubbish she could, making space on the floor ready to swill down. Somehow she managed to shut her mind to the offending sights and smells, and after an hour there were signs of improvement. Worst of all was the closet. It had been unblocked, but it took several buckets of water to remove the surface grime and she began to ache from holding her breath to avoid inhaling the stench.

Eating made Maggie cough, and once she had started the hacking sound went on and on, but at least she wasn't coughing up blood.

'And how long have you had that terrible cough? You must see a physician.'

'How can I see a physician when I ain't got a penny to me name?'

'You could go to a hospital.'

'Never!' Maggie found strength to raise her voice. 'I ain't going to die in no hospital and be buried in a pauper's grave. I'll die at home.'

'You're not going to die,' Sarah told her. 'I shall come every Sunday afternoon and bring you enough food to last the week. What you need is building up. And you're not going out charring till you're stronger. I'll give you whatever money you would've earned, as long as you don't tell Abel.'

'I can't take your money.'

'Why not? I've nothing better to do with it.'

Rubbish she couldn't burn she took outside. She finished cleaning the floor and gathered up washing to put in her basket, deciding anything that would stand laundry treatment she would take to be washed properly. The rest she would dispose of as soon as possible.

Maggie watched nervously. 'What am I going to say to Abel? He'll want to know what's 'appened.'

'Tell him you felt better and did it yourself,' said Sarah. 'Now I'm going to make us some tea.'

Sarah's spirits revived a little as she brewed the tea and searched for decent cups from which to drink it. She had watched her mother die from the lung sickness, but her limited knowledge of the disease made her hopeful that starvation was more likely at the root of Maggie's trouble. What she needed was good food and some good clean air. If she'd had the money she would have paid for Maggie to visit Margate, which was where sickly children from the Foundling Hospital were sent to take advantage of the sea baths, but though she saved a little from her wages now that she was earning more, Sarah certainly didn't have enough for that.

All at once Maggie came out with a quite illogical question. 'Is 'e good to you then?' She was beginning to look slightly better already.

Sarah raised her eyebrows in surprise. 'Is who good to me?'

'James Halden. Him you ran off with all those years ago.'

'I haven't set eyes on James Halden until this week. Whatever made you think such a ridiculous thing?'

'His wife told me. Seems you both disappeared together.'

'James disappeared? And you saw Maud Halden?'

'Don't gawp like the idiot you are. She came 'ere looking for 'im.'

'Good gracious!' Sarah was stunned.

She'd convinced herself of James's insincerity when he'd failed to track her down after Abel Wood's visit to his house. Like a fool she had expected him to reject Maud's account of it, then not stop looking until he found her. For weeks she had waited for some sign that he knew where she was, and understood. But there'd been nothing, so she'd resigned herself to thinking he must have shrugged his shoulders, then resumed his routine. Instead he had gone away without telling anyone. It was unbelievable, yet apparently true. Certainly Maud must have been very worried indeed to have come here.

'When was it Maud Halden came?'

'More'n a week after you left. The poor woman was in a right state, I can tell yer. I can see 'er now.'

'And she had no idea where James had gone?'

'None. 'Cept she was sure it was with you, and I was forced to think the same.' Maggie began to cough again. When she could get her breath she asked: 'Where was yer then if yer wasn't with 'im? Are you married?'

'No,' said Sarah. 'I'm a nurse.' She answered absent-mindedly, her thoughts still on the mystery of James's strange disappearance. He'd said nothing.

'A nurse in an 'ospital? But that's no more'n skivvying.'

'I look after children.'

The truth quickly dawned on Maggie. 'You mean at the bloody Foundling!'

'Yes,' Sarah said. 'I live at the Foundling Hospital.'

'And what good 'as it done yer?'

'I've been able to see Angel grow up.'

The stillness in the room closed in on them, and where Sarah had scrubbed the floor a fungal smell rose up from the rotting timber.

'Has it made you happy?' Maggie asked.

Sarah remembered the long hours she had spent with her stepmother before Corrie was born, and how close they had become. All at once she longed for that closeness now. She needed someone to tell about her disappointment in the child she had idolized, and only Maggie knew of that secret relationship.

'Happy? No. I suppose I expected too much.' She paused, then confided something which she hadn't consciously admitted even to herself. 'Lately I've no feeling that she's mine.'

She talked about Corrie's illness and her stubborn refusal to forgive what she saw as Sarah's betrayal. The pain of the last eleven years poured out, and Maggie listened. Then Maggie talked. Over the next hour so many confidences were exchanged the walls must have buzzed with them, and the bond between the two was renewed.

Just before Sarah left, Maggie said: 'I ain't worried about Abel's boys. John's sensible and

clever with 'is 'ands, and Dick don't need me.'
She put her fingers to her temples as if to press
away worries. 'It's Patrick I'm bothered about.
He's too much like Paddy Byrne.'

'He always did look like my father.'

'It ain't the looks that matter. He thinks like
the Irish, and 'e's getting mixed up with the
wrong company. There'll be trouble before long,
I can feel it coming. Big trouble.'

'Perhaps you're imagining too much,' Sarah
said.

'Perhaps *you* could speak to 'im,' said Maggie.
'He always listened to you.'

To ease Maggie's mind she said that she
would, but in the next few weeks her own life
became too complicated for her to remember
the half promise.

The following Saturday Sarah received a letter
from James.

'My dear Sarah,' she read. The paper trembled
in her hands. 'I thought you would like to know
personally that Anna Beckett has settled here
fairly well and has had no recurrence of the
epileptic attacks so far. I am keeping her
under observation and trying to establish the
seriousness of her condition. Having seen how
concerned you are for her welfare I venture to
suggest that a visit to Anna might be helpful
to both of you. If you would like to accept
my invitation I shall be happy to escort you to
Hanwell on Wednesday of next week. Please let
me know if it will be convenient. Yours sincerely,
James Halden.'

She read the formal missive twice. The first time she could only absorb the pleasure it gave her to have a penned message from him, and it wasn't until she read it through again that she understood he was making a valid excuse for them to meet. The knowledge caused a surge of girlish excitement to course through her body. James was a widower now, free to pay attention to any woman he chose, and there was no reason why she shouldn't write to say she would be pleased to accept.

She had spent an unusually long time in her room poring over her letter, and when she went back on duty there was a string of domestic problems.

'Mrs Morey, there's no more thread to mend the girls' stockings.'

'Jane Pilcher was sick again, Mrs Morey. You said you wanted to know if she was.'

'Mrs Morey, please can you come and see William Bone. He says his voice is too croaky to sing solo any more. Reckon it's breaking.'

She dealt with each minor crisis efficiently, but every now and then her hand strayed to her pocket where the letter nestled. It was still in her pocket when she made her way to the chapel next evening.

The main gates were open and a stream of elegantly dressed visitors passed through them, some on foot, others in vehicles, all pleased to be seen in prestigious company. Through a window Sarah recognized the aging figure of Charles Dickens as he stepped down from a carriage. She had once gone to hear him give a public reading and had been fascinated by the enormous talent of the man who could make his audience laugh one minute and tremble the next at his tales. Such applause there'd been. He rented a seat in the chapel but rarely came any more, and it was sad to see him looking so old.

She went through a small vestibule where memorials to past benefactors buried in the chapel gave a feeling of melancholy. Nahum could have been given that honour if she'd been able to afford a handsome fee. A passage at the far end led to the chapel entrance where a Governor was sitting to receive the usual donations, and here she saw a young man on his own who had obviously never attended a service before. He was being given directions to the eastern gallery. Sarah frowned. His fresh face and plain clothes gave him a countrified air, and something about him revived a memory, but he was swept along with the crowd before she had a chance to place him.

Sarah took her seat among the staff. Today more people than ever were gathered here. A well-known preacher had been engaged to give the sermon, but though he had attracted the public Sarah found him dull and she couldn't concentrate.

The letter from James crackled in her pocket and she longed to read it once more just to bring him closer. What a fool she was. Since seeing him again she was caught up in a web of emotions too complicated to analyse, and Maggie's disclosure that he had left home mysteriously at the time she herself had entered the Foundling Hospital was very intriguing. She pictured him as he had been then, and as he was now. The attraction had increased if anything, and she had only to imagine those heavy-lidded eyes fixed on her to be passionately stirred.

Frighteningly stirred. There was something about the sensuality of James's eyes which had disturbed her greatly the other day, not because they had contained any deep message, but because of their similarity to another pair of eyes seen frequently enough over the years. Sarah pushed away a recurrent niggling fear which was making her lose sleep, but to which she would not put a name.

After the service she walked from the chapel with Teresa Thorpe, the only nurse who had been at the hospital longer than Sarah.

'A young fellow in the east gallery's been looking at you like he ought to know you,' Teresa said. 'Bold as brass he was. Didn't you notice?'

Sarah shook her head. 'I'd things on my mind.'

They had only gone a few more steps when she heard her name called, and she turned to see the fresh-faced young man who had made her pause earlier.

'Mrs Morey?' he said. 'It is Mrs Morey, isn't it?'

'Yes indeed.'

'Can I talk to you, please? I don't suppose you remember me. I'm Edward Wooldridge from Chertsey.'

Sarah's breath caught in her throat. 'Of course,' she murmured. 'I'll walk with you to the gate.'

Amidst the throng of departing people she felt alone with him, drawn to his unhappiness which she could sense immediately. When Anna had spoken of him Sarah had only remembered his name, but now she recognized the boy she'd seen with Peg Wooldridge in the past. She knew why he was here, yet what was she to say to him when Anna had expressly asked that he should not be told where she was going?

'I shouldn't've come,' he said. 'I'll be in fine trouble for taking time off, but I've got to know about Anna. Is she still here? I'd hoped to see her.'

'Anna had to go away,' Sarah said. 'She was ill, as you know.'

'It was all that stupid old woman's fault ...'

'It was no one's fault. Anna has had fits since she was a child and they'd been getting worse. She needs to be looked after properly.'

Edward's face became pale and he stopped, clutching Sarah's arms to make her turn and look at him. 'You've *shut* her away!'

'It was for her own good.'

'No!' He was hurting her in his distress and passers-by paused to make sure there was no trouble. After a moment the powerful grip eased, but he was still angry. 'If you've sent her to a madhouse I swear I'll go and tear the walls down.'

This was a very earnest young man who would not be fobbed off with half truths. Sarah liked his open face in which she could see a resemblance to his mother, and she wanted to be fair to him. He'd risked much to seek out the girl who had shared a part of his childhood and he deserved honesty.

'She's not in a madhouse,' Sarah assured him. 'She's in another hospital having treatment.'

'Which one?'

'Anna asked me not to say. I have to respect her wishes.'

He drew the back of his hand across his eyes as if to wipe away the implication of Anna's request, and Sarah's pity increased. She'd thought they had met by chance, but anyone could see Edward Wooldridge cared very deeply about the girl, and she suspected he must have sought her out as soon as he was able to get to London. Mrs Cobham had said she'd found them in a compromising situation, and there had been an outcry. Kissing, she had declared. She had seen them kissing in Anna's bedroom! Now Sarah wondered how much it had meant.

'I'll find her anyway,' Edward said. 'I must.'

He strode off, shoulders hunched, hands now embedded in his pockets. After a moment's hesitation Sarah felt compelled to follow.

'Edward, I've had a letter from her physician,' she called, hurrying, but unable to catch him up. 'Anna's happy.'

He didn't stop. He went weaving among the brightly coloured crinolines which tipped and swayed along the drive, and was lost from view.

Abel Wood was on his way home just as the sun was about to set. His pockets were empty but his belly made a noise like a full wineskin with every staggering step he took, and his knuckles were raw from hammering on the door of the Finsbury Dispensary on the corner of Woodbridge Street.

'Bloody people,' he swore. 'Thought you were supposed to 'elp the poor. I ain't well, I tell yer.'

'Ain't nothing wrong with you 'cept too much liquor,' scoffed a passer-by. 'And it ain't no good expecting the dispensary to open its doors of a Sunday evening.'

'Get on home to yer missus,' said another.

'Lotta good she does me,' Abel shouted. He swore some more, then informed the world at large that Maggie was a slut who never did nothing but cough.

He reeled half across the street, almost under the wheels of a newfangled boneshaker being ridden by a bloke with no thought for the safety of folk walking.

'Tom o' Bedlam!' Abel bellowed, shaking a fist at the offender. Many more expletives followed, each one coarser than the last.

By the time he'd negotiated Woodbridge Street his thirst had returned and he aimed for the Bell at the junction of Corporation Lane and Plumber Place. There were not so many people around as there had been in St John's Street where he had already patronized the Nag's Head and the Red Lion. Outside the latter he had boarded an omnibus to follow a woman he'd vaguely fancied, but her screams had ensured he was forcibly removed before the vehicle set off once more. At the White Hart in Aylesbury Street he'd fallen foul of a gang of thieves who had easily relieved him of his last penny, but by now he had forgotten that he didn't have the means to buy another drink.

He lurched past several of his cronies who were lounging against the pub wall, deaf to their familiar insults, and fell on to a settle just inside the door. Long shadows made patterns on the sawdust-covered floor which he saw as pointing fingers and he was feeling maudlin as he leaned his head back against the warm wood. He closed his eyes, and it was then he heard Patrick's voice behind him.

'In Manchester it were,' Patrick was saying. Abel turned and saw a group of men reflected in the window, huddled together with their drinks as though they had conspiracy on their minds. 'I read about it. Kelly and Deasy were being taken from a police court to the gaol and the Fenians stopped the van.'

'I'm after tellin' you I was there,' said a man with an Irish brogue. 'Armed we were. We tried to break the door of the van but it was locked from inside so the boy-o next to me fired a shot through the keyhole. Killed a policeman it did.'

Their heads drew even closer together, but their voices still carried in the way that urgent whispering sometimes does to an ear that is tuned to the sound. Abel struggled against the effects of alcohol which dulled his brain, sensing that he ought to pay full attention to what was going on.

'So you got the door open,' Patrick breathed. His handsome young face was eager, alight with a strange keenness to know more of some distant trouble.

'A woman prisoner got the keys out of the officer's pocket and handed them to us.' The man had his back to the window so Abel couldn't see what he looked like. 'It's dangerous me telling you this, but I want you to know we're doing something positive.'

'Where did you take the prisoners to then?' asked another Irishman.

'Now that I'll not be telling you. It's bad enough that five Fenians are being put on trial for the murder of the policeman, and it's lucky I am I'm not one of them.'

Abel closed his eyes and tried harder to concentrate while a discussion went on as to whether or not the five would be given the death sentence. He'd had suspicions about Patrick's activities but had never been able to accuse him of anything. Now he had evidence.

Ever since he'd been lumbered with Patrick Byrne he had hated his guts, but especially after the affair with Sarah Morey when Maggie had dared to protect the boy. Lately he'd been out of the way, sometimes for days on end, but he still called Abel's house his home and ranted on about Maggie needing a doctor. Impudent lout. Well, now Abel knew what bad company he was keeping he would have a weapon to threaten him with if he looked like getting too big for his boots, and he reckoned there was a chance he might soon be able to get rid of him for good.

James arrived in a private carriage on Wednesday afternoon to escort Sarah to Hanwell. Her small hat with the ostrich plume was set at the correct angle above her forehead, and she had arranged her hair so that two long curls hung down her back from a high bun, a style so different from her usual one it caused looks of surprise. Her hands were encased in immaculate gloves, and she wore elastic-sided boots with heels which gave her an added feeling of dignity. No one would have believed that her confidence had never been at a lower ebb.

The treasurer's clerk had welcomed her request to visit Anna Beckett.

'It's very good of you, Mrs Morey, to wish to see for yourself how the girl is settling,' he'd said. 'Foundling children never cease to be our responsibility if they are unable to fend for themselves. Mercy Draper was a case in point. She had the voice of an angel but became sadly deranged and was cared for at the charity's expense for more than forty years. I hope for Anna's sake such measures will not be necessary this time.'

'I'll report to you as soon as I'm back, sir,' Sarah had assured him.

Now the time had come to accompany James she was absurdly nervous, but her manner was cool and she gave no sign of the agitation

336

just below the surface. He stepped down from the carriage, a gig which had served him admirably for many years, and a boy took the horse's reins.

'Good afternoon, Mrs Morey.'

'Good afternoon, Dr Halden.'

With equal coolness he handed her into the vehicle. To anyone watching they were no more than acquaintances, but even through her glove she was aware that the merest touch of his strong hands could still bring weakness to her limbs. He wore a beige cutaway coat with a matching single-breasted waistcoat which was now the fashion, and a brown derby hat tilted at a rakish angle. His hair was longer than it had been a decade ago and in the sun there was still a brightness to it which was made more noticeable against his soft white collar.

They bowled down the drive at a reasonable pace, passing the Coram statue at the main gate, turned left into Guilford Street and straight across Gray's Inn Road into Lower Calthorpe Street. James drove past the North British School, the police station and Vernon Chapel, then carried on past the Union Tavern. Sarah knew very little of London beyond the confines of Clerkenwell, but she sensed that this was a strange route to be taking to Hanwell which she understood to be somewhere to the west of Hampstead.

'It's a fine afternoon for a long drive, James,' she said, opening a parasol to shade her face from the sun. 'Are we leaving town by St John's Street and Islington?'

He had to wait for a cab and several other vehicles to pass before he could cross Amwell Street, and the horse snorted with impatience.

'We're not going as far as St John's Street,' James said while they were waiting.

Sarah frowned. Something was not quite right. Her heart began to beat unpleasantly fast and it was more than the shade from the parasol which turned her chilly. She glanced at him quickly, saw a smile curving his lips, and in that moment knew instinctively that the letter he had sent her had been deliberately misleading. Without doubt James Halden intended terminating their journey at Calvert Terrace.

He flicked the horse with his whip and they crossed into River Street which in turn led to Myddelton Square.

'Stop this minute, James,' Sarah ordered. But of course he took no notice. 'James, I don't trust you. Unless you can assure me this is the way to Hanwell I should like to return to the Foundling Hospital.'

'There's no need to go to Hanwell,' James said. 'I've already told you that Anna Beckett has settled well. You can take my word for it.'

'I believed you when you wrote inviting to take me to see her, but you lied. How can I believe anything else you say?'

Sarah's irritation was expressed loudly, but it was not responsible for the tumultuous feelings in her body which years of dedication to children had almost made her forget. There'd been no man in her life since Nahum's death, and no man other than James had been able to arouse her physically just by his presence. She was acutely aware of details which affected her heartbeats. The hair on the backs of his hands gleamed like threads of gold, freckles on his forehead were as pale as sycamore seeds, and she wanted to trace the fine lines at the corners of his eyes. Her anger increased, but became directed towards herself for letting James Halden upset her once more.

'You can believe that we have things to discuss,' he said. 'Unfinished business.'

'Anything you have to say can be discussed on the way to Hanwell.'

He slipped towards her on the seat as the carriage turned sharply into Myddelton Square. His arm pressed against hers and in pulling on the reins his muscles tightened. Sarah sat rigidly, trying to ignore the signals imparted in that contact which James allowed to exist long after the corner was negotiated.

'I prefer to talk to you in private, where I can give my mind to your answers. What we have to say is so important I want to give it my full attention, and I can't do that if I have to control a horse in traffic.'

'I don't want to go to your home, James.'

'I'm sorry but that's where we're going.'

He drove round to the back of Calvert Terrace, unhitched the carriage and stabled the horse while Sarah fumed.

'There's no need for all this. I shan't be here more than a few minutes.'

'You won't be expected back at the Foundling until this evening.'

'Then my time will be better spent visiting my stepmother who's ill.'

James threw some fresh hay into the stable and fastened the lower half of the door. 'I employ a groom cum odd-job man to see to things when I'm not here. He's Nessie Whittaker's brother Fergal, but like Nessie he's never around when he's needed.'

'You're not listening to me, James.' Sarah was exasperated.

'Not yet,' he said easily. He put a hand beneath her elbow and guided her to the rear entrance of the house. There he paused and turned her to face him. 'We have several hours to call our own, Sarah. Don't you think we should enjoy them? We've had little enough time together.'

She couldn't put up any more resistance. When those hazel eyes rested on her with such candour she lost the will to object.

The house seemed empty. Sarah looked around anxiously, almost expecting to hear Maud's high voice calling from the parlour to know who it was James had brought home. Empty, yet Maud's presence was everywhere. A thousand and one knick-knacks still filled every surface not covered by a dust sheet. Pictures cluttered the walls.

'I keep meaning to get rid of a lot of these things,' James said, following her eyes.

'It would be easier to keep clean,' said Sarah, declining his offer to take her hat and gloves.

'Please sit down.' He jerked the embroidered

340

bell pull beside the fireplace. 'I'll get Nessie to bring us some tea.'

She avoided Maud's favourite chaise longue and seated herself in a spoon-back chair covered in Berlin woolwork, spreading her skirt decorously. What now? James appeared to be perfectly composed, but the atmosphere was charged with rising tension. He stimulated her senses until it was impossible to be alone in a room with him and not shiver inwardly.

'There's always been a strong bond between us,' he reminded her. 'I had hoped it made us truthful with each other.'

'Yes,' she agreed.

'So if I ask you a direct question I can expect an honest answer.' She looked away. He tilted her chin to regain her attention. 'Answer me this, Sarah. Did Abel Wood speak the truth when he told Maud you gave birth to my child after our time together? I've got to know.'

'Why do you have to know? You were not interested in finding out after Abel spread the story. No doubt all that mattered was hiding from your wife's temper.'

'Don't fence with me.'

'Where did you go then when she assumed you and I had run away together? Yes, I heard about that from Maggie.'

James took off his coat and waistcoat, then turned his back on her.

'Put your hand beneath my right shoulder blade,' he said. She stood up slowly, mystified and hesitant. He repeated the instruction, and reluctantly she let her fingers trail over his shirt

341

where she could feel a ridge of flesh which could only be from a badly healed wound. When she recoiled he swung round again. 'So you think I didn't care enough to go looking for you!'

She swallowed down shock. 'What happened?'

'I scoured Clerkenwell. Unfortunately I met up with some ruffians and I had a knife stuck in my back.'

Sarah closed her eyes. 'Oh, no.' Such pain stabbed her it was as if she experienced that long-ago wounding herself. 'You could have died.'

'Then tell me if it was my punishment for having failed you.'

'You didn't deserve that.'

Before any more could be said Nessie came puffing up from the servants' room. The years hadn't been kind to the plain little housemaid. She had put on a lot of weight, perhaps because Maud was no longer around to discipline her and she was left to please herself too much. There was no one to see how much she ate and she had become lazy. If she recognized Sarah she showed no sign. She was far too agitated about another matter.

'Oh, sir, I didn't know you was coming 'ome,' she gasped.

'Do I have to inform you in advance?' James was curt with her. 'I pay you to have things in order whatever time I choose to come.'

'Yes, sir. It's just that ... Oh, sir ...'

'Well?'

Nessie wrung her hands and glanced anxiously at the window. 'I was expecting Fergal back with

342

a visitor,' she said. 'A girl ...'

'Is that so dreadful?' His irritation eased and he smiled to show she had no need to be so worried. 'I'm sure it won't interfere with you getting us some tea.'

'No, sir. I'll get it right away.' She scuttled to the door, then turned once more with tightly clasped hands. 'Oh, I 'ope you won't be cross. I done something awful ...'

With that she left, closing the door after her, and for a moment there was silence. The girl's anxiety had somehow lessened the tension between themselves, and when James looked at Sarah they both laughed.

'What do you suppose she's done?' Sarah said.

'Allowed Fergal to rent a room, do you think?'

'Perhaps she said he could borrow one for the afternoon.'

James's face clouded again. 'If so Fergal had best be careful. One afternoon's amusement can have far-reaching consequences.'

'Is that all it was for you, James? An afternoon's amusement?'

'You know it wasn't.' He clasped her shoulders and looked deeply into her eyes. 'I have my answer then. You did have my child.'

'Yes,' she said.

A fly buzzed in the draped net curtains. The grandfather clock chimed a quarter past the hour. James groaned.

'Why didn't you let me know? I would've helped you.'

'You'd left the country. I went to the hospital and asked for you twice.'

'You could have left a message for me to see you as soon as I got back.'

'No, I couldn't. The man who told me you were abroad was your wife's father.'

There was no answer to that, and he didn't try to find one. After an agonizing pause he took her in his arms and cradled her there.

'I'm sorry,' he murmured, his cheek against her hair. 'It must have been hell for you. Perhaps it's just as well the baby didn't live.'

The warmth of his body moulded against hers lulled her into relaxing her guard. The scent of him, the feel of his skin through the cambric shirt, the pressure of his hands at her waist, all created a luxurious response which made her temporarily forget there was anything beyond this moment. He was the source of every delight, and the strength she sought. For several seconds she surrendered to the purely sensual joy of James's embrace, but his last words slowly penetrated and the years of devotion to Corrie made it impossible to deny her existence completely.

She drew away, raising her eyes to his. 'How can you say that?' she cried. There was a break in her voice as she accused him. 'How can you even think it? Is that all that matters? You don't even want to know if you had a son or a daughter.'

He mistook her reaction for remembered grief and his expression became compassionate. 'My darling, it must have upset you to lose our child,

344

but the burden might have been intolerable. I know how much you would have loved it, and the sacrifices you would have made.'

She flounced away towards the window, unable to bear his condescension. Unable to bear the guilt he was inflicting on her.

'You sound so pompous,' she said.

'Sarah, please don't be angry.' He came up behind her. 'I'm not heartless. Tell me, did we have a son?'

'A daughter.'

'Then if she had lived I would've acknowledged her, and yes, I would have loved her. I've always wanted children.'

She put her hands to her eyes to stem tears, but she couldn't stop the trembling which began in her heart and affected all her body. The silence she had kept for so many years made it impossible to speak of Corrie, especially to James.

'There are things I wish I could tell you,' she said shakily. 'But it's too late now.'

'Too late for what? What else should I know?'

Sarah turned and buried her head against his shoulder, sobbing. Her hat slipped backwards so that it was held only by the elastic beneath her chin, and James stroked her hair. For several minutes neither spoke, but when the storm of weeping had passed he was urging her not to tantalize him with half truths.

'What was wrong with the child? Was she born dead?' he persisted. 'What haven't you told me?'

'She didn't die,' Sarah cried.

His expression hardened as he stared at her almost with disbelief. His deeper feelings he kept hidden. After a few stunned seconds he said: 'So you parted with her.'

'I had to.'

'Then do you know where she is?'

'She works in Myddelton Square, only a stone's throw from here.'

'Have you seen her?'

'Yes,' she murmured. 'Yes, I've seen her, but she doesn't know who I am.'

'What is she like? Damn you for keeping the knowledge from me.'

'Don't speak to me like that.' Sarah was devastated.

There was a commotion outside, a sound of vulgar laughter and voices which were too loud. James frowned at the intrusion and set her away from him so that he could look out of the window to see who caused it. What he saw outraged him, but perhaps he was in need of an excuse for a passionate outburst.

'My God!' he exclaimed. 'So that was what Nessie meant. She's given one of Maud's dresses to Fergal Whittaker's wench.'

Sarah too looked in the direction of the noise. A young couple were walking along Calvert Terrace, the girl clinging to the arm of a man at least ten years her senior and so dandified he would have no trouble attracting the attention of a certain type of female. For a moment Sarah was too busy looking at the dress to study the wearer, but when she did was almost paralysed with shock. The girl was Corrie Palmer.

'Dear Lord, help me!' she breathed. Her face became as white as the cumulus clouds gathering overhead.

If she hadn't known Corrie so well she would scarcely have recognized her. She was startlingly pretty in a coarse kind of way. Her minute waist emphasized the roundness of her breasts enclosed in the tight-fitting corsage of a scarlet dress with a steel-hooped petticoat beneath, and the excessively wide skirt swayed as she walked. The flounces at the hem lifted rhythmically like waves lapping, and it was certainly not the kind of gown worn by an apprenticed servant. She was into the second year of her apprenticeship with a family called Naresby, but she looked like a street woman.

The couple stopped outside the house. Corrie laughed again at something the young man said, dropped his arm and put pressure on the sides of her skirt, tipping up the front to reveal boots with high heels which were laced up the calves of her legs. The dress would have been in fashion at the start of the decade when skirts had been as wide at the front as at the back, but the shape was no longer being worn.

'We have a lot to say to each other, but first I must see Fergal doesn't bring that trollop into my house,' James stormed, and he strode towards the door.

Sarah shouted. 'James! Take care what you say.' She ran after him, immediately defensive in the face of an attack on her offspring. Her temper was rising. Her voice scorched him. 'You want to know what your child is like. Well you can see for yourself. *That*'s your daughter out there in Maud's dress.'

'What!' The word was explosive.

'Now if you'll excuse me I'm going back to the Foundling Hospital,' she said.

She shrugged away from James's angry attempt to restrain her, marched out of the room, through the front door, and past a startled Corrie with her ill-chosen beau.

Storm clouds were banking up over the city and the sun went in.

## CHAPTER 14

'Who *are* you?' James demanded furiously of the girl now sitting in the spoon-back chair.

His initial reaction had been to rush after Sarah, but then he would have lost the chance to capture this hoyden whom she had outrageously labelled as his. He'd nearly frightened Fergal Whittaker out of his wits when he'd made him bring the girl indoors. Whoever she was she bore no resemblance to the woman who had just left, and he could only think Sarah had been taking a subtle revenge when she made that ridiculous statement.

'My name's Corrie Palmer,' the girl said, biting her lip.

Now that she was in the house her manner

had changed and he could see that she was not so coarse as she had seemed. It was the unsuitable dress which gave the wrong impression, and her nervousness showed in the way she gathered the expensive material between her fingers. Fergal would have told her the house was always empty.

'It were my fault, sir,' Fergal said, a rush of words robbing him of his usual affability. 'I've been walking out with Corrie and I wanted to give 'er a present, but I didn't 'ave no money. Nessie said about there being all Mrs Halden's dresses upstairs what nobody wanted, and Corrie being about the same size she thought you wouldn't miss just one. I'm right sorry, sir.'

Maud had been small. This girl was small, and her prettiness relied mainly on her pert little nose, dimpled cheeks and fluttering eyes which she obviously believed could melt the stoniest heart. None of these features could be found in Sarah, and though he knew himself to be a fool he even compared them with his own. Nothing about Corrie Palmer matched up, except perhaps for the colour of her hair and his. So Sarah must have seen this common baggage and blurted out the piece of nonsense either as a strange joke, or to make him look a fool.

He was blisteringly angry. No one had ever tried to dupe him so cruelly, and Sarah's lie caused so much pain it set the scar on his back throbbing. Her provocation was doubly heartless because he had always longed for a child of his own, and it had contributed to the crumbling of his marriage to Maud when she had failed to produce one. Now Sarah had surely taunted him with a terrible falsehood.

Nevertheless, he was not prepared to let the matter rest without further investigation.

'Where do you come from?' he asked the girl, ignoring Fergal's repeated apologies. His tone was razor sharp.

'I'm an apprenticed servant at the Naresbys' in Myddelton Square, sir.'

'An apprentice?'

'Yes, sir. I come from the Foundling Hospital.'

James felt in need of a drink. His mouth was suddenly parched and he loosened the collar of his shirt. 'So you know Mrs Morey who just left.'

'Oh, yes, sir. But I won't tell anyone she was here.'

The hussy. Diffidence left her as she misconstrued the reason for his anger, seeing it as a cover for concern over Sarah's good name rather than a pother over a stolen dress. James had an urge to strike her, but recognized it as a defensive instinct. He feared the way things were adding up.

'How old are you?' he asked.

'Seventeen this month, sir.'

It was getting worse.

'And do you like Mrs Morey?'

This question appeared to make the girl uneasy. Her eyes dropped. 'Why are you asking me about Mrs Morey? I thought it was the dress I was in trouble over.'

Fergal butted in. 'Please, sir, I've said it were all my fault. Can't you let Corrie go and change into her own things and I'll give the dress back. It'll never 'appen again, I promise.'

'You can be sure there won't be a chance for it to,' said James.

His odd-job man continued to shuffle uncomfortably. James wished he could tell him to wait outside so that he could talk to the girl in private but such a move might be misinterpreted and leave him open to blackmail.

He gave her his attention. 'I'd like to know if Mrs Morey was good to you,' he said.

'Are you checking up on her?'

'Perhaps.'

A conspiratory look crossed Corrie's face and she leaned forward a little.

'Well,' she began. Her pretty mouth pursed, and a shadow crossed her brow as she cast her mind back. 'I used to think Mrs Morey was the most wonderful person in the world. I really did. She was married to parson in Chertsey and the woman who brought me up worked for her. She used to give me things, make me clothes and the like, and tell me stories.' For a moment she hesitated, and a little French clock on the table by her side ticked frivolously. 'Just before I came back to the Foundling she made me a promise that I could go and live with her and the Reverend Morey. She hadn't meant it, though. The inspector came and took me away.'

'And that upset you?'

'I reckon I've never trusted anyone since.' She cast a baleful look at Fergal Whittaker.

James scrutinized her and saw how she had once been spoilt by too much love. Disillusionment had been the outcome when she'd been deprived of it by the sound of things, and she had never forgiven Sarah. He felt as if every nerve in his body was raw and exposed.

He turned away, unable to look at her any longer.

'You'd better go,' he barked.

'Yes, sir,' she said with the utmost relief. 'And I'll bring the dress back as soon as I can.'

'Keep it.'

He strode from the room, blind to everything, even the subservient way in which Fergal Whittaker held the door for him. Upstairs he went to the bedroom Sarah had occupied during her brief stay, as if by standing in the spot where he had once looked upon her intimately he would be able to judge better what was truth and what was lies.

The facts given to him by the girl added up to a picture he decidedly didn't want to see. Seventeen this month, she had said. Any child born to Sarah as a result of their union would have been born towards the end of September 1850. It was September now. And if Sarah had been intent on getting Nahum Morey to agree to giving the child a home then she must have been particularly fond of her. She had spoilt her. Of course, it could be that Sarah had been emotionally reminded of the child she had lost and had tried to put another in her place.

Yes, that was it. Sarah had become so devoted

to Corrie Palmer that eventually fantasy had become fact in her mind.

But she had spoken forcefully. 'That's your daughter out there in Maud's dress,' she had said. The words had been flung at him as if they were indisputable.

He'd never understood how she could have given herself in marriage to a man like Nahum Morey, old enough to be her father and physically unattractive. Many a night after he'd first learnt of the marriage he had fumed over the waste, and sought reasons, but none had been apparent except for financial security. The appeal of Nahum Morey's involvement with the Foundling children had naturally never occurred to him.

The more he reasoned, the more incensed he became. No woman with an ounce of maternal love in her would abandon a child to the mercies of a charitable institution, not if she was quite capable of raising it herself. He refused to believe it of Sarah Morey.

He clenched his fists and beat them on the dressing table top. Dust flew. In the mirror he could imagine Sarah's reflection, and was ashamed of the fierce longing for her which heated his blood even more than his temper. Perhaps his desire had never been more than a carnal craving. She was the most desirable creature he had ever met.

He tested the idea that Sarah had willingly allowed their child to be taken from her, but he couldn't reconcile himself to it. It went against every memory of her. If she had been too ill to look after a baby there might have been some excuse, but he had seen her at the Bradfords only weeks after the birth he now knew for certain had taken place, and she had been in fine fettle then.

Another thought caused him further confusion. When Nahum Morey had died that should have been an end to Sarah's connection with the charity, but she had sought work there.

The evidence in favour of her having spoken the truth was overwhelming, yet still James refused to believe it, and he failed to understand himself. Surely he ought to have been overjoyed at being shown the child Sarah had borne him, but all he felt was an urgency to disclaim it. He didn't have the slightest sense of affinity with the girl in Maud's red dress.

He slammed out of the house a few minutes later, his mouth grim and the set of his shoulders witness to his determination not to be taken for a fool. In the minimum of time he harnessed his horse to the carriage, and set out just before the storm clouds settled above Calvert Terrace. The proof of the matter lay at the Foundling Hospital and he would get to the root of it within the hour.

He knew deep within his gut that this Corrie Palmer was not a child of his seed.

When Sarah left James's house she knew that as matron of the Foundling Hospital, and as a mother, it was her duty to visit the Naresbys to have a report on Corrie's behaviour, but she was too overwrought to do it. Nor could she return to Calvert Terrace and try to explain her own behaviour.

The shock of seeing Corrie so unexpectedly and in such a place had thrown her into a panic, coming on top of the frankness James had demanded. The words had been forced from her, and it should have been a relief finally to share the burden, but all she felt was a kind of horror that she had pointed out to James the child he had fathered. Having done it she was terrified of the effect it would have on him, and her flight had been an escape.

She was afraid to see them together.

She had worn her silence concerning her relationship to Corrie Palmer for so long it had become like an old, familiar garment, so the sudden exposure of her past made her feel stripped naked. Now that James knew of Corrie's existence she could expect him to descend on her in high fury. He would challenge her right to have kept the knowledge from him all these years, and she would have to get her answers ready. Her secret had always been her slave. It was about to become her master.

There had been a satisfactory testimony about Corrie from the Naresbys at Easter after her first year of apprenticeship. She was a good worker who responded well to instruction, and her conduct had been praised. It must be the undesirable influence of Fergal Whittaker that had changed her. He'd been going to take Corrie in the house, believing it to be unoccupied, and both had given the impression it was not the first time they'd gone there together. Sarah turned cold at the thought of what would have now been taking place if she and James had not been around.

When she reached Amwell Street the storm cloud released a deluge of rain. Her parasol would give no protection, and she didn't want to return to the hospital looking half-drowned when she was supposed to be visiting with Dr Halden. A cry of frustration escaped her. She couldn't go back yet. She didn't know how long it took to get to Hanwell but she guessed that the journey there and back might take an hour or two, plus a little time spent talking to Anna Beckett. If she returned to the Foundling so soon everyone would know that she hadn't been far, and there would be awkward questions.

The Clerkenwell Parochial Schools building was opposite and she ran across the road to take shelter in one of its doorways. Rain beat against the railings edging the pavement and coursed down the windows behind which boys and girls clothed by the charity were being taught to read and write. Patrick had gone to this school. If she had kept Corrie after her birth there might have been a place for her as well. How different things would have been.

James had loudly voiced his disapproval of mothers who abandoned their babies. He was going to be so angry with her, yet he knew nothing of extreme poverty and a woman's fear for her child's life. She'd been a fool to blurt out a fact which he would never understand.

Tears gathered in Sarah's eyes and mingled

with the raindrops as they ran down her face. She was alone, as she had always been, with no one to talk about the stupid thing she had just done. No one, except Maggie.

It wasn't fair to take her troubles to Maggie when she wasn't well, but Sarah was desperate. As soon as the rain eased she set off with unladylike haste along Amwell Street in the direction of Corporation Lane, dodging puddles and umbrellas. She took a short cut through Plumber Place and glanced at the Clerkenwell News office on the corner of Myddelton Street and Garnault Place to check the time. With a bit of luck Abel wouldn't be downstairs for an hour or two.

She had almost reached Maggie's house when she saw a young man leaving it, the most handsome young man imaginable. He was nearly as tall as James, had black curly hair to his collar, and a confident manner. He thrust his hands in his pockets and started to whistle as he swaggered in her direction, and Sarah's breath caught in her throat, for it was just as if she were watching her father coming towards her.

'Patrick,' she called.

It took a moment for him to recognize her but when he did a smile worth more than gold lit his face and he strode up to her with a lightness of step she remembered from his childhood.

'It's Sarah, begorrah!' he exclaimed, and swept her off her feet. 'I never thought to see you again.'

She feasted her eyes on him. 'I've stayed away

too long by the looks of things,' she said. 'I'd say you're too handsome for your own good. I'll bet you won't want to settle down with a wife just yet.'

'Women cost money, and I've more important things to do with it,' said Patrick.

'Well I hope you're spending some on your mother.'

His eyes dropped from hers and he refrained from a direct answer. 'I was glad you got me message.'

'Sounds like it's the first sensible thing you've done for her. Why couldn't you have sent for me sooner? And more important, why couldn't you have seen for yourself that she was starving? Shame on you, Patrick.'

'I wouldn't be after going in the house this afternoon. Abel ain't in the best of moods. It's meself that has a bad effect on 'im, I'm thinking.'

'How is he treating Maggie?'

'When he's had a bit to drink he beats her. When he's drunk he tells 'er how sorry he is. The man's after bein' in league with the divil, I shouldn't wonder.'

She noted the way he spoke and recalled Maggie's anxious remarks about Patrick's Irish friends. It seemed he admired them enough to imitate them, and there was danger in that, but he was old enough to live his life any way he chose. Guiltily Sarah remembered being asked to speak to him about them, but there'd been so much else on her mind.

'And you're in league with bad company too,

by the sound of it. Patrick Byrne, you're *not* Irish, so why are you trying to make people think you are?'

'I'm half Irish. Me father was Irish so that makes me want to take up the cause.'

'What cause?'

'The only one worth fightin' for. Freedom for the Irish,' declared Patrick, lifting his arm as if he was holding a banner, and Sarah could almost hear the inflammatory voice he was obviously copying, for surely he knew nothing of conditions in Ireland.

She shivered. 'Well, I'm more Irish than you since *both* my parents came from the emerald isle, but I've no great feelings on the matter, and I'd be happier if you didn't take it so seriously yourself.'

He tweaked her chin mischievously, and his smile would have melted an icicle. 'So me big sister's turned up again to tell me what I shouldn't be doing!' he teased. 'Don't worry, I can take good care of meself.'

'I hope so.'

'I make a habit of never taking anything for granted. I check everything I'm told, so I do.' He put an index finger to the side of his nose and tapped it knowingly. 'Things are not always what they might seem to be, you know. Mistakes are easily made.'

The words were like heat applied to a raw, exposed nerve. Sarah was instantly back with her own problems. With extraordinary clarity her recent apathy towards Corrie, her concern for Anna, her reluctance to see James and Corrie together, and her alarm at having made Corrie known to him, all came together and spun round like water being sucked down into a funnel. At the bottom of the funnel she could see Patrick's words written in big black letters. THINGS ARE NOT ALWAYS WHAT THEY MIGHT SEEM TO BE. NEVER TAKE ANYTHING FOR GRANTED.

She turned deathly pale. Thunder rumbled in the distance and the sky was growing dark again. Seventeen years ago she had accepted what she had seen with her eyes without question, but supposing things had not been as they had seemed then. She saw again the never forgotten picture of two women leaving the Foundling Hospital with babies in their arms, one plump and motherly, the other thin and prematurely white-haired with her child hidden in the folds of a patchwork blanket Sarah's mother had made. She had never checked that the baby in that patchwork wrapping was still Angel.

'What's the matter, sis?' Patrick was asking. His voice sounded miles away. He had hold of her arm as if afraid she might fall, and indeed she felt so weak she was glad of his support. 'You ain't going to be taken ill on me are yer? Sarah, what's up?'

Things swam back into focus. 'Can you lend me some money, Patrick?' she asked.

'Money? What I've got I'll be needin' to solve me problems. Is it important?'

'Yes, it's very important. You'd never believe the troubles *I've* got.' Poor Patrick. He was completely bewildered by her sudden strangeness

360

and she could see him wondering if she was right in her mind. She tried to explain. 'I've got to go to Chertsey tonight.'

'Not a minute ago you were going to see Ma.'

'But something you said made me change my mind. *Please*, Patrick. Help me for God's sake.' Seeing her desperation he reluctantly fished in his pocket and produced a handful of coins. She counted them and took what she thought would be enough for the train fare to Chertsey and a cab to get her to the station. 'I'll pay you back, I promise. And please don't say anything to anybody about this.'

As she hurried away, blind to his bewilderment and the curiosity of passers-by, she gave no more thought about what time she should return to the Foundling Hospital. All that mattered was that she should speak to Betty Gilling and Peg Wooldridge before James came with his questions.

On the day following his visit to the Foundling Chapel Edward Wooldridge was called to account for his absence.

'You're a great disappointment to me, Edward,' said Gower Blunt, the farmer he had worked for since he was old enough to be useful. 'I trusted you to do business for me in London, but one taste of the city wasn't enough for you, it seems. I'll not have you sneaking off at the busiest time of the year. Consider your privileges at an end.'

'There was a good reason for me going again,

Mr Blunt,' Edward said.

'Aye, a woman I don't doubt.'

'A very special one. I want to marry her.'

The farmer snorted. 'Quick work, weren't it?'

'I was hoping to come and see you about having a farm cottage, sir.'

A raucous laugh was the answer he got. 'What's wrong with sharing your father's cottage? There's room enough.' A ledger was open in front of him and he put a tick in the margin before counting out eleven shillings and seven pence. Edward's wages for a week's work. 'Think yourself lucky I'm not deducting anything. Until you've calmed down you'd better stay in the fields. All hands'll be needed anyway for harvesting and you're a good scytheman, I'll say that for you.'

Gower Blunt had never invested in a mechanical reaper. Each September he hired an Irish harvesting gang to help out, and mostly the same men returned year after year. They came with their womenfolk who did the raking and binding and stooking after the corn was laid. This year Edward was put in charge of four such men and they tackled the fields with scythes and bagging hooks, managing to cut two acres a day.

While Edward sweated with the effort of wielding his scythe from dawn till dusk his mind was continually on the problem of what to do about Anna. He knew that with a little ingenuity he would be able to find out which hospital she had been sent to, but until he had made some definite plans he didn't want to go in search of her.

Her illness was a fact he had to accept, and he wasn't afraid of it. He knew that if he could obtain her release from hospital he would be able to look after her himself, but to do that he must have a house where they could live on their own. Without one he would never be able to convince the authorities that he was able to provide for her. He would do anything just to have her with him and if it wasn't possible to bring her to the country then he would move to London.

The days passed, and he was haunted by the memory of Anna's collapse. It hadn't in any way detracted from his regard for her, but had made him love her more. Having seen her first apparently in fine health, so gentle and lovely, he knew that the fits were only temporary things. He was prepared to nurse her whenever they occurred, and somehow he felt sure she wouldn't be so troubled by them if she was happy.

He confided in his mother. 'You always loved her too, Ma. She's the sweetest girl you ever saw.'

'But she's epileptic, son,' Peg said. 'What happens when she 'as children? Have you thought of that?'

'We'll face that problem when we come to it. Now say you give us your blessing.'

Peg Wooldridge, fat and pink as the pig Isaac could now afford to keep in the yard, hugged her oldest son, but not to signal the approval he wished for.

'I know how you loved her when she was a child, Edward, and like as not you think you still do, but think carefully before you commit yourself.'

There was no different advice from his father. On an evening when rain dripped from the deep eaves of the cottage and drenched the tiny windows Edward and Isaac sat at the table supping ale, and Edward repeated Gower Blunt's statement that there was room for Anna to move in with the family.

'It ain't that we don't want you, Eddie, but what with the little 'uns still around and George with *his* new wife, this wouldn't be the best place to bring an invalid.' Isaac picked up his youngest child, the last of three more boys surprisingly born to Peg after Anna had been taken from them. 'Yer wages hardly pay for one to eat, never mind two. And you couldn't afford to pay a doctor's bills. No, son. Forget about the girl.'

Forgetting was easy for his father to say. For Edward it was an impossibility. He appreciated his parents' reasons for discouraging him, but nothing would change his mind. He was going to marry Anna and give her the chance to lead a normal life.

The next day he got soaked walking the three miles to the fields. His trousers, tied with whipcords beneath the knees, clung uncomfortably to his legs, and rain from his hair ran into his eyes. The hired Irishman new to the farm this year tagged along as they headed for the fields. His name was Tam O'Mara.

'There was I hankering for the great outdoors like I used to know in Ireland,' Tam said. He was younger than Edward, but had a worldly look about him. 'I'd forgotten what it's like when it's wet, so I had.'

'Is it better in London then?' Edward asked.

'Different. The best place in all the world is Donegal. That's where me heart is.' The fellow's green eyes clouded wistfully.

'So why did you leave it?'

'Why? Well now, it's after being one of the poorest places on earth, I'm thinking, and what's needed is a change in politics. I thought I could be more use to Ireland if I left it. Would you be knowing what I mean?'

Edward didn't know, but he nodded as if he did.

The weather improved after a couple of days and the gathering of the harvest was completed on time. Extra money was paid, more ale had been downed than at any other time of the year, more bread and cheese and onions eaten, and aching muscles were given a chance to relax. There only remained the harvest supper to round off the season, and by then Edward had struck up quite a friendship with Tam O'Mara.

Gower Blunt sat with his wife at the head of a long table in the barn behind the farmhouse for the supper. It had been decorated with sheaves of corn, and flags hung from the rafters. On the whole he treated his workers well as the farm was his own, and this year the highlight of the feast was a freshly boiled ham.

Tam's eyes roved over the girls who had been following in the wake of the threshers all week, but kept settling on Molly Tyler, the one who couldn't understand why lately it was so difficult to entice Edward into the hay.

'It's you she wants, boy-o,' Tam said. 'But would you be mindin' if I take her meself later seeing as you don't seem keen?'

'You'd be doing me a favour,' said Edward. 'There's only one girl I want and it looks like I'm going to have trouble getting her.'

The roguish green eyes of his companion were full of humour. 'Would it be lessons you're needin'?'

'There ain't nothing you can do that I can't,' laughed Edward. But his heart was heavy, and between mouthfuls of bread and boiled ham he told Tam a bit about Anna.

A fiddler had been hired and after supper there was dancing in the barn. For a while Tam O'Mara was missing, and when he came back he was full of smiles. Several minutes later Molly Tyler also reappeared and partnered one of the older men in a reel, but Edward saw her glance flick knowingly over the Irishman.

'Your loss was my gain, boy-o,' Tam said. He downed another tankard of ale as if it had been thirsty work, then became serious for a few moments. 'I've been thinkin'. I'm goin' back to work in the markets. You can earn good money if you put your mind to it. If you'd be after thinkin' it a good idea to move to the city for a while I'll give you my address in Clerkenwell.'

Clerkenwell. Edward remembered standing in St John's Square and how he had felt when he had seen Anna looking for him at the milliner's window. She wasn't there now, of course, but he would be in a better position to start making inquiries, and if he could earn more money he'd be able to save a little.

'That's good of you, Tam,' he said. 'Reckon I'll visit you right soon.'

'It's a bit crowded, mind, but one more won't make a bit of difference. And you'll get along fine with me friends.' The music started up again and Tam tapped his feet in time to it. 'One of them plays the fiddle so well it makes this one sound like a cat fight.'

Edward joined in the dancing, pleased with his luck in meeting up with someone so helpful, and his hopes were revived. In London he could make plans to get Anna out of hospital, and once they were married he would find himself another job in the country, perhaps with a cottage to go with it. He wouldn't be answerable to Gower Blunt any more.

The last time Sarah had been on the train to Chertsey it had been with Nahum a few hours after their wedding. She remembered it vividly because every clickety-clack of the wheels had been taking her nearer to Angel, and her anticipation had mounted with every passing mile. Now she was travelling the same route, but she was filled with dread as to the outcome of this present visit. It was the only way she would find out if she'd made an appalling mistake. Checking Foundling Hospital records was out of the question. The rules regarding access to private documents were so strict that no one other than a Governor had the right to see them, and she knew the crown jewels were hardly locked away more securely. Her only hope lay in talking to Betty Gilling, who must remember what had taken place that day she had gone to collect Angel.

She had started thinking of Corrie as Angel again. It was like giving her anonymity until it could be established for certain that she was who Sarah had always believed her to be. The hours since she had borrowed money from Patrick had been a nightmare and she would have no peace until she knew the truth. Her thoughts were in chaos. She couldn't credit that instinct wouldn't have warned her if she'd been devoting herself to the wrong girl, for surely no mother could feel such love for a child which was not her own.

The houses of London thinned out and gave way to fields. Cattle gazed in water meadows. Church spires pointed to Heaven in clear, smokeless air, and the cottages looked a picture even though Sarah knew they might leak and flood in heavy rain. The storm had been pushed northwards by a rising breeze. She looked at the sky which was already displaying evening tints, and briefly pictured the Foundling children at supper, but distance saved her from suffering any pangs about the furore her late arrival back would cause.

There was one very important thing which Sarah had been trying to shut out of her mind, but it couldn't be ignored much longer. She had to face the fact that if Corrie was not her daughter then someone else was, and that someone could only be Anna Beckett. There, it was admitted at last. Sarah felt awash with confused emotions.

She continued to look out of the window but the scenery blurred into a haze of memories which, in the light of these new possibilities, were as painful as anything she had previously endured. She'd seen nothing likeable in Anna as a child, but that was because she had never looked. She'd been obsessed with Corrie and her golden hair. Anna, she recalled now, had sat by her feet while Corrie had occupied her lap, and in those days there had been adoration in her eyes to which Sarah had failed to respond. Over the years she had been out of patience with Anna on many occasions, but on reflection it had usually been because her faults mirrored her own. And now, so recently, she had stood by while Anna had been condemned to life in a mental hospital.

Guilt gnawed at Sarah's soul.

She'd been blind all these years. Blind because she had seen only what she had wanted to see, and even her disappointment in Corrie hadn't been sufficient to remove the veil from her eyes. Now that she was daring to look at things clearly she saw glaring examples of Anna's likeness to herself, and yet they had never been apparent until this moment. Her height for one thing, and the colour of her hair and eyes for another, stood comparison, though their features were dissimilar. Anna's nose was too big for beauty and her upper lip was finely drawn. My God! In the window glass Sarah imagined a reflection of Anna Beckett and superimposed it on one of James. Nose and mouth were surely identical, added to which were the heavy lids shading both pairs of eyes. She had been blind, blind, blind!

At the London terminus the carriage had been full, but her travelling companions had dispersed at various stops along the way until there was now only a large, ruddy-faced woman with a loaded basket sitting opposite. Every now and then she would smile and nod as she tried to capture Sarah's attention, and at last she spoke.

'Excuse me for asking, but aren't you the widow of Reverend Morey what died ten years or so back?'

Sarah blinked with the effort to bring herself back to the present. 'Yes, I was married to the Reverend Morey,' she said.

'I haven't seen you since we lost 'im. It were a terrible time.'

'Yes, it was.'

'I were one of 'is congregation. Never missed a Sunday. Oh, 'is sermons were something, weren't they? I bet you misses 'im still.'

'Yes, of course,' said Sarah, who could scarcely remember what Nahum had looked like.

Once the woman had succeeded in getting into conversation there was no stopping her, and Sarah was obliged to listen.

'You'll be coming back to see 'is grave no doubt,' she went on.

'Yes.' Fresh guilt troubled Sarah, for the thought hadn't occurred to her, but if there was time she knew she ought to at least pay her respects to Nahum's remains in the churchyard. She changed the subject. 'I also want to visit a Mrs Betty Gilling who used to work for me.'

The woman threw up her hands. 'You'll not know then. Poor Betty Gilling died in the winter eighteen months since of pneumonia. A right sad do that were too ...'

A long, involved tale followed, most of which Sarah didn't hear. If Betty Gilling was dead everything now rested on what Peg Wooldridge would have to say, and she hadn't really wanted to call on Peg. Edward Wooldridge's interest in Anna made the family too personally involved, but having come all this way there was now no alternative but to make for their cottage.

'Where's yer luggage, dearie?' the woman asked when they arrived at Chertsey.

'It should be in the luggage compartment,' Sarah lied.

She lingered on the platform, hoping the busybody would be on her way, but she waited while Sarah was forced to make inquiries about a non-existent case. What a fool she'd been to come. She discovered that there was no late train back to London that night, she had very little change left from Patrick's money, and nowhere to stay. Once again she had acted on impulse, and once again she didn't know what would be the consequence.

'What a shame,' said the busybody. 'Can't trust people to do anything, can yer?'

'They say it'll arrive later.'

'Well then, no use waiting. Me ol' man's at the gate with the cart. It ain't much, but can we take you somewhere?'

Sarah sighed, too tired both mentally and physically to care much more what anybody thought. It had been a long, exhausting day.

'I'd be much obliged if he could take me to Isaac and Peg Wooldridge's cottage,' she said. 'Do you know it?'

'Why, bless you, yes. Along Bridge Street, and that's the way we're going.'

The slow journey in a cart with wheels which wobbled was made no easier by the incessant questions still coming at her like hailstones. How long had she known the Wooldridges, did she know Peg had three boys younger than George, and did she know George was married, and Billy was courting? Sarah's head was aching by the time they arrived at the cottage gate, and she was incredibly thankful to see the last of the woman.

The door stood open, and noise issuing from inside the cob and wattle walls was enough to burst the eardrums. The three boys born after George were obviously indulging in an energetic rough and tumble.

'Anyone there?' Sarah called when her knock went unheard.

A cheeky young face appeared, followed by another, and another. Then there was a lull

372

until all three boys started yelling for their ma to come. Sarah took hold of the door jamb, her aching head seemed to spin until she couldn't focus properly. Her legs felt weak and her mouth dry.

A few minutes later Peg Wooldridge came in from the garden, wiping her hands on her apron and shouting at her sons for not letting her finish gathering blackberries before dark. She bustled through the kitchen, just as Sarah Morey collapsed on her doorstep.

Edward missed Tam O'Mara when he'd gone back to London. The fellow was a rogue but a good-hearted one, and the offer to stay with him in Clerkenwell had been repeated before he'd left yesterday morning. Edward intended to take him up on it before too long.

With the harvesting done he was once more working with the herd, but the evening that Sarah came he escaped from the milking shed early before Molly Tyler had finished milking. The girl's foray with Tam had not diminished her ardour where Edward was concerned, and in dodging her he began to know how a mouse felt when it was stalked by a cat. Tam would have laughed and called him a coward, but his quest for Anna was becoming so important he wanted no more casual flings in the hay.

It was almost dark when he arrived home. He had his own method of entering the garden through a gap in the hedge after taking a short cut across fields, and his little brothers pounced on him before he reached the path.

'Ma's got a woman with 'er,' said the middle one.

'She just fell in a heap on the step,' said the youngest.

'Ain't none of us seen 'er before,' said the oldest. 'But Ma knew 'er.'

Edward was intrigued. He dropped the bundle which had contained his lunch time bread and cheese and walked towards the cottage, the boys following him excitedly.

'Scat!' he commanded, turning to shoo them away.

For a few minutes they played him up, but when Edward was serious he was no fun and they soon got tired of the game and went off. He had a premonition that it would be best not to let his presence be known too soon, so he loitered beside a riot of honeysuckle which almost covered the open kitchen window. The smell of it was so cloying it made him want to sneeze, but he stifled it and stayed undetected.

To his amazement he saw Sarah Morey sitting in Pa's chair. She looked very pale, but Ma had made her some tea and was asking if she felt better.

'Must have been the thundery weather got at you,' she said. 'I've never bin so surprised in me life as when I saw you there. Are you staying in Chertsey?'

'No.' Mrs Morey sipped the tea. 'I came on the train because there's something very important I've got to ask you.'

'Lawks, you do sound mysterious. Now what

374

would you be wanting with me after all these years?'

'It's about Anna Beckett.' She looked up at Ma, and Edward saw the strain in her eyes. His heart began to thud. 'I must know if she was wrapped in a patchwork blanket when you first saw her at the Foundling Hospital.'

Ma looked surprised. 'Now there's a thing!'

'Forgive me, I'm not in the least worried about the blanket, though my mother made it. What I *must* know is which baby was wrapped in it when you returned to Chertsey.'

'Why, Corrie Palmer was,' said Ma. Relief swept across Mrs Morey's face as she closed her eyes and let out a slow breath. But it was short-lived when Ma went on. 'Your mother made it, you say? Fancy that now. It were a pretty thing, I remember. Poor Betty Gilling really took a fancy to it. That's why I said she could have it and I took the other one.'

Mrs Morey spilt tea in her lap and Ma leaned forward quickly to take the cup from her before it got dropped and broken.

'I'm sorry ...'

'You're right upset. I can't think why such a thing should be bothering you after all this time, but if you want to tell me about it I'm here to listen and see if there's anything I can do.'

Edward loved his mother. She was the kindest woman he knew, and many a person had sat where Sarah Morey was now while she gave comfort and advice. But this was different. He found his fists were clenched with tension.

'One of those babies was mine,' Mrs Morey

whispered, almost too low for him to hear. 'I always believed it was Corrie ... because of the patchwork blanket ...'

'Oh, mercy ...' gasped Ma.

'Lately things have happened ... I had to come and see you.'

'You poor thing.'

'Please promise me no one else will hear of this. It's desperately important that no one else knows.'

'I'll not breathe a word to a soul. I swear on the Bible,' Ma promised. 'But what're you going to do now?'

Mrs Morey put her hands to her head, and tears rained down her face. 'Anna's my child, and I let them take her to the hospital in Hanwell. Oh, Anna, I never knew. Anna, forgive me,' she sobbed. 'I've got to make it up to her. I've got to go to her right away.'

Ma comforted the distraught woman, putting a motherly arm round the shaking shoulders. 'You'll not be going anywhere tonight,' she said. She was so wise. She knew all about how people felt. 'Besides, it would be wrong to go haring off to see Anna without considering her first. That poor girl can't stand shocks, so Edward says.'

'I'll be very careful.'

'And if you tell 'er you're her Ma, d'you think she'll be pleased?'

Mrs Morey looked stricken. 'I've no right to expect it, have I?'

'No, Mrs Morey, you haven't. Not knowing the ins and outs of it I can't judge, but I'd say you gave up the right to be anything to Anna

376

other than a friend, and that's the way it ought to be left.'

'But I want to look after her.'

'Reckon she's being looked after well enough.' Ma lit the lamp and it flickered until the flame settled. 'Did you ever let on to Corrie Palmer that you thought she was yours?'

'No, never.'

'Then why should you burden Anna with knowing? It'd make it awkward for everyone, yerself most of all.'

Edward crept away, his legs numb from crouching so long by the window, his thoughts in a whirl. The things he had just heard were so potent he reeled as if he'd taken too much ale, and he needed privacy to sort them out. Later on he would reach some decision about the way he felt at learning of Anna's parentage, but it was too soon yet. What mattered at the moment was that he had discovered, by the sheerest luck, where he could find her, and it was imperative that he should act at once before Sarah Morey could make things any worse. He had never particularly liked her, and now he must get away without her seeing him.

He waited until it was dark then he climbed the apple tree and swung himself over to the window of the bedroom he shared with Billy, the way he'd done when he was a boy. He had some money in a tin box under his bed which he stuffed in his pocket as soon as he had changed to his better trousers and jacket. Minutes later he left the way he had come.

At this hour he knew where to find George,

and he gave him a message to tell Ma where he was going. Then he set off at a brisk walk for the main road to the city.

His luck was still in when he reached the first coaching inn. A young dandy with a carriage and pair was easily engaged in conversation, and an hour later Edward was up beside him in the carriage bowling along towards London.

## CHAPTER 15

When James returned to Hanwell that night his anger and frustration were so severe he had no patience with anyone.

His visit to the Foundling Hospital earlier had yielded nothing.

'I'm very sorry, Dr Halden,' the treasurer's clerk had said. 'I have no authority to let anyone see our private records, not under any circumstances. The only people allowed access to them are Governors of this hospital.'

'I assure you it's very important,' James had insisted.

'Perhaps you can furnish me with the reason. I could bring the matter up at the next committee meeting.'

'But that would take time.' His personal reasons certainly couldn't be divulged.

'I'm sorry.' The man's courtesy had then bordered on rudeness. 'And forgive me but I understood from Mrs Morey that you were taking her to Hanwell Asylum this afternoon to see Anna Beckett. Did you not go?'

'I'm afraid there was a change of plans. Mrs Morey is returning here alone.'

He'd been expecting to catch up with her along the road so that they could talk as he drove her back in his carriage, but there'd been no sign of her. He'd been afraid her arrival on foot might be remarked upon, but her current disappearance had added fuel to his temper and he no longer cared for her reputation.

James had left without another word, and for the first time in his life he'd whipped his horse into a lather in his desire to put distance between himself and the bureaucracy which denied him the right to make certain if a child was his own. So great was his affront he forgot that if anyone had asked to be given access to his own records at Hanwell he would have been equally adamant in his refusal.

It was late when he arrived back on duty and he walked through the long galleries to his room, somewhat soothed by the quietness. It was partly due to his work here that screams and other inhuman sounds were no longer heard. He knew his opinions were often considered too advanced, but there was real kindness at work and cruelty was nonexistent, even though the attendants' duties were tiring, depressing and often downright repulsive.

The quietness, however, didn't last. No sooner had he closed his door than there was a knock on it, and a night attendant was asking him to see a new patient.

'Thank goodness ye're back, Dr Halden, sir. The bloke admitted yesterday's gone berserk. We've 'ad to shut 'im in the padded room.'

James's anger erupted. 'Can nobody do anything here without bothering me? I've had one hell of a day, and now you can't manage to calm a man down without sending for me.'

The woman had never heard him speak with such impatience. 'I'm sorry, sir. It's just he's real violent and we thought you might be able to give 'im something, but I'll go back and see what we can do.'

'No.' He was ashamed of himself. He lowered his voice and apologized. 'Of course I'll come. I'd no right to bring my own problems back here.'

The room in which violent patients were locked, for their own safety as well as for the safety of others, was padded with coconut fibre covered in ticking which was fastened to wooden frames fixed to the walls. The floor was covered with a thick mattress and there was no furniture, only a bolster and two pillows. A wire blind covered the windows, letting in air and light, but ensuring the glass was out of reach, and in this sad apartment James found a stricken creature who wouldn't allow anyone near. He was throwing himself against the walls like a demented gorilla, his eyes staring, his mouth lolling open, and it was plain to see why two women had found it impossible to restrain him.

'What brought this on?' James asked.

'It were this evening, sir,' said the second

attendant. 'He were in the garden talking to that pretty young girl, Anna Beckett, when another bloke tried to take 'er away. This one tried to strangle 'im and there was a bit of a fight until Dr Wilkin came and broke it up.'

'They were fighting over Anna Beckett?'

'Yes, sir. Then this bloke went mad, and Anna Beckett had one of 'er turns.'

James, already tense, felt his muscles tighten even more, and his stomach churned. The day had started with Anna Beckett and looked like ending with her. He had the strangest premonition that the girl was about to become a bigger issue than he had previously thought and he guiltily admitted that it served him right for having used her name to entice Sarah to his house.

With the help of the attendants he managed to administer a sedative to the lunatic, but his mind was now centred on Anna, and though he knew she would have received proper attention already he nevertheless went to her ward as soon as he could. His temper had subsided. In its place was an anxiety he couldn't explain, and he hoped very much that this attack of hers might not have been so severe as the last one.

She had been moved to a quiet room where she was resting on a special low bed with another mattress beside it on the floor as epileptics were known to fall out of bed in a fit. He discovered that she had lost consciousness for a brief period but hadn't become violent, and when he went in she smiled sleepily.

'I ought never to forgive you for making me

381

come here, Dr Halden. I hate it so much,' she said. 'But everyone says you know what's best for me and they're all very kind.'

He sat on the edge of her bed. 'Are you feeling better now?'

'I'm just tired.'

Her blue eyes were drowsy beneath heavy lids and her face was so pale the skin seemed almost translucent. He picked up her hand to test the rate of her pulse, and saw how long and sensitive her fingers were. How sad it was that a girl with such intelligence and creative ability should be afflicted with epilepsy. It pained him to accept that she was incurable.

'How old are you, Anna?' he asked. Some illnesses changed in seven-year cycles and hers had become worse at fourteen. Perhaps there was a chance of improvement when she reached twenty-one.

'I'm nearly seventeen, sir,' Anna told him.

James's heart gave a peculiar jolt. It was the second time today a girl had said those same words, and both were from the Foundling Hospital. He looked keenly at Anna Beckett, scrutinizing every feature as he checked her pulse by the second hand of his gold pocket watch.

Now if Sarah had pointed to this girl and said that she was his daughter he might not have rejected the notion so strongly. But she hadn't. Sarah had pointed a finger with absolute conviction at the girl in Maud's red dress.

'Why are you staring at me, Dr Halden?' Anna asked anxiously. 'Am I getting worse?'

'No, you're doing fine, Anna,' he reassured her, and placed her hand back on the bedcover. He'd had an urge to keep hold of it and to show her some affection but it wouldn't have been ethical. Nor sensible. Such behaviour would be misconstrued, and no one would believe his motive had been of a paternal nature. 'Tomorrow we'll start you on a different treatment. There's got to be something that will suppress these attacks.'

He had never felt such a desperate need to find a means of helping someone. Even when she'd been a child he had felt drawn to this girl. He liked her gentle ways and her courageous smile, and she deserved the very best treatment his knowledge could provide. Just looking at her made him ache with sorrow as deep as if she belonged to him.

What a fool he was. He had allowed Sarah's admission to give rise to preposterous ideas. A mother would never mistake the identity of her child, and there had been nothing in Sarah's manner when she had tended Anna at the Foundling Hospital to suggest that she held any special place in her heart.

Damn Sarah. She had played a wicked game with his emotions and not given him a chance to question her. She was responsible for the ludicrous fancies chasing through his mind, and he hurriedly banished them before his anger returned.

Murmuring goodnight to the girl lying so pale against the pillow, he left her and went to the library. Among the tomes that had been written about epilepsy surely there must be hope of some sort, a guiding light amidst the darkness surrounding the illness. Heaven knew he'd searched long enough, but he would search yet again. Lately John Hughlings Jackson, the neurologist, had been talking of its effect on nerve cells in the brain, and last year Sir Victor Horsley had successfully operated on a patient's brain to relieve focal seizures, but the prospect of Anna being subjected to such drastic measures was unthinkable. Besides her seizures originated from the lower limbs. He'd witnessed them symmetrically extended while the upper limbs were flexed, whereas with a focal beginning the contractions would be asymmetrical. Anna had classic symptoms of *grand mal* which he'd been treating with bromide but he decided to try suppressing her attacks with tincture of herbane to see if that would bring about an improvement.

His reading that night once again revealed little that was new in the way of treatment. But there was one paper which bothered him, nagging at something in the past which was just out of reach of his memory. In 1854 a man called Moreau had spent time investigating instances of epilepsy occurring in the same families, and he had come up with a great number. It hadn't been proved, of course, that the disease was hereditary, but certain links had been found. Anna's background was not known, yet James sat for a long time in that book-lined room, seeking a detail which might give insight to a reason for her debility.

384

The smell of so many old leather-bound volumes aggravated his nose. It was quite distinctive, once breathed never forgotten. Certain smells had that effect. It brought a prickling sensation to his scalp when he unexpectedly remembered the terrible stench of burning flesh and he drew up every muscle in an effort to reject it, but it persisted.

He'd got it. A singular connection was made which couldn't be overlooked, and it shook him. Sarah's father had died in the furnace at Smith's Manufactory. James had been called to attend the man himself, and as if it were yesterday he was able to recall the words of a witness.

' 'E fell, I tell you. One minute 'e had the pot in the tongs, then 'e went like 'e was in his cups, and toppled into the fire.'

Paddy Byrne had not been drinking that day. He had collapsed with some kind of fit.

For a while longer he stayed in the calming atmosphere of the library, feeling in need of quietness to consider this new development. Like Moreau's paper, it proved nothing, yet the disturbance it caused him was long lasting.

On his way back to his room he went to check on the condition of his patient with dementia, but the state of his own thoughts was still so disordered he began to wonder if he would soon be a candidate for the padded cell himself.

The treasurer's clerk had been affected by the anxious behaviour of Dr Halden. He was curious to know why it was so imperative that he should see the admittance records of Foundling children, yet be unwilling to divulge his reason. After James left he sat for a long time in his office puzzling over the matter.

The physician had obviously been under stress. Something had happened soon after he had set out with Mrs Morey, and whatever it was it had caused friction between them, else why would the lady be returning later and alone when he'd been coming back here himself? It presented an intriguing conundrum, one which he felt inclined to investigate, for when two people who were practically strangers seriously disagreed there had to be an exceptional motive.

Besides, he had always found Mrs Morey an enigmatic creature and he welcomed the opportunity to break through that reserve and discover what lay hidden. When he had first seen her he'd marvelled that Nahum Morey had won himself such a beautiful young wife, and he would have bet his last shilling that she wouldn't remain a widow for more than a year. But here she was, still married to her work and growing more lovely every day, yet with never a hint of association with any other man. Her behaviour was exemplary and no one could be more efficient, so there was no reason at all for him to look for faults, unless it was that she was *too* perfect.

Clearly the mystery concerned Anna Beckett in some way. Dr Halden had no interest in any other children in the hospital. His involvement with the case must have caused disagreement between himself and Mrs Morey, for she had cared enough about the girl to defend her when she had been brought before the Governors. No doubt she had also disagreed with the decision to send her to Hanwell, and it could be that she blamed the physician for taking her. Yes, that was where the friction lay.

All the same, it didn't account for Dr Halden's angry demands to look at records. It shouldn't have aroused his temper. If he'd wanted to check on Anna Beckett's background in order to treat her illness he could have asked respectfully, but his manner had been so overbearing it had provoked a negative response.

The clerk felt uncomfortable. Perhaps it would have benefited the girl to relax the rules for once. He twisted his hands together as if washing them, then tapped the knuckles of one against the palm of the other rhythmically, worried in case he had jeopardized Anna's health by being so rigid. He was no medical man but there would be no harm in taking a look at Anna's records. There might be something he could pass on to the physician by way of recompense.

He brought the record books from the safe. There were detailed accounts, of course, charting the progress of each Foundling child from the time it was returned to the hospital, but the book he turned to first was the list of admissions. He thumbed through until he came to the year 1850 and found the section on Anna Beckett under the twenty-fifth of October. As Nahum Morey had done several years before him, the clerk read the words written in sepia ink and saw the mother's name had been Sarah Byrne, and that, unencumbered, she had returned to work

387

for Mr and Mrs John Bradford in Newcastle Place.

At first it meant nothing to him. Certainly there was nothing which might be helpful to Dr Halden. There was no mention of the mother having any disease when she left the child, and she hadn't been a foreigner, though the name Byrne had a slightly Irish ring to it.

He had already closed the book and was searching for Anna's personal records when the name Bradford flashed across his mind again and set his memory working.

'Nahum Morey's sister was married to John Bradford,' he mused. 'And I'm damned if they didn't live in Newcastle Place.'

He stroked his chin above the edging of beard. Mrs Morey's name was Sarah. A tic in the side of his cheek started to work and he was so hot suddenly he had to get up and open the window, letting in a cool September breeze. It was incredible, but no one, neither himself nor any of the Governors, had ever questioned the woman's past before she had become the highly respected wife of Nahum Morey.

He got up and paced the floor a few times, unable to face the evidence which might convict Mrs Morey of unforgivable duplicity. No, he just refused to believe it. The woman couldn't possibly live and work in the hospital without giving some hint that her feelings for a certain child were greater than for all the others, even supposing she had been clever enough to recognize that child as her own.

He put the books back in the safe, locked it

388

and pocketed the key. Then he went through the hospital in search of Sarah Morey, only to learn that she had still not returned from her afternoon outing.

The dandy took Edward as far as Paddington, the journey having lasted most of the night with stops for refreshment. He set Edward down at the Great Western Station with instructions how to get the rest of the way to Clerkenwell by the Metropolitan Railway.

'Threepence it'll cost you and don't get off until you get to the other terminal in Farringdon Road,' the dandy said. 'It's quite a lark. First line ever to go underground, would you believe. If you can stand the smell of coke and sulphur it's an experience not to be missed.'

'I don't know how to thank you,' said Edward.

'The pleasure's been mine. I don't like driving alone.'

They parted without even exchanging names, and Edward continued his journey in the early morning, rubbing shoulders with city travellers and workers of all description making use of the rapid new means of transport. There were so many in the carriage he found himself squashed against a window, but at least he could see out and it helped to ease his apprehension at the prospect of descending into a seemingly endless tunnel.

At first the incline was gradual, passing beneath a wharf, and then it dipped into the cover of great iron girders where all would have been dark if it hadn't been for the gaslight in the carriage. Edward clutched his stomach with nervousness, fearing the roof of the tunnel might collapse on them all, and at every station he half rose from his seat hoping it was the terminal, only to find each time that the small niche he occupied was almost lost as the passengers beside him tried to spread out. The rattle of the wheels echoed loudly in the confined space, and though the seats were cushioned his bones began to hurt from the jolting. In an open cutting at King's Cross he gazed up to the level of the road with awe, and he dreaded entering the next great, dark bell mouth, but the train continued safely along the three and a half miles of track, finally arriving at Farringdon Road Station where everyone alighted.

Thankful to be breathing fresh air again, Edward stood a moment on the platform watching men unload a goods waggon on a doubled line track before he climbed the steps to the station entrance. The clock on top of it said five minutes past nine. People jostled him on all sides, but he was not quite such a country bumpkin as he'd been on the last trip to London, and he felt better than he'd done for the last few weeks, knowing that at last he was doing something positive to help Anna.

The next thing he had to do was ask for directions to St John's Lane, for somewhere near there was the alley where hopefully he would find Tam O'Mara. A man piling fish baskets on top of a cartload of straw wiped his hands on his waistcoat when Edward approached him.

'Saint John's Lane? Spit and likely yer'd hit it,' the man said, gathering the reins of his two carthorses and climbing up behind. 'Cut across Turnmill Street, up Benjamin Street and it's opposite the Albion on yer right.'

The noise of iron-clad wheels rattling over the cobbles drowned Edward's thanks. He set off eastward and was soon searching for his friend amidst the courts and alleys of the most squalid area he had ever seen. Filthy children sat against walls, women leaned against doorposts, and so many looked about to produce further children he doubted there would be room enough soon for them all to sit. Strings of tattered washing hung like flags on a battleground, but the battle here must surely be just to survive.

It was the silliest thing which affected Edward the most. He felt unbearably sad for the mangy-looking chickens pecking between the cobblestones without hope of finding a crumb. The poor things would never know what a field of thick grass and buttercups was like.

He found Paul Place a short while later and was so busy looking at the numbers he almost slipped into the open gutter running down through the middle, but the houses didn't look quite so bad as some he had passed. They all seemed to belong to watchmakers, engravers and the like, having small plates on the doors to announce their professions, and by the noise issuing from them it sounded as if the craftsmen were also good at producing large families.

Edward spoke to a woman dressed all in

391

black. 'I'm looking for a Tam O'Mara,' he said.

'That Irish good-for-nothing!' The woman looked him up and down. 'You don't look the type to be mixing with the likes of 'im.'

A child sidled up to him. 'Tam lives in that one over there, but there ain't room for no more in that 'ouse.'

He gave the child a coin, and immediately other children appeared, but he couldn't afford to waste his money so he went over to the door he'd been shown and knocked.

'What d'yer want?' came a shout from inside.

'Tam O'Mara,' called Edward.

In the blinking of an eye the door opened and he was dragged inside by a girl no older than Anna. He was in a dark passage so he couldn't see what she was like. There was a closet at the bottom of the stairs which smelt worse than a pigsty, and he slipped on water which he shuddered to put a name to before tripping over a dustbin. Eyes peered at him in the dimness. Footsteps scattered. Surely Tam didn't really live here.

The girl led him to a relatively clean room at the back with a small square window looking on to a yard filled with boxes and baskets. Two mattresses were on the floor, and the remains of a frugal breakfast had stuck to two plates on a rickety table.

'Did the Fenians send you?' she asked fearfully as soon as the door was closed.

'No,' he said, not knowing what she was talking about. 'Me name's Edward Wooldridge and I'm from Chertsey.'

She relaxed her shoulders. 'Gawd, you came quick. Tam only told us about you the day afore yesterday.'

'Ain't Tam 'ere then?'

'No. He took a navvy's job working on the viaduct they're building at Holborn.' She tipped her head on one side to get a better look at him. 'It's you what wants to marry a girl who's in the lunatic asylum at Hanwell, ain't it?'

'She ain't a lunatic.' Edward was instantly on the defensive. 'She's epileptic.'

'I know what that is. She 'as fits.'

Now he could see that her dark hair hung to her waist and was in need of brushing, her skin was blemished and her collar bones protruding above the low neck of her dress created hollows deep enough to bake pies in. But with a wash and plenty of Ma's cooking no doubt she'd be quite good-looking.

'Tam said I could stay here while I was trying to get Anna out. I didn't mean it to be so soon, but yesterday something happened and I've got to do something about it right quick.'

'If you stay yer'll 'ave to pay rent to me father, same as Tam and Shaun Connell. We lets this room out, see.'

'I ain't penniless.'

The girl smiled for the first time and the effect was startling. It lit her face. 'I'm Louisa Picken,' she said. 'Me father makes watch dials out of sheet copper in 'is workshop at the front. I 'as to take care of the kids now me Ma's gawn, so I'm always here if you want someone to 'elp you.'

Edward liked her. He had the feeling she was intensely smitten with Tam O'Mara, and hoped the rogue treated her right.

'I 'as an aunt lives at Hanwell,' Louisa went on. 'I 'aven't visited her in ages, but if yer like we could go there p'raps termorrow.'

His spirits soared. 'I'd like that fine. Then p'raps I could visit Anna.'

'Not too fast. Best take a gander at the place first.' She looked as if she would enjoy a conspiracy, and he couldn't believe his luck in having met someone so interested in his problems. Her expression softened and she touched his arm. 'You look tired.'

'I've been travelling all night.'

'Take a rest on Tam's bed,' she suggested. Then: 'I'll lay down with you if you like.'

Although her presence was overwhelming, Edward's mind was fixed on Anna and he had no wish for anyone else.

'It's real nice of you, but if I'm going to make plans I'd rather be on me own.'

'Suits me,' said Louisa. She took his coat and found a nail to hang it on, handed him a dirty glass from the window ledge and filled it with beer from a jug, and plumped up a stained pillow on one of the mattresses. 'Don't worry, Tam'll work everything out for you.'

Her confidence in Tam rubbed off on Edward, and when she had gone he was able to make up for his lost sleep, content in the knowledge that his new-found friends would help him.

Later on the same morning that Edward

Wooldridge arrived in Paul Place, Sarah returned to London. The long curls of yesterday were firmly pinned up in a chignon at the nape of her neck and the veil of her hat hid her swollen eyelids, but there was no sign that she was likely to dissolve into any further tears.

Her head was held high as she went in the main entrance of the Foundling Hospital. No creeping in guiltily through a side door. She greeted some children who were marching in single file from morning classes, and picked up an infant newly returned from fostering who looked so sad it tore at her heartstrings.

'There, there, my precious,' she crooned, planting a kiss on its damp cheek. 'It's not such a bad place here, you know. You'll soon get used to it.'

A schoolmaster brought up the rear of the column. 'Ah, Mrs Morey,' he said. 'If I saw you I was to inform you that the treasurer's clerk would like to see you in his office.'

'Thank you, Mr Randell. I shall be there as soon as I've taken off my hat and gloves.'

'It sounded urgent.'

'I've no doubt it did.'

She went to her room and closed the door, determined not to be daunted by the expected summons. It would be silly to let herself be upset by a reprimand over absence when she had given so many years of exemplary service. All the same, her nerves were agitated after yesterday's events and she needed a little time to calm herself.

Since leaving Chertsey this morning she had

been trying to come to terms with her wretched stupidity and the guilt which, had she dwelt on it, would have driven her to a dangerous despair. Anna, of course, didn't know she had been deprived of the place she should have held in Sarah's heart, and Peg Wooldridge's words echoed through her mind:

'You gave up the right to be anything to Anna other than a friend,' she had said. And: 'Why should you burden her with knowing?'

She'd spoken so wisely. Nothing must be done in a hurry. Perhaps nothing could be done at all, especially as shocks seemed to trigger off Anna's epileptic attacks. But with every breath Sarah took the longing grew to leave the shadows behind and have the truth known.

She hadn't found the courage yet to examine her deepest feelings about Anna. It was impossible to transfer maternal love from one girl to another in a matter of hours, and her love for Corrie couldn't be snuffed out like a candle. Yet she had felt drawn towards Anna over the last few years, enough to feel guilty that as a person she preferred her, and Sarah prayed that if she ever did learn of their relationship Anna would be able to accept it without ill effects. The last thing she wanted was to make her condition worse. That, at the moment, was her greatest fear, the one which would prevent her from belatedly facing up to her responsibilities.

Yes, whatever she did now would have to be in the name of friendship. The whole deception seemed to be starting all over again and it hurt more than ever, but that was something she must accept along with her guilt.

The most incredible thing was that in all innocence she had allowed James to take Anna to Hanwell. Where once she had unknowingly been in her mother's care, she was now in her father's, still unaware, and the course to follow now must be up to James. She would have to be guided by him.

Sarah sat down at a small writing table by the window. The treasurer's clerk could wait. There was something more important to attend to first, and she drew out some writing paper and an envelope, dipped her pen in the inkwell, and started to write without hesitation.

'Dear James,' she wrote. 'I must see you again on a matter of great urgency. Please accept an apology for my hurried departure yesterday. And please, above all, discount my thoughtless disclosure regarding Corrie Palmer. More than this I prefer not to discuss in a letter, but I shall explain in due course. I shall anxiously await your reply saying when we may meet. Yours, in all sincerity, Sarah.'

She read the missive through, folded it, and addressed the envelope to Dr James Halden at Hanwell. A penny postage stamp was affixed and she put the letter in her pocket to post later in the box at the end of the drive where no one would see to whom she had written. That done she rinsed her hands in the bowl on the wash-stand, smoothed her hair and her dress, and went downstairs to the clerk's office.

Her courage began to wilt as she neared his door. His high position at the hospital as spokesman for the Governors made him an awesome figure and no one courted his displeasure, but she knocked with apparent confidence and entered when bidden.

'Good day, sir,' she said. 'I hope I haven't kept you waiting.'

'Good day to you, Mrs Morey.' He had piercing grey eyes which assessed her demeanour at a glance. 'Please sit down.'

She decided it would be best to take the initiative. 'I'd like to apologize for being away without your permission. I know it was wrong of me, but there were reasons ...'

'Have you come also to report on how you found Anna Beckett yesterday?'

Sarah coloured. The clerk clasped his short, square fingers and dropped his hands on to the leather-edged blotter with the air of throwing down a gauntlet. It was going to be worse than she had thought.

'I'm afraid, sir, I didn't go to Hanwell after all.'

'I've been made aware of that.'

'A ... family matter came up unexpectedly,' she faltered.

His gaze didn't leave her face. 'Indeed. We've always understood that you had no family.'

'I have a stepmother who is ill.'

'And that is where you went?'

It was obvious that he was testing her, perhaps hoping to catch her out in a lie. Something had happened since she'd last seen him, and a chill stole through her, though the room was warm. It warned her to answer everything with care.

'No, I went to Chertsey, my late husband's parish.'

'May I ask why?'

Her anxiety grew. 'Sir, I've been working here for eleven years and this is the first time I have been away from the building for more than a few hours. Please will you accept my apology, and my assurance that it won't happen again.'

The clerk looked down at his hands, deliberating. If there was something serious on his mind she wished he would voice it so that she could know what charge she faced.

'Mrs Morey, I had a visit from Dr Halden yesterday,' he said, studying her once more. Sarah's heart skipped a beat. 'It was quite a surprise as I had supposed he was on his way to Hanwell with you.'

'Our plans were changed.'

'So he informed me. He was also considerably troubled, and from what he said I thought it might be to my advantage to consult our hospital records.' He paused, now showing slight discomfort. 'Mrs Morey, I dislike having to ask a delicate question, but I must. A girl called Sarah Byrne was taken pity on by the Governors of this hospital on 25 October 1850, and we accepted her child. Were *you* that girl? Though I find it difficult to credit I have reason to believe that you were.'

She couldn't speak. There was a pain at the back of her tongue and a choking sensation in her throat. Her chest hurt. She tried to clutch at the edge of the desk but it seemed to be moving away from her, and still the wretched man stared as if he would drag the truth out of her without a shred of compassion.

'Your silence is confirmation,' he said after several moments.

'Yes, sir,' said Sarah.

He stood up. 'This matter is too serious for me to handle. I shall have to inform the Governors. They may want to refer the case to a court of law as you have wilfully deceived us over a number of years.'

'I've made no claims ...'

'You have allowed a child to be brought up at our expense when you were perfectly able to provide for it yourself. That, to my mind, is a criminal offence.' He cleared his throat. 'Did your husband know of this child's existence?'

'No, sir.'

The clerk raised his eyes to the ceiling momentarily. 'Poor Nahum Morey,' he murmured, and his fingertips met in a prayerful gesture.

Sarah pressed her own fingers to her lips to stop them trembling. He couldn't have said anything to express his condemnation more powerfully, and all argument was swept away.

'You will be called before the Governors when they meet again on Saturday,' he went on. 'Until then, please consider yourself relieved of your duties.'

She didn't know how she was going to get to her room. Outside in the corridor she leaned against the wall and waves of desolation swept over her. The boys' choir was singing in the chapel, their high voices drifting towards her with unbearable sweetness, and a certain chord touched her soul, releasing a flood of fresh tears.

A nurse asked if she was feeling ill and offered to help, but she shook her head. No one could help. She had been betrayed by the man she had always loved. His name should have been Judas instead of James.

She took a deep breath as sudden, passionate awareness of his treachery drove out grief. The panelled walls were a dark background for her thoughts, and she stood up straight. Soon the whole hospital would know that she was about to be dismissed, and there would be ugly gossip, but when she left the Foundling it would be with her head unbowed and shoulders firm. Worse things had happened in the past and she would come through this new crisis just as she had done the others, by keeping her dignity.

The letter to James was still in her pocket. She took it out and went to the kitchen on the far side of the building, her steps now as confident as always. Several saucepans were boiling on a long, black range and she held the envelope near one of them to steam it open.

'I need to add something to a letter I've just written,' she said to an assistant cook who eyed her curiously. 'I don't see the point of wasting a penny stamp.'

She went back to her room and tore the note she had previously written to James into tiny pieces, then once again sat at the writing table and took up her pen.

'James,' she wrote this time. 'Your cruelty to me is beyond belief. Am I so wicked that you felt it necessary to expose me to the treasurer's clerk? I have suffered greatly, as no doubt you intended, and now I have lost everything.

'You have no conception what it is like to see a beloved child dying from want of nourishment. I loved my baby more than words can say, but I gave her up to save her life. A part of me died when I left her here at the Foundling Hospital, but it was the only way to make sure that she lived, and I schemed and sacrificed to be always near the little girl I believed to be mine. How ironic that on the very day you learnt of her existence I discovered that my heart had been given to the wrong child. Perhaps it was meant that we should find Anna together.

'You may think that I've got what I deserve, but I honestly believe that what I did was right at the time. Now that you know Anna is our daughter do you propose to punish me for ever? You must take some responsibility for the deception since you spared no thought for me after you had taken what you wanted. And now you have also taken Anna.

'Thanks to your meddling I am to be dishonourably dismissed from my post. I do *not* ask your forgiveness for anything. I expect your assurance that I may be given the chance to devote the rest of my life to Anna, in whatever capacity she will let me.

'Your heartless betrayal has finally convinced

me that you have never wanted any part in my life. Nor do I want any part in yours, but unfortunately we must meet to decide Anna's future. Please write by return giving a time and day. Yours truly, Sarah Morey.'

James knew that the Foundling Hospital Governors always met on Saturdays, and he guessed that Sarah would be brought before them this morning. His own commitments had made it difficult to leave Hanwell early, but he'd started out in his own carriage as soon as he could, knowing that he would be late for the start of the proceedings. All he hoped was that he would get there before the committee passed judgement.

The usual impressive meeting day collection of vehicles was drawn up at the top of the drive when he arrived. He tethered his horse to a post, brushed some of the highway dust from his shoulders and entered the building in haste. When he knocked on the door of the secretaries' office he could hear faint mumblings from the direction of the Court Room which was next to it, so the conference was still in progress.

'I'd like to speak with the Governors,' he said to the skinny youth who nervously admitted him.

'Oh, no, sir,' said the youth. 'I'm afraid you can't. There's a very important meeting going on.'

'I know. I have vital information relevant to the meeting so will you please let them know that I'm here. I'm Dr James Halden.'

'I ...'

'Now, if you please. There's no time to waste.'

The youth scuttled away, probably not knowing who scared him most, this arrogant physician or the assembled Governors. James saw him give a timid rap on the Court Room door and creep inside, shoulders hunched to make himself less obvious. He followed.

The door was ajar and he could see a line of interrogators sitting at the long, highly polished table, the warm rose colour of the walls reflecting in their faces. At a glance he recognized Lt Col Hyde in military uniform, who had been a Governor since 1862, and others who were uniformly attired in black jackets, white collars and black neckcloths looking like a line of magpies. One with brown, thinning hair was Charles Plumley, another thin-faced man with ears flat to his head and the sides of his white hair brushed forward also looked familiar. The secretary was there, and the treasurer himself. Not one of them smiled.

For a moment the memory of Anna lying on the floor unconscious after these men had declared her insane made James tense every muscle, and his thoughts briefly deviated from his reason for returning here. He hadn't known who she was then, but he had felt instinctive irritability that their well-meaning decision had led to her collapse. They were good men, but like all governing bodies their power gave them a certain omnipotence, and he saw the same inflexibility in their manner again today.

Sarah was in the same chair that Anna must have used. She had her back to him. A current of air from the open door disturbed tendrils of hair at the nape of her neck, and he was reminded of the urgency of his visit, but his gaze failed to make her aware of him.

The youth whispered to the treasurer's clerk and he scowled.

'No,' James heard him say in an angry undertone.

'But the gentleman insists, sir,' said the youth.

'Tell him to wait in my office and I'll speak to him later.'

James was out of patience. He strode across the turkish carpet, his head seeming near to the exquisite stucco ceiling, and Sarah looked up. His expression gave no indication of his mood as he sketched a formal bow in her direction. Shock registered in her lovely face.

'Gentlemen, forgive me,' James said, approaching the inquisitors' table. 'I know I'm uninvited, but I came as quickly as I could when I heard that Mrs Morey was in trouble.'

'And may we ask what business it is of yours, sir?' asked the military man.

'I knew this lady when she was married to the Reverend Morey. She is very brave, and very dedicated. I understand from my informant that certain things to do with her past have become known.'

'You're right, Dr Halden,' said the treasurer's clerk. 'Investigations have proved that her character, in our opinion, leaves much to be desired.'

'That's because I'll warrant she won't speak in her own defence. She is also a very modest lady.'

Charles Plumley addressed Sarah. 'Mrs Morey, in all the years this hospital has been here it has never been abused. Its good work is renowned. But you, by your own admission, knew your own child was being raised here on charity. You tried to make us all look fools.'

'I've tried to explain, sir,' said Sarah. There were dark circles under her eyes and she looked very tired.

James thumped his fist on the table and leaned towards the Governors. 'But I'll bet she hasn't told you that *I* advised her silence on the matter many years ago.'

There was a gasp. Muttering. Neighbours exchanged whispers. Sarah turned very pale, her eyes widened and her hands cupped her chin in amazement.

'*You* knew?' An immaculately turned-out man raised a heavy eyebrow. 'We've been supporting this woman's child when she was perfectly able to do so herself, and you admit to abetting her! This is scandalous, sir!'

'Allow me to enlighten you,' James said. 'Mrs Morey's loyalty to her late husband may not have let her speak of the debts he left on his death, but I am quite prepared to do so. She came to me, as a doctor and as a friend of the Bradford family, admitting for the first time that she had a child and wanted it restored to her. Gentlemen, she was even less in a position to support it than she had been before.'

406

'Is this true, Mrs Morey?' asked the colonel.

Sarah took a breath and answered very quietly. 'Nahum left me something far more valuable than money, and that was a love for the children he had beggared himself to help.'

How clever of her. She had neatly evaded telling a lie.

'This was what Mrs Morey said when she applied for a job as a nurse,' agreed the treasurer's clerk helpfully. 'At the time I found it very commendable.'

James sensed a slight turning of the tide and quickly took advantage of it. 'You will all be aware that her daughter is Anna Beckett, the girl who, sadly, suffers with epilepsy and is now in my care. I examined her when she was brought back from fostering, you may remember. When Mrs Morey expressed the wish to raise the little girl herself, with no money and no home, I couldn't allow it. The child's life would have been at risk.'

'You took a great deal upon yourself, Dr Halden,' said the clerk. 'We should have been consulted.'

'I realize that now.'

'And did you also advise Mrs Morey to embark on further deception?'

He cast an impersonal glance at Sarah, avoiding her eyes. 'Gentlemen, this lady loved her child so much she was prepared to make the ultimate sacrifice, not once but twice. She relinquished all hope of ever being able to make herself known to Anna, and instead devoted her life to helping other abandoned children.'

'For Nahum's sake,' said Sarah. 'I wanted to carry on with his work in the only way I could.'

'So you see, you need to be open-minded in your judgement. I hope I've been able to assist you.'

The committee was nonplussed. They shook their heads in bewilderment, stampeded into reversing their thoughts by a man who was giving them no chance to do otherwise.

'You're making out Mrs Morey has no case to answer,' said the colonel. 'Yet the fact remains we have supported her child, *and* paid her a wage. Can that be right?'

'I'm deeply sorry, sir,' Sarah said. 'I'll find a way to repay the money.'

'That won't be necessary.' James knew they would consider his extraordinary intervention in a different light later, perhaps even surmise the true reason for it, but victory, at the moment, lay in the speed with which he wound up the matter. 'This morning I have paid a considerable sum to the Foundling Hospital charity which will more than cover the expense of providing for Anna Beckett. And from now other financial arrangements will be made for her care. I hope this will be agreeable to you.'

The clerk's mouth dropped open and his beard brushed his neckcloth. His cheeks had become almost puce where the heat in the room had aggravated the broken veins in them.

He turned to his colleagues. 'Are we to let the matter rest here, gentlemen?'

Charles Plumley was a man of sense. 'I think

we have no choice,' he said. 'If we pursue it there might be a scandal. And I take it, Dr Halden, that your generous donation to the charity will be withdrawn if Mrs Morey's past is made public.'

'That's so.'

He turned to Sarah. 'Then, providing you give us your resignation, Mrs Morey, I am obliged to say that no further action will be taken.'

Sarah looked on the point of collapse herself. Her blue eyes were brimming with tears of relief and she hurriedly found a handkerchief to dab at them.

'How can I thank you?' she said, her voice shaking with emotion.

James placed a hand beneath her elbow and helped her to her feet. 'This lady has been under very great stress for the past few days and I recommend that she leaves immediately.'

Half an hour later James stowed a trunk containing Sarah's clothes and possessions beneath the seat of his gig. The weather was changing and scudding clouds sent shadows to plunge the Foundling Hospital in shade. Sarah was already seated, facing Lamb's Conduit Street, and she stared ahead impassively.

'Where are you taking me?' she asked.

'Where do you want to be taken?'

'There's nowhere I can go except to Maggie's.'

He swung himself up beside her and took the reins, steadying his horse when it was anxious to go. Sarah was looking weak and helpless, but he hardened his heart.

'Does she still live in Corporation Lane?'

'Yes.' She dabbed at her eyes again and he saw that her handkerchief had become a small, wet ball. 'James, I just don't know what to say to you. You've rescued me yet again.'

'Perhaps that apology you refused to give might be in order,' he suggested. 'Now that I've perjured myself on your behalf and risked my reputation you must know that your letter hurt me very much.'

'I didn't know ...'

'You jumped to the conclusion that I informed on you to the treasurer's clerk. I did no such thing. My love for you is great enough to overlook far worse sins than the ones you seem to think you have committed, but I can't forgive your lack of faith in me.'

'James!'

'I wanted to see the hospital records. Not for one minute did I believe the girl you had pointed out to me was my daughter. The clerk refused my request and I left, but I'd said nothing to arouse his suspicion. I swear it.'

'I'm sorry, James.' She was so sorrowful and full of remorse he almost capitulated, but his furious reaction when he had received her letter had not abated. 'You said you love me ...'

'I did. But that doesn't mean I can overlook your accusations.'

'I'm sorry I made you so angry.'

He couldn't look at her. If he did so his fine resolutions to resist the effect she had on him would crumble away and he would be comforting her in his arms. He flicked his whip over the horse's rump and the carriage set off briskly.

'I can't take you to Maggie's,' he said. No matter how cross he was with her he couldn't deposit her in the clutches of Abel Wood. 'I know of rooms in Wilmington Square which will be suitable.'

'But, James, can't I go to Calvert Terrace?' She placed a hand lightly on his arm. 'You won't be there, and I won't be any bother. I'll keep the place clean for you and you can get rid of Nessie Whittaker. I'll be your housekeeper.'

She was so anxious to appease, but he wouldn't be won over.

'I'm sorry, but that's not possible.' He saluted the porter at the lodge gate and turned left into Guilford Street. 'I intend to install Anna in the house in Calvert Terrace as soon as I can arrange for a private nurse to look after her.'

'James, *I* can look after her. I always have.' She came to life, her woes cast aside in the sudden vision of cosy domesticity he refused to contemplate.

'When I feel the time is right for our daughter to come to terms with the confusion you have caused in her life I'll let you come to see her,' he said. 'Until then, Sarah, I'm afraid you must stay away.'

And though she continued to argue he drove resolutely towards Wilmington Square.

# CHAPTER 16

The singing in the chapel of Hanwell Asylum bore no comparison to the glorious voices heard at services in the Foundling Hospital, but what the congregation lacked in musical ability it made up for with enthusiasm. Only Anna, sitting among more than three hundred patients at Sunday prayer, couldn't feel any reason to give thanks. If it wasn't for Dr Halden she would be wishing she could die.

She looked around at the people near her. Some couldn't keep still, some had staring eyes and a few had dribbles of saliva seeping from their lips, but there were others who appeared so normal she wondered why they were here. She'd been working in the kitchen and hardly known which were staff and which were patients. It turned out that only the cook, two kitchen maids and a dairy maid were employed, while the others who kept the large, lofty kitchen so clean were inmates. Male patients worked in the garden, in the farmyard and the blacksmith's shop, and women helped in the wash-house, the drying room, laundry and storeroom. Everything was orderly and quiet, yet Anna hated it.

She spent much of her time doing needlework. When it was warm enough she took her sewing outside in the garden, or sat under one of the large screens erected to keep off the sun. Since coming to Hanwell she had made sets of baby clothes in fine cotton, stitching tucks in gowns and edging bonnets with lace so exquisitely they were quickly sold to visitors who came to the bazaar room in the centre tower ward of the female wing. The organ in the chapel had been purchased from the proceeds of fancywork done by patients, so she had the satisfaction of knowing that at least some good would come out of her occupation.

When she left the chapel that morning, the day after Sarah's departure from the Foundling Hospital, she went to get her needlework from the ward she shared with other epileptics. She was still feeling tired from her latest attack, but otherwise none the worse for it, and her resentment at being forced to live in this huge institution was heavy on her mind. The rest of her days loomed ahead of her without hope of normal living, and she visualized herself becoming a babbling idiot through sheer boredom and lack of intelligent conversation.

She sat on her bed and vowed that somehow she would maintain her sanity. Some of the epileptics here were far worse than she was, their brains suffering from continued convulsions and limbs subject to nervous twitching day and night, so she supposed she really did have something for which to be thankful. She decided to read whenever possible, particularly the newspapers so that she could keep up with events in the outside world which seemed so far away. Also, it might help her to stop thinking too often of Edward.

413

Meeting Edward again was just about the most cruel trick that Fate could have played. It had been so wonderful to see him. Nothing could compare with the joy she had felt at the sight of him, and at night she could lull herself to sleep by remembering those brief, ecstatic moments when he had held her in his arms and kissed her. Thinking about him gave her strength, just as it had done all those years ago when she'd been taken from the Wooldridges to the Foundling Hospital, but it also brought back the pain of separation, and some days she felt it was too great to bear. To have found him again, and then lost him, had been such a blow to her delicate system it felt as if her heart had been torn out.

She took from her pocket the little wooden doll Edward had made her. Surprisingly she had managed to keep it. The rule of shared possessions had meant it had been taken away many times, but she'd always found a way to get it back, and when she had become too old for toys she had hidden it among her few personal things, praying that she would never lose it permanently.

She had the doll in her hands when Dr Halden found her.

'I came to check on you, Anna,' he said. He looked drawn and worried, as if something had happened which had affected him deeply, yet his expression softened when he looked at her. 'I was away all day yesterday. Did you behave yourself?'

She smiled. 'I did my sewing.'

'No headaches?'

'Not really.'

'And you took your medicine?'

'I always do whatever you tell me.'

He smiled too. His lightly freckled skin was something she always remembered about him, and she was sad to see that his once reddish-gold hair was losing its brightness. But nothing changed the concern for her that warmed his eyes.

He opened his hand for her to put the doll on his palm, knowing the mistake it would be to take anything from one of his patients. She gave it to him, trusting him implicitly. The little wooden figure now had clothes made of tiny pieces of cotton, each miniature garment minutely embroidered.

'This is beautiful,' he said. 'The doll seems to mean a lot to you.'

'Edward Wooldridge made it for me just before I left Chertsey.'

'That was kind of him.'

'Yes,' said Anna. She'd not reached a stage yet where trust extended to confidentiality so she didn't want to talk of Edward in terms of their recent relationship. It hurt too much anyway to dwell on him. She took the doll back. 'All the family was good to me. I loved them very much.'

'So much so that you had your first major fit when you had to leave them.'

'Yes.'

Dr Halden looked at her keenly, the lines on his brow deepening into a frown as he asked several more questions about what her life had been like at Chertsey. Perhaps the events of her past would lead to hopes of a cure in the future if he could discover what made her have these hateful convulsions. Oh, if only he could work a miracle.

'I'm hoping to move you soon,' he said. 'As soon as I can make some special arrangements.'

Immediately her heart began to jerk at the thought of another change. 'Where to?'

'Somewhere much quieter where you won't have all these other patients around you.'

She didn't want to know any more. She got up and walked away, brushing past him rudely in her haste to escape before he could tell her anything unpleasant which would start up the strange sensations in her stomach and limbs. Lately, too, she would get a dreadful taste in her mouth which warned her she was about to suffer another attack of unconsciousness.

Perhaps she was getting worse, in spite of his assurance to the contrary. How terrible it would be if he'd decided she must be shut away from the other patients because she might become violent. Somewhere quieter, he had said. No, she wouldn't think about it. It only made her frightened when she thought too much about her illness, and being frightened was bad for her.

She hurried outside where she always felt better, not slowing down until she came to the female airing ground. Five women were sitting on one of the large rocking horses, moving it back and forth in a gentle rhythm which had sent one of them to sleep. Some could forget their troubles with ease. She pressed her lips together and prayed that she would never become demented. While she could still worry about the state of her mind there was nothing seriously wrong with it.

Visitors were arriving through the great archway at the entrance to the grounds. Anna could see a pony and trap, and several people on foot making their way up the main drive, so she changed direction and went indoors again to the bazaar room. Sometimes strangers would hold a conversation with her and she could ask for news of London, so she quickly found some sewing and asked permission to sit by the window.

It was mostly ladies who came to buy fancy goods. Today, however, she saw a young man accompanying his heavily pregnant wife who held his arm as they approached the entrance. The wife was dressed in black and wearing a hat with a thick veil. The husband had on a brown tweed sack coat and brown hat, and he looked so much like Edward it took Anna's breath away. Her mouth went dry and her sewing fell to her lap.

The couple came in. Anna froze. Edward, for there was no doubt now that it really was he, was looking round idly, as if seeking the best table. He whispered something to his companion and they stopped where he could survey the room while at the same time examine some of the articles. Then he saw her. Their eyes met, his inscrutable in the crevices created by squinting as he toiled long hours in the sun.

He made no sign that he knew her, but held

her gaze for several seconds without any change in his expression. His dear face looked so out of place here that she wanted to cry, and she had to will herself not to rush over and welcome him rapturously. His stern countenance forbade it. He turned again to the veiled girl at his side, and Anna felt like a leaf curling up in the heat, the sap evaporating into a dry fear that he might have come to mock her. She had no idea who the girl might be, but she seemed totally dependent on Edward. Anna trembled as her fear increased. If this woman was his wife, then everything he had told her in Clerkenwell had been a lie.

He took off his hat and the light fell on his silky brown hair and the broad planes of his face. Farm work had given him a powerful build, and his short neck looked uncomfortable in a high collar and neckcloth. He spoke to one of the assistants, then glanced casually in Anna's direction once more as she was pointed out to him. A few moments later the pair wandered over, and when they were close enough to be unobserved Edward winked at Anna and put a finger to his lips. She was so relieved she went to get up but he shook his head.

'I'm told you make the best layettes,' he said loudly. 'My wife is anxious to have an infant gown made specially for her. Could you have it done by next Sunday?'

His voice was imperious, quite unlike the usual slow, country accent she remembered, and she was confused. Suddenly she wanted to laugh. She didn't need to pretend hesitation.

418

'I ... I think so. Yes.'

'There, my dear, I promised you something beautiful and I'm sure this young lady will be able to produce it,' he said to his companion. 'Do you have the instructions?'

'Yes, dearest.' The girl opened a reticule and took out an envelope. It was impossible to see her properly through the thick veil, but when she handed the letter to Anna their hands touched briefly. 'I want everything to be just perfect, so please read this carefully.'

'I'll do my best,' Anna promised. It was a wonder they couldn't see how erratically her heart was behaving.

'Thank you,' said Edward.

There was no one near so he, too, touched her hand, and the feel of his rough fingers against her skin sent shivers coursing along her spine. A quick pressure accompanied by another wink was enough to assure Anna that she was about to become involved in some plan of his, and excitement sent a glow of colour to her pale cheeks. She didn't know what he was up to, but whatever it was she had to play along, for surely he was trying to help her.

When they had gone she opened the letter, her fingers clumsy with the urgent need to read what Edward had written before anyone was curious. She saw at once that he had left nothing to chance. There were two notes in the envelope, one detailing the fancywork required on a baby's gown; the other, which she hid straight away in her pocket, was meant for her eyes only. And she had not hidden it a minute too soon.

'May I see what the young couple are wanting you to do?' the assistant asked.

'I don't think it's too difficult,' said Anna, passing over the first note. She was so nervous she couldn't look at the woman.

The assistant agreed about the work. 'You'd better start today, though. I know how quick you are but there's plenty to be done in a week.' She handed the note back. 'Strange young couple. The wife appears to be in mourning for a close relative. Very sad.'

There would be no privacy in the ward to read her other letter so Anna was forced to take it to the closet. She leaned with her back against the door as there were no locks, and unfolded the first personal letter she had ever received.

'My darling,' she read. 'Be at the shrubbery near the west wing tower next Sunday at one o'clock. Don't let anyone see you, and wear a black dress if you can. My friend Louisa and me and another friend will come. Don't be surprised at anything. Remember that I love you and I'm going to marry you very soon. E.'

For a moment Anna held the precious paper against her breast, wishing she could keep it. Like the doll it was a tangible reminder of Edward, but she didn't really need it when he lived in her heart, so for safety's sake she put it in the water closet and flushed it away.

She didn't know how she was going to have patience to wait until next Sunday at one o'clock. Somehow the long days in between had to be filled, but she could think of Edward all the time she was stitching the baby gown for his friend Louisa.

Sarah was determined that James should not monopolize Anna, but for the moment she didn't know how to prevent it. He had made stipulations which she was in no position to argue with, considering his generosity, and until he had come to terms with his own relationship to Anna she would have to bide her time.

She couldn't go to see her daughter. Not yet. James had forbidden it for one thing, and for another she didn't know what she would say to her. Everything had changed so much in the last few days she felt emotionally drained.

Nor could she go to Calvert Terrace. Her offer to keep house for James Halden had been refused so decisively she wouldn't dare to suggest it again. Come to that she didn't even know if it was something she wanted to do. She'd suggested it without consideration, but now she'd had time to think it over she knew it wouldn't be wise to enter his house once more on such terms.

One thing was clear, though. After being left on her own for most of Sunday to brood she knew she couldn't stay in Wilmington Square. Her rooms were on the first floor of a large house belonging to a pleasant enough elderly lady, but they were dreary and she hadn't seen another soul. Her life had always been so busy. Now suddenly there was going to be nothing with which to fill the tedious hours, and she greatly resented the way James had left her here without a single thing to do.

The old lady appeared to have a much higher regard for James than Sarah did.

'Dr Halden is a saint,' she said the first evening. Her name was Mrs Elbert and she resembled an owl. Her dark, unblinking eyes were set in a round face framed by an abundance of white hair, and her soft skin had a suggestion of fluffiness like a baby bird's. 'He took my husband to Hanwell when his mind went, and I declare the wretch has never been so happy. Come to that neither have I. It's all due to that dear doctor.'

A saint was certainly not what Sarah would have called him, but she had to admit that he had done everything he could to save her reputation with the Foundling Hospital Governors.

'He's very good to his patients,' she'd agreed.

'And will he be coming up here to visit you often?' The question had been asked delicately, but the addition of a knowing smile had left Sarah in little doubt as to the real issue.

'I think not. The dear doctor has banished me here so that he won't have to see me.'

'Oh dear.' Mrs Elbert's disappointment would have been amusing if Sarah had been in a better mood.

On Sunday evening she walked as far as Myddelton Square to attend the service at St Mark's Church, wearing a gown she had made some time ago in purple brocade with a white lace collar high at the neck. Her lavender crêpe bonnet was tied with purple ribbon, and a black velvet cape covered her shoulders. The grey matron's gown had been discarded for ever.

She found an inconspicuous place at the back. It was when the congregation sat down after the singing of the first hymn that Sarah saw Corrie. She was sitting behind an austere-looking family who had a private pew and she was dressed in black housemaid's garb the same as three other girls who were with her. The golden hair was covered by a large white mob cap.

Throughout the service Sarah's eyes scarcely left the small black-clad figure. For seventeen years she'd believed she had given birth to her. Now that she knew differently she had expected her maternal feelings for the girl to wither away, but they were still there. Corrie Palmer hadn't changed. She was exactly the same, mercifully ignorant of the trauma affecting Sarah, and it was impossible to shed love like sloughing off an old skin. A terrible sadness engulfed her, and she left the church immediately after the Blessing so there would be no risk of meeting Corrie.

All night she fretted about her predicament and the mess she had made of everything. By Monday morning she was wallowing in self-pity, convinced that no one needed her, until she remembered Maggie. She hoped to see Patrick anyway to repay the money she had borrowed, so she made up her mind to set out after breakfast.

The weather had changed. A cool wind heralded the onset of autumn. It funnelled down the narrow street between twenty tenement houses and the wall of the House of Detention in Corporation Lane, almost knocking her off her feet as she turned the corner. Children were already playing hopscotch in the street. A muffin seller was shouting his wares and she bought some, almost overloading the basket she'd been filling at food shops along the way. It was a relief to put it down as she knocked on Maggie's door.

Abel Wood came.

Sarah felt as if she had come face to face with the devil himself. Such revulsion flooded through her she took an involuntary step backwards. Tufts of sparse grey hair stood out like horns at the sides of his bald head, his beak of a nose was more pronounced than ever where his cheeks had sunk in, and his chest was a hollow createed by the permanent sag of his shoulders.

'You don't 'ave to act like I've got the plague,' he said. 'I ain't got a hankering for the likes of you these days.'

Indeed she doubted he could do much except lift a glass to his lips, but at least she had come early enough to find him sober.

'I've come to see Maggie,' Sarah said.

'Well yer can come in. And bring them vittles with you. We can do with 'em.'

She plucked up courage and went inside. It was the first time she had seen him since he had visited Maud, and his vicious stirring that day had changed the course of her life. She would never trust a word that he uttered, but for Maggie's sake she had to be brave.

'I hope Maggie's better.'

'The lazy cow won't get up,' Abel grumbled, his language deteriorating even more as he went on to complain that yesterday he'd had no dinner.

'She's ill,' said Sarah. 'Have you no pity at all?'

'A good thrashing's what she'll get if she don't get up off 'er backside.' His tongue moistened his lips as he looked at the food in the basket. ' 'Bout time you repaid the meals we gave you, madam.'

'You'll not have any of this, Abel Wood. It's for Maggie.'

Sarah marched into the kitchen, gaining confidence, and when there was no sign of Maggie she went straight up the stairs, praying he wouldn't follow. Her heart sank when she saw a mound under the grubby blanket and she feared the worst, but there was a movement when she softly spoke her stepmother's name. The blanket was lowered and Maggie peered out, her face lighting up at the sight of Sarah. She scrambled up.

'You're a sight for sore eyes and no mistake,' she said. Incredibly she looked much improved. 'I thought yer last visit would've put you off coming again.'

'Quite the reverse.' Sarah gave her one of the muffins which she ate ravenously. Starvation was likely at the root of her weakness. 'Now tell me why you're skulking here when you ought to be keeping the place tidy.'

'I get up as soon as *he's* out of the 'ouse. Not before.'

Sarah went over to the window and opened it, letting in a cold wind to freshen the stale air. 'I've got some meat and vegetables to cook if there's a fire to heat the stove.'

'Reckon you'll 'ave to do it yerself.'

'Isn't Patrick around?'

'Paddy leaves at daybreak to get down the market, and 'e don't show 'is face again till night.' Maggie swung her stick-thin legs off the bed. 'I'm worried about 'im, Sarah. He keeps real bad company. Abel says 'e saw 'im with a load of Irish layabouts what were talking trouble. I don't like it, that I don't.' She inclined her head in the direction of the prison. 'He'll land up in there one of these days.'

From the window Sarah could see into the House of Detention yard where a solitary prison warder was patrolling. Everything was so quiet beyond the wall until exercise time at three o'clock and it made the rowdiness in the street incongruous. She remembered Patrick using his acquired Irish accent and talking a lot of nonsense about fighting for the cause. Maybe Maggie was right to be worried.

'Life would be much simpler without our children,' she said.

'Hmm!' scoffed Maggie. 'And what would *you* be knowing about that?'

Sarah picked up the basket. 'I'm going down to get a meal for you. Seems like I only just came in time the other day to save you starving to death and I'll not let it happen again.'

'You're good to me, Sarah.'

'At the moment you're all I've got.' She

426

stooped and planted a kiss on Maggie's greying hair. 'I need to talk to you as soon as Abel's gone out.'

She couldn't deny Abel Wood a share of the food, much as she begrudged it, but at least she had the satisfaction of seeing him grateful. And after he had eaten he lumbered out of the house, heading for the nearest pub.

'Now,' said Maggie, the minute he had gone. 'Why ain't you working on a Monday?'

'I've lost my job,' Sarah told her. 'They found out about Angel.'

She related most of what had happened leading up to her dismissal from the Foundling Hospital. She had never called her child anything but Angel when speaking of her to Maggie, and she continued to do so now. It saved having to explain what a fool she had been over the mix-up. But she spoke of Angel's illness.

'She's epileptic, Maggie. I never told you before. Now James has got her at Hanwell.'

'The lunatic asylum!'

'It's where they take epileptics if they're really bad, and after Angel had a violent turn the Governors decided that was where she had to go.'

'And now James Halden knows who she is?'

'He found out.'

'Gawd, what a mess.' Maggie huddled over the first fire there'd been in the grate for months. 'What about Angel?'

'She still doesn't know, and James says she's not strong enough to be told. He intends to take her to Calvert Terrace and employ a private nurse.'

'The devil 'e does! And 'e won't let you see 'er?'

'No.'

Sarah covered her face with her hands. The relief at being able to speak of it almost broke her.

'I want her, Maggie,' she breathed, her voice no more than an anguished whisper. 'She's *my* daughter too, and I want her.'

'Then tell Dr High and Mighty Halden you want 'er. He ain't got no more right to 'er than you 'ave. The biggest mistake you ever made was letting that man 'ave 'is own way to start with.'

There was no arguing with that. Endless trouble had resulted from a few thoughtless moments of pleasure, but nothing could be done to change things. What had happened had happened, and that was that. Sarah took a deep breath and made a determined effort to think positively instead of wallowing in misery. She'd never been a pessimist. It was time she tried to beat James at his own game.

She got up. 'Maggie, you're marvellous. I've got a bit of money saved, enough to rent a decent house where Angel and me can be together. And both of us are clever with our hands. I reckon we could start up a little dressmaking business.' The idea was so simple and so good she didn't know why it hadn't come to her before. 'Yes,' she cried, 'that's what we'll do.'

It was not so easy to find a woman with all the qualifications James was looking for. He wanted someone with nursing experience but as most nurses were drawn from the domestic servant class the ones he had interviewed so far were all too rough to be considered. The type of woman he needed was one who could also be a companion to Anna.

The most promising had been a sister from St Thomas's Hospital who had once been head servant with a very respectable family. She'd struck him as a responsible person, reliable when it came to issuing medicine and efficient at domestic duties, but when he'd explained Anna's condition she had turned the job down for the most extraordinary reason.

'Epileptics scare me,' she'd said. 'They see things, don't they?'

'Most certainly not.'

'In the Bible they call it an "unclean spirit". I don't reckon I could work with one of them.'

So the woman had gone, and James had spent the rest of that morning feeling dejected and frustrated by people's ignorance.

As the week progressed he found himself wanting to spend all his spare time near his daughter, but he had to refrain. She seemed to have been in a tense state ever since he had mentioned the probability of moving her, and he was afraid of acting too rashly. Not only that, he was afraid his excessive interest in her would attract gossip, and that was the last thing he wanted. One day he would proudly acknowledge her, but while she was at Hanwell their relationship had to be a closely guarded secret.

The trouble was the more he saw her, the more difficult it became to hide his feelings.

Every time he looked at Anna a rush of love warmed his heart. He wanted to put his arms round her and express the wonderful emotion she inspired in him just by giving her trust. He would look at her when she was unaware, marvelling that she was his flesh and blood, and all the paternal tenderness he had stored for Maud's poor stillborn children welled up to the point of overflowing. Anna belonged to him.

But she was also Sarah's child, and that made her doubly precious.

His feelings for Sarah had never been more complicated. He couldn't deny that he loved her, but she had behaved with such stupidity he was completely out of patience. In fact he couldn't even bear to think about it. He would never forgive her for keeping the existence of his child from him all these years so that he had missed the joys of parenthood.

If only she had tried again to find him after Anna was born. He would have done everything to help her. She could have had a little house somewhere convenient and enough money to bring up their daughter in comparative luxury. Then he would have been able to visit at least twice a week, and when Maud had died he would have married Sarah as soon as a suitable time had elapsed. The thought stirred him.

He was free to marry her now, but he was

no longer certain it was the right thing to do. If anyone had said he was punishing her for the torment she had caused he would have ridiculed the suggestion and countered with the fact that he must be punishing himself at the same time, but it was true. He didn't think she deserved to have a hand in caring for Anna, not when she had been too blind to recognize her from infancy.

By Friday not one of the women he had interviewed was suitable. But that afternoon a woman came, recommended by a titled lady who unfortunately had no further need of her services now that her husband had died. At last James felt confident. She had all the right qualities, and she was of a reasonably companionable age to please Anna. Prudence Windham had a gentle, unassuming manner and had been resident in other well-respected homes to do private nursing prior to her latest post.

'Miss Windham, I can't tell you how relieved I am to find you. I was beginning to despair.'

'You won't need to worry, sir. I'll look after the young lady like she was my own. Is she a relative of yours?'

James had reached the first awkward hurdle. 'I'm her guardian,' he said. 'Now tell me, can you start tomorrow?'

He wanted no more delay. The sooner he could finalize arrangements and move Anna away from Hanwell the better. Saturday would be an ideal day with regard to his work. The most important thing at the moment was to get her happily established in his Calvert Terrace house without risk to her health, and then he would be able to prepare her gradually for the revelation about her parentage.

'Oh, I'm sorry, sir,' said Miss Windham. 'I have to pack, and last-minute arrangements to attend to with her ladyship. Will Monday be all right?'

He sighed. Another three days really didn't make any difference, except to his patience. 'Very well, that will have to do. Monday it is.'

They shook hands on it, and half an hour later Prudence Windham departed.

He felt good now. Anna would soon be going home.

At noon on Sunday Edward, Louisa and Tam O'Mara set out from the house of Louisa's aunt, Miss Emma Picken, which was situated between Hanwell Station and the Wharncliffe Viaduct. They made a strange trio.

Edward was again wearing his brown tweed coat with a patch on the sleeve which his Ma had stitched on after he'd used it to put out the fire at Miss Cobham's shop. This time he carried a canvas bag. Tam was in the old trousers and shirt he wore for navvying in Holborn, while Louisa, who couldn't stop giggling, waddled between them with the large bulge at the front of her black skirt raising the hem several inches to show her boots.

'It's a good job that veil covers your face,' Edward said. 'If you laugh when we get there the game'll be up.'

'I won't laugh, I promise. But I feel so silly.'

432

'I've a great desire to make you look like that really,' said Tam with a twinkle in his eye.

Louisa scolded him. 'Stop yer Irish blarney, Tam O'Mara.' But she lifted the veil and the look she gave was an invitation.

Hanwell was a pleasant area after Clerkenwell with plenty of open spaces bordering the River Brent. Edward felt much more at home than in the city and he wished he didn't have to take Anna back there, but it wouldn't do to stay near the asylum. He was worried enough that their plans could go wrong. It was taking such a risk, especially as Anna's health was so unpredictable, but he banked on her love of adventure carrying them through.

Before crossing the Uxbridge Road, Tam left them.

'I'll be off on me own now,' he said. 'It's a good walk round to the canal.' All trace of humour was gone and he took Louisa's hand. 'Sure and you'll be takin' care. Remember not to run, and I'll be waitin' for you below the coal wharf.'

'We've done jobs together before, Tam. I know what to do.'

'Good luck,' said Edward.

He waited a few minutes until Tam was out of sight, then he and Louisa approached the entrance to the asylum, she now clinging to his arm with genuine need for support. The same porter as last week came out of the lodge.

'My wife and I have come to collect the layette we ordered from one of the seamstresses,' Edward said. 'May we go in?'

433

'That's all right, sir.' The porter was a family man and he gave Louisa a sympathetic glance. 'Lucky it's not quite so warm for the lady today, ain't it.'

Edward felt one of Louisa's giggles threatening and he pressed her hand in warning. He said: 'The sun's still strong enough to trouble her, though, so we shall keep to the shade.'

'Very wise,' said the porter, and went back inside the lodge.

The large brick building which was Hanwell Asylum lay ahead of them as they walked close to the hedges along the drive. To the right was the men's airing ground with a bowling green where several male patients were enjoying the exercise. On the opposite side was a similar space with a summerhouse. Edward passed them by and turned towards the tower-like building on their left where the shrubbery was dense. He paused a moment, as if anxious about Louisa, and looked around. There was no one close enough to observe them, and careful stock of the bank of windows in the tower made him fairly certain they couldn't be seen from there. Seconds later they were hidden from view among the bushes.

Edward looked at his watch. It was five minutes to one.

A muted whistle told Anna where they were. She came straight away, wearing a black skirt as he had requested. There were bits of twigs in her hair, her cheeks were pink, and excitement shone in her eyes. He was so pleased to see her he was tempted to clasp her in his arms,

434

but there was neither the time nor the room so he had to make do with giving her hand a reassuring squeeze.

'Thank goodness,' he breathed, with relief.

'I was so afraid you wouldn't come,' Anna said. But her eyes widened in alarm when she saw the rotund figure of Louisa. 'Is it safe for you to be here?'

Louisa pressed her fingers to her lips to stifle laughter. 'I'm about to give you me burden,' she said, undoing her skirt which was held across with a large pin to keep one of her Aunt Emma's cushions in place. She stepped out of it.

'Quickly, Anna,' urged Edward, 'there's no time to lose. Take the cushion from Louisa and let's fasten it the way she did.'

'I can't!' Anna gasped. 'Oh, Edward, no, I'd be too embarrassed.'

'Shhh, my darling, it's all right,' he murmured. The colour in her face increased and he was so afraid of bringing on one of her attacks. If that happened all was lost. 'I'll help you. Soon I'll be your husband, so you mustn't mind.'

Louisa was already pulling a pair of Tam's old trousers over her pantalooned legs. 'Just give a grin,' she said. She took a cap from the canvas bag and pulled it on, stuffing all her hair up inside. 'It's a real lark and no mistake, people feeling sorry for you an' all.'

'Don't let me down, Anna.'

A pony and trap was coming up the drive. The three of them sank down, holding their breath in case the driver was seated high

435

enough to look over the hedge and see them. The horse's hoofs sent gravel in their direction. Iron-clad wheels rattled past.

When it seemed safe Louisa stretched up to make sure they were out of danger. 'It's all right,' she said, hurriedly donning a black greasy jacket, then turning to Anna. 'I'm ready. Now I'll help you.'

Together they secured the cushion beneath Anna's skirt and covered her shoulders with a black mantle which also belonged to Emma Picken. Finally the hat with the heavy veil was pinned to Anna's hair, and the transition was so successful it was hard to tell she was not the girl who had walked up the drive fifteen minutes earlier.

It was Anna's turn to giggle. 'I feel like a barrel.'

'You look like a balloon, but if anyone sticks a pin in you they'll get covered in feathers.'

'It's just perfect,' said Edward. He looked at his watch again. 'D'you think we've been long enough to have bought something?'

From inside the front of her blouse Anna produced a white baby's gown which even someone as inexperienced as Edward could see was beautifully made.

'This was a labour of love for Louisa's baby,' Anna told them, and all three had a job not to laugh.

The little gown was placed in some paper just inside the canvas bag which now contained Louisa's discarded clothes. A few minutes later she cautiously emerged from the shrubbery and pretended to inspect the leaves for blight while surveying the immediate neighbourhood.

Some women were fairly close. Edward could hear them. They waited. Another minute ticked by. His heart was pounding as he took Anna's hand and the wait seemed interminable until Louisa gave the signal that it was safe to leave. The girl in navvy's clothes strolled nonchalantly away in the direction of the Grand Junction Canal which ran behind the asylum, while the young man in the brown tweed coat, supporting a heavily pregnant wife, started walking slowly back down the drive to the lofty entrance.

'How will Louisa get away?' Anna asked anxiously.

'We worked it all out. She'll walk round the side and through the burial ground to the canal. Tam O'Mara's waiting for 'er where the barges unload coal, and 'e'll get her away sure enough.'

'They're taking such a risk. It's very kind of them.'

'Tam's Irish,' said Edward, as if that explained everything.

He made a point of speaking to the porter. 'We're so pleased with the needlework,' he said, giving the man a glimpse of Anna's fine sewing. 'So sad the poor woman who did it isn't quite right in the head.'

'That's the way it goes.' The porter shrugged, and went over to some other people seeking permission to enter the grounds.

It was a great temptation to hurry once they had left the asylum behind, but Edward

437

regulated his stride so that Anna could appear tired beside him. In truth she looked it, but she was free, and as long as he could get her safely to Miss Picken's house all would be well.

'We belong together now,' he said, smiling into her eyes. 'I've got a licence in my pocket so we can get married tomorrow.'

'You think of everything.'

Love and admiration gave her a special kind of glow, and he caught his breath with wonder at her loveliness. The doctor who had condemned her to life in an asylum was a heartless monster, and if ever he met him Edward vowed to tell him so in the strongest terms.

## CHAPTER 17

The peace and quiet of early Sunday evening was shattered abruptly when Dr Halden learnt that no one could find Anna Beckett. His voice could be heard throughout the female wing.

'What the hell do you mean she's missing! She can't be missing. There are attendants around at all times, and she couldn't just walk out of the main gate without the porter seeing her. When was she last seen?'

'Around midday, sir,' quaked the assistant who had been on duty in the bazaar room. 'She said she had to put the last few stitches in a baby's gown.'

'Did she have any visitors?'

'No, sir, not to our knowledge.'

'And when was the matter reported?'

'Not till three o'clock, sir. She's not the sort of young lady what needs full-time watching, so we didn't realize she'd gone.'

James had never shown his authority with such force. Other patients had been known to wander away and there was usually a hue and cry until they were brought back, but never a display of bad temper like this. The corridors were ringing with it.

'Bring the porter to me,' he commanded, and strode off to his office in the centre octagonal tower, near to the one John Conolly had occupied during his time in residence.

Too fraught to sit down he stood by the window looking down the drive, and banged clenched fists on the sill until the pain jarred. He was so angry he felt ready to explode. In all his years as a physician to the mentally sick he had never before shown lack of patience. He knew his outburst had shocked the staff, but his control had snapped when he'd heard the news.

He knew what must have happened. That was what was so utterly infuriating. Sarah had visited the hospital and had somehow managed to spirit her away, though he didn't know how she could have done it when everyone was so vigilant. He had expressly forbidden her to see Anna until he judged the time was right, but she had gone against his wishes. Heaven alone knew what damage she might do if she decided to enlighten the girl.

439

His head was throbbing. He grasped a handful of his hair and tugged at it until his scalp pained more than his knuckles. He had never been so angry. The reason eluded him while he was too enraged to think clearly, but he gradually calmed down enough to see that he was being absurd. Having just discovered his daughter he had become obsessive about her and he had been jealously preparing for her to come under his sole protection, but he didn't have that right.

He prayed that Sarah wouldn't do anything foolish.

James had spent most of Sunday at Calvert Terrace. As well as engaging Miss Windham he had earlier arranged for a cook to take up residence, and Nessie Whittaker had cleaned the house from top to bottom. The finished result pleased him. Anna's room, the one which Sarah had used, was once again pretty enough for a girl. The last dust covers had been removed, the whole place was aired, and he couldn't wait to see her happily installed. He'd been going to tell her tonight and take her there tomorrow. Now his plans had been thwarted.

The porter was hurrying up the drive, and the young assistant skipping along beside him was obviously filling him in on the reason for the summons. The day had produced a beautiful sunset, shades of lavender, peach and gold staining the sky long after the giant ball had sunk out of sight. A mellow light shone in James's eyes, but it did little to soften his mood.

'I want to know if you admitted a tall, rather

striking woman with dark hair, possibly dressed in grey,' he said to the porter.

'I didn't let any woman in on her own, sir.'

'In a carriage perhaps, or a cab?'

'Not that I can recall, sir.'

'Did any cabs bring visitors this afternoon?'

'Two, I believe.'

'And did they wait for the occupants to return?'

'They did, sir.'

James fired questions like bullets, but got no satisfaction. Sarah had made an unremarkable entrance, and her departure with Anna had caused not the slightest suspicion. It was so galling he felt like shaking the poor man.

He tried one last time. 'You're expected to note the number of people in every vehicle,' he said. 'Are you absolutely certain one didn't leave with an additional passenger?'

The porter squared his shoulders resentfully. 'I've been 'ere seven years, sir, and never once 'ave I let anyone through them gates I didn't know about. If there'd been anyone trying something on I'd've known.'

'I'm sorry,' James apologized. 'The fact is one of our epileptic patients is missing and she must be found.'

'I 'ope she is right soon, sir, for 'er sake, but I certainly ain't responsible for 'er leaving.'

There were other patients to see, notes to catch up on, a dozen and one things requiring his attention, but James Halden restricted himself to urgent matters only, detailing everything else to more junior physicians. There was nothing so important as finding Anna, and he couldn't waste time.

It was dark when he ordered his gig to be brought round, and he set off to journey once more along the Uxbridge Road, through Ealing and Acton, into London via the Bayswater Road, and thence by the shortest route to Clerkenwell. It was a distance of ten or more miles but he covered it in record time, having been provided with a fresh horse.

The sky was not so clear as it had been in Hanwell and gas lights flared through a veil of mist creeping in from the Thames. The air had a distinctly autumn feel to it and leaves from the trees in Kensington Gardens were beginning to collect in the gutters. Pedestrians were sporting coats. James had to curb his speed as he entered the city, far too many vehicles being abroad for a sabbath night, but he made good headway along Oxford Street with its tall houses at the western end complemented by the Marble Arch at the entrance to Hyde Park. He didn't stop until he reached Wilmington Square.

Mrs Elbert came to the door in answer to his peremptory ring.

'Why, Dr Halden,' she exclaimed with surprise.

'I wish to see Mrs Morey,' James said.

'My dear sir, she's not here.'

'And when will she be back?'

The woman's smile flickered like the light outside which was bothered by a quivering aspen tree. 'She didn't spend much time here at all. I'd thought she might be company, her being on her

442

own the same as me, but she was more often out than in. Then yesterday she packed her things and left altogether.'

James felt his temper rising again, dangerous as a river at the equinox which threatened to burst its banks with each high tide. Sarah was forever taking flight. He was exasperated with her whims and totally out of love with her. In fact he bitterly regretted the fact that she had ever come into his life.

'Where, pray, has she gone?' he asked.

'She didn't say. Secretive she was. I couldn't make her out at all.'

'You're not the only one, Mrs Elbert.'

It was no use expecting to find any clues in her room. He knew without looking that Sarah would have left the place so clean a speck of dust wouldn't dare to settle, and she had a knack of covering her tracks expertly when she didn't want to be found.

He returned to his house in Calvert Terrace, surprising Nessie and the new cook. He was far too tired to make a fourth journey along the Hanwell road in one day.

'Beggin' yer pardon, sir, but you look real unhappy,' Nessie said when she brought a cup of hot chocolate to his room. 'Has the lady you was going to marry called it off?'

Her audacity had annoyed Maud, but James had always tolerated it. Nessie was a cheerful, hard-working creature who meant no harm, which was why he hadn't dismissed her after the rumpus involving her brother Fergal.

'Did I say I was thinking of getting married?'

'No, sir. But with all the fuss that's been going on this week I thought we was preparing for a bride to come.'

He smiled for the first time since the news had reached him of Anna's disappearance. 'I'm allowing a young, invalid relative to live here. I'd hoped she would arrive tomorrow, but there's been a change of plan.'

'Oh, I'm sorry, sir. Reckon it's made you cross after all the bother you've been to.'

'Yes, Nessie, it has. Very cross indeed.'

His room was at the back of the house. It had been his study when Maud was alive, and after her death it had been the only room kept ready for occupation so he'd arranged for his bed to be moved in. The oak-panelled walls were book-lined, the heavy maroon velvet curtains kept out winter draughts but could be looped back to admit summer sunshine, and his desk was the most important piece of furniture. There was a wonderful relaxing atmosphere about it which soothed his mind as soon as the door was closed. When Nessie had gone he leaned back in his deep leather chair and filled a pipe with sweet-smelling tobacco, a luxury heartily condemned by Maud in her lifetime.

He would find Sarah. She no longer had the semi-cloistered retreat at the Foundling Hospital in which to hide.

What worried him was that she had Anna with her and he prayed there would be harmony between them. Anna had not shown a particular fondness for Sarah the only time he had seen them together and it surprised him that she

444

had been persuaded to leave Hanwell with her. The only reason could be that she looked upon Hanwell as a prison, and any method of escape must have seemed preferable to being kept against her will.

Early in the morning, before returning to the hospital, James paid a brief visit to Corporation Lane. Not that he expected Sarah to be there, but every possibility had to be explored. The hag who opened the door gave him short shrift and it took him several moments to realize that it was Maggie.

'So you're looking for Sarah,' she said. 'Well she ain't here, and if she was I wouldn't be telling you. When 'ave you ever cared?'

Seeing the squalor beyond the doorway he knew Sarah wouldn't have brought Anna to share it, so he didn't linger. There was something about the street which made his skin feel tight and his stomach queasy.

He didn't know where to start looking next. He drove round the area just as he'd done in the days after Gabriel Smith had saved his life, his eyes alert for the slightest clue which might lead him to Sarah and Anna, but doors and windows were closed against him, offering nothing in the way of help. Sick at heart, he knew he was completely wasting his time.

Having made a futile tour of Clerkenwell he came down Sekford Street and past St James's churchyard on his way to Clerkenwell Green, from where he intended to leave for Hanwell.

A sound of merriment was coming from the direction of the church. Someone was happy. He glanced across the grass and gave a somewhat wistful smile when he saw a small wedding party about to go inside.

On the Friday prior to Anna's disappearance from Hanwell, Sarah managed to find a house which she could afford to rent. On the Saturday she moved in. It was a modest house in Sekford Street, part of an elegantly curved terrace, and she could see no reason for James to object to it, unless he took exception to its proximity to Nicholson's Distillery. Outside all the doorways were different, the windows were pleasant, and there was fancy brickwork coping. Inside she knew she could make it a comfortable home and she planned the coloured curtains she would make to replace the dull brown ones already there. The advantage, which surely he would appreciate, was its nearness to the Finsbury Dispensary if an occasion should ever arise when she needed urgent help for Anna.

She spent all Sunday cleaning, and on Monday morning she felt satisfied that everywhere was fresh and attractive. Sarah was in a tense state, alternating between optimism and the terrible feeling that this move was going to be a disaster. Questions continually plagued her, the most important being how Anna would react if she was told of their relationship. It frightened her to think about it.

She had never been so nervous before, and she prayed over the outcome. Anna was suddenly like a complete stranger. They would have to get to know each other in a totally different way

446

and learn to live together. She didn't think it would be all that difficult to persuade her to leave Hanwell, but it was going to be a bigger problem convincing James to let her go. She kept telling herself that now he'd had time to get over the initial shock he couldn't possibly stand in her way.

With this thought firmly in mind she walked to Calvert Terrace to check whether Anna was already installed there with a nurse. Nessie Whittaker, who had never known quite what to make of Sarah, was glad of someone to tell about the morning's incidents.

'Lor, ma'am, there's no young lady here,' she said, folding her arms. 'And the master left in a right lather, I can tell yer. Seems 'is young relative ain't coming after all, and 'e ain't too pleased about it, not after all the bother 'e's been to.'

'Do you know why?'

'No, ma'am. He's gone awf back to the 'ospital now and I don't know when we'll be seeing 'im again.'

This was a puzzle. Sarah chatted for several minutes, learning that a new cook had started and the house had been completely opened up ready for occupation, but then James had returned unexpectedly last night in a terrible temper, and had left again with it scarcely improved. So it seemed that if she wanted to speak to him she would have to go to Hanwell herself. This being so she set off by train later in the day, tired and more anxious than she had let Nessie see. Something had gone wrong with James's plans, and the only thing she could think was that Anna had become much worse.

It was drizzling with rain when she arrived at Hanwell station and though she had an umbrella she got quite wet walking to the asylum. The enormous building was daunting and she hesitated a moment, looking nervously through the great arch. She ought to have written to James and made an appointment to see him, or better still asked when it would be convenient for them to meet in Clerkenwell either at his house or her own in Sekford Street. Yes, that would have been much more sensible, for then he could have seen for himself the surroundings to which she proposed to bring Anna. Too late now.

'I wish to see Dr James Halden very urgently,' she told the porter at the lodge.

He brushed off the request. 'I'm afraid the doctor's very busy, madam.'

'I'm sure he'll see me. My name is Mrs Morey and I want to speak to him about Anna Beckett.'

It was as if she had turned a magic key. The man's attitude changed and he eyed her with new interest. 'Anna Beckett you say? Well yes, I reckon Dr Halden might like a few words with you.'

He gave her directions to James's office, though she was warned he would probably be in another part of the hospital and she would have to wait. She didn't mind that. A secretary asked her questions when she entered the central tower and she was told to wait in an anteroom.

She sat down, her heart beating faster than it had done when she'd been brought before the Foundling Governors. She wasn't afraid of James, but confronting him here where he was obviously a very important person made the coming interview too official and she felt at a disadvantage before she even saw him. She removed her damp gloves and clasped her hands anxiously.

When he came he looked so imperious she thought he must have been given a wrong message, and his opening remark was quite inexplicable.

'How did you do it, may I ask?' he thundered. No greeting. No smile of welcome. No expression of pleasure at seeing her.

'You *do* seem out of sorts. I hope nothing's wrong.'

He said: 'I'll speak to you in my office.' His back was ramrod straight and his eyes like ice. When the door was shut he started a tirade. 'It was very clever of you to spirit Anna away without anyone's knowledge. It was also very stupid and shows you have no thought for your daughter. I hope you've not come expecting my approval or understanding. I demand that you return her to me.'

Sarah turned cold. 'I haven't got Anna. I came to ask you if I could see her. I want her to live with *me*. James, I've found a nice little house where I can look after her.'

He held her gaze, no doubt deciding whether she lied or not. Then he swallowed hard and she saw the Adam's apple rise and fall in his throat.

'She isn't here,' he said. 'I was certain you must have taken her. She couldn't have left on her own.'

The atmosphere was charged with tension. Sarah took a deep breath, holding back resentment and a dreadful foreboding. So this was why he was in such a state.

She rebuked him coldly. 'You misjudged me, James.'

'I'm sorry.' He closed his lids with thumb and index finger, as if to erase the wrong conclusions, but he was still suspicious. 'When she was reported missing I drove straight back to Clerkenwell and tried to find you. No one could tell me where you were, so what was I to think?'

'I wouldn't have gone against your wishes.'

'Then where is she?'

'If I knew that would I have come here?'

She could see that he had suffered. The strain was in his eyes and etched across his brow. There could be no doubt that James had come to care deeply about his daughter in a very short time, and it made her ashamed that it had taken her so long to feel the same way.

Shame made her even sharper with him. 'You took her from the Foundling Hospital and now look what's happened. I'll never forgive you if she's come to any harm.'

'Take care who you blame,' James said. 'When I recommended she should be brought here neither of us was aware who she was. There's a lot I can say about that.'

He went on to voice his opinions in strident

450

tones, all the anger he had felt last night finding voice even though she was not guilty of removing Anna from his care. He called her many things, none of them complimentary, and rejected every plea she tried to make in her own defence.

'You were irresponsible. All you thought about was taking the easy way out. I'll never forgive you for turning my child into a foundling.'

'Then *you* should have given a thought to the possible consequences of the time we spent together. If Maud had given you children would you have cared anything for your bastard?'

'I didn't know she existed.'

'You weren't there to be told.'

'Is that why you rejected her? Did you hate me so much you couldn't bear to love our child?'

'I *did* love her. I loved her too much.' His lack of understanding was so infuriating she raised her voice. 'I couldn't give her anything, James, not even milk from my body. She would have died.'

Her passion moved him to act. He was breathing fast as he snatched her to him and his mouth was hard and fierce in its demands. When she struggled he clamped her face between his hands and kissed her until she cried out for mercy. All the years of suppressed emotion culminated in a tempestuous display of force which would have ended in his possession of her if they had been anywhere other than his office. Sarah found a reserve of strength which at last enabled her to break free, and they faced

451

each other like wild animals in combat.

'Don't ever touch me like that again,' she hissed.

She took up her umbrella and was tempted to strike him with it before turning towards the door with a swish of her skirts.

'Sarah!'

'When I find Anna you will be the last to know. Goodbye.'

She made a regal exit, her head high, her shoulders drawn back, and she didn't pause to say anything to the surprised secretary who started to patter after her. She walked down the drive with unladylike strides, covering the ground as if devils were after her.

This vitality lasted until she reached the station. The building represented a haven, a way back to sanity, and she hurried to the ladies' room where she collapsed on the wooden seat completely exhausted. Luckily there was no one else around. Sobs shook her.

The awful, unbelievable thing was that in the midst of that shocking outburst she had discovered that she loved him more than she had ever thought possible. There had never been anyone else who could inspire such craving or make her so aware of her body. But more than that, she felt something beyond the physical attraction which had drawn them together from the start, and she began to understand something about love which she had never known before. It was selfless.

As she sat alone in that dreary station waiting room she saw a picture of herself which she hoped no one else had ever seen. She had married poor Nahum for what he could do for her. The love she had professed for him had been a selfish covering for her real desire to be near her child. And that had been a fiasco. Her obsession with Corrie Palmer had not been love. The child's infant beauty had blinded her to every obvious sign that it was Anna who should have been loved. Her pride had been hurt when Corrie rejected her at the hospital, and still she hadn't seen what a fool she was.

It was James who had demonstrated the true meaning of love many years ago when he had risked ruining his marriage to give her a refuge from Abel Wood, and again in lying to save her reputation at the Foundling Hospital. He had almost lost his life for her when she'd not had the courage to stay and face the trouble Abel had caused. She didn't deserve his love.

Fresh tears filled her eyes and spilt over. 'Oh, dear, will I *ever* do anything right?'

Love was very powerful. It drove men to great lengths. All at once Sarah had a vivid picture of a large young man catching up with her outside the Foundling Chapel one Sunday evening demanding to know where Anna had gone and declaring his intention of finding her.

She raised her head. She knew where Anna would be.

But the following day, after dragging herself once more to Chertsey, she was no nearer to the answer.

'All I know is Edward upped and left the same night you was here,' said Peg Wooldridge. 'I ain't seen 'im since, but he's a grown man and knows how to take care of 'imself.'

'But didn't he say where he'd be staying?'

'No, dearie. He just left a note saying 'e was off to work with Tam O'Mara in London, but that didn't mean anything. Tam O'Mara was a restless young Irish vagabond with more charm than sense and I don't reckon he'd stay anywhere long.'

So Sarah returned to Sekford Street and wandered round the house she had made so pretty for her missing daughter. She had never felt so lonely, or so helpless. London was full of Irishmen and if Edward Wooldridge had come under the influence of one of them it would have put love right out of his mind. She knew that by the way Patrick had talked.

James had little known how close he was to Anna when he saw the wedding party entering the church near Clerkenwell Green.

Anna's wedding day was the happiest of her life. She borrowed a dress from Louisa and decorated a bonnet which had belonged to Louisa's mother. Everyone was so kind. The Pickens' house was overcrowded and none too clean, but the hearts beating within its walls were of pure gold.

'There's a room in the attic you can rent when yer married,' Mr Picken had said when they arrived from Hanwell. He was bow-shouldered and his hands were scarred from working with sheet copper but he was still a man with decent looks. 'It'll be nice to 'ave a young couple up there. What we usually get is the likes of Tam O'Mara and Shaun Connell.'

'And where would you be without us, I'm asking?' Tam slapped him on the back good-naturedly. 'We pay our rent now, don't we, boy-o.'

'And involve us in yer escapades to boot, though I must say this was one of yer better ones.'

Tam, Shaun and Mr Picken were at the wedding along with Louisa and two of her young sisters. They walked to St James's Church where Edward had arranged for the short ceremony to take place at eleven, but before they went inside they were joined by another friend, a very good-looking young man with black hair and blue eyes.

'Anna, this is Paddy Byrne,' Tam said. 'If Edward's got any sense he'll not be letting you anywhere near the man. It's a fine reputation he's got with the girls.'

Paddy shook Anna by the hand. 'I don't take 'em from me friends,' he said, putting all his charm into the smile he gave her. 'But it's lucky for Edward he saw you first.'

'Paddy's found me a job in the market, Anna,' Edward told her. 'It were right good of him. I never 'ad a bean left after buying the licence.'

'Oh, Edward, I'm sorry ...'

'Perhaps in a few months we can go back to Chertsey, but we'd best stay here for a while 'till I've made a bit of money.'

Paddy Byrne tweaked her ear playfully. 'I'd never forgive 'im if 'e took you away too soon.'

Anna liked him. He was as saucy as Tam and better-looking into the bargain, but her eyes were only for Edward.

She looked at him all through the ceremony, drawing her strength from his love, and she made her vows in a surprisingly strong voice so that none should be in any doubt as to her pride in becoming his wife. When he put the ring on her finger her heart was singing and she'd never thought she would know such happiness, especially lately.

They came out of the church into a patch of sunshine which had struggled through cushions of fluffy cloud to touch the spot where bride and groom would stand a moment. She had gone into the church as Anna Beckett, a foundling who had never belonged to anybody. Now she was Anna Wooldridge, wife of the most wonderful man in the world, and she would never be unwanted again. Edward kissed her cheek and she turned her head so that his mouth came to rest for a few delicious seconds on hers.

The wedding party went from the church to the Crown Tavern at the corner of Clerkenwell Close and the Green, and there were such noisy celebrations Anna several times buried her head against Edward's chest and covered her ears to shut it out. Not that she disliked it. She loved every minute, but harsh sounds brought on frightening symptoms and she was so afraid something would happen to spoil the first night alone with her husband.

Paddy Byrne had a fiddle and he played it like a master. Soon everyone was dancing. When they tired of that there was singing, all the old London songs almost lifting the rafters as the beer flowed.

When he gave up fiddling Paddy came and sat next to Anna. 'My old stepfather told me there used to be a mummified cat in here once, in a glass case with a curtain round it.'

'Don't be telling her such things,' said Tam.

'It's true though. Seems workmen found it bricked up when they were pulling down the old church walls. A right face it was making.'

'Well, wouldn't you be making a worse face than the one you've got if you were buried alive?' said Shaun.

'Stop it. I don't want to hear any more,' Anna cried. But she laughed just the same at the way they ragged each other. They were all the best of friends.

She sipped lemonade and watched anxiously as Edward, along with the others, became more than a little drunk. Louisa was no better.

'You'll not 'ave 'im bothering you tonight, dearie,' she said, inclining her head in Edward's direction and giving a lopsided grin. 'Reckon 'e'll snore till morning, and 'e's got to be down the market by six termorrow.'

It was dark when they finally staggered back to Paul Place, still singing, and the party had grown by another dozen.

'Come on in,' said Mr Picken, extending his

arms to encompass them all. 'Plenty of time before morning.'

'Plenty ... of ... time,' sang Tam and Shaun together, their arms round each other's shoulders.

Louisa broke them up and caught Tam round the waist. 'Time for you and me, Tammy boy.'

'Oh Tammy boy ...' sang Paddy, 'the pipes, the pipes are call ... ing ...'

Anna had hold of Edward's hand, hoping he wouldn't drink any more. His face was red and he was acting as silly as the rest but she didn't want to say anything to spoil the evening for him. They all went inside, laughing and squabbling good-humouredly over who should use the closet first.

Edward went and stood on the stairs. 'I want to thank ... you. Thank ... you all ... very much,' he said swaying slightly. Then he focused on Anna and saw how tired she looked. 'I think my wife and I would like to go to bed now.'

The ribald laughter was followed by crude remarks which Anna didn't fully understand, and she was glad to get away. The stairs creaked as they climbed. Up and up they seemed to go, a lighted candle in Edward's unsteady hand producing frightening shadows at every bend. She clung to the rope rail, ready to break his fall if he stumbled. The attic room was hot and stuffy. Flies buzzed round their heads and a moth flew in, straight to the flame, when she opened the tiny square window, but there was a jug of water and a chipped basin on a table by the bed. Once Edward had sluiced his face he sobered considerably.

She made him sit on the bed and undid his collar and necktie, helped him to slide out of his jacket, and remembered how she had loved doing things for him when he'd been a boy. She knelt down to remove his boots, and he took her face between his hands.

'Ummm.' The sound between a sigh and moan rumbled from his throat. 'I love you, Anna.'

'I love you too, but you've had too much to drink. Lie down and sleep it off and we'll talk tomorrow.'

'Who wants to talk? I want *you.*'

There was only just space for the narrow bed and the table in the room and she had to be careful not to bump her head on the eaves. She took off his shirt and touched his smooth, broad chest tenderly, letting her fingers slide over the skin which shone with perspiration in the candlelight.

When he was undressed except for his trousers his mouth sought hers hungrily and she became a captive in his arms. He drew her down on to the bed beside him and she gave a small gasp as his tongue parted her lips, but the novelty was so exciting she allowed him to continue. He opened the top of her dress and his lips trailed down over her throat. By the time they reached her breast she was beginning to feel more intoxicated than he was and she responded feverishly. Time and place dissolved away.

He lifted her shoulders and slipped her dress

down until it came over her feet, then undid the waist buttons of her petticoats and discarded them as well so that she was left in only her chemise, ankle-length drawers and stockings.

'Put out the candle, Edward,' she implored.

'I want to look at you,' he murmured.

She trembled when he removed his trousers. The sight of him proud and eager for her was so daunting she buried her face in the pillow, but he coaxed her with surprisingly gentle hands. His fingers and lips produced currents of glorious sensation which cascaded through her body. She twined her arms round him and pressed herself close.

'I'm afraid I might frighten you.' His mouth was against her ear, and shivers ran down her spine.

'Make me your wife,' she urged. 'Nothing'll frighten me.'

'Shock makes you ill.'

'Silly!' She pulled off her drawers and stockings, and pressed herself against him, knowing that if he'd been sober she would have been too shy to make any such movement. 'Edward, I want you. I love you.'

The feel of his skin against hers was warm and inviting, more wonderful than anything she had imagined. It felt so familiar, yet so exquisitely different, and fires seemed to be burning in every secret part of her. He took her with great care, leading her into the union with a love which feared for her yet could not be suppressed, and though she cried out initially the pain was but a memory within seconds. She

460

was so deliriously happy she drew her muscles tight to keep him there even after he was spent.

They lay in each other's arms afterwards, Anna with her head against his shoulder and the blanket pulled up over her head to shut out the rest of the world. This was the only place she wanted to be for the rest of her life. There was no better place on earth than here in bed with Edward.

The noise downstairs was spilling out into the street and riotous laughter echoed through the house. Neighbours had joined the party. Gin was flowing along with the beer, and girlish shrieks told of male advances. But inside the tiny attic room there was peace.

'We belong together properly now,' Anna said. 'I can forget I never had a mother or father. For the first time in my life I've got someone of my very own and you're all I want.'

Edward had been lying on his back, but he turned towards her sleepily.

'You have got a mother,' he grunted.

'Somewhere, yes. But whoever she is she couldn't get rid of me quick enough.'

'Mrs Morey's your mother. The cow!'

For a moment Anna didn't move. Edward was still drunk. His eyes were closed, his speech slow, and he was talking a lot of nonsense. All the same, she wondered if he was sensible enough to repeat what he'd said.

'Say that again,' she prompted.

'Say what?'

'Tell me about Mrs Morey.'

'She's your mother. I heard her talking to Ma not long since. That's why I had to come and find you, because *she* wants you and she can't have you. You're mine.'

She had to lean up on one elbow to hear what he was saying as the words got slower and sleepier, but there was no doubt he was speaking the truth as he knew it.

'Shouldn't 'ave told you,' he muttered. 'Never meant to tell you.'

Anna felt the old familiar tingling start in her foot and quickly spread to the rest of her body as a convulsion of enormous proportions shook her. The candle seemed to be revolving round her like an orbiting star, and foam bubbled from her mouth. She heard Edward calling her name. Calling, calling, calling. All night he seemed to be calling her but she couldn't answer.

When at last she was able to open her eyes it was daylight and he was bending over her, fully dressed and so worried he seemed to have aged overnight. There was a salty taste in her mouth and her tongue was sore where she had bitten it. She smiled at him and tried to stretch out her hand but she'd no strength, and her head ached intolerably.

'Rest quiet, love,' Edward murmured, bathing her head with cool water. Louisa was hovering by the door. 'You're over it now.'

Sudden fear shook her. 'You won't make me go back to the asylum, will you, Edward?'

'Never,' he promised. 'It were all my fault. I'll never forgive meself.'

Slowly she recalled what had brought on the attack, and she closed her eyes again, unable to cope yet with news of such magnitude. If it was true that Sarah Morey was her mother she couldn't bear to think about it. The woman had be the cruellest, most heartless, selfish creature on earth, and Anna's bitterness was worse than the blood that had been in her mouth. She felt as though she had been deprived of milk from birth and had been fed instead on sour wine.

## CHAPTER 18

In the weeks which followed her meeting with James, Sarah continued to live in the house in Sekford Street, taking in sewing to pay the rent. She'd known she would have to do it but had imagined Anna being with her to share the work so that they could build up a little business. Without her there was no incentive.

On Sundays she took a basket of food to Maggie, who was now well enough to go out charring again and should rightfully have had enough money to buy her own, but it made a reason for going, and Sarah needed Maggie's company. She had written to James giving him her address so that he could let her know when there was any news of Anna, but he hadn't visited, and she didn't seek him out again. It seemed they were destined to meet only in a crisis.

October ended with dismal weather, and the dark evenings felt interminable. She missed the Foundling children more than she would ever have thought possible and longed to hear their voices ringing through the dormitories. She missed the exercise. She had always walked long distances through the corridors and the grounds. And she missed the singing. Every Sunday she went to a church service but it was never the same, and she daren't go to the Foundling Chapel as a visitor in case she was told that she wasn't welcome.

Her only interest, apart from sewing, was to read the newspaper so as to keep in touch with what was happening in the world. She saw the *Clerkenwell News* at least once a week, sometimes picking up work from the advertisements, and if she could afford an extra penny, which was double the price, she would sometimes buy the *Illustrated London News*. It was in one of these she read about a trial in Manchester involving some Fenians who were accused of murdering a policeman. She recalled the conversation she'd had with Patrick that traumatic day when she had borrowed the money to go to Chertsey, and she felt a twinge of uneasiness. She hadn't seen him since she had left the Foundling Hospital. Patrick had vanished, almost as mysteriously as Anna had done, and no one seemed to know where he had gone.

A few days later she had a worrying conversation with Maggie.

'Paddy 'ad a row with Abel,' Maggie said. 'A terrible row. I was so 'appy because Dick was

464

'ome that day for the first time in months, but Abel was drunk and I wonder Paddy didn't kill 'im for the things 'e said.'

'What things?'

'About 'im being mixed up with the Irish and killing a policeman. A load of nonsense it were. The ramblings of a drunken old sod. But Paddy took it serious and went for 'im, and Abel said he were never to come in the 'ouse again.'

'Where did he go then?'

'I don't know. Paddy never tells anyone anything. A law unto 'imself, that one. Why can't 'e be decent-living like 'is brothers? John ain't never caused me a minute's worry.'

Privately Sarah thought Patrick was worth two of either of Maggie's other sons in spite of his wildness, and she continued to worry about him. The Fenians were an unlawful bunch who had gained notoriety and she hoped he wasn't fool enough to be mixed up with them. He wasn't truly Irish so he ought not to pretend that he was, but she'd seen by his swagger that he was flattered to be thought a worthy fighter for the cause, as he'd put it.

For a while Sarah scoured the news for the outcome of the Manchester trial. It helped to take her mind off Anna and James. But then, one foggy November day, she had the most unexpected visitor, and Patrick's affairs were cast aside.

It was a Saturday afternoon and the sound of vehicles along St John's Street was muffled by the dampness in the air. The parlour was dark and she was sitting by the window so that she

465

could see to stitch some tucks. A steady drip on the window ledge splashed the glass and distorted people passing by with their heads hidden beneath umbrellas, and when someone knocked on the door she pricked her finger. She put her sewing down carefully so as not to mark it, and went to see who it was.

The girl on the doorstep was Corrie Palmer.

They looked at each other with embarrassment for a moment, neither saying anything. Sarah was almost too surprised to find her voice.

'Corrie, you're wet. Come on in and let me make you a hot drink.'

'Thank you, but I can't stop long. I wouldn't have come on a day like this but I don't get another off for a fortnight and I wanted to see you.'

She was neatly dressed in black, a cape covering her uniform skirt and blouse, and when she slipped off the hood her bright hair was drawn into a tidy knot on top of her head. She sat down by the table and Sarah lit the lamp even though it was early.

'Mrs Morey, I had to go back to the Foundling Hospital recently and the girls were talking about you. They said you'd been dismissed. I couldn't believe it.'

'There was bound to be talk,' Sarah said.

'I must be frank with you. There's a rumour that it was because you once left a baby at the hospital yourself. I've come to ask if that's right.'

The girl had courage. It must have taken a lot of it to bring her here with such a question,

466

and it deserved a truthful answer.

'Yes, it's right,' Sarah said quietly.

Corrie looked down at her hands; neat, small hands which had never had any aptitude for needlework or anything requiring patience. She clenched them tightly together.

'Then I am your child?'

'No.' Sarah searched for the right words to explain. She could see by Corrie's face that she had agonized over the possibility for days, but there was no clue as to whether she wished it to be true. She said: 'I always believed that you were my daughter. I married the Reverend Morey so that I could live in Chertsey and be near you. When you rejected me it nearly broke my heart.'

'You smothered me with love when I was little. Then you let me down and I was afraid to trust you again.'

'Perhaps it's just as well. I seem to have made a dreadful mess of everything.'

Silence fell between them, the subject too deep for trivial chatter. A coal fell out of the narrow grate and into the hearth, disturbing the bright warm glow. Sarah picked up the tongs and replaced it, but there was no longer the same comforting heat. The heart of the fire had sunk.

'I'm glad you're not my mother,' Corrie said. 'If you were I'd be feeling guilty, and I might even hate you. I'd rather not know the woman who deserted me.'

Until recently Sarah hadn't really thought beyond her own side of the situation. She

467

had never envisaged the complications that would arise from her decision to let the Foundling Hospital take her child. Now she had suffered James's condemnation, and today she was discovering how it felt to *be* a foundling child. For the first time she was aware that her sin had not been the abandoning of her baby. It had been her selfish need to stay near her and watch her grow up. She thought of the old saying that you can't eat your cake and have it too, but that was what she had always been determined to do. It was time now to pay.

'I've hurt everyone,' she murmured. 'But no one deserves it except me.'

Corrie's damp skirt was beginning to steam, and the material had a peppery smell. She patted it studiously, avoiding Sarah's eyes.

'It's Anna Beckett, isn't it? She's the one.' When Sarah neither confirmed nor denied it she showed impatience. 'I'm not so frivolous as you think. I gave up seeing Fergal Whittaker and I returned the red dress. Nessie told me where to find you. I care about things, Mrs Morey, and I always cared about Anna.'

'Then you can tell me whether you think Anna would also rather not know the woman who deserted her.'

'You haven't told her then?'

'No, I don't know where she is.'

Their roles were reversing. This girl had all the answers to the questions Sarah wanted to ask because she saw things from the opposite side of the fence.

'Well, I hope you *don't* find her. I think

the shock would make her illness worse if she found out you're her mother. You've never done anything for her all these years. She wouldn't want you to start now.'

'You think she would resent me?'

'I'm sure of it.' Corrie stood up. 'If you love her you'll stay away and leave her in ignorance. It's the kindest thing you could do.'

She left not long afterwards, but the strange meeting had brought a measure of understanding. When Corrie Palmer got to the door she put her arms round Sarah impulsively and quite unexpectedly.

'Thank you for loving me once,' she said.

'I never stopped loving you.'

'Ah, but you did, and it was my own fault.' She pulled the hood over her head ready to go out again in the fog which was growing thicker as dusk approached. 'May I come and see you again?'

A surge of joy made Sarah catch her breath.

'Yes, Corrie.' How she had once yearned for such an opening as this. Even now it was not too late. 'Oh, yes, *please* come again.'

Anna took several weeks to fully recover from the epileptic attack on her wedding night. She wasn't physically ill. In fact those around her assumed she was better long before she felt anything like her old self again, except for Edward who quickly came to recognize the signs of her illness. He blamed himself for having brought on such a bad attack, but she was cross with him for even thinking it.

'Of course it wasn't your fault. Things just upset me sometimes and I never know when it's going to be.'

'But if I hadn't mentioned Mrs Morey ...'

'It's done, Edward.' She was lying in his arms on the lumpy bed. 'Now don't let's talk of her ever again. I never want to see her or hear of her, so let's just forget about it.'

She was blissfully happy with her husband. He was so kind and gentle, and he worked from dawn till dusk at Covent Garden for a miserable wage which barely paid for their room. She knew he was fretting. He wanted to take her out of London, back to his mother in Chertsey, but Anna was content to stay where she was. In Chertsey there would be reminders of Sarah Morey.

'This is our home,' she told him when he worried that she was too pale. 'I like it here. We've got good friends and a warm bed. What more could we want?'

'I want the best for you, Anna,' Edward said. 'This is a hovel. I know we couldn't afford much better in the country but at least you'd be breathing clean air.'

'I've always breathed London air. It doesn't do me any harm.'

She would have been content to live anywhere as long as it was not in the asylum. The wonderful moment when she had walked away from Hanwell would stay in her memory for ever, not only because Edward had been so brave in rescuing her, but because she could live a normal life. But there was one thing

470

which marred her happiness a little. She missed
Dr Halden. He had been very kind to her over
the few weeks she had been under his care,
and she had trusted him. No doubt he too had
trusted her. It worried her that she hadn't been
able to let him know where she was and that
she was all right, but there was no guarantee
that her marriage meant she couldn't be taken
back there.

Anna rarely went out. The busy streets of
Clerkenwell made her nervous, so she stayed at
home and dressed dolls which Louisa made and
sold in a local street market. But one Saturday
evening in early November she plucked up
courage and went with Louisa to the market.

She had never seen the streets so crowded. The
whole population seeming intent on spending
what little money it had. She was tempted to
warm her hands at a hot chestnut stove with fire
shining crimson through the holes, but Louisa
wouldn't let her linger. The closely packed stalls
were mostly lit by grease lamps, the smell from
them stinging her nose, and from all sides came
shouted appeals to buy everything from apples
to bloaters. There were saucepans and shawls,
turnips and tin trays, a whole gamut of bargains
too good to miss if the bawling and cajoling
vendors were to be believed.

Louisa stopped in a doorway near a stall lit
by candles stuck in swedes.

'Reckon we can sell some 'ere,' she said, and
began to shout as loud as the rest.

Anna was fascinated. It was all so exciting,
a wonderful way to help Edward financially,

and she wished she had come before. But Louisa hadn't been there five minutes before a decrepit woman gave her a shove which sent her reeling against a barrowload of whelks. The dolls scattered in the gutter.

'Get awf me patch,' the woman yelled.

Louisa picked up the dolls and they moved down further, selling one for a penny to a costermonger's child. Everyone else was either too busy proclaiming his own wares, or too engrossed in buying Sunday's dinner.

Louisa shouted: 'Come and look! 'Ere's the best dolls you ever saw. Come and buy.' Two children tugged at their mother's dress and made her stop, their faces puckering when their requests were refused. 'Beautiful dolls, lady, for the most beautiful children I ever saw.' Louisa appealed to the mother. 'Don't say no and make 'em cry.'

Her sweet-talking brought two more sales. Louisa shouted louder, and Anna joined in. But women with money were filling their bags with vegetables, and men thought only of beer shops.

It was while they were still trying to attract attention that Anna saw Sarah Morey. Her heart skipped a beat. She was only a few yards away, intent on selecting a cabbage, and Anna pressed herself into a dark doorway so as not to be seen. Her limbs felt paralysed, her stomach knotted and she had a job to breathe.

She watched Mrs Morey surreptitiously, seeing the same poised, beautiful woman she had always admired, but as she stared she experienced the strangest sensation. It was as if she could see inside that graceful body and was once again curled up inside a protective, life-giving womb. There was warmth and nourishment, and there was love. She could feel it.

She'd heard it said that epileptics sometimes saw things. It had never happened to her before, but in that moment she saw and almost understood how her mother had felt with a child inside her which she feared would die if she kept it in poverty. She felt bound to this woman for just an instant by an invisible tie, strong as an umbilical cord. And as if she too felt the pull of it, Sarah turned, her eyes seeking the source of something which made her draw up her shoulders. Anna stayed hidden.

The feeling passed. She watched Mrs Morey walk away without buying anything from the stall, and all the bitterness flowed back like stagnant water which had been temporarily held in check. And with it came the headache she had been suffering since Edward had told her.

'Are you all right, ducks?' Louisa became aware that something was wrong and she put down the tray of dolls on the path. She looked worried. 'You ain't 'aving one of yer turns, are you?'

'No,' said Anna. 'I'm fine.'

It was quite ridiculous. No one ever felt as close to another person as she had just done. Her mind had been playing tricks. She'd never had such an experience before in all the years she had known Mrs Morey, and nothing like it would have happened now if she hadn't been told that they were mother and daughter. The suggestion had been put into her mind and she had embroidered upon it, just as she did when she was given a piece of fine, new linen.

One Saturday at the end of November Patrick was delivering some flowers to an address near Bow Street when he saw someone under escort being taken to the police station in a prison van. A small crowd had gathered.

'What's going on?' he asked the man closest to him.

'Irish troublemaker,' the man said. Luckily he was the chatty type who seemed to know everything, and liked everyone to know that he knew. 'Bloke called George Berry, but they reckon 'e's Colonel Burke of the Fenians.'

'Get-away!' exclaimed Patrick. He was immediately all attention. 'When was 'e arrested?'

'Last Wednesday week. Didn't you 'ear about it? Right struggle there were. The constable threatened to shoot 'im if 'e tried to escape.'

'He was violent then?'

'Not 'arf. Had another bloke with 'im called Casey. Reckon they'll both do time.'

Patrick passed on the news to Tam and Shaun as soon as he got back to the room in the Pickens' house he'd been sharing with them ever since Abel Wood had turned him out.

'I heard about it, boy-o,' said Tam, which was disappointing. Patrick had hoped to be the first to tell them something important, and it was that all right. 'It's serious. The Colonel's a good man come from America. The revolution needs him, so it does.'

'What can we do?'

'Nothing yet. But there'll be a meeting soon enough, when we know what's happening.'

A group of Fenians met secretly the next week, Tam, Shaun and Patrick among them, but though passionate words were spoken no plans could be made until word got round that both Burke and Casey had been sent to the Clerkenwell House of Detention while on remand. Another meeting was called. Somehow they had to be got out, even if it meant taking desperate action, and for the first time since Patrick had become a supporter of the cause there was talk of using explosives. His heart raced. This was excitement which stirred his blood to fire.

'We need Richard Burke,' said the leader of the party, Captain James Murphy. 'Ireland *must* be free, and to fight for freedom we need guns. The Colonel has the means of getting them, and I've had orders from Dublin that they're both to be got out before the trial.'

'T'was a sad day for us when he was caught,' said another, a man in his forties, Timothy Desmond by name and a tailor by trade.

'It'll be a sadder day for those who did the catching when we blow a hole in the wall of the prison.'

'You don't mean it!' cried Tam.

'I mean it full well. It's the only way.'

'It would be easy enough in Corporation Lane,' said Patrick, daring to speak up. 'The wall's right by the exercise yard.'

'And would you be knowing what time it's used?' asked the only woman in the group.

'Between three and half past four o'clock every day so they are.'

Murphy was taking no chances on Patrick's reliability. Burke and Casey were allowed visitors in the House of Detention and he ordered the woman to go and talk with them the next day.

'I want to know everything you can find out about the movements of the warders, how many are on duty in the yard and the exact length of time the prisoners are allowed exercise.'

There was a lot of talk about obtaining gunpowder and the best place to position it. Someone would have to light the fuse, others would need to keep watch, but nothing definite could be arranged until the woman had reported on her visit, so the meeting was adjourned.

When they got back to Paul Place, Tam and Patrick were intoxicated with the excitement of it all but Shaun, who had a reputation for cunning, was much more realistic.

'If there's going to be trouble we three ought to split up,' he said. 'Heaven forbid the police'll be after us, but if such a misfortune should occur they'd have good pickings with all of us together in one hole.'

They could all see the sense of it, but couldn't agree as to who should move out.

'I ain't got nowhere else to go,' said Patrick. He'd got used to his mattress on the floor and the way the fleas jumped out of it when he sat down heavily.

'And I found this place first,' Shaun stated.

Tam poured himself some ale from a pitted jug. 'Well, I'm after staying here, and I reckon I've the most right since I'm courting Louisa.'

They argued plenty, but in the end Shaun and Patrick had to concede that Tam had priority. Louisa wasn't in on all their plans, but what little she knew was safe with her, and if they needed help at any time it was best to keep on the right side of her.

'Looks like it's you and me'll have to find somewhere else to live, Paddy, me boy,' said Shaun.

A week of December had gone when Patrick collected his belongings together. He had an idea it might be useful to live in Corporation Lane again, so he chose a time when Abel wasn't likely to be there and paid his ma a visit. She was still thin, but the hollows in her cheeks had filled out a little and she had tidied herself up.

'Look what the cat's dragged in!' she cried. 'Paddy Byrne if I ain't mistaken.'

'Now, Ma, I ain't been away that long.'

'And you ain't staying either. Abel'd do me a mischief if I let yer.'

'I need somewhere to live.'

'Then go to yer sister. She's got plenty of room.'

This was news to Patrick. He didn't know Sarah had left the Foundling Hospital, or that she had a house of her own. He hadn't seen her since the day she'd borrowed money off him, and as he hadn't got it back he reckoned she owed him a favour. Armed with the address, a respectable one in Sekford Street which might be even better, he set off again, keeping close to the gloomy wall of the House of Detention which broke the force of a high wind cutting through. And every few yards he pictured where would be best to blow a hole in it.

Sarah welcomed him with a little more pleasure than his mother had done, though she was cautious.

'What brings you here, Patrick?' She showed him in to a cosy parlour. 'No one's had sight nor sound of you for weeks.'

He swung her off her feet, making her squeal, and when he hugged her she gave his cheek an affectionate kiss. The house was warm and comfortable, the plain furniture decked with lace-edged covers and antimacassars to make it look like a toff's, but though it was too fussy for his taste it was several steps up from the one where he'd been living and he wouldn't mind settling for a while. He wondered what gent was keeping her in it.

He decided to play for her sympathy, knowing she could always be relied upon to support him if she felt he wasn't being treated fairly.

'I'm a bit down on me luck,' he said. 'I couldn't pay the rent for me last room and got turned out.'

'So you need the money I owe you. I would've given it to you long ago if you'd been around.'

She turned to pick up a purse from the table, but he stopped her.

'No, it ain't the money. I need somewhere to sleep. Ma won't let me stay there because of Abel. It ain't fair. It's me home.'

Sarah didn't respond the way he expected. Her lovely blue eyes became hard and she drew up her graceful neck like a swan about to protect its territory.

'I see. You think you can vanish for weeks without letting anyone know where you are, then turn up like the prodigal son for the fatted calf.' The way she put her hands together reminded him that she'd been married to a parson. 'Well let me enlighten you, Patrick. You've been a trial to your mother. Why should she go against her husband's wishes and give you a bed? She's been ill.'

'I know.'

'You know! More to the point, do you care? Your mother needed food. She was starving nearly to death but you didn't spare a farthing of your wages to get anything for her, so why should she help you now?'

'Sarah ...'

'Then there's the stories your stepfather heard about you mixing with bad company. I'd like to know what you've been doing.'

'Don't say you believe anything Abel says. You of all people should know he's a right bastard.'

'Then why did you let him turn you out if you'd nothing to hide?' Her temper was in full flood and she gave him no chance to defend himself. 'Your mother made a lot of sacrifices for you, Patrick. The least you could've done

479

was see that Abel Wood didn't spend every penny on drink, leaving her with nothing.'

'Sister Sarah, where were you when Ma needed someone? Seems to me you didn't come near any of us for ten years.'

Patrick had always loved his half-sister, but he wasn't a child any more and he wouldn't be treated like one. She thought about it for a moment, lowered her lids, then smiled ruefully.

'All right,' she admitted. 'I'm no better than you so I've no right to stand in judgement. I'm sorry.'

As soon as the atmosphere seemed more hopeful he appealed to her again.

'I really wish you'd let me have a room,' he said.

She was mellowing. 'I might let you *rent* the extra bedroom. I won't have you living here for nothing, and I don't want it spoilt.'

'You're good to me. You are 'n all.' He pecked her cheek. 'I promise I'll stay out of the way when you're ... entertaining.'

She pursed her mouth primly. 'If you're referring to gentlemen callers I can tell you there won't be any. And I've only said that I *might* let you stay.'

'A beautiful colleen like you, begorra, and no man in her life!' Patrick teased. 'Just wait till I tell that to Tam O'Mara.'

Sarah's face suddenly turned very pale and she clutched a handful of her taffeta skirt, crushing it.

'What name did you say?'

'Tam O'Mara. He's after being one of me friends.'

She was quite agitated. A variety of emotions chased across her face which he couldn't make out at all. She was such a complex creature, always full of secrets. They were alike in that way, sure enough. They were both full of secrets, and always had been.

'Sit down, Patrick, and I'll make some tea.'

'I haven't got time for tea.'

'Then you'll make some time. I want to hear all about Tam O'Mara.'

'Now why would you be interested?'

'I want to know if he has another friend called Edward Wooldridge.'

This was a puzzle and no mistake. He started to tell her: 'I know Edward Wooldridge. I went to 'is wedding a few weeks since.' Understanding slowly began to dawn as he made the connection. 'His wife was a foundling from that hospital where you were ...'

He would have told her more, but Sarah's eyes filled with tears and she sank down on to the hearthrug with her skirts spreading round her like a fallen flower.

'So Anna's married,' she said.

'I told you, I were there at the wedding.'

'Does she know you're related to me?'

He bent down beside her, growing more curious by the minute. 'I don't talk much about meself, girl. You should know that.'

'So she doesn't know?'

'No.'

'Then will you swear on oath not to tell her

481

before I can get to visit?'

Patrick cupped her chin in his hand, forcing her to look into his eyes, and he grinned. 'If I do, will you definitely let me have the room?'

'You're a devil, Patrick Byrne, just like your father was. Yes, you can have it.'

'I knew you would. I'll be after leaving me things then.'

He couldn't have felt more pleased with himself. It had turned out to be a very successful visit.

Sarah's thoughts were in turmoil after Patrick left. She needed to see James and ask his advice, but after the last stormy meeting she was reluctant to contact him. She'd declared he would be the last person to know if she found Anna, and she didn't know if she ought to tell him at all. It would be yet another betrayal if she gave him the address and he went straight round to insist on Anna's return to Hanwell.

Since Corrie's visit she had been seeing things differently. Sarah didn't have the right to visit her daughter herself, even if she had the courage, and now that Anna was married to Edward Wooldridge she herself had less claim on her than ever. She'd seen that for Anna's sake she must stay away and never again try to become selfishly involved in her life again. Certainly she would be better off not knowing the self-indulgent, designing, stupid creature who had given her birth.

But one thing worried Sarah very much. She'd been brought up in Clerkenwell and knew the district well. Paul Place was among a labyrinth of alleys near St John's Lane, all of which were unsavoury, and she dreaded to think of Anna living in similar conditions to the ones she had known herself. She had given her up partly to save her from poverty and disease, and she didn't know what the Wooldridge boy could be thinking of to take her there when he had a family in the country who would surely make room for them.

Something else concerned her even more. Marriage was a big undertaking for any girl and the physical side of it could be quite frightening. She dreaded to think what effect it might have had on Anna, who was delicate and quite inexperienced. It was this which finally decided her that James must be told.

She wrote a note to him, giving no details.

'Dear James,' she wrote. 'By sheer coincidence I have learnt where Anna is living. Please come to see me as soon as you can. Sarah.'

She addressed the letter to him at Hanwell and posted it on Wednesday morning, 11 December, hoping he would get it the next day, then if finding Anna meant as much to him as he had professed he would come straight away.

He came on the afternoon of Friday, 13 December.

A cab stopped outside just before noon and James stepped down, soberly dressed in black coat and grey trousers. From behind the curtain Sarah saw him pay the cabby, survey the house, then remove his top hat before knocking on the door with the silver knob of his cane. She waited a suitable time, then went to let him in.

'Good morning, Sarah.'

'I'm glad you could come,' Sarah said.

She hadn't realized how the sight of him in her parlour would affect her. He gave her his hat, gloves and cane, and sat down in the only armchair, asserting his authority before a word had been spoken. Her head was dizzy. Her hands became damp and she couldn't seem to find her voice.

'You told me very little,' he reproached her. 'I oughtn't to have left Hanwell today, so I hope what you have to tell me will justify my absence.'

'Prepare yourself for a shock, James.' She was determined not to let his overbearing manner put her off. 'Anna is married.'

He digested the news without immediate comment. It didn't send him into a rage or ruffle him in any way that she could see. He let several seconds tick by, his elbow on the chair arm and chin resting in his palm as he studied her and thought about it.

'All right, tell me how you heard, and everything else I should know.'

He listened without interruption while she related all she knew about the Wooldridges and what she had learnt from Patrick. His expression hardly changed.

She finished with: 'I didn't think of Edward Wooldridge until I was on my way home from seeing you. It came to me that he must have helped Anna to leave Hanwell, but I couldn't

484

find out where he was, and never for one minute did I think he would marry her.'

'And now I suppose you've already poked your inquisitive nose into Anna's new life.'

'I haven't done anything except write to you.' He was insufferable. Indignation flared and she wished she'd left him in ignorance.

'Why didn't you let me know as soon as you suspected this Wooldridge fellow?'

'There was no point. You wouldn't have known where to look for him any more than I did.'

'Weren't you worried?'

'Of course I was worried. If I hadn't been I wouldn't have got in touch with you.' She felt like a servant in her own house being quizzed by the master. If only he wouldn't look at her like that. 'I want you to go and see where she's living. I'm so afraid it's a dreadful place.'

'Why haven't you been yourself? Why leave it to me? I thought you objected to my interference before.'

She didn't know why he was being so difficult. At one time he would never have spoken to her like this, but then, of course, he hadn't known about Anna. His attitude hurt her and she was trembling, but the discussion had to be kept dignified.

'I've been doing a lot of thinking since I saw you,' she said, trying to make him understand. 'I realize that I've forfeited the right ever to see Anna again. I long to see her, but for her sake I've got to stay away. I've failed her too often and I'm sure she wouldn't want to see me anyway.'

'Noble sentiments,' he scoffed. 'Are they to cover up a cowardly reluctance to pursue the matter now she has a husband?'

'No!' The trembling gained momentum, affecting her visibly, and she wrung her hands together. 'Please don't keep blaming me. I need you. I must know if ... if marriage ... suits her. I'm afraid for her, and I don't want her to have to go back to Hanwell.'

He stretched out his hand and drew her towards him. 'Sarah, if Anna's happy she won't need to go back to Hanwell. I watched her for several weeks and while she was contented she was well. Perhaps marriage is the very thing she needs. We all need someone to love us, just as much as we love them. It should make us better people.'

His strong fingers bound hers and the masterful clasp sent shivers up her arm. She drew a quivering breath, hoping he was unaware of the chaotic sensations his slightest touch caused.

'What would you know about that?' she demanded, dragging her hand away.

'Nothing. You've seen to it.'

'I don't know what you mean.'

He sat forward. 'You've denied me the happiness that love brings. You denied me my child, and you only need me to get you out of difficulties.'

'That's not true ...'

'If Anna has found love then she's lucky and

486

it's the best thing I could wish for her. You have never had any to give.'

She darted away from him, broken-hearted, and rushed to the foot of the stairs. 'You say such cruel things to me, James, and I can't stand any more. Please leave at once.'

She gathered up her skirts and hurriedly climbed the stairs to her room, intending to indulge her misery in private, but James had no intention of leaving and he followed her with great strides. His foot was in the bedroom door before she could slam it.

'What a fool you are, Sarah.'

'Don't you dare come in here.'

But she couldn't hold out against his strength. He put his shoulder to the wood and eased the door until there was room for him to slide round it. Her heart was hammering. His head almost touched the low ceiling and the floorboards rocked. She was breathing so fast her lips parted to draw in air and there was pain in her breast, but she was able to push him away when he attempted to take her in his arms.

'Stop fighting me,' he commanded.

'Get out of my bedroom!'

He clutched her wrist so firmly she couldn't drag away. 'Sarah, I'm trying to tell you that I've loved you all these years and you've never once shown that it meant anything to you.'

Those hooded eyes held hers with such sensuality she felt as if her very bones were melting. She couldn't look away.

'I didn't know I seemed like that. I never meant to hurt you.'

487

'I need someone to love me. I need *you.*'

'I *do* love you.' She shouted the words at him in exasperation. Then tears filled her eyes and she went limp. Her voice became a caress. 'Oh, James, let me show you how *much* I love you.'

He began to kiss her very gently, his lips playing over hers, scarcely touching, yet producing such feeling Sarah lost awareness of everything else. Small sounds of delight escaped her. Her fingers sought the back of his neck, kneading upwards through his hair, and she pressed herself as close to him as she could while his teasing mouth drove her wild with anticipation.

'You bewitch me,' he murmured.

His mouth moved down to the curve of her neck. His tongue touched the lobe of her ear. She laughed at the ecstasy and stretched her head back so that he could explore further. Her skin had never felt so responsive to touch, so tinglingly alive. Waves of overpowering excitement stimulated every part of her body, and she moved with luxurious abandon.

'I've been waiting so long for you,' she breathed, breaking away to grip his hand. She tried to lead him towards the bed.

His feet were firmly planted on the spot where he had caught her and he was as immovable as a rock.

'Shame on you,' he teased gently. He drew her back into his arms and kissed her again, but with more fervour. His mouth was hard against hers, moulding her lips to his own with luscious promise, and with one hand at the small of her back he pressed her to him until she was aware that he was equally aroused. Then he let her go. 'No, Sarah. Remember what happened before. I'm not going to make love to you until we're married.'

'But James ...'

He kissed the tip of her nose. 'We'll set the date for next week. I'll make the arrangements and let you know.'

'I haven't said yes.'

'In the last few minutes you've said it a hundred different ways, so don't torment me, woman.' He opened the bedroom door and cold air from the passage cooled her cheeks. 'Now, to set your mind at rest, I'm going to see Anna.'

She was immediately alarmed. 'What will you say to her?'

'Don't worry, I'll visit her as a physician, and I promise there'll be no mention of Hanwell.'

'You'll let me know how she's living.'

'Of course I will. I'll call in on my way back.'

'And, James, may I go and tell Maggie that we're getting married?' She was just bursting to tell someone. 'I'll be back before you are.'

'So the answer is definitely yes?'

'You know it is.'

When he left, Sarah leaned on the window sill and watched until he was out of sight. Her breath steamed the glass, and with childlike joy she drew the shape of a heart on it with her finger, then hurriedly wiped it off before anyone passing should see.

She dropped the curtain quickly as two

constables appeared. They were being vigilant, glancing about them as they walked down Sekford Street, and for some reason a quiver of apprehension momentarily marred Sarah's happiness. In a foolish moment her thoughts immediately flew to Patrick. How silly. He was a bit irresponsible but he wasn't a criminal.

The constables turned the corner into Woodbridge Street just as the clock on her mantelpiece chimed three.

## CHAPTER 19

James entered the alleys warily, a slight throbbing beneath his shoulder blade reminding him to keep his eyes peeled for suspicious-looking characters with evil intent, but when he reached Paul Place he was slightly relieved to see it was not quite as bad as some of the other courts and alleys in the area, though bad enough. As he turned in he could feel eyes upon him, but being a cold December day they were behind the dirty windows. A few barefooted children played in the gutter and seeing his fine clothes came after him, begging, but he brushed them aside and stopped at the address Sarah had given him. It had taken rather longer than he had anticipated to find it and when he looked at his watch he saw it was getting on for three o'clock.

'I wish to see Mrs Wooldridge,' he said to

the urchin who answered his knock. He'd almost forgotten what name to ask for. The child seemed struck dumb so he stepped inside, and a handful of other children appeared from a door at the back, round-eyed and open-mouthed. 'Where will I find her?'

'Upstairs.'

James climbed the rickety stairs carefully, hoping none of the mildew would rub off the wall on to his coat sleeve. He felt sick at the thought of Anna living in this squalor, and he knew he would have to do something about it. At the top of the first flight he called her.

'Anna!'

When there was no response he called again and after a moment there was a noise above his head. He looked up the next flight of stairs and saw her leaning over a precarious rail. She gave a cry of pleasure which turned to alarm.

'Dr Halden, how did you know where to find me?'

'Can I come up?'

'I'm looking after Edward. He's sprained his ankle and can't walk.'

'Never mind anyone else, it's *you* I've come to see. How are you, Anna?'

He continued climbing, having to lower his head when he reached the attic room into which Anna had gone. A strongly built young man with brown hair and a pleasant face was lying on the bed with his trouser-leg rolled up and a cold compress tied round his ankle. He struggled to get up. The only other furniture in the room was a table which was strewn with torn strips of material and sewing things.

'Now look here,' the young man said angrily, 'if you've come to take Anna back to that asylum I forbid it. She's my wife now.'

'Edward,' Anna warned.

'I haven't come to take Anna anywhere,' he said. 'And don't you think I'm the one who should be making statements? You abducted her. I could make things very unpleasant for you.'

'I know that, but I love her and I'll risk anything for her.'

James sat on the edge of the bed so that he wouldn't have to stoop, and he unwrapped the compress. 'That's a nasty sprain. You'll have to stay off your feet for several days.'

'I can't. I've got to work so I can get Anna out of here. I want to take her to Chertsey.'

'If you try to walk far you'll make it worse.' James began to feel the damaged limb which was swollen and bruised, but Edward hardly flinched as his expert fingers painfully investigated. 'No bones broken, thank goodness. Give me the bowl of water, Anna, and a fresh piece of cloth.'

When the ankle was bound firmly Edward tested it. 'I'm much obliged,' he said, though he could still hardly stand. 'Now p'raps you'll tell us what brings you.'

'And how you found us.'

James was on treacherous ground, but while attending to Edward he had been surreptitiously regarding Anna and he was pleased by what he saw. She radiated happiness. There was colour

492

n her cheeks and her eyes were healthily bright. He'd never seen her looking so well and knew he'd been right in what he'd said to Sarah. Every touch and every glance assured him that Anna was very much in love with her husband.

And from what he'd seen of him he had to approve of Edward Wooldridge. All the way to Paul Place he'd been dreading what he would find, but this was no uncouth lout. Of course, in normal circumstances he would never have permitted such an unsuitable match for his daughter, but there had never been a less normal situation than this, so he had to be grateful that she had chosen a kind, loving man.

'It was all a coincidence,' he told them. 'I believe you have a friend called Patrick Byrne.'

They both frowned, then Edward said: 'You mean Paddy. He's been living downstairs with Tam and Shaun.'

'Well Paddy is Mrs Morey's stepbrother.'

The lovely colour drained away from Anna's face and Edward reached for her hand. James hadn't expected Sarah's name to have such an effect. It obviously distressed her deeply to hear it mentioned, and he looked from one to the other, seeing that the young man shared her anxiety.

'It's all right, love,' Edward said, drawing her down beside him on the bed. The springs creaked. He put his arm round his wife's shoulder and kissed her temple, then turned to James. 'So Mrs Morey couldn't wait to tell *you* to come interfering.'

'It wasn't like that at all. I've known Mrs Morey for very many years and she came to me because she wanted to make sure Anna was well.'

'How like her not to come and see for herself.' Anna's voice had turned cold, and she moved deeper into the shelter of Edward's arm. 'Not that I ever want to set eyes on her again.'

'I'm sorry you feel so strongly,' James said. Caught up in a conflict of loyalties, he was provoked into telling them a piece of news he'd had no intention of revealing. 'You see, I've just asked Mrs Morey to marry me.'

She gasped. Her eyes grew round with surprise and after a moment she covered her mouth with her hands. 'Oh, my goodness,' she breathed.

In a rapid change of mood she pulled away from Edward and he swung his feet to the ground to follow her. The pressure on his sprained ankle made him swear mildly before he drew her close again to show James that they were united against him.

'Dr Halden, I must tell you that Anna knows Mrs Morey is her mother.'

The words cut through the stuffy air like a knife blade. There was a strained silence until James said: 'Then you must know that she loves you very much, Anna.'

He had no means of expressing the extra-ordinary emotions coursing through him, for in learning that she knew her mother he jealously longed to reveal his own identity. But he was not left in that position for long.

'I don't want to talk about her,' she said.

494

She shook off Edward's restraint and came to James's side, a curious light shining in her eyes. 'You're my father, aren't you? You don't have to tell me. I know it. I can feel it inside me.'

'Anna, what are you saying ...' Edward was horrified.

'Tell me if it's true.'

James looked at her and loved her. The heavy-lidded eyes, as blue and beautiful as Sarah's, reproached him. Her mouth, so like his own, drew into a stubborn line he recognized as a sign that she would not be taken in by evasion. She was so near that he could touch her, but it wasn't permissible. From the moment he admitted the truth there was going to be a time of testing which would require all his strength of mind and he didn't know how he would come through it. He wanted to help these young people, to buy a cottage for them in the country, somewhere near enough for him to keep an unobtrusive eye on Anna's health, for she would never be completely free of the debilitating convulsions. He had to make it possible for them to have a good life together, but such things would have to be taken slowly. First he had to win their trust, and that was not going to be easy.

He didn't know how to answer her question without making excuses for himself, and for Sarah. He didn't know how he could ever make up to her for all the years he hadn't known of her existence because he hadn't been around when Sarah had needed him. So many things wound so tightly round his heart he felt that it bled.

'Tell me if it's true,' she repeated.

'I humbly admit it,' James said.

Again there was silence in the tiny attic room. Anna didn't move and Edward was too uncertain to offer support, not knowing to whom his wife would now turn. James waited.

'How long have you known?' Anna asked.

'A matter of weeks.'

'And how do you feel about having an epileptic daughter?'

She wasn't rejecting him, or showing signs that the revelation upset her. She seemed to be cautiously offering herself. He felt womanish tears pricking the back of his eyelids, something he rarely experienced, and there was a prayer in his heart that he might be given the right words.

He said: 'I'm so proud of you. I never expected to have a daughter. You can't imagine how I felt when I discovered this courageous, beautiful girl was mine.'

'Then why didn't you tell me straight away?'

'How could I?'

'You're right,' said Edward. 'And why should she accept you? She owes you nothing.'

'Except my life,' she murmured. 'Hush, Edward. Hush, my darling.' She put a gentle finger on his lips, then gave James her attention. 'I've always had an affection for you, Dr Halden. You were my only regret at leaving Hanwell, but perhaps now we can get to know each other as father and daughter. I should like that.' She paused. 'However, I shall not commit myself in any way until I learn why my mother felt compelled to desert me. I've judged her harshly, but I ought to be fair so I need to know whose fault it was. Please understand.'

How wise she was. How dignified. Sarah couldn't have handled the situation with any more poise. Dr James Halden, a senior physician at Hanwell Asylum, had never felt so humbled.

'I beg you to let her tell you herself.'

'In a little while ...'

At that moment the house rocked on its foundations, shaken by a terrible explosion somewhere to the north of them. The attic window, already cracked and loose, fell out of the warped wooden frame. It shattered into fragments with the vibration and glass flew everywhere.

Anna screamed and both men protected her with their broad bodies from the effects of the blast which was so loud and so unexpected it sent everyone flocking into the alley to know what had caused it.

It was well past three when Sarah set out for Maggie's house, her hooped skirt flowing out behind her as she hurried. The plaid material was lightly brushing the cobbles and the front was lifted a little so that she wouldn't trip in her haste. She was deliriously happy. James Halden had asked her to marry him and she wanted to shout it to the world.

It only took a few minutes to walk through Woodbridge Street to Corporation Lane. Quite a lot of people were about, and the constables she had seen in Sekford Street now appeared to be keeping a watch on three men and a woman loitering by the wall. The group dispersed before Sarah got to it, dissolving quickly into the murky weather. She smiled to herself, wondering what they were up to, but for the moment she was seeing through a haze of contentment which coloured everything with innocence, so she soon forgot.

Before opening Maggie's door she stopped to rebuke some boys who were playing with lighted paper.

'That's a dangerous game,' she said.

'It ain't a game, miss. We're smoking it.'

'When you're old enough to smoke you can have pipes of tobacco.'

'It ain't none of your bloody business.' Her interference was a waste of time and only earned her a mouthful of abuse.

Maggie was in the kitchen, and for the first time in months she was looking clean and tidy. Sarah had renovated a dress for her and the grey hair was tucked under a neat lace cap she had bought second hand.

'You timed yer visit right, ducks,' Maggie said. 'Abel's gawn upstairs to 'is workroom though I doubt 'e'll do any work in it. Got a bottle hidden away, I shouldn't wonder. Well, what brings you at this hour?'

'Maggie, I've come to tell you James Halden has asked me to marry him.' Sarah was too excited to worry about Abel. She caught the older woman by the waist and swung her round.

'Say you'll come to my wedding.'

'Hmmm!' sniffed Maggie when she got her breath. 'That's a turn-up. What brought this on?'

'Oh, Maggie, there's so much to tell you.'

'I'll put the kettle on then. I ain't sitting around thirsty while you babble on. But first I want to know if Paddy came round to you? That son of mine'll be the death of me.'

There was nothing for it but to wait until Maggie had unburdened her troubles, and Sarah curbed her impatience.

She became curious about what was happening outside while she cleared a space on the table under the window, only half listening to complaints of Patrick's neglect and thought-lessness. A man was rolling a three-foot barrel along the road. He stopped opposite the house next door, stood the barrel on end against the wall of the House of Detention, and covered it with what looked like a piece of oilcloth. Then he struck a match and appeared to light something at the side of it before going away. A minute or two later another man came along with a squib in each hand and went over to one of the boys Sarah had spoken to earlier.

'Gimme a light, son,' she heard the man say in a reedy voice. He had light-coloured hair and side whiskers, and was quite well dressed in a brown overcoat and a black hat.

The boy looked nervous of the stranger but he allowed him to light one of the squibs from his paper. Some people walked by, obscuring Sarah's vision for a moment, and boys gathered round the barrel. The next thing she saw was the man bending down to thrust the end of the squib into the barrel.

'Maggie, there's something strange going on outside,' she called. 'Put the teapot down and come and look.'

The fuse, for that was what it was, started burning. Maggie scurried to Sarah's side, anxious not to miss anything, but by that time the man was hurrying away, pursued by everyone who had been nearby, and all that was left was the barrel with the burning fuse which fizzed and crackled like a firework.

Realization flashed into Sarah's mind. She went rigid with fear.

'My God, it's gunpowder!' she screamed. 'Run, Maggie. Run for your life.'

She dragged Maggie away from the window and headed for the back of the house, not knowing where to go for safety but determined to put as much distance as she could between them and the deadly barrel. They'd reached the back scullery when a deafening explosion sent them reeling from one side of it to the other. The window burst in. Bricks, iron and glass fell around them. Dust covered them.

Sarah lay under the debris in a welter of blood, and the last thing she knew was the terrible silence which followed.

Patrick was not important enough among the Fenians to have been given a leading part in the conspiracy, but he knew the plans and found it difficult to concentrate on his market job that day. He wished he was there. It wasn't until gone two o'clock that it occurred to him his ma's house might be in danger if the gunpowder was strong enough to blow more than a hole in the wall of the House of Detention.

As soon as the thought crossed his mind he left everything and hurried from Covent Garden towards Corporation Lane, intending to make some excuse to get her out of harm's way, but as soon as he turned the corner he saw Sarah talking to some boys smoking paper, then going inside the house. He didn't know what to do. Sarah was not gullible like his mother and the last thing he wanted to do was arouse her suspicions. His life wouldn't be worth living if the plot failed because of his careless tongue.

His mind was made up for him when he saw one of the Fenians being dogged by a constable. In fact there were officers at every turn. His heart started hammering. Such a show of the law must mean word had leaked out and the attempt to rescue Burke and Casey was off. Best not to stay in the neighbourhood even though anyone local would vouch that he lived in the Lane if he was apprehended.

Curiosity and anxiety made him linger. He dodged into a doorway and spent some time watching developments but not daring to show his face. He saw three Fenians he recognized separate and go different ways, engaging the attention of the police officers in three different directions, and as soon as they were out of sight things began to happen. The plan had not been cancelled after all.

Patrick's contribution to the plot had been to procure a truck from Covent Garden, a task which would have earned him severe penalties if he'd been caught stealing it. Timothy Desmond wheeled the truck out of a passage two doors up from Ma's house, and there was a barrel in it. He left it on the pavement and went back up the passage, followed by a constable. Patrick held his breath so long it caused a pain in his chest. No sooner had the pair gone than James Murphy appeared, rolled the barrel on its end over against the prison wall and put a lighted match to something at the top. Then he left it, going back to the shadow of the gloomy tenements.

Fog was creeping in, yellow and dirty in the soot-filled air. At any moment Patrick expected a spurt of flame and a loud bang to disperse it, and he covered his ears. Nothing happened.

It was about half past three and people were walking past the barrel. The boys smoking paper took no notice of it. A few moments later a man in a smart brown overcoat and black hat walked over to the boys. It looked like the one they'd called Michael Barrett at the last meeting, a bit of a toff compared with the others, and thick as thieves with Murphy. He spoke to one of the boys and took a taper from him, using it to light one of the fuses he carried. He stuck the fuse in the side of the barrel and then made off at speed down Corporation Lane, staying close to the wall. His speed alerted others and everyone started to run after him. A glimpse of his face as he passed showed that he expected the second attempt to be successful.

Patrick was suddenly terrified. He was sweating, though it was cold and damp enough to chill through to the bones. He ought never to have come. He was desperate to get away and was about to leave his hiding place when a police officer set off in pursuit of Barrett, so he had to stay a moment longer. In that moment the most terrible explosion rent the air. The officer was blown off his feet, and Patrick was flung out in the road where he lay stunned but relatively unhurt. The noise had almost split his eardrums. A smell of gunpowder stung his nose. And as he landed in the road he saw the building burst apart opposite to where the barrel had been placed, bricks and mortar shooting skywards, then falling into a devastated heap.

There was a deathly silence for a while. Then it was broken by the agonized shrieks and screams of the injured and dying, a great wailing which became a crescendo, and it was the worst sound Patrick had ever heard. It was like a battlefield.

He was choked with dust. His eyes hurt and he felt as if every part of his body was bruised. When he struggled to his feet and saw the terrible damage he'd had a hand in creating he wanted to die on the spot. Through thick smoke he saw that the house which had been completely destroyed was the one next to Ma's, and the rest of the street was in ruins.

In a daze he wandered through the debris, urging his feet to hurry, but they wouldn't obey. The broken body of a little girl was lying in the gutter, her face destroyed by glass. Patrick vomited.

People appeared from nowhere. A mob of them, panic-stricken. Ironically there was a hole in the wall of the House of Detention through which no one had escaped.

He pushed through the crowd that had gathered and found strength at last to start climbing through the rubble to reach Ma's kitchen. When he looked up he saw the wall of Abel's workroom with a fire still burning in the grate on the third floor. Abel Wood was lying dead in the ruins below, but there was no sign of Ma or Sarah.

Patrick began frantically digging with his hands.

Louisa Picken was in a tavern on Clerkenwell Green looking for her father when the explosion happened, and it was as if a giant hand shook the shelves, tipping off all the bottles and glasses. The place shuddered, and everyone ran outside in terror.

'It's the artillery. They've gone mad,' someone yelled.

'They must be shooting people,' screamed another.

Indeed the sound had been like great volleys of artillery fire. Shock stunned people into temporary immobility.

'It's the end of the world,' muttered one old woman, swigging gin from a bottle on the assumption there would be no tomorrow.

News travelled within minutes. A boy came

haring out of Clerkenwell Close.

'It were a barrel of gunpowder. Knocked 'ouses down in Corporation Lane,' he cried. 'And a bloody great hole in the prison wall an' all.'

There was pandemonium. Louisa picked up her skirts and sped towards home, her heart thudding hard enough to burst. Knowing something about the conspiracy, she had to make sure Tam was safe, but it was no good following everyone else to the scene of the explosion because he wouldn't be there. He'd been used as a decoy, told to lead the peelers off the scent. Trouble was, if he was caught he'd be found as guilty as the rest.

There were more people about than on Guy Fawkes night when there'd been a parade. They were all heading in the opposite direction to Louisa and she had to push her way through, shouting and swearing when her way was barred.

If they'd taken Tam in she didn't know what she would do. Houses down was real serious. It could mean there were a few deaths, and death meant a murder charge. She thought of the tales she'd heard about Fenians being executed in Manchester for killing a peeler, and she tried to go faster but her legs were trembling too much.

She'd never dreamed it would turn out like this. It had all been a bit of a lark till now, a bit of excitement to liven things up. She'd felt important being involved. And she'd come to love that great oaf Tam O'Mara more than anyone on earth.

The blast had found the weak spots in property for streets around, and glass littered the pavements. Her boots were through at the soles and slivers of glass spiked her toes, but she kept on running until she reached Paul Place. Bits of wood and glass were everywhere. Those who hadn't gone running to see what had happened were standing around talking about it in high-pitched voices.

'Have you seen Tam?' Louisa called.

'Ain't 'e working on the viaduct?'

'Not today 'e ain't. Oh, Gawd, what's 'appened to 'im?'

'Are you reckoning the blast was 'is fault then?' asked a blowsy woman from across the way who was a troublemaker if ever there was one. 'If it ain't to do with the Irish I'll eat me 'at.'

'Of course 'e ain't got nothing to do with it.'

At that moment Tam turned the corner with purposeful strides, though not as if anyone was after him. There was none of his usual shillyshallying. None of his Irish nonsense. No roguish smile.

'I've come to get me shovel,' he said. 'I've been talking to the police so I have, and they need every man they can get to start shifting rubble in Corporation Lane. It's a dreadful business.'

Anna was so afraid she might have one of her attacks. She sat down on the bed, trying to breathe steadily, and it was the greatest relief when none of the frightening symptoms started up in her limbs. No frightful taste in her mouth. She was going to be all right.

A lot of shouting was going on below. Dr Halden was leaning through the hole where the window had been, and what he heard made him draw back hurriedly, his face taut, his movements suddenly urgent.

'They're saying there's damage in Corporation Lane,' he said. 'I must go. Sarah was there visiting her stepmother. And if there are people hurt I'll be needed.'

He bumped his head on the rafters in his haste, but before he could leave Anna caught hold of his sleeve.

'Wait,' she cried. 'I'm coming with you.'

'No!' yelled Edward.

'Sarah Morey's my mother. I want to go.'

'Stay where you are, Anna,' the doctor commanded.

He didn't think for a minute she would disobey him. He was already on his way down without a backward glance, his long legs carrying him over the shallow stairs two at a time.

Anna pulled her cape off the nail on the door and flung it round her, drawing her hood up over her head.

'Anna, I forbid you to go out.' Edward put his feet to the ground and attempted to catch her, but she was away before he could reach her.

'I'll be all right,' she called over her shoulder, and dashed after the man she now had to think of as her father.

She ran through the alleys after him. He was

way ahead of her and there were crowds of people about, but she could see his distinctive head above everyone else. No hope of catching up with him. She just had to keep him in sight so that she would know where to go.

He'd been terribly worried as soon as he had realized Mrs Morey was in danger. There could be no doubt that he loved her. He had asked her to marry him. Anna wondered whether the love was mutual and found herself hoping very much that it was. She knew nothing of the circumstances of their separation but her parents must have loved each other once, and now they had a chance to be reunited surely they would take it. Having found such happiness herself Anna couldn't help but wish the same for them, no matter what trouble their problems had caused.

He took such long strides, but she didn't lose him. Her skirt and petticoats clung to her legs as she got hot from hurrying, and a smell of dust and smoke began to sting her nose. She had never seen so many people. The street was thick with them, and cabs were trying to get through.

'Move yerselves,' one cabby cried, using his whip to make room.

James Halden took hold of the bit of a horse which was whinnying with fright at the commotion and threatening to rear up. He led it along himself, clearing the way as he went. Anna wondered why the hansom cabs were there, dozens of them, seeming to cause more confusion. It wasn't until she turned the corner of Corporation Lane and looked down the brick-strewn length that she saw the reason. They were being used to carry the dead and injured to hospital.

The sight which met her eyes was unbelievable. And so terrible. A whole street of tall houses had collapsed like playing cards into a heap of rubble, one completely demolished, the others with the fronts blown out only partially standing. Everywhere people were shouting and trying to help, some digging frantically with anything they could find. The Metropolitan Fire Brigade commandeered the cabs as they came along, while a huge body of police were trying to create some order out of the chaos.

Anna clambered over bricks in the road and finally caught up with James.

'Which house was my mother in?' she gasped. It was a job to make herself heard above the noise.

He was surveying the ruins, his eyes moving from house to house as he tried to distinguish which one Sarah had been visiting. He seemed not to hear so Anna went up and slotted her arm through his.

'I'm sure she'll be all right,' she said. 'Perhaps one of the cabs has already taken her to hospital.'

'I told you to stay where you were,' he roared. 'Don't you know what a risk you're taking? There's enough trouble here without you adding to it.'

'I *had* to come.' It was no good him getting angry and playing a heavy father role yet. 'Look, there's Paddy Byrne. Didn't you say he's Mrs Morey's stepbrother?'

'Point him out to me.'

'This way,' she said.

The dust was choking her and she prayed her strength would hold out, though she didn't know what good she could do. She didn't even know why she had come. It didn't really matter if Mrs Morey was alive or dead.

They pushed nearer to the debris surrounding the great gaping hole in the prison wall, and the damage to the houses became progressively worse. There was a mob surrounding the wall, trying to push inside for some reason.

'Move away or we fire,' shouted a thick-set man in high-ranking uniform.

When the panic-stricken mob continued to force their way through he issued an order and there was a volley of musketry as the police fired blank cartridges above the heads of people to get them out of the exercise yard. Everyone around took to their heels, including Anna with James's arm round her protectively. But once it was certain there wouldn't be another salvo they all crept back like starlings returning to settle after being frightened away by a loud noise.

'I saw Paddy, I know I did,' Anna said through the racket. 'Yes, there he is over there.'

Paddy was helping some firemen to shift rubble from a house. His black hair hung in his eyes, his clothes were torn and he was working feverishly.

'Paddy, is Mrs Morey in there?' Anna

scrambled over the fallen masonry to reach him, tearing her skirt. James was close behind.

'She went to visit Ma. I saw her go in,' Paddy sobbed, but he didn't look up. 'They would've been in the kitchen gossiping. And this *was* the kitchen.'

There were cuts on his face, and one hand was bleeding quite badly.

'Patrick, you need something round that hand or you'll get blood poisoning. Come here, man,' said James.

He pulled his shirt tail from the top of his trousers and tore a strip of it off, forcing Paddy to stop what he was doing.

'Dr James Halden!'

'The same. Have you heard anyone calling in the ruins?'

'Not a sound.'

Two firemen were working through what had been the passage, gradually clearing timber and bricks which barred the way to the back of the house. Suddenly one gave a shout.

'There's a couple in here. Two women.'

James and Paddy climbed together over the mountain of rubble. Anna stayed where she was, watching them help to lift a beam clear so that they could get into a room which was blocked with debris.

She felt sick. Her head was aching. Time passed. People around her were working like beavers but all she could do was sit and wait, her hands pressed to her mouth. She wanted to go over and work with them, but she was afraid. Not for herself. She knew she'd passed the stage where shock could bring on one of her fits. By the grace of God she had been given strength to avoid it and she prayed that she could stay calm until all this was over.

In spite of everything it was Sarah Morey she feared for. It mattered very much that she should live. Anna would never have believed she could feel such anxiety for anyone, least of all for the woman who had given her birth then cared nothing for her all her life. She had cruelly wished her dead when she had first found out who she was. Now, with all her might, she was willing her to be alive.

Pictures came tumbling into her mind as if the pages of an open book were being flicked over in front of her eyes. Mrs Morey in the garden at Chertsey. Sewing a dress for her. Cuddling children at the Foundling Hospital, herself included. And then the flickering stopped at a vivid memory of Mrs Morey kneeling in front of her when she had come round from that violent fit she'd had after learning she must go to the asylum. She'd held her in her arms and there had been tears in her eyes, but Anna had remained rigid, wanting her comfort and sympathy yet rejecting it because she had always been afraid of fresh heartbreak if she hoped for too much.

'Don't die,' she murmured. 'Mrs Morey, please don't die. I couldn't bear it if you died and I'd never got to know you.'

Misty rain dampened her clothes. The careful digging went on, careful because if masonry was dislodged with too much haste it could cause a lot more to collapse and bury those underneath. Anna held her breath every time a piece was removed. After considerable time James reappeared, now covered in dust and as dirty as the rest, but hope shining clearly in his eyes.

'It's all right, Anna, they're alive,' he called to her. 'We're just getting one of the doors out to use as a stretcher. Can you make sure there's a cab waiting? They must be got to St Bartholomew's as quickly as possible.'

At last there was something useful she could do. She willed herself to keep going as she ran shouting to a constable with James's message. Her heart was pounding furiously but everything around her was still steady. Her mother was alive.

'There's two injured women to be taken to St Bartholomew's,' she said. 'Can you have a cab ready?'

A cab-horse snorted nearby. 'I'll hold on to this one,' the constable said, clearing a space for it to move closer.

Hope had given Anna fresh energy. She climbed over the rubble, agile as a mountain goat, until she reached the opening the men had made to release the trapped women. She could look now.

James was picking his way down there. He managed to squeeze through the narrow hole leading into the darkness of a tiny, dust-filled room. Anna lay on her stomach, straining to see inside. It was getting dusk and men were lighting flares. She could just see a thin woman with grey hair pinned under a pile of bricks. Sarah Morey was trapped by a welter of wood, her face dirt-streaked and ashen, her eyes closed.

'Mrs Morey!' Anna called. Her voice was shaking. 'You're going to be all right, Mrs Morey.' The eyelids flickered, and Anna willed her to hold on: 'Mama. Ma,' she called. Then she began to cry in earnest. 'Ma, I need you. I need you so much.'

Sarah's eyes opened, so blue they put the gloomy grey sky to shame, and she looked up at Anna with a warm, gentle expression.

'Mama, I love you!' Anna shouted, just as James reached the bottom and started to move the restraining planks.

When Sarah first regained consciousness she couldn't remember where she was or what had happened, and she thought she was in some sort of tomb. There was hardly any air, the blackness was suffocating, and her throat felt choked with dust. Then she remembered dragging Maggie along the passage to get as far away as they could before the gunpowder went off, but they hadn't gone further than the scullery when there was an explosion like the end of the world had happened.

'Maggie,' she managed to call hoarsely.

When there was no answer she felt around, trying to draw herself up so that she could look for her stepmother, but a pile of wood was trapping her. It was balanced precariously across loose bricks which could easily slide away

514

at the slightest disturbance, and she daren't move any more for fear of dislodging it. Fear added to the dryness in her throat. It rended her motionless.

Maggie still didn't answer, but a groan from nearby assured Sarah that she was alive.

After a few minutes her eyes became accustomed to the blackness and she saw cracks of dim light above her through the tangle of wood and fallen masonry. Beyond she could just see the rest of the scullery which was still partly intact, but she daren't try to reach it, and when she attempted to shout not a sound would come. The pressure seemed to make it impossible to draw enough breath.

Whoever was responsible for this terrible outrage ought never to sleep again. They had to be caught. Hanged. There must have been people killed, which made it murder, and as she lay there she kept seeing again the man with the fuse and the innocent boy with the lighted paper. It had all been a plot to get someone out of prison. She didn't doubt that had been the intention, but whoever was responsible for organizing it was a madman without any idea of the strength of gunpowder.

After a while she heard noises above. There was a lot of shouting, then thumping and banging which echoed through the debris and hurt her ears. Perhaps help was coming. Please, God, let help come. Still she couldn't get enough breath to shout that they were here.

Maggie's groans grew louder. Maggie had been worried about Patrick. She had asked

Sarah to have a word with him and to try to make him keep better company. Now she desperately wished she had found out more about what he was up to instead of being so wrapped up in her own problems. Abel had said Patrick was mixed up with the Fenians and the killing in Manchester. If he'd had anything to do with this she wouldn't lift a finger to stop him getting the punishment he deserved. It was too awful to think about.

She tried to keep awake by thinking of James and how much she loved him. And Anna ...

She couldn't think at all. There was pain in her head which blurred everything and she drifted away again into the strange realms of semi-consciousness while sounds above her intensified.

Such wonderful dreams she had. She heard James calling her. Then Anna's voice. Perhaps she was dying. The most beautiful words of all came from Anna. She was calling her Mama. Ma, she was shouting. Ma.

Sarah struggled to open her eyes, fighting the heaviness which made her lids feel weighted down. Men were moving the debris, a brick at a time, enlarging a hole they'd made above her until now it was big enough for someone to get through.

'Ma, I need you.'

She could still hear Anna's voice. Perhaps the space and the sky she could see were not real. Rain had gathered in a little pool on a ledge about two feet up and when it was pulled away the water spilt on to her face. Her dry tongue moved round to locate a few drops. The dampness revived her spirits, reassuring her that she wasn't imagining the voices.

'Ma, I love you,' called Anna, and Sarah smiled. They were the sweetest words she had ever heard and her heart suddenly felt like beating wings. It pounded in her ears.

Someone was coming down. Legs appeared through the gap the men had made, easing slowly towards her.

'It's all right, Sarah. I'm coming. Don't move, whatever you do.'

James's voice, surely. In another moment he was beside her, his face and hair covered in brick dust, his shirt ripped.

'James, help Maggie. She's over there and I think she might be badly hurt.'

'I'm getting *you* out first.'

He took hold of one end of the obstruction and began to lift it gradually while someone above leaned in and managed to help. No one spoke. An inch at a time it moved, and the pile of bricks supporting the other end teetered dangerously. One careless move and the whole lot could be down on her, but she wasn't afraid any more. Now that James was here nothing could go wrong. He always got her out of difficult situations.

'When you get me out of here I promise not to be any more trouble to you,' she said.

He grinned. 'I'll never dare let you out of my sight.'

The sleeves of his shirt were torn. Sweat ran down the corded muscles in his arms which hardened like iron as he took the weight of the wood for several seconds until the men above had a firm enough hold to draw it clear.

'Pull away,' he ordered.

'We've got it.' The man who had been handling the other end poked his head through the gap as soon as it was safe. 'Hang on, sister Sarah. We'll have you out in no time,' said Patrick. Thank goodness he was helping with the rescue, so he couldn't have had anything to do with causing the diaster. Sarah's eyes filled with tears of relief. 'Can we reach me ma yet?'

'I think she was knocked unconscious by the blast. But there's nothing on top of her.'

Sarah had found her voice, but it was shaky. She tried wriggling her legs cautiously and discovered she could move them. They were suffering from nothing worse than terrible cramp which made it feel as if red hot needles were piercing the soles of her feet when she tried to put weight on them. How lucky she was.

'I'm going to lift you up now,' said James. He raised her gently until she was able to stand in the tiny space he had made. His body was hot, his hands strong, and for a moment she was crushed against him. 'Remember I love you,' he said.

Somehow he managed to slide her up on his shoulders inch by inch, and from there she was able to clasp Patrick's waiting hands. Moments later she was in the open air. The winter day was drawing in. The police were lighting flares for the rescuers to see by and they shimmered

518

in the cold, misty, dust-filled air.

Anna was waiting a little way back now so as not to hinder anyone. The dirt on her face was streaked with tears, but her eyes were shining.

'Oh, Ma!' she breathed.

She took off her cape and came over with it, wrapping it round Sarah's shoulders. Sarah was trembling so much she felt as if she was going to fall, but Anna's arms reached out and suddenly they were clasping each other tightly.

'Did you mean what you said just now?'

'Yes,' said Anna. 'I meant it.'

She touched her daughter's face gently, wiping away the tears with tender fingers like a blind person seeing with the senses. Her own cheeks were awash with tears. This was surely the most precious moment of her life.

'Forgive me, my darling,' Sarah wept. 'Please forgive me? I love you so much.'

'I know. I know.'

Someone had found an old door which firemen used as a stretcher to carry Maggie as soon as she was lifted free of the rubble which had once been her house. She was muttering incoherently, swearing most likely. Patrick held her hand and walked beside her as she was lifted over to the road.

A few minutes later James swung himself up from the debris and came straight to Sarah and Anna, bending to kiss the top of each tangled head.

'We can't stay here,' he said. 'Sarah, I must see you've come to no harm. I'm taking you both home.'

'To Sekford Street?'

'To my house. It's time we were all together as a family.'

Anna broke away. 'I can't come. I've got to go to Edward.'

'I'll go and fetch him now, as soon as you and your mother are safely in a cab. She must be got to bed.'

James picked Sarah up and carried her over the rubble to the next available vehicle, his arms taking her weight as easily as if she were a child, and she leaned against his chest for several precious seconds before he deposited her into the cab.

Anna still hesitated. 'I really don't know if I should. Edward might not want to come, and I belong with him.'

Leaning back against the leather seat, Sarah was so tired she could hardly keep awake, which was infuriating when there was such a lot to do and talk about. Her life could so easily have ended in the ruins of Corporation Lane, instead of which she hoped it was just beginning. She closed her eyes.

'Will it make you happy to look after your mother?' she heard James ask. Voices seemed to sound miles away. 'She mustn't travel alone.'

'I want to go with her, of course,' Anna said. Then: 'Yes, it'll make me very happy.'

'In that case you may be sure that husband of yours won't have the slightest objection. Let me help you up.'

Anna climbed in beside Sarah and the cabby took his seat up behind.

'Take them to number seven Calvert Terrace,' James said to him. 'And then I'd be obliged if you can come to Paul Place. There's a young man with a sprained ankle coming with me to the same address.'

'Right-o, sir,' said the cabby, and flicked his whip.

There was not much room in the hansom. As they set off Sarah was acutely aware of the girl sitting stiffly beside her, inhibited now that there was no longer any danger. After they'd been travelling a few minutes she cautiously took her hand, and was relieved when the slight pressure of her fingers was returned, but as yet there was nothing they could say.

This Large Print Book for the Partially sighted, who cannot read normal print, is published under the auspices of

## THE ULVERSCROFT FOUNDATION

## Other MAGNA General Fiction Titles In Large Print

FRANCES ANNE BOND
Return Of The Swallow

JUDY GARDINER
All On A Summer's Day

IRIS GOWER
The Sins Of Eden

HELENE MANSFIELD
Some Women Dream

ELISABETH McNEILL
The Shanghai Emerald

ELIZABETH MURPHY
To Give And To Take

JUDITH SAXTON
This Royal Breed